ESCAPE FROM ZOBADAK

ESCAPE FROM
ZOBADAK

Brad Gallagher

Mackinac Island Press
for the love of reading

To my wonderful wife, Julee, for her constant support, guidance, encouragement, and most of all for stubbornly believing in me even when I didn't

—B. G.

Text Copyright © 2010 by Brad Gallagher

A Mackinac Island Book
Published by Charlesbridge
85 Main Street
Watertown, MA 02472
(617) 926-0329
www.charlesbridge.com

Library of Congress Cataloging-in-Publication Data
Gallagher, Brad
    Escape from zobadak / Brad Gallagher
        p. cm.
    Summary: With his sister Sophie and their friends, Chris and Maggie, Billy decides to explore deeper into this impossible place. What they don't realize is that someone else is looking for it too.
    ISBN 978-1-934133-32-3 (hardcover)
    ISBN 978-1-934133-33-0 (paperback)

This is a book of fiction. Names, characters, places, and events are works of the author's imagination or are used fictitiously. Any similarities to any person is coincidental.

Cover design and art by Tom Mills

Printed March 2011 by Lake Book Manufacturing, Inc. in Melrose Park, Illinois, USA

(hc) 10 9 8 7 6 5 4 3 2 1
(sc) 10 9 8 7 6 5 4 3 2 1

Mackinac Island Press
for the love of reading

Switzerland, August 13, 1793 (near the southern end of the Black Forest):

"There's a storm coming."

"Yep."

"Did you bring the horses in?"

"How many times are you going to ask me that? Yes, I brought the horses in. Are you going to sit down and eat or are you going to stare out the window all night?"

Gerda made no move to come back to the table. Her husband, Otto, tore a chunk of bread from the loaf in the middle of the table and dipped it into his stew. He took a bite, and then scooped up a potato with his wooden spoon and glanced up at Gerda again.

"What are you looking at?" he asked.

"I don't know," she answered. "Something's wrong."

It was twilight and the wind whipped the branches of the trees back and forth at the edge of the forest. They almost seemed alive as they flailed about, like creatures caught in a trap and unable to run away. But it wasn't the trees Gerda was looking at. She leaned to her left, tilting her head through the window opening as she tried to see up the grassy incline at the edge of their property. Through the deepening gloom she could see the ghostly yellow flickering of lamplight at the top of the hill.

"He's still working," she said. "He never stops working."

"Who, Bosch?"

She nodded. "Yes."

"So what? A man has to make a living. Why does he always worry you so much?"

"I don't like him. He scares me."

"He's an old cabinetmaker," Otto said, taking another bite. "And he's crippled. What's to be afraid of?"

"I don't know."

Thunder rolled across the sky from north to south, heralding the approaching storm front. A sudden gust of wind whipped around the eaves, causing them to whistle and then howl. The little one-room cabin creaked around them.

"Gerda, close the shutter now. You're letting in a draft. Come sit down. You worry too much."

"I suppose." Gerda sighed then closed the shutter and latched it. She shuffled to the table and sat down. Ladling some of the stew into her bowl, she stared down at it.

"Blue is in the barn, right?"

"Yes, Blue is in the barn. All the animals are in. The hay is down. The door is bolted. Everything is safe and tight. I don't understand you, Gerda. You were never afraid of storms before."

"It's not the storm." Gerda stood up, her chair scraping the wooden floor. Then she sat back down. Abruptly, she stood up again and looked toward the window. A flicker of lightning illuminated the outline of the window and door. Thunder crashed directly over the house and the rain began to patter down on the roof.

"I'm not afraid of the storm. It's—" her voice trailed off.

"It's what?"

"I don't know. Something is going to happen. Can't you feel it?"

"Feel what? You're not still worried about old Zulus Bosch, are you?"

Gerda crossed the room to the window and stood listening with her ear close to the shutter.

"I think he's some kind of witch or warlock," she said softly.

"Don't be foolish. He makes furniture. That's all."

"No. There's more going on up there."

"You better be careful with that kind of talk. You don't want to go around accusing people of witchcraft. You know what could happen to them."

"It's not just furniture. He's doing something else up there. I think he's doing something unnatural."

"Now, Gerda, you listen to me. I want you over here at this table right now. We're going to eat our dinner and then get ready for bed. Tomorrow is going to be a busy day and I have to get up very early. I don't want to hear any more of your crazy talk."

Another crash of thunder shook the sky, rumbling away into the distance. As the thunder retreated, another sound took its place. It was a strange, deep groan that rose and fell and rose again, ascending in pitch and volume until it was a high shriek. Then it abruptly cut off.

Gerda and Otto looked at each other, speechless. Rain pelted the house and the wind lashed through the trees.

"Did you hear that?" Gerda whispered.

Otto nodded and put down his spoon.

"It's the werewolf," she breathed. "It's coming."

Otto stood and hurried to the corner where he kept his long gun behind the chair. He always kept it loaded.

"Snuff the candles," he ordered.

Gerda moved silently to the table. She blew out the two candles there, then rushed to the stove and the nightstand, blowing out the others. Otto stood at the window, slowly opening the shutter. He peered out toward the forest and Gerda joined him.

"Do you see anything?" she whispered.

"No," he said. "It could be wolves. Henrik saw a pack of wolves last month."

"That wasn't a wolf, Otto. Have you ever heard a wolf sound like that?"

He didn't answer. They squinted into the forest, looking for any sign of movement among the wide trunks of the trees. The rain poured down at a sharp angle, curtains of mist blowing across the clearing. Beyond the first row of trees, the forest was as black as charcoal.

"It might go after the horses," Gerda whispered, her voice trembling. "If it smells them, it could break into the barn."

"I know. I'm going out."

"No," Gerda shook her head. "Don't go out there! Please, Otto!"

With his gun clasped tightly in his hands, he moved to the door.

"I have to go out. I can't see the barn from here. You stay. Lock the door behind me."

"Otto . . ."

He slid back the iron bolt on the door and pulled it open. A gust of wind and rain blasted through the open doorway, knocking Otto back a few steps. He snatched his hat from a hook next to the door and put it on his head. With shaking fingers he checked his gun a second time. Then he stepped through the doorway and was gone.

The sound came again—deep and hollow—so deep that the shutter vibrated on its hinges. Another sound joined it, a drawn-out, high-pitched squeal that quivered and skittered about. Then two other sounds, wailing and moaning, rising and falling, creating a nightmarish chorus.

A chill ran down Gerda's spine and back up to her neck. She felt the hairs prickling on her arms and scalp. It didn't sound anything like an animal. It sounded almost like wood—like the scream an oak tree makes when it falls down. Almost.

The noise stopped. But immediately behind it came a crashing, banging, and tumbling, as if something very large were falling down the hill toward their house.

Otto suddenly came through the door, walking backward into the house, face white as parchment. The gun fell out of his hands, clattering on the floor. He slammed the door shut and pushed the bolt over.

"It's coming!" he shouted.

"Otto! What is it? What's going on?"

He ran to Gerda and grabbed her arm, pulling her away from

the window. She glanced out but could see nothing through the dark veils of rain and mist. But the sound grew louder—crashing and booming, shrieking and banging, like a hundred large wooden boxes tumbling down the hill.

"Get away from the window!" Otto screamed. "It's coming! It's coming!"

He pulled on her arm, dragging her across the room. His wet hands slipped on her skin and he fell backwards, knocking over a chair. Turning himself over, he crawled across the floor to the far corner.

"It's coming! It's coming! It's coming!" he screamed over and over as he flattened himself against the floor and squeezed his body under the bed.

"What's coming?" Gerda shouted to him, unable to stop herself from moving toward the window. She couldn't help herself. It was right there, only two steps away. Just one look before hiding. She had to know what she was hiding from.

Gerda took the two steps across the floor to the window. She looked out—to the right—up the hill toward Bosch's place. The sound came from up there.

When the thing came into view, tottering, reeling, looming beneath the flickering clouds, she didn't understand what she was seeing. Nothing about it made sense. Parts opening and closing. Whatever it was, she had to crane her neck and look up through the gale to see it pass by. Whatever it was, it was big.

It crashed through the trees, disappearing into the dark forest.

Gerda stepped back, her legs gave way, and she slumped to the floor.

"Lord help us," she whispered, covering her mouth with a trembling hand to hold back the scream.

It was no werewolf. It was a thing not of this earth. Gerda wept as she prayed. It could be only one thing. Only one thing could be that big. It had to be the devil himself that had just walked by.

1

Greenhaven, Michigan, May 1st of this year:

It drove Billy's mother crazy every time Uncle Gary came over to visit because he left little trails of sawdust wherever he went.

She usually made him stand on the porch and shake himself off before he came into the house. That helped, but there was always more—the faint dust-prints on the dinner table where he rested his elbows, the scattering of tiny wood flecks on the chairs he sat in, the little piles left here and there about the house, shaken loose from his trouser cuffs. When he went into one of his coughing fits, he seemed to rain fine clouds of sawdust from every part of this body—especially his hair.

Eleven-year-old Billy Fyfe and his little sister, Sophie, nine and a half, couldn't have cared less about the sawdust. They loved Uncle Gary's visits. Today's began like any other, with the sound of his old, green station wagon sputtering and rattling up Fairlane Avenue and into the driveway.

"Uncle Gary!" they shouted in unison, running out the front door.

Uncle Gary, tall and lanky, black and gray hair uncombed, jumped out of the car with a huge grin on his face.

"Kids!" He ran over and hugged them both together in his long, skinny arms, sprinkling them with sawdust.

"Billy," he said, shifting his ever-present toothpick from one side of his mouth to the other. "Did you get your pirate cannon back from that kid Justin?" His expression was one of genuine concern. He actually cared; he wasn't just pretending, like most adults.

"No," said Billy. "He says he doesn't have it. But I think he does, because I saw him showing something to another kid at recess. I didn't get a good look at it because he hid it in his pocket when he saw me coming."

"Hmmm," said Uncle Gary. "You need to make sure he really has it. I have an idea. Next time you see him, say this: 'Hey Justin, guess what. I found my pirate cannon!' Then watch his face very closely. He might look confused and nervous. Don't say anything else. Just watch him and report back to me what he does."

"Okay," Billy said, smiling. The thought of making Justin nervous was rather enjoyable.

Then Uncle Gary turned to Sophie.

"I found out something important about fairies."

"You did?" said Sophie, hazel eyes wide.

"Yep. Listen to this. If you're ever in a forest and see mushrooms on the ground, look at them very closely. If the mushrooms grow in a little circle, with an empty spot in the middle, that means a fairy slept there."

"Really?" Sophie was so excited she momentarily forgot to breathe.

"Yep. And if you are very, *very* quiet, sometimes you can move the dead leaves out of the way and the fairy will still be sleeping there."

"Really?" Sophie was jumping up and down now, her sand-colored ponytail bouncing behind her faded blue cap.

Uncle Gary nodded, then raised his finger and a serious look came over his face. "But don't ever try to touch one. Fairies are very, very delicate. Their wings can get damaged easily. And if they see you trying to touch them, they will get scared and think you are attacking them. But if you do *not* try to touch them, they will trust you and they might not fly away."

"Wow!" Sophie squealed. "Did you hear that, Billy?"

"Yeah," Billy said with a grin.

"Hey, I have something for you guys," said Uncle Gary.

He went back to his car, opened the passenger side door, and took out two small wooden boxes. He often brought them unusual little gifts, even if it wasn't their birthdays. The gifts always came in beautiful wooden boxes that Uncle Gary made himself. The boxes were strange—each had a little metal handle on one end, and below each handle was a small metal plate with a number etched on it. He never explained what the handles or numbers were for. The tops of the boxes always opened on hinges, and the kids never knew what to expect when they looked inside.

Uncle Gary handed a long, narrow box to Billy and a small square box to Sophie, nodding, "Go ahead, open them."

Billy opened his box. Inside was a tarnished metal tube that looked old and worn. Billy lifted it out.

"Careful," said Uncle Gary. "Don't touch the lenses on the ends. Do you know what that is?"

"I think so." Billy turned it over in his hands. He pulled on one end and two smaller tubes extended from the main tube. It was a retracting telescope. "A spyglass!" Billy's eyes lit up.

"Not just any old spyglass." Uncle Gary shifted his toothpick solemnly. "That's an authentic telescope from the Navy of Norway during World War II."

"Wow!" Billy shouted. "Do you think it was the captain's?"

"I don't know. Probably. It's solid brass, and I think there are some initials stamped on the tube there."

"S.R.K.," Billy read.

"It's not a toy, so be careful with it," Uncle Gary warned. "Don't let that kid Justin get a hold of it. In fact, I think you should use it to spy on him. Find out what he's up to. Can you see his house from here?"

"I can see it from my window upstairs," Billy said excitedly. "Thanks, Uncle Gary!"

Uncle Gary gave Billy's short brown hair a quick ruffle, and Billy ran into the house and up the stairs to his bedroom. Uncle Gary looked over at Sophie, chewing on his toothpick.

"What about you?"

Sophie opened her box. Inside was something that looked like a round blob of dark yellow glass. She lifted it out and held it up to the sunlight. The blob turned the color of honey.

"What is this?" she asked, breathless.

"That is a piece of amber. Do you know what amber is?"

"No." Sophie moved the object back and forth, watching the sunlight dance inside of it.

"Amber comes from tree sap. It's the goopy, sticky stuff inside a tree. It's what they make syrup out of, only amber is millions of years old. It gets hard like a rock. And sometimes a bug or a small animal gets stuck in the tree sap. When the sap hardens, the bug is still trapped inside. Do you see that little wing there by the edge of the piece?"

Sophie nodded.

"I could be wrong about this." Uncle Gary lowered his voice to a whisper. "But I think that's a prehistoric fairy wing."

Sophie brought the amber closer to her face, peering inside, enchanted.

"Really? But it's so small."

"You're right, it is small. Most people don't know this, but some kinds of fairies are very, very tiny. Only as big as a fly."

"Oh, my gosh! I have to show Mom!" Sophie ran onto the porch, pulling Uncle Gary along behind her. "Mom! Look what Uncle Gary brought me!"

Just then, Mom opened the door, folding her arms across her chest. Her smile belied the order she gave.

"Wait just a minute, Mister," she said. "You are not coming in this house until you shake yourself."

"Hello, Molly," said Uncle Gary, smiling back at her. He was genuinely fond of his sister-in-law. "Why, of course I'm going to shake myself." He began dancing around crazily, shaking his head back and forth, rubbing his hands up and down on his clothes and making weird monkey noises with his mouth. Clouds of saw-dust came off of him, drifting like ghosts across the front yard.

Sophie giggled helplessly. Mom laughed too.

Neither Billy nor Sophie, nor even their mom and dad, had any idea that this would be his last visit to the house, ever.

2

Billy propped the telescope on his windowsill and squinted into the eyepiece, looking across the street and down the hill toward Justin's house. He had to look between the branches of the big oak tree in his front yard, but the telescope was powerful and brought Justin's front door right up close. There was no sign of activity.

Justin Carbuncle was Billy's friend for a total of three days. He was a large boy, with long stringy hair that always hung in his eyes. They played football and soccer outside a couple of times, but Justin was always too rough, taking every opportunity to shove Billy to the ground. And he was always giggling—an irritating, high-pitched, almost girlish laugh.

One day Billy brought Justin inside to show him his bedroom. His cannon—a small replica of a pirate cannon—was sitting on his dresser. It was a gift from Uncle Gary, who said it was a one-of-a-kind item carved out of a whale tooth by a real pirate—one of Captain Morgan's crewmen. Billy didn't know if that was true or not, but it didn't really matter. It was his most prized possession at the time.

The cannon disappeared that day. Billy didn't actually see him take it, but after Justin went home, Billy never saw it again. That is, until that day on the playground at school.

He had wanted to approach Justin on the playground but he didn't dare. Billy was what someone like Justin might unimaginatively call a "loser." He wasn't quite at the bottom of the school popularity ladder. That spot was reserved for hopeless cases like Gil Huskins. Billy was one step up from that, at least. On good days he could go unnoticed, which was usually easy enough for him. Light brown hair, large brown eyes, scrawny and shorter than average, with no distinguishing characteristics to speak of. He had become an expert at disappearing into the woodwork.

Billy had exactly one friend—Chris Toffler. And Chris wasn't with him that day on the playground. So, really, approaching Justin and his gang of friends was not even remotely an option.

Billy moved the telescope to the right and looked at the large picture window over the front porch. Blurry shapes moved back and forth inside but he couldn't tell who it was or what they were doing. Just as he was trying to focus the telescope better, his dad called from downstairs.

"Billy! Come on down, buddy! Time for dinner!"

"Dang it," Billy whispered.

Pushing the three sections of the telescope back together, he carefully replaced it in the box and closed the lid. Then he put the box in his closet, on top of the stack of other boxes Uncle Gary had given him: he had exactly thirty-four of them now, all different shapes and sizes, carefully organized with their handles and numbers facing out. The numbers seemed random. The telescope box was number 4,947. He nudged it carefully into place on the appropriate stack.

"Billy, come down here!"

It was his mother this time.

Under normal circumstances it seemed like all Uncle Gary wanted to talk about was wood and furniture making. He could go on for hours about oak or cherry or teak or mahogany. Sometimes he would bring over small pieces to show them, pointing out unique grain patterns that looked like ocean waves or animals or boiling lava. Sometimes the wood was incredibly beautiful, like the leopard wood and the zebrawood and the quilted maple. Billy remembered even stranger names like cocobolo, gaboon, tambootie, bubinga, timbo, and wandoo, and he often tried to imagine what exotic lands those trees grew in.

When Uncle Gary started talking about furniture, he would get excited. His dark eyes would light up, and he would stand up and draw invisible pictures in the air with his fingers. Especially when he talked about joinery. Billy wasn't exactly sure what "joinery" was. He just knew it had something to do with the way wood pieces were put together.

Mom would stare at the little tendrils of sawdust, falling from Uncle Gary's sleeves as he waved his arms around, and take mental notes of where each grain fell so she could retrace his path later with the vacuum cleaner. She loved Uncle Gary, but furniture making wasn't really her thing. Besides, she liked a clean house.

Dad would smile, nod his head, and make an occasional comment. The two brothers had built furniture together as teenagers, and Dad always tried to keep up his end of the conversation, but he usually ended up mostly listening with a vaguely puzzled look on his face.

But there was one thing that never made any sense to Billy. If Uncle Gary spent all his time making furniture, where in the heck was it all? Billy could not remember ever seeing a single item Uncle Gary had made, besides the wooden boxes, of course. Not one chair or table or even a stepstool.

"I'm sorry," Uncle Gary was saying. "I know I said it wouldn't happen again. But I don't know what else to do."

He seemed nervous about something. He chewed on his toothpick without even taking it out of his mouth when he ate. Not that he was eating much anyway.

"Gary, this is the third time this year," said Dad. "I don't understand it. You make okay money at your regular job. And anyway, making furniture isn't that expensive. You're asking me for ten thousand dollars. That's a lot of money."

"This should be the last time, Henry," said Uncle Gary. "I promise. And I hate asking you for it. But I'll be able to pay you back by the end of summer." He rapped his knuckles on the wood of the table, as was his habit whenever he spoke of the future.

Dad closed his eyes and rubbed his forehead. Then he looked across the table at Uncle Gary.

"I need to ask you something."

"What is it?" said Uncle Gary.

"Shouldn't you be making money from selling your furniture? I mean, at least enough to pay for your wood?"

Uncle Gary chewed his toothpick and looked down at his plate. He seemed embarrassed. Billy had never seen him like this.

Uncle Gary sighed, then looked back up at Dad. Finally he said, "It's complicated."

"Why is it complicated?" Dad asked in a bewildered voice.

"Because, well . . ." Uncle Gary seemed to be searching his mind for something. Maybe for the right words. Or the right joinery to put the words together. Billy half-smiled at his own thoughts, even though he felt sick at the thought of Uncle Gary having no money.

"I haven't been selling the furniture."

Dad's eyebrows went up. "Why not?"

"Because . . . because it's not done yet."

"Not done yet?" Dad was almost shouting. "What are you talking about? How can it not be done yet? It's all you do!"

"It's just . . . not done yet." Uncle Gary looked down at his plate again.

Dad's mouth dropped open. He could not have looked more confused if Uncle Gary had put on a clown wig.

"But," Dad groped, "if you haven't sold anything, where are you keeping it all? Your house isn't that big. And…and, anyway, why aren't you selling it? You're the best wood craftsman I've ever seen. People would buy your stuff in a second. What have you been doing all this time?"

Uncle Gary's eyes were closed, his toothpick sticking out between clenched teeth. For a long time no one spoke. Billy looked back and forth between Uncle Gary and Dad. He was scared. He didn't understand everything the two brothers were talking about but something was clearly wrong.

Finally Uncle Gary broke the silence. "Like I said, it's complicated. I mean, really complicated. The thing is—"

Suddenly there was a soft thump. It seemed to come from outside, on the porch.

Uncle Gary spun around and looked toward the door, one hand clenched on the back of his chair.

"What was that?" he asked.

"Oh, it was probably just the newspaper," said Mom. "The paperboy throws it up to the porch."

"Are you sure?" Uncle Gary stood up and walked quickly to the front window, next to the door. He peeked out between the curtains.

"Gary, what's going on with you?" Dad asked. "Why are you so nervous?"

Uncle Gary looked back. He smiled at his brother's family seated around the table, but to Billy it looked like he was having a hard time pulling up the corners of his mouth. And his eyes looked scared.

"I'm sorry," Uncle Gary said. "I have to go. Listen, I'll call you later, Henry. We shouldn't be discussing this at the dinner table. Please think about the money. You know I wouldn't ask for it unless I had no other choice."

"But you've barely touched your food." Mom looked worried.

"I'm sorry. The food is delicious, Molly. But I just can't eat anything right now. I really have to go."

He went to Sophie and hugged her. Then he walked around the table to Billy and hugged him. Tighter than usual.

"Bye, everybody. I love you guys. Henry, I'll call you."

And then he was out the door. They heard his old station wagon roar to life and rattle away up the street.

They finished their dinner in almost complete silence.

Later, while Mom and Dad were cleaning up the dishes, Billy opened the front door and looked out onto the porch, out of curiosity. There was no newspaper in sight.

3

Billy reached the top of the rope easily. Hanging on with one hand, he smacked the bell that was fastened to the ceiling. He looked down at the other students gathered around the floor mat, watching him.

"Nice job, Billy! That was 25.62834 seconds! That's a new class record!" announced Mr. Guyback, the Greenhaven Elementary gym teacher, holding up his stopwatch as if Billy could see it from the ceiling.

Grinning, Billy lowered himself back down to the mat.

Chris Toffler, Billy's friend, patted him on the shoulder as he stepped back into the group.

"All right, Billy!" said Chris, his gray-blue eyes alight. "That was awesome!"

"Come on, Jethro!" Mr. Guyback shouted. "Up you go!"

The rope climb was the only activity in gym class that Billy excelled at. Being small he was hopelessly out-played in most sports and, of course, he was usually one of the last to be picked for teams. In fact sometimes he felt like the rope climb was the only thing he was good at, in or out of the gym. His grades certainly weren't anything to brag about. Sophie was the smart one. School always seemed so easy for her. Billy often found it almost impossible to keep his mind from wandering in class. And it showed on his report cards with comments from the teacher like, "Billy needs to stay on task" or "too easily distracted" or "The day-dreaming must stop!"

He could sure climb a rope though. Whatever good that would do him.

As Billy and Chris moved to the back of the crowd, they heard a familiar voice.

"Nice job, Billy!" mocked Justin in a high-pitched, nasal whine.

Justin had made it roughly three feet off the ground in his attempt to climb the rope. After slipping off and falling on his butt, he had stomped off the mat angry and red-faced. He was still sweating.

"What do you want, Justin?" snapped Chris.

"Get lost, Ringo," Justin waved his hand dismissively at Chris.

He sometimes called Chris "Ringo" because his thick mop of brown hair made him look a bit like one of the Beatles. Billy was surprised Justin even knew who the Beatles were.

"You looked just like a real monkey up there, Billy," Justin sneered, flipping his greasy hair away from his face with a toss of his head. "Come to think of it, you look kind of like a monkey down here too!" He laughed his usual screechy giggle.

"Justin, you're such a jerk!" Chris burst out.

"Forget it, Chris," said Billy, low. Working up his courage, he turned to his tormentor. "Hey Justin, I've been meaning to tell you something."

"What's that, monkey-boy?" Justin stepped toward Billy, looking down at him.

Billy swallowed. Justin had to be at least ten inches taller than he was. "Do you remember that pirate cannon? The one I showed you when you came over to my house?"

"Yeah, what about it?"

"Well, I found it."

"So what? So you found it. What do I care?"

"I mean I thought it was lost but now I found it," said Billy.

"Who cares, monkey-boy? I don't even know what you're talking about! Why don't you go climb a tree and tell the other monkeys about it?"

Billy didn't think this was how it was supposed to go.

"I know where it is," he stammered. "I just wanted to let you know that."

"Oh yeah? And where do you think it is?" Justin pushed his chest out and bumped it against Billy, forcing him backward. "Huh, monkey-boy? I got an idea! How 'bout if I just tell you where it is? It's in my bedroom on my dresser, that's where!" Justin laughed with delight at the look on Billy's face. "You gonna do something about it? Huh, monkey-boy?"

This was definitely not how this was supposed to go.

"Give it back, Justin," Billy said, trying to remain calm, but feeling the frustration rising up inside him.

"What if I don't want to?" Justin bumped his chest against Billy again, harder this time.

"It's mine, Justin! I got it from my uncle! You stole it!"

"Oh, yeah? You got it from your uncle, huh? Hee-heee-heeeee! You wanna know what I heard about your uncle? Huh, Billy-monkey?"

Billy glared at him.

"I heard your uncle is married to a piece of wood!" Justin chortled with glee, as if he'd just made the funniest joke ever.

"Shut up!"

Unable to contain himself Billy pushed Justin away.

Justin came right back, thrusting his chest into Billy.

"Uh-oh! Monkey-boy is getting angry! I'm scared!" Justin advanced, forcing Billy back toward the bleachers. Billy tried to push him away, but it was no use. He was too heavy. He seemed unstoppable. Chris grabbed Justin's arm, but Justin yanked it away.

"What are you gonna do, Billy-monkey? Look at you. You can't do nothing! You might be able to climb a rope, but so what? What good is that? You can't play football, and you can't play basketball, and you can't fight, and you can't get your pirate cannon back, either! So what are you gonna do, huh Billy-monkey? Bunky! Heee-heee-heeee! Hey, Bunky!"

Several of the other kids, mostly Justin's friends, had turned to look at them. Some of them began laughing and pointing. Billy backed away, but Justin kept pressing forward, puffing his chest out and yelling down at him. Billy clenched his fists, the anger building.

"Come on, answer me! What are you gonna do, Bunky? Bunky can't do nothing! Hee-heee-heee! Bunky can't…"

Billy shoved as hard as he could against Justin's chest, but Justin was like a mountain. He took one small step back, then advanced on Billy again.

"Is that the best you can do?" Justin snarled. "Here, let me show you how to do it."

Justin's hand came up and smacked the side of Billy's head with such force that Billy toppled over, landing on his shoulder and banging the other side of his head on the gym floor. Immediately his ears began ringing as he sat up and rubbed his head. For a moment, he was afraid tears were going to start falling from his eyes, but he was able to hold them back. He heard Justin's voice calling, "Whoopsie! Bunky fell down! Hee-hee-hee-heeee!"

Abruptly Justin's chortling stopped. Billy watched in amazement as Chris leaped onto his back and wrapped his arms around the bigger boy's neck.

"Leave him alone!" Chris shouted, straining in vain to pull Justin to the floor.

Justin began turning in circles, trying to throw Chris off. He reached over his shoulder and grabbed a handful of Chris's hair.

One of the girls began yelling, "Mr. Guyback! Mr. Guyback!"

Mr. Guyback appeared seemingly out of nowhere, lifting Chris off of Justin's back.

"That's enough! Break it up!" he barked.

"Billy started it!" Justin whined, shaking strands of Chris's brown hair off his sweaty hand.

"I very much doubt that, but I don't particularly care," said Mr. Guyback. "All three of you are going down to the office! You can explain it to Principal Wiggins."

The three boys trudged silently to Principal Wiggins' office. When it was Billy's turn, he left out the part about the pirate cannon. It seemed silly now, and what was the point, anyway? What did Uncle Gary think talking to Justin was going to accomplish? He hadn't been able to trick him, and he wouldn't be able to get his cannon back. Justin didn't care.

Fortunately, since no one was seriously hurt, they were all given a stern warning and told to go back to class. Justin snickered and made little monkey sounds under his breath as they walked down the hall toward their classroom.

Billy ignored him. He made a mental note to tell Uncle Gary the plan had backfired really, really badly. But at least he knew for sure now: Justin had the cannon.

4

A month later, during the second week of summer vacation, Billy and Sophie got their birthday cards in the mail. They were from Uncle Gary. Billy's card had a colorful picture of a ship floating above the clouds with balloons instead of sails. Sophie's card had nine fairies flying through a forest, each one holding a candle. The kids opened them and read the messages.

"Happy Twelfth Birthday! Love, Uncle Gary," read Billy's card.

Sophie's card was just as simple. "Happy Tenth Birthday! Love, Uncle Gary."

"Mom," said Sophie, pushing the bill of her cap further back on her head, her brow furrowed in confusion. "Why did Uncle Gary send us birthday cards? My birthday isn't for another—" She counted on her fingers. "Six months. And Billy just turned eleven a couple of months ago."

Mom took the card from Sophie's hand and looked at it, front and back.

"That's strange," she said. "I don't know."

As Billy examined his birthday card, he noticed something else that was strange. A small number was handwritten inside the card, at the bottom near the left-hand corner. It was the number 2,317.

"Why is this number written here?" Billy asked, pointing to the number and holding it up for Mom to see.

Mom frowned. She looked at Sophie's card. "There's a number in this card too."

"What does my number say?" Sophie asked, standing on her tiptoes to see the card.

"It says 48,615," said Mom. "Hmmm. I'm sure it doesn't mean anything. You know how Uncle Gary is. He puts numbers on everything."

It was true. All the boxes he gave to the kids had numbers on them. The little carved wooden animals and people he gave as gifts to their parents had numbers etched into their bottoms. All of his clothes had little numbers written somewhere on them in permanent marker. Even the pencils sticking out of his shirt pockets had little numbers written on them.

Uncle Gary made his own toothpicks, which he carried around in a little wooden toothpick case he'd also made. Billy couldn't remember ever seeing him without a toothpick in his mouth. According to Uncle Gary the toothpicks you bought in stores were made of birch. Birch was fine, but it got soft too fast. He preferred maple or oak, so he made all of his own toothpicks in his basement workshop. And sure enough, every one of his toothpicks had a tiny number carved into it.

But Billy couldn't remember ever seeing a number written on any of his birthday cards before. It just seemed odd, that's all. Billy had a bad feeling about Uncle Gary. Something wasn't right.

That evening, around 10:00 p.m., when Billy was supposed to be asleep, he got out of bed and crept out to the landing at the top of the stairs. He could hear his parents talking down in the kitchen, his dad murmuring, "He never answers his telephone anymore. . . ."

Billy listened to their voices trail off, and then he crept back to bed, silent and scared. It was a long time before he fell asleep.

5

Three months later there was still no word from Uncle Gary. It was around the end of summer vacation when the police began coming to their house. Every time they came, Mom and Dad told Billy and Sophie not to worry—to just go play somewhere—while they went into the office to speak privately with the police officers.

One evening Billy listened outside the door. He couldn't hear much—only little snippets of conversation. The policeman's voice was deep and rumbling, with a sinister quality Billy didn't like. At one point he heard Dad say something about the money Uncle Gary owed a wood company to pay for some kind of rare wood.

"From Tasmania or something," Dad said.

Sophie came into the room holding a mermaid doll and they stood listening together. She pulled the bill of her cap lower over her eyes.

"What's going on?" she asked.

"I don't know," said Billy. "Sshh. Just listen."

For a moment, Dad's voice could be heard clearly, saying, "The last time I talked to him was the day after he came here. He called me on the phone. I asked him if he was in some kind of trouble, but he wouldn't answer. Then he said something strange. He said, 'Listen, brother—no matter what happens, I love you. And your wife and the kids, too. Will you tell them that for me?' And I said, 'Of course, I will.' And that was it. He hung up and I haven't heard from him since."

Billy and Sophie looked at each other, wide-eyed.

The policeman said something in a low, gravelly voice that Billy couldn't make out. Billy turned away from the office door. He didn't want to hear any more. Sophie followed him into the living room.

"Do you think Uncle Gary's dead?" she asked suddenly.

"What? No, of course not!" Billy said, shocked and angry. How could she ask a question like that? He looked at her.

Sophie had tears on her cheeks. She was staring down at the mermaid, twisting its purple hair around her finger.

Billy's anger vanished. He knew exactly what she was feeling. He had thought the same thing many times over the last few weeks but he had always pushed those thoughts out of his mind. He didn't even want to consider they might be true.

But he knew now that something was seriously wrong. Mom and Dad weren't talking about it in front of the kids, but he could tell just by looking at their faces. They both seemed worried all the time. There was very little conversation over dinner. Dad spent many hours in his office, on the phone. Sometimes he would start shouting into the phone and have to close the door. Billy just wished they would tell them what was going on.

Suddenly Billy realized that he too was about to cry.

"I have to go to the bathroom," he said, walking quickly away. He didn't want Sophie to see how upset he was and he didn't think he could keep the tears from coming.

6

"Billy. Sophie. Come here for a minute. We want to talk to you."
Dad waved his hand, motioning them over to the dinner table,
where he sat next to Mom. "Sit down."

"Kids," Mom began. "You've probably noticed that things
have been a little weird around here lately."

Here it comes, Billy thought. He looked down at his hands
and waited.

"It's about Uncle Gary," said Mom. "He's—well—he's missing."

Billy looked up. He had been prepared for the worst, but this
actually sounded a little bit hopeful.

"Missing?" asked Sophie.

"We haven't seen him in over four months," said Dad. "The
police have been searching for him for the past two months. But
so far they don't have any clues as to where he might be."

"So he's not dead?" asked Billy.

"Dead? No, of course not," said Dad. "I mean, we don't know
anything for sure but—well—no, he's not dead. It's like the police
say, nobody's dead unless there's a body."

Billy pondered this for a minute, thinking he should feel more relieved, but somehow this news didn't make him feel much better. He still had the impression that his parents weren't telling him everything.

"The police are going to find him, right?" asked Sophie.

"We sure hope so, baby," said Mom. She put her arm around Sophie.

"There's just one problem," said Dad. "Uncle Gary owed a lot of money to a lot of people. The bank is going to take his house away because nobody is paying for it. Do you understand that?"

Both kids nodded but neither fully understood what their father meant. Where were they going to take the house? You couldn't just move a house, could you?

"If Uncle Gary comes back—I mean, *when* he comes back," Dad continued, "he'll probably have to live with us for a while until he gets another home."

"That's okay!" said Sophie, her face suddenly brightening.

Dad smiled. "I knew you guys wouldn't mind that. So, here's what we're going to do. This weekend, we're going over to Uncle Gary's house. You guys are going to come and help us. We have to take everything out of his house. We'll throw away all the junk and keep all the things that we want—the important stuff. We have to get all the furniture he made, even if it isn't finished. It's probably sitting in the basement. I'm going to rent a big truck so we can bring everything back here. We need all the help we can get, so if you have any friends who would like to help, tell them I'll pay them ten dollars each for a short afternoon's work, okay?"

"Okay," said Billy and Sophie together.

Billy wasn't sure how he felt about everything. It seemed like too much information all at once. Uncle Gary missing. His house being taken away. All his stuff coming back here. Billy felt relieved, scared, hopeful, worried, excited, curious, and confused, all at once. At least Uncle Gary wasn't dead. Well—that is, at least there wasn't a body.

Lying in bed that night, Billy's thoughts were running in circles around his head like horses at a racetrack. But there was one thing his mind kept coming back to. He had never been inside Uncle Gary's house. *What's it like in there?* he wondered. *All those strange and wonderful gifts he's given us over the years—they all came out of that house.*

And then, *What else might be in there?*

Dad backed the truck into Uncle Gary's driveway as the kids watched from the backseat of Mom's minivan at the curb.

"Henry, stop!" Mom shouted out the window.

Dad stopped the truck, looking over at her, confused.

"You're going to hit that tree!" she shouted, pointing.

Dad nodded, pulled the truck forward, and straightened it out. He started backing up again and there was a loud crunch as the back wheels rolled over Uncle Gary's mailbox. Bills and junk mail spilled out onto the street and began fluttering away.

Dad continued up the driveway as Mom got out of the minivan and started picking up the mail.

Sophie and her best friend Maggie Margaret were in the third-row seat of the van, playing mermaids and paying no attention to what was happening outside; the mermaids were in grave peril. Maggie was half-Asian, her other half unknown because she had been orphaned as a baby. Her mother had adopted her when she was one year old. She had freckles and short, curly, dark red hair and called herself a freak because she was the only Asian on earth with red hair.

Billy didn't think she was a freak, and he was pretty sure she wasn't the only Asian with red hair. He liked that she was different. He actually thought she was cute, though he would never admit it to anyone.

"Does your dad know how to drive that truck?" asked Chris. "Umm," said Billy. "I think so."

"Henry, stop!" Mom screamed from the street as the back wheels of the truck rolled up onto a bush, squashing it flat.

"I don't think so," said Chris.

"Me neither," Billy admitted, wincing.

Finally Dad got the truck back on the driveway and turned off the engine.

Mom came back to the minivan and said, "Come on, kids. Everybody out."

Uncle Gary's house was a small, red brick ranch on a street where all the houses looked exactly the same. Billy had seen it before from the outside but had never been in it.

Dad opened the back of the truck and pulled out a stack of empty boxes. He dropped them on the driveway, wiping away the sweat already forming on his brow. It was humid and unusually hot for late September.

"Come on over here, kids," he said. "Okay, listen up. Most of the stuff we're going to take out of here is furniture. Gary's been making furniture for over twenty years, so he might have a hundred pieces in the basement. I'm not sure how many, exactly, or how close to being finished they are. I have some guys coming over to help me carry it all out. What I need from you four is to take these boxes and put all the small stuff in them. Like dishes and silverware and small tools and whatever you can find. If it looks like garbage, just leave it in the front room and we'll take it out later. Everybody understand?"

The kids nodded. Dad looked at Mom, who was still holding a stack of mail in her hands.

"You ready, Molly? Let's go take a look at what we're dealing with."

They walked toward the back of the house. As they went around the corner they both suddenly stopped, staring in shock at what they saw.

"What happened here?" Mom asked.

"I don't know," said Dad. His mouth came open as if to say something else, then it closed again and he tilted his head, frowning.

The kids ran over to see what they were looking at. It was the back door. Torn off its hinges, it was lying on the overgrown grass of the backyard. But that wasn't the strange part. Somehow, the door was no longer flat—it was bent into the shape of a "U," vertically along its length.

8

"Who would do this?" Mom asked.

"I don't know," said Dad. "It doesn't make sense. There are easier ways to break into a house. Why would someone do that to the door? How did they do it?" He looked around, as if there might be an answer floating in the air over the backyard.

"Well, there's nothing we can do about it now," he said. "I'm going inside to check the place out. You guys wait out here for a minute."

He went inside the house. Soon he reappeared in the doorway and said, "Everything looks about the same. Come on in, everybody."

Billy, almost dying of curiosity, went to the door first, followed by Chris, Sophie, Maggie, and Mom. The first thing he noticed was the sawdust. It was everywhere. Every surface was covered with a layer of it, like snow. Across the center of the kitchen floor were trails of footprints where Uncle Gary had walked back and forth. In the corners and along the walls, the sawdust was drifted up ankle deep or higher.

"Uck!" said Mom. "How could he live like this? Didn't he ever vacuum?"

"I don't think he owns a vacuum," said Dad. "This is the saw-dust from ten years or more of woodworking. Now you know why I never wanted to come over here."

"How are we going to get this place cleaned up?" she asked no one in particular.

"We're not," Dad replied. "All we need to do is get Gary's things out. It's the bank's problem to clean it up. It's their house now."

"Hey, Billy! Think fast!"

A clump of sawdust hit Billy in the back of the head, explod-ing into a cloud of wood particles that rained down around him. Chris shrieked with laughter as he began to gather up another handful of sawdust.

"Oh, you're in trouble now!" Billy stooped over and scraped together his own clump.

"You two, stop that!" Dad called, a trifle irritably. "You're going to get that stuff in your eyes."

"Aw, man!" said Billy, dropping his handfuls of sawdust.

Maggie began sneezing.

"I'm—achooo! I'm—achooo! I'm—allergic to—ACHOO! Dust—ACHOO!" said Maggie, wrinkling her nose, freckles twisting.

"Sophie," said Mom, "why don't you and Maggie go outside to the backyard? Maggie can't stay in here like this."

"ACHOO! It's okay, Mrs.—ACHOO!" said Maggie.

"No, really, I think you should go outside. It doesn't look like there's going to be very much in here to pack up anyway," Mom insisted.

"All right," said Sophie. "Come on, Maggie, let's go see what's in the backyard!"

"ACHOO!"

Mom disappeared into the back hallway to check out the bed-rooms while Dad and the boys went to the living room. The saw-dust was even worse here. A small couch in the middle of the room was covered with so much sawdust they couldn't even tell what color it was. It looked like nobody had ever sat on it. On the other side of the room was a big round ball of sawdust as high as the kids' waists.

"What's that?" pointed Chris.

"It's probably the TV," said Dad. He found a remote control on the mantle. When he pushed a button, the ball of sawdust began to glow with an eerie blue light.

A voice from inside of it said, "Thunderstorms tonight and continuing into tomorrow. Expect showers and strong winds possibly as late as Sunday evening. Travelers are advised to . . ."

Just then, Mom came out of a back hallway from the bedroom. Her face was pale.

"Did you see his bed?" she asked, eyes wide with horror.

"I don't think I want to," said Dad.

"You're right, you don't," Mom replied, shaking her head and walking back into the kitchen. "Henry, I don't know how we're going to do this. I don't want to bring all this stuff to our house. We'll never get rid of all the dust."

"Don't worry," said Dad. "Most of this is garbage. The important stuff is in the basement. I don't really care about anything up here."

"Have you been down there yet?" asked Mom.

"No, I'm a little afraid to," admitted Dad. "If Gary never sold anything, it's probably packed with furniture from one end to the other."

"Well, you'd better get started," said Mom. "You heard the weather report."

Dad nodded. "My buddies should be here any time now to help with the heavy stuff. Come on, boys," he nodded at Billy and Chris. "Let's go take a look."

9

The basement stairs creaked under their feet, and Billy felt like an explorer descending into an Egyptian tomb. This was a place no one but Uncle Gary had ever seen. The smell of old dust and mold hung in the air, and cobwebs drifted lazily over their heads.

At the bottom of the steps was a door. It was unlocked, and Dad turned the handle and pulled it open. He felt around and found a light switch just inside, next to the door. He flicked the switch and then just stood there, motionless.

"Dad, what is it?" Billy tried to peer around him into the basement.

"I . . ." Dad began to speak, but the words never found their way out. He took a step forward, then stopped again.

"What's in there, Dad?" Billy insisted.

"Umm," said Dad. "Just, uhh—just stay close to me, okay? Don't play around."

He began to walk slowly forward, and something in his tone of voice told the boys—even Chris—that they had better pay attention. Billy followed him through the doorway.

The basement was a world of sawdust.

A narrow pathway led from the door into the basement. On both sides of the pathway was a wall of sawdust piled straight up to the ceiling.

"Don't touch it, you guys. It could collapse and bury us," Dad warned.

Slowly and carefully, they followed the path to the middle of the basement where it opened up to a circular clearing, maybe twelve feet across. The small area was swept clean but was surrounded on all sides by the near vertical mountain of sawdust. At the opposite side of the clearing was a workbench with tools scattered across its surface. Other large woodworking tools were scattered around the perimeter—a table saw, a band saw, a lathe, a router.

In the exact center of the clearing was a nightstand. Nothing special, really. Its square top was about two feet by two feet across. It had two drawers and was stained a dark reddish brown color.

"Dad?" said Billy. "Um. Where's all the furniture?"

"I don't know," Dad replied absently. He was looking around at the walls of sawdust.

"You don't think it's buried under there, do you?"

"No, I doubt it. But . . ." He didn't finish his sentence. He grabbed a broom that was leaning against the workbench. Holding it by the brush end, he approached the wall of sawdust and gingerly poked the handle into it. He pushed it all the way in and moved it around, feeling for anything that might be buried inside.

"I don't know," he said again. "I don't think there's anything in there but more sawdust." He sounded lost.

"We could dig," suggested Chris, holding up a snow shovel he'd found leaning against the other end of the workbench.

"No," said Dad. "This is too dangerous. If these walls fall in, we'll suffocate. You guys shouldn't even be in here. Let's clear these things out and then I'll see if I can dig around a little." He looked around again, shaking his head. "This is unbelievable. Where did all the sawdust come from if there's no furniture?"

"Henry, are you in here?" Mom's muffled voice came from the direction of the doorway. They hadn't heard her come down the stairs.

"Yeah, honey. Just follow the path."

They heard her feet shuffling up the pathway toward them.

"You guys shouldn't be down here."

"I know," said Dad.

Mom entered the little round workspace, her mouth hanging open in disbelief.

"What was he doing in here?" she asked.

"Well, a lot of woodworking, obviously."

"But where's all the furniture? Do you think it was all stolen? By whoever broke the door?"

Dad shook his head. "I don't think so. Because—well—where would it have been stolen from? There's no room down here for anything." He gestured at the sawdust on all sides. "And there's no sign of anything upstairs being moved either. I think we're going to have to get some of this sawdust out of here. We don't know what could be buried underneath."

"Well, we'll figure that out later," said Mom. "Right now I want everybody back upstairs. This is an accident waiting to happen."

Dad nodded.

"Yeah, you're right. Come, boys. Let's get out of here."

Billy was looking at the nightstand, running his hand over its smoothly polished surface. He admired the grain of the wood that swirled in intricate patterns and seemed almost three dimensional.

"Can we at least take this up?" Billy asked. "I don't want to leave it here. I can use it in my bedroom," he added as an afterthought.

"Yep. I'll get it," said Dad. "You guys go on up."

He wrapped his arms around the nightstand and lifted, straining.

"Man, oh, man," he gasped. "This is a lot heavier than it looks."

It took him almost fifteen minutes to waddle back across the floor, painstakingly making his way up the stairs and carrying the nightstand out to the backyard where he put it down, huffing and puffing.

Just then, two cars parked in the street and four men got out and came walking up the driveway. They were Dad's friends, arriving to help.

"It's going to be a short day," Dad said to them. "There are some tools and things from the basement I want to bring up, but that's about it."

The four men headed for the back door.

"Oh, and Stanley!" he shouted at one of them. "Put that cigarette out!"

10

The rest of the afternoon was spent putting things in boxes and carrying them out to the curb. Dad and his friends loaded the tools and woodworking equipment onto the truck. There were a few other small pieces of furniture from the main floor—things Dad said Uncle Gary didn't make. Mom found some papers in the bedroom and a wooden box of homemade toothpicks in the kitchen, but everything else was garbage.

Dad and his four friends had dug around—carefully—in the basement, tossing up garbage bags full of sawdust, one after the other. They didn't even come close to emptying it all, but it was enough so they could push the piles back and forth to see if anything was buried underneath. Billy kept imagining them discovering Uncle Gary's body buried under all that sawdust. To his great relief, they didn't find anything but a few scraps of wood and a lost screwdriver.

Outside, the sawdust hung in the air, creating a fog that surrounded the house. It clung to everybody's clothes and hair. Maggie couldn't escape it, the sawdust speckling her red curls like bad dandruff. Her sneezing became a running joke among the movers. She would sneeze three times—no more, no less—exactly every five minutes. You could almost tell what time it was by counting her sneezes.

The girls had spent most of their time collecting black feathers they'd found scattered about the backyard. They had a whole shoe-box full of them, but when Mom saw it, she made them throw the feathers away and wash their hands.

Billy and Chris were carrying bags of sawdust to the curb when Chris said something shocking.

"Man, Billy, your uncle was crazy," he said, matter-of-factly.

Crazy. The word was like a wasp that suddenly flew out of some dark hole to sting him. Billy had never thought of Uncle Gary as crazy. He was just Uncle Gary. But now, after what he had seen inside the house, he wasn't so sure anymore.

He remembered how Uncle Gary used to talk when he came over—how he'd go on and on about the different projects he was working on. About all the different types of wood he used and all the different styles of furniture: Victorian and Gothic and Queen Anne and William and Mary. And the technical things like joinery and marquetry and parquetry and tracery. So many mysterious words. Billy hadn't understood them all, but he'd loved to listen to the talk. Loved the sound of Uncle Gary's voice.

But now he wondered if maybe it was all a lie. Maybe Uncle Gary was just making everything up. What if he really spent all his time just grinding up wood to make toothpicks?

Suddenly, it seemed to Billy that he didn't really know Uncle Gary after all. This person whom he used to love so much and who seemed to love him and Sophie so much in return. Maybe he was really a complete stranger. Still, Billy couldn't help defending him.

"He wasn't crazy," he said to Chris, dropping his sawdust bag onto the pile at the curb. But he said it quietly.

Thunder rolled across the sky and a sudden sharp wind sent leaves tumbling and skittering down the street.

"Come on, guys!" Mom shouted from the top of the driveway. "Let's finish this up before the rain comes!"

Everyone was suddenly scrambling. The men tossed a few remaining items into the truck and slid the door closed. Then they all piled into their vehicles and drove off. Mom took the girls in the minivan and Billy and Chris rode in the truck with Dad. By the time they were rolling up the street, the rain was pouring down, and lightning raced across the sky, chased by thunder.

They dropped Chris off at his house and Dad handed him a ten-dollar bill.

"See you tomorrow, Billy!" Chris shouted as he climbed down. "Thanks, Mr. Fyfe!"

"Bye, Chris!" Billy shouted back.

When the truck was moving again, Billy said, "Dad? What do you think happened to all the furniture?"

"I don't know, son."

"Was it stolen by whoever broke the door?"

"No, I don't think so. I just called Officer Carlson a couple hours ago to ask him about it. He said when they searched Gary's house last month, the door wasn't broken. And he told me there was no furniture in the house besides the few things upstairs. And the nightstand in the basement. So I'm guessing that Gary must have sold it all."

"But he said he didn't sell anything."

"Yeah, I know. Maybe he felt he had to lie about that for some reason. I'm sure he had a good reason but—you know—sometimes. . . ." Dad's sentence drifted off. When Billy looked over at him, he appeared to be lost in thought.

Lightning flashed in the darkening sky, illuminating his face for just a second. For some reason, Billy's dad suddenly looked much older. Maybe he was just very tired.

"Dad?" Billy asked.

"Yeah, son."

"Umm. Was Uncle Gary crazy?"

"What? Crazy? No, of course not! Why would you ask that question?"

"You know," said Billy. " 'Cause of the sawdust and all that. And the way his house looked. And the way he was acting that last time he came over to our house."

"Billy, I'm going to tell you something very important." His dad reached out and gently touched his shoulder for a moment. "There are a lot of people in this world, and each one of them is different. Some of those people are very different, and they might seem strange. But strange and crazy are two completely different things." He shook his head and said softly, "Your Uncle Gary was the smartest person I've ever known. Ever since we were kids he could do incredibly complex math problems in his head. And when we got into furniture building, I saw him do some amazing things with wood. I used to work on projects with him but it was always Gary who figured things out and made the plans. Usually, I just did what he told me and I didn't really understand most of it. As we got older, he started doing things that were totally over my head, but he made some of the most incredible pieces of furniture I've ever seen."

"Like what?" Billy asked.

"He made this library desk with revolving shelves full of books inside." His dad's voice warmed with the memory. "You could open up different panels to get to them. It had desktops and stools that slid out on four sides and little compartments for storing pens and paper. And another time he made a cabinet with a crank on the side and, when you turned the crank, a mirror and vanity and jewelry case came up out of the top. There was a music box inside that played music while the mirror came up. It was all beautifully inlaid with scenes of a garden with butterflies. That was when he was still in his twenties. Very few people make furniture like that anymore." Dad sighed. He wore a faint smile that seemed both happy and sad at the same time.

"When we grew up, I went to college to study engineering and got a job in the automotive industry, like so many other people in Michigan. Then I had a family. I did everything the traditional way. And I don't regret anything, of course, but sometimes I miss the artistic stuff. But Gary—he was always so focused on what he was doing—he had so many things going on inside his head, he never really had time for anything else. That's why he never married, never had many friends, Billy." Dad glanced over at him. "You know, he had a lot of problems with money and with his jobs. But that doesn't mean he was crazy. It just means his mind was too busy thinking about other things."

Billy thought about this for a long time, watching the raindrops roll diagonally across the side window.

Finally he said, "Do you think Uncle Gary's dead?"

Dad took a deep breath and blew it out slowly. "I don't know, buddy. I sure hope not." He paused, listening to the low rumble of thunder. Then he said, "No, I don't think he's dead. I think he might be in trouble because of his money problems. But I don't think he's dead."

When they got home Dad took only one thing out of the truck: the nightstand Uncle Gary had made. He carried it, with much grunting, straining, and a little cursing, up the stairs to Billy's room where he placed it next to the bed.

For a long time that night, Billy lay in bed staring at the wood of the nightstand, his eyes following the lines of the grain across its surface, exploring the many curves and swirls and oblong circles, the knots where branches had once been. He imagined the lines to be the walls of little hallways running back and forth and the circles to be little irregularly shaped rooms. He pictured himself walking around in those little hallways, trying to find a way into the rooms, trying to find Uncle Gary, wherever he might be.

11

About two weeks later, on the second day of October, Billy was awakened in the middle of the night by a sound. Something went THUMP. Or maybe it was more like a CLUNK.

He opened his eyes and looked around the dark room. His door was still closed. The house seemed quiet. Something must have fallen somewhere. That's what it sounded like—something falling.

Holding his breath, he strained his ears to listen. He heard a few clicks and ticks—the noises of the house settling, his dad always said. He heard the furnace coming on. A car drove by outside on the street. Then he heard a creak.

Billy sat up. The sound came from somewhere inside his bedroom. It sounded like it came from right next to his bed. He looked at the nightstand. In the darkness, he could just make out the two drawers, the lamp and a book sitting on its polished top. He could almost see the swirl of the wood grain that stretched across its surface.

There came another creak. It was definitely coming from the nightstand. Billy stared at it, eyes straining to see in the darkness, heart pounding. He wanted to jump out of bed and run for the door, but he was afraid to move. He watched and waited. And waited.

Minutes passed with no other sound: fifteen, twenty, maybe

more. After a while Billy's eyelids began to grow heavy and he lay back down, pulling the blanket over his head so that just a small opening was left for him to breathe and see out of. He told himself that he would stay awake and listen carefully, with his eyes closed. But after a minute and a half, he was asleep again.

When he opened his eyes, the sunlight was streaming in his window and he felt a little silly for being so scared the night before. It was Saturday morning. No school. Billy relaxed into his pillow. Looking at the side of the nightstand, he studied the grain pattern again. In the daytime, the pattern looked different. It almost looked like a face—sort of a long, stretched out face, with one dark eye and one light eye. The mouth was open.

Billy reached up and pulled open the bottom drawer. Looking at it from the side, he could see where the front of the drawer was attached to the board on the side, with a back and forth pattern that looked like puzzle pieces fitting together. That was joinery, he was pretty sure. What Uncle Gary always used to talk about.

"There's magic in joinery," he used to say, but he never explained exactly what he meant by that. Looking at it now, Billy still didn't understand, but in a strange way he believed. He pushed the drawer closed, then reached up and opened the top drawer. Something was written in pencil on the side of the drawer.

Billy sat up and leaned in close to read it. It looked like a child's writing, crooked and a little shaky.

It said, "THE Bigy Bigy BugLu dror."

What did that mean? Billy frowned, reading the words again and trying to decipher what the writer meant by them. Maybe they were misspelled words. "Dror" seemed to mean "drawer," but what about the others? Billy climbed out of bed and stood up. He pulled the drawer all the way out of the nightstand and set it on his bed, turning it around to study the other three sides. There were no other words. There were a few papers inside, drawings Billy had made and put into the drawer. He pushed these around but found nothing unusual about the inside of the drawer.

"Hmm," he said.

Turning back to the nightstand, he pulled out the bottom drawer, setting it next to the top one, and looked at all three sides. There were no words written on this one.

"Strange," he muttered aloud.

Out of curiosity he got down on his hands and knees and looked inside the nightstand. There was no bottom, so when he looked through the drawer openings, he could see down to the floor. On each side ran two sets of small ledges for the drawers to slide in and out on.

Something shiny caught Billy's eye, on the left. It was a small metal hook, toward the front of the nightstand, a few inches above the lower drawer ledge. It looked like something was meant to hang from it. To the right of the hook a small number was written—"2,317."

The number seemed familiar, but he had no idea why. It seemed like he had just seen that number somewhere. . . .

"Billy! Are you awake?" called Mom from downstairs.

He jumped, his heart suddenly racing. He had been so lost in thought, the sound of her voice startled him.

"Yeah!" he called back.

"Come on down and have something to eat!" Mom's voice floated toward him. "We have to go out and run some errands this morning, so get dressed before you come down."

"All right," he answered. *Darn it,* he thought to himself. He hated it when they drove around, running errands. Everything seemed to take forever.

Carefully he put the drawers back into the nightstand. Then he sighed, reluctantly got dressed, and went downstairs.

12

Later that day, as they were walking past the book aisle of the supermarket, Sophie spotted a book about fairies.

"Mom, can I get this?" she begged, pushing up the bill of her cap as she hurried to catch up with them. She held the book up for Mom to see.

"I don't know, Sophie," Mom shook her head.

"Pleeeeeeaaase!"

"How about a new hat? I'll buy you a new hat," Mom offered. She was always trying to get Sophie to wear a new hat. She couldn't stand the raggedy old blue cap Sophie was so attached to. Three years ago, Sophie had found the hat in the street. It had a darker circle in the front where some unknown patch had once been.

"No, thanks," Sophie answered. "I'd rather have this book."

"It's an expensive book. Maybe you can get it for your birthday."

"What if it's gone by then? I really, really, reeeeaaallly want it! Look at these pictures!"

"It won't be gone," Mom said firmly. "If you want it that bad, we can get it for your birthday, but we just don't have enough money today. Okay? Your birthday is coming up."

That was when it hit Billy.

"Mom?" he said.

"Yes, Billy."

"Do we still have those birthday cards Uncle Gary sent?"

"I guess so. Why?"

"Well, do you remember the number Uncle Gary wrote inside my card?"

"I have no idea," she answered, pushing the shopping cart around the end of the aisle. Sophie put the book down, pouted, and followed.

"Was it 2,317?" Billy asked.

"I have no idea, Billy," she repeated.

She wasn't even thinking about it. Billy could tell. She didn't think it was important.

"My number was 48,615," Sophie suddenly said.

"How did you remember that?" asked Billy, astonished.

"Easy. It was the same number that was on one of my boxes from Uncle Gary."

"Really?" His heart skipped a beat.

"Yep."

"Which box? I mean, what's in it?"

"A little music box. It plays 'You Are My Sunshine.'"

Billy remembered the music box. It was white, with a small picture of a girl and a cat on the lid. Billy's thoughts churned: did he have a box from Uncle Gary with the number 2,317 on it? He couldn't remember, but it seemed familiar. Or was it just his imagination? He had to check the birthday card first to find out if that was the number written in it. Was Uncle Gary trying to send them some kind of message? Sophie's music box seemed like it might contain a message, but what about his? That is, if he even had one that matched the number in his birthday card. And what would it mean if it were the same number from the nightstand?

Aaaaaggghhh! Inwardly, Billy screamed.

He searched his memory for all the gifts Uncle Gary had given him. There was the telescope of course. And there was the fossil, the beaver skull, the Civil War bullet, and the old compass. There was the rhinoceros beetle. And that old map of Antarctica. Also a couple of books and the hematite and the pieces of eight and the old railroad photographs. What else? There were thirty-four boxes in all.

"Mom?" he said.

"Yes, Billy."

"When are we going home?"

"As soon as I finish shopping."

"Yeah, I know, but—are we almost done?"

"Please don't nag, Billy. I don't want to be here any more than you do. We'll be done when we're done."

"Okay, but—can we hurry?"

"Why are you in such a hurry to get home all of a sudden?"

"I don't know; I just—I need to check something."

"Well, you're going to have to be patient."

Patient. How could he be patient? Billy hated that word. He didn't have time to be patient. He tried to tell himself to relax; all this probably meant nothing. It was probably just his imagination making all kinds of connections where there really were none. Even so, the shopping trip seemed to go on and on, and every time he thought they were done, they'd go down another aisle.

Even when they finally finished and pulled in the driveway, the torture continued. He and Sophie had to help unload the bags and bring them into the kitchen. Putting the last bag on the kitchen counter, Billy said, "Mom . . . where's my birthday card from Uncle Gary?"

"Oh, I'm not sure, honey. Go check in the drawer there—next to the pencil drawer. You know, where we keep all our papers."

Billy ran to the drawer and opened it. Bills, school papers, magazines, coupons for oil changes. Junk, junk, and more junk. It wasn't there. He started back at the top and began digging through the pile again, more carefully.

"Mom, it's not here!" he shouted.

"Then I don't know, Billy," she said, irritated. "But I don't have time to look for it right now. I have to get this food put away."

She didn't understand how important this was. Billy looked around, trying to think of where else it could be. At that moment, Sophie walked up with the birthday card in her hand.

"Here, Billy," she said, handing it to him.

Billy grabbed the card.

"Where did you find it?" he asked, incredulous.

"Right there on top of the china cabinet," she answered, smugly. "Where we put them after we got them."

"Oh." Billy might have felt embarrassed, but he didn't have time for that. He opened the card—and there it was—"2,317," written very small near the bottom corner, at an angle. The same number that was written inside the nightstand, next to the little hook.

Gripping the card in his hand, he ran to the stairs and began leaping up them, two steps at a time. Sophie followed close behind.

"Billy, what's going on?" she shouted after him.

"Nothing! I mean, I don't know! I mean, none of your business!" he shouted back. Reaching the top of the stairs, he ran down the short hallway and into his room, turning to shut the door.

"Just tell me," Sophie said breathlessly, catching the door before he could close it all the way. She stuck her foot in the opening.

"Don't be a nag," Billy retorted, pushing on the door.

"Why does everyone keep calling me a nag?" said Sophie.

"I'm the one Mom called a nag, not you." He pushed harder.

"Uh, uh. She called *me* the nag." Sophie was remarkably strong for her age and didn't give an inch.

"Okay, if you want to be the nag so bad, then you're the nag. Just leave me alone." Billy's teeth were gritted.

"Stop pushing and tell me what you're doing first!"

"Quiet!" Billy hissed. "I don't want Mom to hear." He had no choice, so he relented a bit. "Why do I have to tell you what I'm doing?"

"Because I'm the nag," she said, laughing. "Nag, nag, nag, nag." She stuck her hand through the door opening and flicked her fingers in Billy's hair, repeating, "Nag, nag, nag, nag, nag. . . ."

"Stop it!" Billy shouted, his frustration boiling over.

"Quiet, or Mom will hear." Sophie's eyes danced. "Just tell me and I'll stop!"

"Okay, okay, I'll tell you." Billy released the door and stepped back, letting Sophie come into his room. "But you have to keep it a secret. You promise not to tell anyone?"

"I promise!" she said, giddy with excitement.

He shut his door. In a hushed voice he told her about the nightstand and the words "THE Bigy Bigy Buglu dror." Then he told her about the hook with the number 2,317 written next to it.

"Do you have a box with 2,317 on it?" she asked.

"That's what I was trying to find out when you interrupted me."

Sophie stuck her tongue out at him. They went to Billy's closet, opened the door, and began scanning the numbers on the small metal plates, just below the knobs affixed to one end of each box: 571 . . . 7,566 . . . 33,285 . . . 1,608. . . .

"There it is!" said Sophie, pointing—"2,317! That little box right there!" It was a small box near the top of the right-hand stack.

Billy took it down and looked at it. It was his smallest box, not much bigger than a deck of cards. As soon as he held it in his hands, he remembered what was inside. He swallowed, his stomach fluttering. The mystery had deepened.

"What's in it?" Sophie asked.

Billy opened the lid of the box and they both looked at the small object lying inside. A skeleton key. He lifted it out and held it up. It was a very old key, its metal brown with age. It had a fancy bow with three metal loops, the bow being the part you held onto when you turned the key, as Uncle Gary had once explained to Billy. The bit, which was the key end, was a notched rectangle sticking out from the side of the shaft.

"What do you think it's for?" Sophie breathed.

"I have no idea." Billy glanced at the nightstand. There were no keyholes in the drawers, but the key, the nightstand, and the birthday card all had the same number. Could it really be a coincidence, or was Uncle Gary trying to tell him something?

"Which one is the Bigy Bigy Buglu drawer?" Sophie asked and giggled. The words sounded funny.

"The top one." Billy pulled the top drawer out and showed her the writing. Then he pulled out the bottom drawer and pointed to the hook inside the nightstand. Sophie leaned in close to see it. Billy hung the skeleton key from the hook, and they both looked at it dangling there, swinging back and forth.

"Hmm," said Sophie. "It looks like it belongs there."

"Yeah, I guess so," said Billy, his mind racing.

This doesn't make sense, he thought. *Why would there be a key if there were no lock?* He decided to ask Dad about it later when he got home. Maybe he knew something about the key.

Billy didn't tell Sophie anything about the sounds he had heard during the night.

13

The following Friday night, Billy woke up again. It must have been 1:00 or 2:00 in the morning. Mom and Dad were asleep. He lay there, staring up into the darkness of the ceiling, listening. The house was quiet.

No, not completely quiet. Something had awakened him. He couldn't remember what it was now, and his thoughts were fuzzy. He'd had a dream about doors. A door slamming. Or had he actually heard a door slamming somewhere? He wasn't sure.

But wait: there it was again. A door closing. But . . . where? It didn't sound like Sophie's room, or his parents' room, or any other door in the house. It sounded very far away. But it was inside his room at the same time. There it was again. Right next to his left ear, like it was coming from the nightstand.

I must still be dreaming, Billy thought. He sat up, crawled out of bed, and turned on his light, his eyes blinking from the sudden brightness. Shielding his eyes with his hands, he looked at the nightstand.

"What's going on?" he whispered quietly. His hands were shaking with fear, but somehow he managed to pull out both drawers. He looked again at the strange words on the side of the top drawer as he set it on his bed. *THE Bigy Bigy BugLu dror.*

Billy knelt and looked into the openings where the drawers had been. All he could see were the insides of the nightstand. It looked the same as it had the day before. He saw the skeleton key still hanging from its little hook. His eyes wandered around, across the back and over to the right side. He saw nothing unusual.

He brought his hand up into the nightstand from beneath, waving back at himself through the drawer openings. Then he felt around inside, across the back and up and down both sides. He ducked his head underneath and craned his neck to look up into the darkness inside the nightstand. His eyes had to readjust, but after a few minutes he could see the inside of the nightstand from below. Again, nothing unusual. Plain old wood, smooth, with two sets of ledges on both sides for the drawers. The underside of the top board was a single, wide piece of wood. There were a few pencil marks where Uncle Gary had taken measurements or something.

As his eyes explored the inside of the nightstand, he suddenly noticed something on the top board, up near the front edge. It was a small hole, an odd-shaped, elongated hole.

He sat up, with his head inside the nightstand, and brought his face closer. The hole was round on one side, with a narrow rectangle shape sticking out of it.

Is that . . . ? Billy thought, straining his eyes, bringing his face even closer and touching it with his fingertip. *Is that a—keyhole!* His mouth fell open as he looked to his right, where the skeleton key hung on the hook, inches from his face. *Could it be?*

With trembling fingers, he reached up and took the key from its hook. He had to poke around several times before the key slid into the keyhole. He twisted the bow of the key and it began to turn around counter-clockwise. When it was halfway around its rotation, he heard a muffled click. He turned the key the rest of the way, then pulled it out.

What now? he thought. *What did I just open?* Without thinking, he pushed up on the top board and lifted it. For some reason, Uncle Gary must have put hinges on the top of the nightstand so it could be raised up. *But what's the point of that?*

Extending his arm he pushed the lid up all the way, until it was vertical, a sudden musty smell of old wood pouring over him. He squinted up into the darkness above.

Wait a minute . . . this doesn't make sense. Lowering his head, he looked out into his bedroom where the light was still on. If the lid of the nightstand was open, shouldn't he be looking up into his lighted bedroom? He glanced back up into the nightstand, but there was only darkness above him.

Carefully, with his hands held out in front of his face, he got up on his knees, then stood up. Half his body was inside the nightstand and he was completely surrounded by darkness. He felt around and his fingers met four walls surrounding him.

Dropping back down onto his hands and knees, he crawled out and stood up, feeling dizzy. From the outside, the top of the nightstand was still down flat, looking the same as it always had. The lamp and book rested peacefully on its surface.

This was impossible. How could this be? He had pushed open the lid from within.

He waved his hand in the air above the nightstand, as if he would be able to feel something invisible there. Which was nonsense, of course.

I'm still dreaming, he thought. *That's it. I'm asleep. Silly me.* Shaking his head at all the silliness of this silly dream, he crawled back under the nightstand. He reached up and pulled the lid back down. It closed with a hollow clunk, and he put the key into the hole again and re-locked it. Then he hung the key back on its hook and put the two drawers back in. The Bigy Bigy Buglu drawer and the regular drawer.

Still laughing silently to himself, he sat down on the bed, pulled the covers up, and leaned back against his headboard. He decided to wait until he woke up in the morning. Once he was awake, things would make sense again.

In his dream, he sat there wide awake with his bedroom light still on, staring across the room until the first rays of the sun found their way through the space between his curtains. He watched the specks of dust glowing in the sunlight as they drifted through the air. He heard Mom and Dad get up and start rattling around in the kitchen below. Making coffee. Rustling the newspaper. Talking quietly.

Billy stood up, almost losing his balance as the exhaustion cascaded down over him like a fuzzy, confusing waterfall. He tried to remember when, exactly, he'd awakened. That was when he began to realize that maybe it wasn't a dream after all—maybe he hadn't been asleep all night dreaming about being awake.

14

"What's the matter, Billy?" Dad asked, taking a bite out of a piece of toast.

"Huh?" said Billy. He wasn't sure if he understood the question. He was so tired everything seemed a bit watery and distant.

"Are you feeling okay?" asked Dad. "You've been so quiet."

"I was wondering the same thing," said Mom. "You've barely touched your food. What's wrong?"

"Oh, nothing's wrong," said Billy, yawning. "I'm just tired. I didn't sleep very well last night."

Mom came around the table and put her hand on Billy's forehead.

"He's not warm," she said, walking to her chair and sitting down.

"Um, Dad?" said Billy poking at his eggs with his fork. "Did Uncle Gary—did he ever . . ." Billy wasn't quite sure what he was trying to ask. He couldn't even think of how to ask about the nightstand.

"Did he what, Billy?" Dad said, looking at him with eyebrows raised.

Sophie was watching him across the table.

"Nothing," Billy shrugged. "I forgot what I was going to say."

"Are you sure you're okay?" asked Mom. She looked worried again.

"Yeah, I'm fine. Just tired, that's all." He picked up his fork and began eating, not because he was hungry but because he didn't want them to worry anymore.

"Maybe you should take a nap today," she said.

"I think I will."

After breakfast, up in his room, Billy spent fifteen minutes just sitting and staring at the nightstand. He had to know if what he had seen last night was real or a dream. But for some reason, he just couldn't bring himself to approach the nightstand. Maybe he was afraid it really *was* real.

And maybe he was afraid he was going crazy. *Like Uncle Gary?*

No, not like Uncle Gary, he argued with himself. *And he wasn't crazy, by the way. In case you weren't paying attention to what Dad said.*

He was just afraid, that's all. He felt like he needed someone with him—a companion or a witness or whatever.

Billy got up and went to the top of the stairs. He could hear Sophie somewhere down in the living room. Descending halfway down the stairs, he saw her playing with her mermaids, swimming them through the ocean of blue carpet. With her tattered blue cap pushed back on her head and her tongue sticking out of the corner of her mouth, she pitted the dolls in an intense battle against some invisible sea monster. The battle included many sound effects of explosions, roaring, and screaming.

What a weirdo, Billy thought. *Half tomboy, half fairy princess.*

"Sophie!" he whisper-shouted. She didn't answer, so he said it again a bit louder. "Sophie!"

"What?" she yelled back, engrossed in her adventure.

"Come here."

"No."

"Just come here for a minute. I need to show you something."

"Why are you whispering?" Sophie shouted.

"Ssshhhh. Because it's a secret."

"All right, but just for a minute. Maggie's coming over." Sophie got up and came to the stairs. Billy motioned for her to follow, and went back up to his bedroom. When Sophie came into the room, he looked out, listening to make sure no one else was coming up the stairs. Then he closed the door.

"So what's the big secret?" she asked.

Without a word, Billy went to the nightstand and pulled out both drawers. He took the key from its hook and, looking back at Sophie, took a deep breath.

"Billy, what is it?" she said, eyebrows raised.

Billy got down and crawled under the nightstand, twisting his head around to look up. And there it was: the keyhole. At least that part wasn't a dream. He put the key into the hole and turned it, hearing the soft click.

Then he pushed. Sure enough, the lid went up. Immediately, he noticed the smell of wood that came down from above.

"What are you doing under there?" said Sophie.

Billy ducked back out and stood up. Turning to Sophie, he pointed at the nightstand.

"Look," he said.

Confused, Sophie removed her cap and tossed it on the bed. Then she crawled under the nightstand and looked up. She was quiet for a long time.

Finally, she said, "That's really weird. How . . . ?" She stopped in mid-sentence, and Billy heard her suck in a quick breath of air as she realized what she was seeing.

"Wait a minute! How can this be?"

"I don't know," Billy replied, feeling a strange mixture of relief and fear. He wasn't crazy after all, and they had just discovered something truly strange and unexplainable.

"What's up there?" Sophie asked.

"I don't know," he answered. "It's too dark. I can't see how high up it goes."

Sophie stood up inside the nightstand. It looked strange—like some kind of optical illusion—to see her legs and feet under the nightstand, with the rest of her body disappearing inside of it.

"There's a ladder," came Sophie's voice from within. She squatted down and crawled back out.

"You should go up there, Billy."

He stared at it for a minute, working up his courage.

"Okay," he said finally. "You have to be the lookout. Make sure no one's coming. If you hear someone coming up the stairs, cough or something."

She nodded and went to the bedroom door and peeked out.

"All clear," she said.

Billy crawled under the nightstand and stood up. Sure enough there were metal bars attached to the front wall of the inner shaft. Taking a deep breath, he reached up, grabbed one of them, and pulled himself up. The nightstand rocked back and forth a bit as he struggled to find a foothold. He put a foot into one of the drawer openings and pushed himself up higher, grabbing the next rung.

Then he climbed. It was complete darkness above him, except for the small amount of light coming in from his bedroom below. The shaft was narrow—about two feet by two feet—the same dimensions as the nightstand. Climbing slowly he counted the steps. When he got to five, he bumped his head on something.

"Ouch," he said, rubbing his forehead.

With one hand he felt around and discovered he was at the top. The passage seemed to have reached an end. Groping around above him, his hand met with something cold and metallic. It was a handle of some kind, like a small doorknob.

"There's something up here," he called down to Sophie, his

voice sounding strangely flat in the tight compartment.

He grabbed the handle and twisted. It was a little tight, but it turned. He heard the click of a bolt being drawn back. He pushed, and the panel of wood opened up.

Billy knew, even before he saw anything, that he was on the verge of a discovery so incredible it would change his life forever. His heart was pounding so hard it almost seemed he could hear it echoing back at him. His breath trembled as it tore in and out of his lungs.

"Sophie," he said in a shaking voice. He didn't know what else to say. Maybe he just wanted to make sure she was still there.

"Yeah," she answered, her voice muffled.

Placing his foot on the next rung, he pushed himself up into the opening above him. Somehow there was more light here, and he realized he could see, but what he saw defied all logic.

The opening was a trapdoor in the floor of a hallway. The hallway was made entirely of wood: the floor, the walls and the ceiling. Behind him, the hallway simply ended. But in the other direction, it stretched away from him for about twenty feet where it appeared to open onto a "T," with another hallway going right and left.

"Billy, what is it?" called Sophie from below.

"I—I'm not sure," Billy answered. "You have to come up here."

"All right. Come on down so I can get in there."

"No," said Billy. "Just come up." He pulled himself all the way up onto the floor of the hallway and slid away from the trapdoor, sitting on his butt. He was afraid to stand up—afraid the whole thing, nightstand and all, would tip over. Of course, that made no sense. But none of this made sense.

As his eyes became adjusted to the dim light inside the hallway, he noticed something strange about the walls. There seemed to be little handles sticking out all over the place.

Sophie's head came up through the trapdoor.

"Oh, my gosh," she said, looking around. "This is—impossible. Billy, what is this? Where are we?"

"I have no idea," he said.

Sophie climbed up and sat across the hallway from him, looking around.

"What are those little things on the walls?" she wondered aloud.

Billy turned to the wall behind him to get a closer look. Sure enough, they were little knobs or handles made of brass. Beneath each handle was a small metal plate with a number etched into it. He suddenly realized what they were.

"These are drawers!" He pulled on one of the handles and a drawer slid out of the wall. Inside was a large white tooth shaped like a triangle. An index card, yellow with age, lay in the drawer next to the tooth. Several words were typed on it: "Tooth of Great White Shark — Australia — 1906." Billy lifted the tooth out of the drawer and held it up, studying it.

"Wow," he whispered. "This is *cool*."

Closing the drawer, he opened the one next to it. In it was a rock gleaming with long, slender purple crystals. It looked so fragile, Billy was afraid to touch it. He closed the drawer and opened the one above that. It contained a small jar of light gray powder. The index card read: "Volcanic Ash — Krakatoa — 1883."

Behind him, Sophie began opening drawers.

"Eww!" she said. "An animal skull!" Then a few seconds later, "Oh, my gosh! Look at this ring!" Then, a minute after that, "Wow! Billy! There's an old compass in this drawer! It has Chinese letters on it!"

Billy found a stone arrowhead, a torn shred of dirty, red cloth, a small green glass bottle, and a pocket watch. The index card for the pocket watch said it had belonged to Benjamin Franklin.

There seemed to be no organization to the items. A rolled-up map in one drawer was right next to an animal tusk in the next, with a rusty blacksmith's tool just below. There were hundreds of drawers lined up from the floor to the ceiling, higher than either child could reach.

"This is amazing!" Billy marveled.

"Did Uncle Gary make all this?" Sophie suddenly asked. That made sense, of course, but for some reason it hadn't occurred to Billy until Sophie asked the question.

"I guess he did," Billy said. "Maybe this is what he has been working on all this time."

And maybe he wasn't lying after all, Billy thought suddenly. He tried to remember exactly what Uncle Gary had said that day at the dinner table, the last day they'd seen him. He'd said something like, "I haven't sold anything because it's not finished yet." Maybe he was talking about this nightstand. Maybe this was the *only* thing he'd been working on.

"Um, Billy?"

He was so lost in thought he didn't even hear Sophie's voice.

"Billy?"

He looked up. Sophie was standing at the end of the hallway, where it branched off in two different directions. She turned back toward him and the look on her face was one of pure disbelief—or was it fear? Whatever it was, Billy had never seen that particular look before, and he wasn't sure what it meant.

"Come see."

He went to the end of the hallway where she stood. She pointed out toward the other hallway. Billy peeked around the corner. His jaw fell open and his breath stopped halfway to his lungs.

The other hallway stretched on into the distance as far as the dim light allowed him to see. The wooden walls here were also covered with rows of drawers from floor to ceiling. Square openings led into other hallways that branched off to the right and left. He turned to look in the opposite direction and saw very much the same thing. In the distance, barely within range of his vision, it looked like the hallway came to an end, but other hallways branched off this one as well. As far as he could tell, each held drawers. Drawers everywhere.

"Billy, how big is this place?" Sophie's voice trembled slightly as she spoke.

He could only shake his head.

"I think we should get out of here," she whispered.

Billy nodded. They turned and tiptoed to the back end of their little hallway where the trapdoor stood open, leading down into Billy's room. The wooden floor creaked under their feet. Sophie went down first. Billy watched her from above until her head disappeared from beneath the nightstand. Then, lowering himself down into the square shaft, he closed the upper trapdoor, went down the five rungs and dropped to the carpeted floor beneath the nightstand.

Crawling out into his room, he was temporarily blinded by the brightness of the light coming in his window.

"What are we going to do?" said Sophie, blinking and rubbing her own eyes. "Should we tell Mom and Dad?"

"I don't know. Yeah. I think we should."

"They're not going to believe us."

Billy pondered this for a moment, knowing she was right. They would just have to get them to come upstairs without telling them anything in particular.

"Let's just say we have to show them something important in my room. Is Dad home?"

Sophie nodded. "He's outside. Cutting the grass."

"Okay, come on."

Motioning for Sophie to follow, moving quickly, now that they'd made their decision, Billy led his sister into the short upstairs hallway and together they ran down the stairs.

15

They found Mom in the kitchen, preparing sandwiches.

"Are you guys getting hungry?" she asked.

"Um," said Billy. He realized he was starving. "Yeah, I guess so. But can you come upstairs first? We need to show you something."

"What is it?"

"It's—well—we kind of have to show you. It's really important. We have to show Dad, too."

"Fine," she said, "but can it wait until after lunch?"

Sophie and Billy both shook their heads.

"My, you two sure are serious. What's going on?"

"We can't really explain it," said Sophie. "We just have to show you. Both of you."

"Okay, but it's going to have to wait. Your father's not going to stop cutting the grass until he's finished with it. And I'm right in the middle of something, too. Why don't you go wash your hands and get ready to eat? We'll go up there later."

"Mom, this is really important," Billy said, growing frustrated. He didn't know how to make her understand that this wasn't just kid stuff. This really was important, in a big person kind of way.

"Billy, I said we'll look at it later."

"But—"

At that moment, there was a knock on the door. A very loud knock. It sounded like someone banging a rock or a hard stick against the door three times.

"Oh, now what?" said Mom, putting down the butter knife she was using to spread the mayonnaise. "Sophie, wasn't Maggie supposed to come over?"

"Yeah, but—I don't think that's her."

"Well, you guys go check. It's probably one of your friends. I'll make an extra sandwich for them if they want."

Billy and Sophie walked to the front door. Three more knocks sounded, louder than before. It definitely wasn't Maggie. The knocks seemed to come from high up on the door. The kids looked at each other. Then Billy shrugged and opened it.

On the porch stood two very strange-looking men. They both wore brown suits, and even though their features were different, they could have been brothers. Both were very tall and very thin with an unusual grayish-brown cast to their skin and, judging by the deep wrinkles and crags on their faces, very old. The one in back actually seemed older, as his wrinkles were deeper and more pronounced. They stood straight and stiff and looked down at the kids with round, unblinking brown eyes.

A sour smell came off of them, strong enough to make the kids recoil. It was a smell of garbage, or spoiled food.

"Gary Fyfe, please," said the one in front. His voice was dry and rasping. There was an odd quality to it, almost a wheezing or a squeaking that came out beneath the words.

"Uhhhh," said Billy. "Hang on a minute." He turned toward the kitchen and shouted, "Mom!"

It seemed to take forever for Mom to get from the kitchen to the front door, and all the while the two men stood completely still, staring down at the children. Finally, she came up the hallway to the front door, drying her hands on a towel.

"Can I help you?" she said to the men on the porch.

"Gary Fyfe, please," the first man repeated. He had an odd accent.

"Kids," said Mom, wrinkling her nose. "Go get your father."

They ran across the house and out the back door, where they found Dad pushing the lawnmower through the tall grass along the back fence. They waved their arms to get his attention, and when he saw them, he shut the mower off.

"Dad, there's someone here," shouted Billy. "Come quick!"

"Who is it?" Dad said, looking irritated. "Can't your mom handle it? I'm busy right now."

"They're asking for Uncle Gary," Sophie shouted.

A shadow seemed to fall over Dad's face. Absently brushing grass clippings from his shirt and jeans, he came across the back-yard and into the house. The kids followed behind, stopping to watch from the hallway as Dad approached the front door.

"What's going on?" he said.

"I told them we haven't seen Gary for almost six months," said Mom.

"Told who?" Dad turned to the open doorway. "Excuse me. Would you mind telling me who you are?"

"My name is John and his name is Bob. We represent the Zobadak Wood Company. May we come in?"

Even from the hallway, Billy could hear the strange, high creaking sound coming from the porch.

"No. I don't think so," Dad replied. He looked appraisingly at the men, unable to keep the scowl from his face at the smell wafting off of them. "What exactly do you want?"

"We are looking for the Gary Fyfe. Are you his brother?"

"Yes, but like my wife already told you, we haven't seen him in six months. We don't know where he is."

The tall man in front stooped over, bringing his head under the top of the doorframe and peering into the house.

"He's here," the man said.

The other man, behind him, bent stiffly over at the waist, leaning to the right and also peering into the house.

"What?" said Dad. "What do you mean, 'He's here'?"

"The Gary Fyfe accepted a shipment of wood from our company. The wood was very rare and expensive. It was not paid for. We have been trying to contact him."

"How much money are you talking about?" said Dad. "I'm not responsible for my brother's debt. I hope you aren't coming here expecting to collect money. You're not going to get it."

"We don't want money," said the man, and the creaking sound came again. "We need to get the wood back. The shipment was made in error."

"I'm sorry, I don't know anything about any wood. My brother never said anything about it."

The man in the back spoke.

"He's telling the truth."

"Of course I'm telling the truth." Dad's voice was exasperated. "Look, I don't know who you guys are, but if your company made a mistake with one of its shipments, I'd have to say that's your problem."

"Yes, that is correct. It is our problem," said the man in front. He leaned over further, stooping so that his face was at the same level with Dad's.

"May we come in?"

"No, I already told you. You can't come in. I've answered your questions. Now I think you should leave."

The men began looking around inside the house, turning their heads slowly back and forth, up and down. The man in front craned his neck to peer up the stairs. The one in back looked down, and his eyes seemed to follow the baseboards around the floor of the foyer. Billy noticed an odd dark bump protruding from the right side of this man's forehead.

Finally, the front man tilted his expressionless face back up to Dad. He reached into an inside pocket of his jacket, pulled out a business card, and handed it through the doorway.

"My name is John. If you find him, please call us right away and we will come back."

Dad took the card but didn't say anything. The men continued to stand there motionless, staring at him.

"I'll tell him," said Dad.

As he pushed the door closed, they heard the voices of both men say, "Bye."

Dad went directly to the front window and looked out. Mom followed him, and a moment later both kids ran over to the window to look. They saw the two men walking across the front lawn. Their movements were slow and stiff, the way a person might walk if both legs had fallen asleep.

There was an old, mud-spattered, black truck parked at the curb. It was like a large pickup, only its cab seemed taller, sort of stretched out. It had a flatbed in back with metal posts around the sides. It was the kind of truck that might deliver lumber. A crow perched on the roof of the truck took off into the air as the men approached. They climbed awkwardly into the truck. As the engine roared to life, a plume of black smoke shot out of its smoke stack. Then the truck lurched and rumbled away up Fairlane.

Mom let out a long breath of air, as if she had been holding it.

"That was weird," she said, waving a hand in front of her nose. "Ugh. That smell. They smelled like rotten meat."

"Boy, you're not kidding," agreed Dad. "I can still smell it."

"And did you hear that sound—that high squeaky sound whenever they talked? What was that?"

"I don't know. I couldn't tell where it was coming from." Dad was looking down at the business card, turning it over in his hand.

"And what's with those brown suits?" Mom continued. "They looked like car salesmen from the seventies. And did you notice their shoes? They were long and pointy. Where would they even buy shoes like that?"

"Look at this." Dad handed the business card to Mom. The kids turned their attention to the card also. It looked like a piece of very thin plywood. The words "Zobadak Wood Company" were sloppily written on it in smeared, splotchy black ink. Below the words were the numbers 164-453.

"That's not even a phone number," said Mom. "What is that?"

Dad only shrugged and shook his head.

"Do you think we should call the police?" Mom asked.

"No. We have no reason to. They didn't break any laws."

"I guess you're right. But I still don't like it," said Mom. "This whole thing makes me very uncomfortable."

Dad looked like he was going to say something. He glanced down at Billy and Sophie, paused, and then changed his mind. At that moment, there was a knock at the door and all four of them jumped.

"I'll get it," said Dad. He opened the door and there stood Maggie.

"AaaaCHOO!" she scream-sneezed so loudly that Dad winced. "Hi, Mr. Fyfe. Some old, ugly truck left a big black stain in front of your house. It made a trail all the way down the street. Can Sophie play?"

"Hi. Come on in, Maggie," Dad said. She came in, walking into the living room where the others stood.

"Hang on a second, Maggie," said Sophie. She looked reproachfully at Billy, as though he'd forgotten all about their mission. "Mom, Dad, we have to show you something up in Billy's room."

"Not right now, Sophie," said Dad. "I have to talk to your mother. Why don't you show us later, okay?"

"But you really need to see this," said Sophie.

"Um, Sophie," said Billy, shaking his head at her. "Never mind. Let's show them later. I need to talk to you first."

"Can I see it?" said Maggie. Without waiting for an answer, she headed for the stairs.

"No!" shouted Billy.

"Yeah, sure, come on," said Sophie. The girls took off up the stairs and Billy followed closely behind, yelling for them to stop.

16

Two blocks from the Fyfe house, the truck stalled and black smoke belched from under the hood, swirling around the cab where the two tall men sat. The driver began turning a rusted metal crank on the dashboard until the engine coughed, chugged, and shuddered back to life. The passenger sat stiffly upright, facing sideways toward the driver, his narrow, deeply-lined face devoid of expression.

"I thought we agreed," the passenger said, rubbing the dark bump on his forehead. His voice was barely audible above the roar of the engine. "I was going to be John."

"What's the difference? John, Bob, Don, Rob. They're all the same."

"They're not the same. Everyone knows Johns are the leaders. And Johns do all the talking."

"How do you know that?"

"Because of John Wayne."

"Okay," shouted the driver. "I did all the talking, so what's the problem? I'm John."

"But I was going to do the talking," said the passenger. "I was going to be John."

"Why?"

"Because I saw the John Wayne movie."

"Well, I got to the porch first. The person standing in front always does the talking. Even Brope said that." The two men sat in silence for several minutes as the truck rumbled out onto the main road. The other vehicles on the road swerved and sped up to get away from the billowing cloud of smoke streaming behind it. Every time another car honked its horn, the driver of the truck responded by honking his own horn and waving.

"Who is John Wayne, anyway?" said John, the driver.

"He's a cowboy famous man guy. The person at the television store said all men wish they were like John Wayne. He's a real man."

"Why were you at the television store?"

"I was doing research. Brope told us to do research. I think you forgot. We are supposed to get better. Movies show people how to be."

"I did research," said John. "I went to the mall."

"The mall?"

"It's where people go to get rid of their money. It's an important place to them."

The passenger opened his mouth to respond, then slowly reclosed it. He stared at the driver for a long time. Finally the passenger spoke again.

"Okay, John. What are you going to tell Brope?"

"Nothing, Bob. We're not going back yet. We can't go back without the wood."

"I know that. Then what do we do next?"

"It's in that house. Didn't you feel it?"

"Of course I felt it."

"We have to go inside that house."

There was another long pause in the conversation, as John, the driver, waved to three consecutive cars, whose drivers were waving at him. It was the "driving wave," which was different from the standing or walking wave. They were learning these things.

"Tomorrow," said Bob.

"Tomorrow," said John, leaning forward over the steering wheel.

"And I get to be John tomorrow," said Bob.

"We will see who gets to the porch first," replied John.

They drove in silence for another ten minutes before turning off the street and onto a small dirt path that led back into a field. The truck bounced over holes and ridges.

Then Bob said softly, scratching the bump on his forehead, "He should have let us take the Truck."

"What?" shouted John.

"I said he should have let us take the Truck. The real Truck, I mean. The big one."

John looked at him for a long time, his wrinkled face a twisted mask of surprise and confusion. Slowly a stiff smile stretched his lips and he began to laugh. It was a dry, rasping, splintered laugh that almost sounded like pebbles rattling around in a wooden box. And even above the noise of the truck's engine, the high-pitched creaking sound could be heard.

17

"How is this possible?" Chris marveled, pulling himself up through the trapdoor and sitting on the floor. He looked around at the walls of the little hallway, and all the drawers, and at Billy, Sophie, and Maggie as though he'd never seen them before.

"Sshhh. Keep your voice down," whispered Billy. "We don't want anyone to know about this yet."

"Okay," Chris said, lowering his voice. "But how is this possible?"

"I'm not sure. I think it has something to do with joinery. My uncle used to talk about it."

"What's joinery?" Chris could not have looked more confused.

"It's some kind of magic," said Sophie helpfully, looking around with obvious pride on her face. "Uncle Gary made this."

Chris shrugged.

"How big is it inside here? How far back does it go?"

"We're not sure yet." Billy looked back over his shoulder at the other hallway branching out from the end of the one they sat in. "We started going down that hallway to the right when we heard you yelling. We didn't want Mom to come up here and start looking for us."

"What's in all the drawers?" continued Chris, opening one and looking inside. "There's a little black book in this drawer. *'Bestiary,'*" he read on the cover of the book. "Aw, cool. It has drawings of creatures in it."

"Every drawer has something different," said Maggie excitedly. "I found a drawer full of seashells and a funny-looking pinecone. Oh yeah, and a snow globe with a little castle inside."

"I found a little stone statue made by the Aztecs!" said Sophie.

"And a fossil of a trilobite! And a pair of sealskin mittens!" said Maggie.

"And a handkerchief with a whole bunch of birds sewn into it with all different colors and—"

"Come on, you guys. Keep your voices down," Billy whispered. "What if Mom's out in the hallway?"

Chris was looking in one drawer after another, occasionally making comments like, "Whoa!" or "Look at this!" or "What the heck?"

"Billy," said Sophie, suddenly serious. "Why don't you want Mom and Dad to know about this?"

Billy thought for a moment before speaking. "We'll tell them about it. We will. But just not yet."

"Why not?"

"Well—you know those two guys that came to the door? Those tall creepy guys who were looking for Uncle Gary?"

Sophie nodded.

"I'm a little bit worried about those guys," he said. "I didn't like them at all. They scared me."

"Well, they scared me too, but what does that have to do with this nightstand?"

"I don't want them to find out about it. I was afraid if Mom and Dad knew about it, they might say something. Or . . . or I was afraid those guys will know if Mom and Dad are trying to hide something. You know, if they ever come back."

"But Uncle Gary's no—" Sophie suddenly stopped talking and her eyes grew wide. Her mouth fell open as she looked at him. "You think Uncle Gary is in here somewhere?"

Billy nodded.

"Then he's not dead?" she said, her voice rising again.

Billy put a finger to his lips. "I don't know anything for sure. But maybe he's been hiding inside here the whole time."

Maggie and Chris had stopped opening drawers and were staring at Billy from further down the short hallway. Both of them looked a bit frightened.

"I'm just saying—it's maybe possible," Billy finished.

"Well, wouldn't he have heard us and come over here?" said Maggie.

"Not necessarily," Billy answered. "The thing is, we don't know how big it is inside here. Maybe he's too far away to hear us."

"This is just too weird," said Chris, shaking his head. "I don't think I wanna be in here anymore." He began moving away from the bigger hallway, back toward the trapdoor. "If it's that big, anything could be hiding inside here."

Maggie followed closely behind Chris, saying, "Don't leave me back there by myself."

"Wait a minute," Billy said. "You guys, wait. Listen to me. I keep telling you, I don't know anything. It's probably not that big. I think we should take a look around. I bet that hallway comes to a dead end in both directions and that's all there is. Let's just check it out. If it's too big, we'll come back. Okay?"

"Come on guys, let's check it out," urged Sophie, her voice full of excitement.

Maggie and Chris were silent for a minute, but finally they both nodded.

"You guys have to promise something though," said Billy. "And I mean super-promise. Like, the biggest promise you ever made."

"What's that?" Chris asked.

"This has to be top secret. You cannot tell *anyone* about it. And I mean, not even your mom or dad, or *anyone*. You promise?"

They nodded.

"Say it."

"We promise," they both said together.

"You too, Sophie."

"Okay, I promise," she said impatiently. She tightened her ponytail and adjusted her cap. "Can we go now?"

"Yeah. Come on, let's go."

18

They moved in single file, Billy and Sophie in front, Maggie and Chris bringing up the rear. The floor occasionally creaked as the boards shifted under their feet. At times, the entire hallway seemed to tilt ever so slightly to one side or the other. From the short entrance hall that they agreed to call the "Lobby," they decided to turn right into the main hallway and follow it to its end.

There were three openings on the right side, each one a short hallway, dead-ending about ten feet back, just like the Lobby. Rows of drawers, some significantly larger than the small, average-looking drawers they'd seen so far, were lined up across every wall, from floor to ceiling.

Billy had to resist the urge to go in and start opening drawers. There would be time for that later. Right now, they had to scout out the place and see exactly how big it was. And see if Uncle Gary was in there somewhere.

That idea seemed a little silly, now that he thought about it. But then again, everything about this situation was crazy. He wasn't even sure what the word "crazy" meant anymore. Could a *thing* be crazy or were only *people* crazy? Was the nightstand crazy? Was Uncle Gary crazy for building it? One thing for sure, he had to be a genius, too. Could a person be crazy *and* a genius? Was "crazy" how a person thought or what a person did? *Am I crazy,* thought Billy, *for going deeper into this place without telling Mom and Dad about it?*

Crazy, crazy, crazy—what a silly, stupid, crazy word. His mind whirling a mile a minute, Billy suddenly realized how completely exhausted he was. He remembered how he had sat up in bed most of last night, wide-awake. But even though he was physically tired, he couldn't have slept for anything.

When he came to the hallway on the left side, he stopped. He could clearly see the end of the main hallway now. It didn't end after all, but turned right into what looked like a very dark, narrow passage. They'd explore that later, he decided. Standing at the opening on the left side, he took a deep breath and peeked around the corner. No Uncle Gary. But this hallway went back for a few feet, then made another turn to the left. The others were whispering to each other and Billy turned around and put his finger to his lips.

"Ssshhh!" he hissed. He tiptoed into the left-hand passage and looked around the next corner. The passage continued on for another five or six feet, then turned right. There were no drawers here.

His stomach clenched with anxiety, he started down the drawerless hallway, motioning for the others to follow. A musty smell assailed his nostrils. Behind him Maggie began to sneeze.

Billy whirled around, glaring at her. "Ssshhhh!"

"I can't help it," Maggie whispered. "AaaCHHOO!" She clamped her hands over her mouth and under her nose to hold back the next one.

Billy rolled his eyes. *If there's anybody else in this place, they sure know about us now,* he thought.

"Come on," said Chris, nervously. "Let's just keep going."

Billy nodded and they continued. The floor here creaked even louder, as if the boards were loose. Arriving at the point where the hallway turned to the right, Billy and Chris both poked their heads around the corner. For some reason, Billy expected another dead end. He couldn't have been more wrong.

The hallway stretched into the distance almost as far as he could see. In the shadows of the far end, it seemed to either stop or make a turn, but it was too dim to tell. On the left side, he saw a series of at least ten branching hallways, one after another. It reminded Billy of the aisles in a library.

"It doesn't end," said Chris. Softy, they crept along the passage.

"Oh, my gosh," Sophie whispered. "This place is *huge*."

They came to the first opening on the left. The walls here were lined with drawers, just like the main hallway behind them, only these were wide and shallow and each drawer had two knobs. Billy could not see the end of the hallway. A section of wall maybe five feet wide stood before the opening of the next aisle. It had decorative wooden panels, but no drawers. The next aisle was the same as the first.

"There must be thousands of drawers in here," whispered Billy.

"Thousands of thousands," Chris corrected him in awe.

They stopped at the third aisle and Sophie took a few steps into it, looking upward.

"I think the walls are higher here than they were in the other hallway. How would anybody reach those drawers up at the top?" she asked.

"I don't know." Billy followed her into the aisle. Using both hands, he opened one of the drawers.

"Oh, man." Inside was a collection of butterflies, each one stuck with a pin to the corkboard covering the bottom of the drawer. Their wings displayed every color and pattern and size imaginable.

Some he recognized, like the monarch butterfly. Others he had never seen before, like the huge green, blue, and black one near the back corner, its fragile wings spread wider than his hand.

Closing the drawer he opened the one below it. This drawer contained a collection of moths, hundreds of them, their furry bodies and wings striped and spotted with blacks, oranges, browns, and whites. Some of the spots looked eerily like eyes staring back at him. There were no tags identifying them. Like the butterflies in the drawer above, the moths were not lined up in orderly rows. They were arranged in symmetrical patterns, creating an intricate, curling design.

Chris had moved farther down the aisle and was opening a drawer in the next section.

"Wow!" he said. "Billy, look at this." His drawer contained a collection of walking sticks, prehistoric-looking insects shaped like green tree branches with legs. Some of them were as long as Billy's forearm. He had never seen insects so big.

"This is getting creepy," Sophie commented.

"Was your uncle a bug collector or something?" Chris wondered.

"Not that I know of," Billy shook his head. "He never mentioned it."

"Where does all this stuff come from?" said Sophie. "I don't get it."

Billy couldn't answer. He felt like he was trapped in a bizarre dream that kept getting bigger and stranger and more confusing.

"Hey, you guys," came Maggie's voice from the main aisle. "Come here."

They went back out to where she stood.

"I went to the end of this hallway," she said. Her eyes were watering from her allergies and she was making a funny face, trying to hold back another sneeze. "There are eight more aisles like this. And at the end, it turns left and goes back that way. I think it's like one big long room with all these aisles in it."

"Let's go all the way around it," said Sophie.

"Yeah, okay," Billy said. "Then we'll at least know how big this section is."

"Should we draw a map or something?" Chris asked.

"Nah," said Billy. "We won't get lost. I know exactly how to get back."

They continued down the hallway, passing one aisle after another on the left. At the end the hallway turned left and ran back parallel to the other ten aisles. Drawers covered both sides. In the dim light Billy could just make out the back end of the room. It was hard for him to estimate the distance, but it seemed like about the same length as the soccer field at school. For the first time, he noticed where the light was coming from. Bare light bulbs hung from short cords in the ceiling. At least half of them appeared to be burned out, which was why this section was so much dimmer than the main hallway.

Not only that everything seemed much older in this room. A layer of dust covered the floor and walls, cobwebs hung in the corners, and the floor creaked with nearly every step. The air was heavy with a stale, musty smell that reminded Billy of his grandmother's basement. She kept stacks and stacks of old newspapers down there and he and Sophie used to pretend they were mountains and climb on them. No wonder Maggie was having an allergy attack. They started down the aisle, toward the back corner of the big room, sticking close together.

"Do you think there's a drawer full of spiders here?" Maggie said. "I'm afraid of spiders."

"Scaredy-cat," joked Chris in a whisper. "Meeooooww." He dragged the sound out in the quiet corridor.

"I'm not a scaredy-cat," she answered. "Just don't open any more drawers, that's all."

When they were halfway down the aisle, Billy could clearly see the back end, where it turned left. He sped up his pace a little. Even though he didn't want to admit it, he was pretty scared too. Suddenly, more than anything else, he wanted to go back to the main hallway and return to his bedroom. This whole thing was just too strange—too unbelievable. Billy wanted to get out of this dark place to go outside and feel the sun.

Finally they reached the corner, and the passage went back toward the first aisle. Just like the wall at the front end, the wall on their right was adorned with dark, rectangular wooden panels outlined in fancy trim. Billy couldn't help but admire the strange, swirling patterns of the wood grain on these panels.

"Come on, keep going," urged Chris. "What are you doing?"

"Now who's scared?" Maggie choked out, fighting back a sneeze. "Aaaa . . . aaaaa . . ."

"Don't sneeze!" Sophie whispered.

"I won't . . . aaaa . . . aaaaa . . ."

"I'm not scared!" said Chris.

"Aaaa*CHHOO!*"

"Hey! Look at this!" cried Billy. They all stopped talking. Billy was staring at one of the panels.

"This wood," he said. "There are faces in it. Look, right here in the middle—and two more here."

"What are you talking about?" said Chris. "It's just a piece of wood."

"No, I'm serious. Come here and look at this."

Sophie, Maggie, and Chris came closer. The light was dim, but they could still see the patterns in the wood. Billy was pointing to the center of the panel.

"These are the eyes—and right here is the mouth."

"Oh, my gosh!" said Sophie. "I see it!"

As Billy pointed out the various features of the faces, they became so distinct and realistic that it seemed almost impossible for them to be random patterns in the wood grain. The large face in the middle had a long beard, a hooked nose, and eyes that seemed to be staring right out at them. Of the other faces, one looked like a child laughing and the other looked like a woman with wild hair sticking straight up.

"That's really weird," said Maggie, as Billy reached up and touched the panel, tracing the outline of the large face with his finger.

"It's amazing," said Billy. He pressed his hand against the panel. With a shriek of wood scraping on wood, it swung inward and all four kids jumped back. Chris shouted.

"Whoa," Sophie said. "What is that?"

"I don't know." Billy approached the panel again and pushed. The panel swung in farther. Behind it was a small passage running straight back into darkness. It was barely large enough for an adult to crawl through.

"You found a secret passage!" Chris exclaimed.

Billy strained his eyes to see in the dark passage, but beyond the first couple feet it was pitch black. The four kids stepped forward and peered into the darkness.

"Where do you think it goes?" Maggie asked.

"I don't know," said Billy.

"What's that smell?" asked Chris. "Do you smell that?"

A strong, spicy smell came from within the passage, and Billy and Sophie were both surprised to discover they knew exactly what the smell was.

"Cedar," they said together.

"What?" said Chris.

"Cedar is a big evergreen tree," Billy explained. "The wood has a certain kind of smell. Uncle Gary used to make us smell it. He said the smell of cedar was magic and could heal people. Some of the boxes he gave us are made from it."

Chris looked blank. His parents both worked in a factory, and Chris didn't know much about trees.

"We should have brought flashlights," Sophie said absently. She poked her head into the opening of the passage. For a moment, Billy thought she was getting ready to climb in and start crawling away.

"Hey, you guys?" whispered Chris. "This is enough. Can we go now? I think we should go."

"Meeeoowww," Maggie teased, but she did it in a whisper and didn't sound very sure of herself.

"Stop it, Maggie," said Chris. "I'm serious. I think we should go back down and tell your parents about this. I have a bad feeling all of a sudden."

"Hang on a second," said Sophie. She leaned farther into the opening, stretching her arms out in front of her, into the darkness.

"What are you doing?" said Billy.

"I think I see something," she answered.

"Sophie, don't," Maggie whispered urgently.

Suddenly there was a loud THUD, like some kind of heavy object landing on a wood floor. Maggie screamed and Chris jumped straight up and whirled around. Sophie backed quickly out of the passage.

"Sophie, what did you do?" said Billy.

"Nothing! I didn't do anything. The sound came from out here."

"Out where?" Billy asked, looking around.

"It came from above us," Maggie corrected.

They all looked up and froze. Footsteps were coming from above. Someone was walking on another floor above them, starting in the back corner and moving across the ceiling. There was an odd limp to the footsteps. And they sounded as if they were made by two different shoes, one soft and one hard, making a kind of CLUNK-THUMP, CLUNK-THUMP, CLUNK-THUMP sound.

"That's enough. Can we go now?" cried Chris. Without waiting for a reply, he began walking, then running, back toward the front of the room. The others took off after him. They ran past the ten aisles on their left. When they got to the corner, they turned and ran up to where the entrance was. They still heard the footsteps moving across the ceiling—CLUNK-THUMP, CLUNK-THUMP—going off in another direction now, to the right.

The kids pushed and jostled through the short passage leading out to the main hallway. They ran back to the Lobby, crashing into each other as they all turned left at the same time.

The footsteps seemed to have faded into the distance, but no one was really sure that whoever had made them was truly gone. Their breathing was so loud it was impossible to hear anything else.

The girls climbed down first through the trapdoor, with the boys nearly tumbling down on top of them in their rush to get down the ladder and back into Billy's room. When everyone was out, Billy slammed the inner lid closed and shoved the two drawers back into the nightstand.

The four of them stood there, breathing hard and looking at each other. Then Chris burst into laughter. The others looked at him, confused.

"Oh, man!" Chris said between breaths. "That was really scary!"

"You're not kidding," said Billy, his hands on his knees as he fought to catch his breath. "So why are you laughing?"

"I don't know," he responded, sitting down on the floor. "I guess I must be freaking out a little."

"You are a freak," said Maggie, dryly. Turning to Billy, she asked, "Who do you think that was? Was that your uncle in there?"

Billy shook his head. "It didn't sound like his footsteps. He doesn't limp like that. And whoever that was, it sounded like he was wearing two different shoes."

"Uncle Gary never wore two different shoes," said Sophie.

"But if it's not Uncle Gary, who would it be?" asked Billy.

"Who or *what?*" said Chris meaningfully.

"Stop it, Chris." Maggie glared at him.

"And what if he comes down here after us?" Chris continued.

They all stared at Chris, then looked at each other in silence, considering the idea. Maggie moved away from the nightstand, closer to the door of Billy's room.

"We have to tell Mom and Dad," said Sophie, pushing up the bill of her cap.

Billy thought about it for several minutes. Then he shook his head.

"I don't think so," he said. "Not yet, anyway. Think about it. If we tell them, they're going to handle it the way adults always handle things. They'll get the authorities involved. They'll call the police and then the news will find out, and pretty soon the nightstand will be swarming with people. They'll wreck everything. They'll probably take it away to a laboratory or something. And—and the other thing is—" He took a deep breath. "I think Uncle Gary is hiding in there. He must be hiding for a good reason," he said to the shocked faces around him. "I mean, maybe he's afraid of something. What if something bad happens to him because we told people about the Buglu Drawer? We would never forgive ourselves. What if the wrong people find out?"

"Like who?" asked Chris.

"Like those two men who came to our house earlier," Sophie answered gravely.

Billy nodded. "Yeah. Or that policeman. Do you remember that guy, Sophie? I didn't trust him either."

Sophie nodded, deep in thought.

"Billy's right," said Maggie. "We have to keep it a secret."

Billy took another deep breath, then said it. "I think we have to go back in there and look for Uncle Gary."

The other three stared at him.

"Uh, excuse me?" said Chris. "Did you say we have to go back in there?"

"Yeah," Sophie answered for her brother. She stood up. "But you guys don't have to come. Billy and I will do it."

"Well, of course we're coming with you," said Maggie. "Right, Chris?"

"Uh—" Chris hesitated, then said, "Yeah, that's right." A pause. "But, uh, you don't mean right *now*, do you?"

"No, not right now," said Billy. "Let's go back tomorrow."

The others nodded. Chris looked visibly relieved.

"Tomorrow," they said together.

Suddenly Billy's bedroom door opened up and all four of them jumped. Sophie, Maggie, and Chris screamed. It was Mom. She looked irritated.

"Where have you guys been? I've been looking everywhere."

"Oh, we were just playing hide and seek," said Billy, looking at the floor. It was kind of the truth. In a way.

"No more play time today," said Mom. She smiled at Maggie. "Your mom called. She wants you home. And Chris, your mom called twice. She didn't even know you were here. She sounded pretty mad. I think you'd better hurry home. And you two," she turned to Billy and Sophie. "Get cleaned up and come give me a hand downstairs. It's time for dinner."

The entire afternoon was gone. Had they even had lunch? The four friends looked at each other as Mom left the room, sober with the knowledge only they shared.

"Tomorrow," Sophie whispered to quiet nods all around.

19

When Billy and Sophie came downstairs Sunday morning, Dad was doing something to the front door with a screwdriver. He had a puzzled look on his face.

"The door is sticking," he said. "Ever since yesterday afternoon."

When he swung it closed to demonstrate, the outer edge bumped against the doorframe. When he opened it back up, the door scraped against the frame. He picked up the screwdriver again and began tightening the screws of the hinges.

"Is everybody ready to go?" Mom walked in from the kitchen. "Get your jackets, kids. It's a bit chilly today."

Every Sunday, the Fyfes drove to the Meat Tree Family Diner for breakfast. Dad always ordered the meat-master omelet. Mom usually got the spinach and cheese omelet. Billy and Sophie ordered the ham scram with hash browns.

"Sophie, take that filthy hat off," Mom said when the food came. "How can you stand that thing?"

Other than that there was not much conversation. At least, not at first. Mom and Dad were unusually quiet, and Billy wondered if something had happened that they didn't want to talk about in front of the kids. Billy and Sophie, sitting across from each other in the booth, were also quiet. Thoughts of the Buglu Drawer, and what they might find when they went back in today, consumed them.

Finally, halfway through his omelet and on his seventh cup of coffee, Dad broke the silence.

"I did a search on the internet for the Zobadak Wood Company. Nothing. Not one reference to it anywhere."

"So you think those guys were making it up?" Mom asked.

"Maybe. Maybe there's no such thing as the Zobadak Wood Company. I checked with a bunch of different business directories too. Nobody lists them." He chewed his omelet thoughtfully.

"They could be so small and private that only a few people know about them by word of mouth. Who knows? Anyway, yesterday, on my way to the hardware store, I stopped at a pay phone and called that number on the Zobadak business card. Just to see what would happen."

"And?" Mom lifted an eyebrow.

"It was weird," he said. "It rang three times and then stopped. There was no voice or anything but I could hear noises on the other end. It almost sounded like factory noise—but it was strange. And then there was this groaning and squeaking noise. It sounded like wood. You know how a big tree sounds when it falls down? How it sort of shrieks and squeals? But the whole time, there was a lot of static so it was really hard to hear anything clearly. After that, there was a sliding noise, like something big and heavy sliding across a floor. Then the line went dead."

Billy and Sophie looked at each other.

"Very strange," said Mom. "It must have been a bad connection. Actually, I'm surprised you got anything at all. It's not even a real phone number. At least not an American one."

"Yeah, I know. This whole business makes me nervous. If those guys show up again, I'm going to call the police."

Mom nodded. "I think that's a good idea."

There was another long silence. When Dad finally spoke again, his voice was so low the kids could barely hear him.

"Molly," he said. "I don't want to jump to conclusions or anything, but I think that company had something to do with Gary's disappearance."

"What? You think they abducted him or something?"

"No. They're still looking for him. But I think he's hiding because of them. And not only that," he lowered his voice even more. "I think they're the ones who broke into Gary's house."

Mom's eyes widened.

"Henry, I don't like this," she said. "Not one bit. You should call the police right now."

"We can't jump to conclusions just because of a feeling. The police won't do anything unless we know something definite."

Mom sighed and put down her fork. She pushed her plate away, leaving half of her omelet on the plate. She took a sip of coffee.

"Where do you think Gary would be hiding?" she said.

Dad shook his head and shrugged his shoulders.

"I have no idea."

Billy looked at Sophie, and Sophie stared back at him, wide-eyed. She cocked her head ever so slightly at their parents, and Billy saw with horror that she wanted to tell them. He shook his head very slightly, so that Mom and Dad wouldn't notice. Sophie subtly nodded yes, silently arguing with him. Billy opened his eyes as wide as they would go, screaming at her with his stare. It was an eye-scream. Their eyes locked, both defiant.

"Wouldn't he have told us what was going on?" Mom asked.

"Maybe, maybe not," said Dad, oblivious to the looks his children were exchanging. "He always was a loner. He didn't always tell me everything that was going on with him."

"Yeah, but come on. I think this is kind of important."

Billy picked up the squeeze bottle of ketchup and furtively drew the word "NO" on his hash browns. He set the bottle down decisively on the table.

Dad looked out the window, deep in thought.

"The thing is," he said, "I think Gary tried to tell me he was in trouble the last time I talked to him. But I didn't listen."

Sophie grabbed the ketchup and wrote "YES" in even larger letters across her potatoes.

"Don't start blaming yourself," Mom said, reaching out to touch his hand. "This is not your fault."

Snatching the plastic bottle of mustard, Billy made a yellow exclamation point after the word "NO!" and then drew a circle around it.

Dad didn't respond. He continued staring out the window.

Still holding the ketchup bottle, Sophie slowly tilted it forward until the nozzle was pointed across the table, directly at Billy.

"Listen," said Mom. "Gary was a smart guy. Don't you think he would have found a way to contact us?"

"But he hasn't," Dad said, his voice heavy with frustration.

Billy quietly aimed the mustard bottle across at Sophie, tightening his fingers in preparation for a counterattack. They eye-screamed at each other. Daring Billy to stop her, Sophie turned toward Mom and Dad, opening her mouth to begin telling them about the Buglu Drawer. The next words out of Mom's mouth made her stop.

"Maybe he has," Mom said. "Maybe he has tried to contact us, but we haven't been paying attention. Just think about it, that's all I'm saying. It seems to me like he would have done something."

Sophie turned back toward Billy. The expression on her face communicated surprise, amazement, realization, and a few other things Billy didn't quite recognize. She lowered the ketchup bottle back to the table, then calmly picked up her fork and began smearing away the "YES" on her potatoes. When there was nothing left but a thin red layer, she began eating.

"You're assuming Gary's still alive," Dad said to Mom.

"Of course," Mom responded. "And so should you."

"Mom," Sophie said around a mouthful of toast, "are we going straight home when we're done eating?"

"Yes, dear, we are. Now please don't interrupt. We're having an adult conversation."

After breakfast, as they were walking out of the restaurant, Billy and Sophie lagged behind. Billy tugged on Sophie's sleeve and whispered, "What's going on with you?"

Sophie smiled.

"I think I know how to find Uncle Gary. *Sssshhh.*"

20

Billy knew something was wrong even before they got to their street. He had a strange feeling in the pit of his stomach as Dad was turning the car into the neighborhood. Something wasn't right. He wanted Dad to hurry up—drive faster—even though he couldn't explain why.

Then he saw the trail of black oil in a crooked, weaving path down the middle of the street. Dad must have seen it at the same time.

"Look at that mess," he said in disgust. "It's from the truck those Zobadak guys were driving yesterday."

"I don't remember seeing so much of it this morning when we left for breakfast," commented Mom.

"Hmm," said Dad. "I don't either."

Billy felt the car speed up slightly.

"Look at all those birds," said Sophie, pointing out her window.

Leaning over so he could see through the window on Sophie's side, Billy saw a dense flock of black birds circling in the sky. There were hundreds of them, and Billy wasn't sure what they were, but they seemed larger than average birds. They appeared to be several blocks away, flying in circles over the rooftops.

"What are those?" he pointed.

"They look like crows." Dad craned his neck to see.

"What are they doing here?" Mom asked no one in particular. "We don't usually see crows around this neighborhood." After a moment of silence, she spoke again. "Henry, they look like they're over by our house."

Dad didn't say anything, but the car sped up a little more. He turned left on Sycamore Street and went over two blocks, then turned right onto Fairlane Avenue. Their house was still two blocks away, but they could now see the birds clearly. There was no question about it; the birds seemed to be flying directly over their house.

Billy noticed large splotches of black oil on the street as Dad accelerated more. People were standing on the sidewalks on both sides of the road, pointing down Fairlane Avenue at the circling flock of crows.

"What's going on?" asked Sophie, her voice tight with anxiety.

Nobody answered. Looking out his side window, Billy saw Maggie riding her bike on the sidewalk. She was pedaling away from their house but she put on her brakes when she saw their car passing by.

Billy turned around to look out the back window and saw her staring back at him, wide-eyed. She waved her hand in the air, then turned her bike around and began to follow, standing on the pedals to gain speed.

Dad slowed down as they approached the house. There were people everywhere—mostly neighbors, standing on their front lawns—looking at the Fyfe residence.

Billy had to rub his eyes to make sure he wasn't seeing things. The roof of the house was covered in a blanket of crows so dense it had virtually disappeared. Crowded and fighting for space, they hopped about and pecked at each other, flapping their wings. Their claws scraped on the gutters. Some took off to join the flock in the air while others landed. They filled the tree on the front lawn, their black feathers standing out against the bright orange leaves. Many more were scattered on the lawn itself. They gathered in clusters on the porch and on the driveway and on Mom's mini-van. The harsh cawing of the birds drowned out almost every other sound, and Dad quickly rolled up the car windows.

"Henry?" said Mom, her voice rising. "Why are they doing this?" She was trying to sound calm, but her voice trembled.

Dad didn't answer. He pulled up to the curb in front of their house and put the car in park, leaving it running.

"You guys stay in the car," he said, turning back to face them. "Do you hear me?"

They nodded and he opened the door and got out. The next-door neighbor, Philip, immediately ran over to the car. The kids could hear his voice because he was shouting over the noise of the birds.

"They just left!" Philip yelled. "I called the police! They should be here any minute!"

"What are you talking about?" Dad shouted back. "Who just left?"

Philip pointed to the front of the house and Billy felt his stomach sink. The front door was split into pieces and lying on the porch.

"Oh, no," Mom said, opening her door and climbing out.

"What happened?" Dad yelled to the neighbor.

"These two guys came in a truck!" Philip shouted. "They drove right up onto the front lawn there! They walked up and broke down the front door! Right here in broad daylight! They were in the house for about twenty minutes. Maybe more, I'm not sure. All these crows started to come while they were in the house! I called the police as soon as I saw it!"

Dad ran across the lawn toward the porch.

"Henry! Be careful!" Mom shouted.

He disappeared into the house without looking back.

Staring out the car window, the kids saw the deep tire tracks the truck had left on the lawn. There was a large black stain on the grass where oil had leaked from the truck.

"Billy," Sophie began, "those guys came here to find Uncle Gary."

"I know," said Billy.

"Do you think . . .?" She couldn't finish her sentence.

Billy didn't need her to finish. He knew what she was going to say—he was thinking the same thing. He hoped she wouldn't say it out loud. The idea was almost too much to bear. But then she did say it.

"Do you think they took the nightstand?"

Billy couldn't answer her. It was his fault. If the nightstand was gone, they might never find Uncle Gary. Those horrible people would have him. And it would be all his fault because he had wanted to keep it secret. How would he ever forgive himself?

The crows were dispersing. More and more were taking off to join the flock overhead. And in increasing numbers the birds were separating from the flock and flying away toward the north. The racket was quieting down and the kids could hear the conversation between Mom and the neighbor, Philip.

"Did they take anything?" Mom asked.

"I don't know," answered Philip. "When I ran home to call the police, they drove away."

A crow landed on the roof of the car, its claws screeching against the metal. Mom screamed and waved her arms, and the crow took off, flying across the lawn before joining the flock.

"They were already driving away when I came back outside," Philip continued. "I couldn't tell if they had anything on the back of the truck."

"I'm getting out," said Billy. He opened his door, expecting Mom to yell at him to stay in the car. She didn't say anything, so he climbed out and stood on the edge of the lawn. Sophie scrambled after him. The flock overhead was now much smaller and there was a steady stream of birds flying away. Most of them were in the air now, with only a few stragglers left on the roof of the house.

Maggie stood on the sidewalk next to her bike. She motioned for them to come over as police sirens sounded in the distance.

"Did you see anything?" Sophie asked her.

"It was the same truck that was here yesterday," Maggie said. "You could hear the birds all the way from my house, so I came over to see what was going on. That truck was on your grass," she pointed. "And its engine was really loud, and black smoke was just pouring out of it. There was so much smoke it was hard to see what was happening. And your house was completely covered in birds."

"Did they take anything when they left?" Billy asked.

"I don't know; I didn't stay," she answered. "The smoke was making me cough and the birds were freaking me out. So I started going back home to tell my mom about it."

Dad suddenly came out of the house, using a pillow to shoo a crow out of the doorway. It appeared to be the last of the crows, and it took off into the sky, following the path of the others.

Dad stopped on the porch, looking across at Mom. His face was pale, his expression utter confusion. Mom ran across the lawn to him and they began talking quietly. Dad made strange and urgent gestures with his hands.

At that moment, two police cars arrived, sirens blaring and lights flashing.

The rest of the day was a blur of activity and chaos as police officers searched the house, spoke with Mom and Dad, and filled out paperwork. Neighbors and friends came and went, offering help as they tried to satisfy their curiosity. Mom was on the verge of panic because of the mess and the smell of rotten meat permeating the house. She wandered from room to room spraying an air freshener while Dad, between outbursts of anger, kept fussing over the broken door and the deep tire ruts in the lawn.

The moment Billy and Sophie were allowed to enter the house, they ran upstairs to Billy's room. To their enormous relief, the nightstand was still there. From what they could tell, there was only one thing missing from the house: the banister. It was torn away from the supporting spindles from the bottom to the top of the stairs. As Dad kept repeating to the police officers, it made no sense. Why would they take the banister?

But that wasn't the only thing that made no sense. Something had happened to the wood in the house. Quite simply, it had warped. The baseboards were bent and some had separated from the wall and were sticking out. The doorframes were slightly crooked, which meant many of the doors would no longer close. Even the wooden dinner table was twisted—not much, but enough so that one leg was raised up and the table rocked back and forth. Wooden chair arms were bowed this way or that, window sills were slightly rippled, picture frames were twisted. Some of the wood was split and cracked from the strain.

Dad worried about the structure of the house. He was afraid the two-by-fours and the two-by-sixes that made up the skeleton of the house had been affected. Billy believed he might be right. Something felt different about the house. He couldn't put his finger on exactly what it was. Maybe the rooms weren't quite square anymore. Floors not quite level. Walls not quite vertical. Everything just a bit off. Not enough to see, but Billy could feel it. Things were just different. As if that weren't enough, a profusion of black feathers and bird poop made Mom's formerly clean house a distant memory.

Billy overheard Dad telling the police about the two men who had come the day before. The intruders had left another business card on the landing just inside the front door—"Zobadak Wood Company 164-453"—so he knew it was the same people. The police told him the men shouldn't be hard to track down since they'd left a trail of oil behind them. He expected them to be in custody by the end of the day.

Billy decided to tell his dad about the Bigy Bigy Buglu Drawer. But not until after the police left.

21

The truck bounced over holes and rocks and tree roots, engine banging, then coughing and snorting in a cloud of black smoke that billowed out from under the hood.

"If it wasn't for your—*problem*—we would have had more time in the house," accused John, fighting to hold the steering wheel straight.

"It's not my fault," said Bob, twisting his face into a frown and lifting his arms up in the air. "He didn't have to use walnut. He could have used elder wood like all the others."

"Maybe you should tell him that when we see him," sneered John.

They were both quiet for a long time. The truck snarled and lurched, tree branches scraping and clawing along both sides. Bob rubbed the dark bump on his forehead. It was larger than yesterday.

Bob said, "Since your name is John, I suppose you're going to do all the talking when we see Brope."

"Yes, I'll talk. I'll tell him how we had to leave before we finished because of your birds."

"And I'll tell him how you had to take the banister even though it had nothing to do with why we were there," countered Bob.

"That's a personal matter. You can't tell him about that."

"Explain it to me again and maybe I won't," offered Bob. "What was your reason for taking it?"

"I told you two times already. I recognized it. It belongs to my family."

Staring at John, Bob opened his mouth wide and made a loud screeching, rasping sound that went on for over twenty seconds.

"What's so funny?" said John, tightening his grip on the steering wheel.

"Your family," Bob said, then screeching again.

"Stop it. That's very irritating." John pouted as he slowed the truck down. It grew suddenly darker outside and he had to lean forward to see out the front window.

"Are you going to tell him we found the Gary Fyfe?" Bob asked.

"Maybe," John replied, almost too quietly to hear. "You're sure he's there?"

"I'm sure."

"But we don't know where he is exactly," said John.

"I know he's in the house," Bob said. "I know he's in the upstairs room."

Neither of them spoke for several minutes as the truck tilted forward. The outside world went black as the windows became caked with mud and tree roots dragged across the windshield.

"Do you think he'll let us take the big Truck?" Bob finally asked, his voice creaking. "The Ballagahaldo?"

There was another long pause.

"No. I don't think that's possible. I don't think so."

22

Four days later, Billy still hadn't told his parents a thing.

The world of school and homework had taken over, Dad wasn't coming home from work until late, and Mom was constantly busy, trying to erase the damage the flock of crows had done to her once-immaculate house.

Billy approached them on several occasions, but it was never the right time. Dad would be on the phone with the police or the insurance company or some other important official discussing serious matters. "Billy, can't you see I'm on the phone?" Or he would be trying to fix a door or the banister or the mantle or some other thing, muttering, "Billy, not now—I'm right in the middle of something."

And Mom never stopped moving—in a frenzy of cleaning and wiping and sterilizing, often with a phone attached to her ear: "Billy, I'm busy. Go talk to your father. So anyway, Mildred, there were crows in my house! Can you imagine the germs? I've never been so disgusted!"

By Thursday, Billy decided he would have to write them a letter. He was a little surprised Sophie hadn't been bugging him to hurry up and tell them. She had been unusually quiet all week. They hadn't even talked about the Buglu Drawer since the day of the crows.

Well past bedtime, Billy sat at the desk in his bedroom with a blank sheet of paper in front of him, trying to think of how to start the letter. He had already thought of ten different beginnings, but he couldn't imagine his parents taking any of them seriously. He was tired and his thoughts were murky. Finally he decided that he would write simply: "Dear Mom and Dad, I know where Uncle Gary is. Love, Billy."

Just as the pencil touched the paper, there was a soft knock on his door. It squeaked as it opened partway and Sophie peeked in.

"Are you awake?" she whispered.

"Yeah." Billy put the pencil down.

She came in, wearing her pink fairy pajamas, and shut the door behind her. She had just come out of the shower and her sandy hair was brushed down and uncovered, which was an unusual look for her.

"I heard Dad talking on the phone with the police," she said. "I could hear him through my vent. He sounded really mad."

"Did you hear what he said?" Billy turned around in his chair to face her as Sophie knelt on his bed, bouncing.

"Not all of it. But the police didn't find those Zobadak guys yet."

"I thought it was going to be easy," said Billy. "They left a trail."

"I know. I heard something about a forest. They lost them in a forest or something. Dad started yelling at them, and he wanted them to send a policeman to our house for protection. But it sounded like they weren't going to do it because there was no evidence that the men were dangerous. And then Dad shouted, 'Am

I supposed to wait around until someone in my family gets hurt?' And then he slammed the phone down and swore."

"Whoa," said Billy. He and his sister looked at each other in silence for long time.

Then Sophie said, "You didn't tell them anything yet, did you?"

"No," Billy answered. "I tried about four or five times, but they were always too busy. I was just getting ready to write them a letter."

"Maybe you should wait," she said.

He looked at her quizzically, eyebrows raised.

"I don't know," Sophie continued. She seemed restless and frustrated. Her feet swung to the floor. "I've been thinking about this all week. I just don't know if telling them is the right thing to do. I mean it makes sense to tell them. I can think of all kinds of reasons we should do it. But then another part of me keeps saying, 'Don't do it! Don't tell them yet!' And I don't have any good reasons to listen to that part of me, but—it just seems like there is a good reason, but I haven't thought of it yet." She studied his face for a moment. "You probably think I'm crazy."

"No," Billy said, shaking his head. "I don't. The weird thing is, I kind of know exactly what you're talking about. Maybe there's a reason why *I* haven't been able to tell them anything yet. It seems dangerous. I'm not even sure why—it just seems like if we tell them, it could be a really bad mistake."

"Yeah," said Sophie. "That's how I feel. And when Uncle Gary sent us those birthday cards, I think he was sending us a message. And I don't think he wanted Mom and Dad to know about it. Why else would he do that?"

Billy nodded, deep in thought.

"Sophie," he said, "when we were leaving the restaurant that day, you said you knew how to find Uncle Gary. What did you mean by that?"

She hesitated, and for a moment Billy thought she wasn't going to tell him anything.

"Well," she said finally. "It might not mean anything. But I was thinking about the birthday cards. Your birthday card had the number 2,317 written in it, and that turned out to be the clue we needed to find the key and get inside the Bigy Bigy Buglu Drawer. And when we were in the restaurant, Mom said something about how maybe Uncle Gary already sent us a message but we haven't seen it yet. That's when the idea came to me. Maybe the number in my card means something too."

"Your number matched one of the boxes you got from Uncle Gary," said Billy. "There was a music box in it, right?"

"Yeah. Maybe there's something about the music box that's important. Or maybe . . ." Her sentence trailed off.

"Maybe what?"

"Well—all the drawers in the nightstand have numbers too. Maybe the number matches one of those. Maybe Uncle Gary meant for us to find a certain drawer."

Billy sat bolt upright at his desk, suddenly wide awake. He looked across the room at the nightstand. It actually made sense. He was even a little embarrassed that he hadn't thought of it. Maybe his own number—2,317—had more significance too.

Suddenly, the entire situation seemed more critical—even more desperate in a way. For some reason, Uncle Gary needed to hide. But he didn't want Mom and Dad to know about it. He sent the message to the kids because he wanted *them* to find the Buglu Drawer. He was depending on them for some reason. But why?

Billy suddenly felt like he had been wasting too much time. People were breaking into their house, looking for his uncle. He should have taken this more seriously. They had been incredibly lucky the Zobadak men hadn't found the nightstand. After all, that was surely what they were looking for. If those men came back again, they would probably find it and take it. And if that happened—well, Billy didn't even want to think about it.

"Go get your box—the one with the music box in it," Billy said to Sophie. "Be quiet; don't let Mom and Dad hear you."

Sophie left the room. A moment later she came tiptoeing back, holding a rectangular wooden box about the size and shape of a small shoebox, which she set on Billy's desk. Like most of the other boxes, it was made of oak and stained a deep rich brown color. Just below the brass knob on its end was a small metal plate with the number 48,615. Billy picked it up and looked at the bottom and the sides. The wood grain made dark, U-shaped stripes across the lid, from one end to the other. He lifted the hinged lid to reveal the music box inside.

Oval shaped, made from white ceramic, on its lid was a painting of a little girl sitting on a picnic blanket with a cat. There was a small crank on the side to wind it up. When you lifted the lid, it began to play "You Are My Sunshine." Inside was a little statue of the girl sitting in the middle, while a tiny cat chased a red ball in circles around her.

Billy closed the lid and turned the music box over. Printed on the bottom, in tiny black letters, were the words "French Quarter—1885."

"What does that mean?" Billy asked, pointing to the words.

"I don't know," said Sophie. "I guess it's where the music box was made. And the year it was made."

"That's not much help." Billy looked inside the box for any writing, anything at all that might suggest a message of some kind, but there was nothing. He put the music box back inside its container and closed the lid. Turning in his chair, he stared for a long time at the nightstand.

"So when do we go back in?" Sophie asked.

Billy shrugged. "I don't know. As soon as possible, I think.

We have to try to find him before those men come back."

"What about those footsteps we heard? Aren't you worried about that?"

"I don't know. Yeah. Of course I'm worried. But maybe it was Uncle Gary. For all we know, he's just down the hall waiting for us. We only explored one direction. I mean, he's probably wondering what's taking us so long."

"And what if it wasn't him? It didn't sound like him and you know it."

"Well," said Billy thoughtfully. "Then I guess we ask for directions."

"Billy, this is serious. Don't joke around."

"I'm not joking. You don't have to tell me how serious it is. I don't even care about the footsteps anymore. We just have to try to find him."

"You're not thinking about going in tonight are you? It's a school night."

He sighed. It was getting harder and harder for him to take school seriously. Lately it was almost impossible for him to pay attention in class. Ms. Haggerty had yelled at him three times already this week for "daydreaming." And the other kids had been making fun of him, calling him "crow boy." That didn't exactly help take his mind off things.

"No, not tonight. But maybe tomorrow night. Tomorrow is Friday."

"Should we get Chris and Maggie to come with us?"

"I don't know." Billy rubbed his eyes and yawned, feeling waves of exhaustion come over him. "I don't want them to be in any danger, but . . ."

"But what?"

He looked up at her.

"But I want them to come."

"Yeah, me too. We might need them."

A little while later, as Billy lay in bed, exhausted but unable to sleep, he turned on his side and stared at the pattern of the wood grain on the side of the nightstand. The face stared back at him. It seemed more realistic every time he looked at it. Stretched long, mouth open, one dark eye, one light eye. It was like a person calling for help, trapped inside the wood. It made him shiver, and he rolled over to his other side and pulled the blanket up over his head.

For some reason, the same words kept repeating in his mind over and over: "French Quarter—1885, French Quarter—1885 . . ." What did it mean? Did it mean anything at all?

When he finally fell asleep, his dreams were dark and restless.

23

"Caaawww! Caawww! Caaawww! Hey, Crow Boy!"

It was Justin. He stood across the playground with his little gang of buddies. They all laughed at his antics as he flapped his arms up and down, shouting, "Caaww! Caaww! CAAWW!"

Soon, the other boys joined in, creating a chaotic chorus of terribly unrealistic crow sounds.

"Ignore him, Billy," advised Chris, steering his friend toward the play structures and away from the jeering boys. "He's such a jerk."

"Ignore who?" said Billy, looking up. "Oh, you mean Justin? I didn't even realize he was over there."

"Caw! Caaww! Caaww!"

Sophie and Maggie arrived, and the four of them huddled under the slide at the end of the play fort.

"What's wrong with those guys?" Maggie said, perplexed.

"Justin's a loser. You want me to beat him up, Billy?" Sophie offered, pulling her cap lower over her eyes.

"Forget it. Listen, we have to make a plan," said Billy. "We're going back in tonight. We're going to try our best to find Uncle

Gary. I was thinking you two could ask your parents to sleep over at our house."

"Did you ask Mom and Dad if it was okay?" Sophie asked him.

"No, not yet."

"What if they say no? They're still freaking out over what happened last Sunday. They might not want extra kids in the house. And Chris and Maggie's parents might not want them staying over either. They might think it's dangerous."

As usual, Billy was amazed at how smart Sophie was. She always thought of things he never would have considered. She had a talent for finding important perspectives on situations.

"And even if they can stay over," Sophie continued, "our parents always come in our rooms to check on us before they go to bed. They're going to find us gone and then *really* freak out."

"Caaww! Caaww! Caaww! Crow Boy! Hey, Crow Boy! Caaww! *CAAWW!*" At least ten other boys were now flapping their arms and cawing like Justin. They ran in circles around the play fort. "Caaww! CAAWW! *CAAWW!*"

"We might have to do it tomorrow instead," continued Sophie.

"I'm worried about those wood company guys," Billy admitted. "They came the first time on a Saturday. What if they come back tomorrow?"

"I don't know," she said. "I'm as worried as you are. But what else can we do?"

"If they come back," said Billy. "They're going to find the nightstand. And I have a feeling they don't care if our family is at home or not. There's something really weird about those guys. Sophie, you know what I'm talking about. They're not right. They don't even seem like people."

"Okay, now you're really starting to creep me out," Maggie put in.

"Yeah, come on you guys," Chris said. "Don't start getting ridiculous."

"No, he's right," said Sophie. "You'd have to see them up close to know what we're talking about. They look fake. And they make this weird creaking sound when they move and talk. And they smell really bad."

"*CAAWW!* Caaww! Caaww! Hey, Crow Boy! Caaww! *CAAWW!*"

"So, what are we going to do then?" Maggie asked.

"I think we have to get the nightstand out of the house. As soon as possible," Billy emphasized, rubbing his forehead. "And you guys have to come over and help us. It's really heavy. Chris, maybe we can move it to your house," he suggested. "But we have to do it without anyone seeing us."

"I don't want the Zobadak men coming to my house!" Chris protested.

"They won't," said Billy. "They don't know anything about you. They came to our house because we're related to Uncle Gary. They think we're hiding him in our house."

"And we are," added Sophie. "At least we think so."

"Caaww! Caw! Caw!" Just like the real crows that had come to their house on Sunday, the boys of the mock flock slowly began drifting off to pursue other activities.

"Okay. I hope you're right. So, when do we move it?" Chris asked.

"I don't think we can do it tonight," Sophie thought out loud. "By the time we're done with dinner, it's starting to get dark. Mom and Dad are going to be cleaning up the kitchen and walking around the house. They'll see us."

"How about tomorrow morning right after breakfast?" said Billy. "You know how they always go out on the patio and drink coffee and read the newspaper Saturday morning."

"Yeah," said Sophie, her eyes brightening. "That's perfect. We'll move it while they're in the backyard."

"And later in the afternoon we can meet at Chris's house and go inside to look for Uncle Gary."

The others nodded. It sounded like a good plan—or at least the best plan they had.

"We need to be prepared this time," Billy said. "Everybody should bring a backpack with supplies. Bring a flashlight. And maybe some tools or something. You never know what we might need."

"Bring a sandwich and a juice box," offered Sophie. "We could be in there awhile."

"Caw! Caww! Caw . . ." Justin was the only crow left. He stopped running and stood there panting and staring at them, arms dangling at his sides.

"Maybe I can get my brother's pellet gun," said Chris, his eyes lighting up.

Billy thought it was a pretty good idea until Sophie said firmly, "No guns." And, of course, she was right.

The bell rang, signaling the end of recess.

"Think about what else we can bring," said Billy as they made their way back to their respective classrooms. "We'll talk about it more later. Come over right after breakfast, you guys. We'll move it then." The afternoon shuffle was closing in, and he had to raise his voice to be heard.

None of them noticed that Justin was walking several feet behind Billy, still breathing hard, and listening with great interest to Billy's words.

24

"They're both in the backyard! Okay—they're sitting down—now they're drinking coffee." Sophie jumped down from the chair in front of her bedroom window, where she was looking down over the backyard patio. "Let's go!"

The nightstand teetered on the edge of the top step, creaking.

"Wait! Hang on a second. I don't have a good hold on it." Billy, standing with Chris on the steps below it, shifted his hold on the bottom edge of the nightstand.

"Are you ready?" Maggie appeared, holding on to the other side of the nightstand at the top of the stairs. Sophie joined her.

"I think so. Are you ready, Chris?"

"Umm."

"Okay, here it comes."

The nightstand tilted forward. Billy and Chris strained to lift it. Above, Sophie and Maggie struggled with their end. The legs came up off the floor, but just barely high enough to clear the steps.

"Let's go," Billy said. He and Chris took a backward step down, then another, the girls following.

"Be careful," said Sophie. "Go slow."

One step at a time, they went down. The nightstand was much heavier than it looked, and Billy kept imagining them tripping and falling with the nightstand tumbling down on top of them. Then he began to wonder what would happen inside the nightstand if it fell. Would all the drawers fall open, spilling their contents? Would it be like an earthquake? Would Uncle Gary be hurt?

"Wait, stop!" said Chris. "Set it down for a second."

They carefully lowered the nightstand until the back two legs rested on a step. They were almost halfway down. Chris turned around, putting his back against it to hold it up, and wiped his hands on his pants.

"My hands are sweating," he said. "I thought it was going to slip."

Billy took the opportunity to rest his own hands, putting his shoulder against the side of the nightstand. He thought he heard a thump from inside, like something falling, but he wasn't sure. It was very faint.

"Are you ready?" he said to Chris.

"Yeah."

They both gripped the lower edge of the nightstand and lifted. They went down two more steps. At that moment, the back door opened, then slammed shut. They heard Mom walk into the kitchen.

"Wait, stop," whispered Billy.

They put it back down.

"Sophie!" called Mom. "Where are you!"

"I'm upstairs, Mom!" she called back. "With Maggie."

"What are you doing?" Mom shouted.

The four kids looked at one another. Chris wiped his hands on his shirt again, his shoulder pressed against the nightstand, his teeth clenched.

"Nothing!" said Sophie.

"Can you come down here for a minute?"

Startled, Sophie looked at Billy. Billy looked back, trying to come up with an idea. His arms were beginning to hurt and it was impossible to think clearly. The nightstand felt heavier and heavier. He shifted his position and there was a high squeak of wood. Beads of sweat broke out on his forehead.

"Umm," said Sophie, equally at a loss.

They heard Mom's footsteps coming up the hallway toward the stairs.

"Sophie, did you hear me?" she called.

"Yeah, Mom! Uhhhh, I have to go to the bathroom! Really bad! I'll be there in a minute!"

"You left your mermaids on the kitchen table," said Mom. "You know how I feel about that. As soon as you come out of the bathroom, I want you to come and get them." Her voice faded away.

"Okay, Mom!"

Mom's footsteps receded back into the kitchen. Billy realized he was holding his breath and he let it out in one long gust. His arms were shaking.

"Hang on a minute," he whispered. "Wait till she goes back outside."

They listened. Dad's voice drifted in from the backyard. They couldn't tell what he said, but then Mom answered him from the kitchen.

"Excuse me?" she called. "Did you say 'crows'? Henry, don't even tell me that! I can't deal with that again!"

Billy and Sophie stared across the nightstand at each other, instantly sharing the same thought.

"They're coming back," they both whispered together.

"Who's coming back?" said Chris. "You mean the crows?"

"No," said Billy. "I mean, yeah. But not just the crows—the Zobadak men. They're coming. We have to go. Right now."

Chris wiped his hands on his shirt again, then wiped the sweat from his forehead using his shirt sleeve.

"Let's do it," he said.

They lifted together, straining under the weight of the nightstand. One step at a time they descended. Each time they took a step down, the nightstand tilted forward and nearly its entire weight shifted onto Billy and Chris. Billy thought his arms were going to explode, they hurt so much. Sweat ran into his eyes, stinging them, and he squeezed them shut, going backward and blind down the steps.

"I don't think I can hold it," said Chris, his voice trembling.

"You're almost there," said Sophie. "Keep going."

"My hands are slipping," he cried.

The nightstand bumped against the new banister Dad had put in, scraping the paint. Billy's left foot got tangled with his right foot and he almost stumbled and fell backward, but somehow he was able to catch himself.

"Careful," urged Sophie. "Just three more steps."

"I can't. . . ." moaned Chris.

"One—two—three."

Suddenly they were on the floor of the foyer and the nightstand came down with a loud THUD!

Billy and Chris released their hold, gasping for breath and their aching arms, trying to get the feeling back into them.

"We did it!" Maggie exclaimed.

"Not yet," said Billy between breaths. "Sophie, you go get your mermaids. I'll get the wagon and bring it to the front door. Maggie—there's an old white sheet under my bed. We need it to cover up the nightstand. Will you go get it?"

The three of them took off in different directions, leaving Chris behind to guard the nightstand. Billy ran out the front door, stopping for a moment to look up and down the street for the truck. It was empty and quiet, except for a dog barking somewhere. He ran around to the garage where he kept his wagon. It was a wooden Radio Flyer with removable red sides. Quickly pulling off the sides and tossing them in the corner, he grabbed the handle and ran back around to the front door. Back inside, Sophie, Maggie, and Chris were waiting for him.

"Mom and Dad are in the backyard," said Sophie. "They're looking up at the sky, but I couldn't tell what they were looking at."

"Okay," said Billy. "Let's hurry."

25

Five minutes later they were pulling the wagon down the drive-way with the nightstand lying on its back beneath the white sheet. It almost slid off when they started going too fast and had to make the right turn onto the sidewalk; Maggie made a quick grab and slid it squarely back on.

Billy and Chris pulled the handle of the wagon, while Sophie and Maggie walked on either side, holding the sheet-covered nightstand steady. Chris's house was on Magnolia Drive, down the street and around the corner, a little over two blocks away.

The wheels of the wagon made a steady THUMP-THUMP ... THUMP-THUMP ... THUMP-THUMP sound as they rolled over the lines and cracks of the sidewalk. They also squeaked loudly and Billy began to worry the sound would attract attention.

Remembering the crows he looked up, scanning the sky.

"Does anyone see any crows?"

The others looked. A large oak tree in the neighbor's front yard, with brilliant red autumn leaves obscured much of their view. When they got past it, there was a clear view in the direction Mom and Dad had been looking.

Sophie pointed. "There!" she said.

In the distance, they saw a flock of black dots, hovering in the sky over the rooftops.

"Are they crows?" Maggie wrinkled her freckled nose.

"I'm not sure," Sophie answered. "They're too far away."

Billy's heart was racing in his chest, and it wasn't just from the exertion of pulling the heavy wagon. He kept imagining the black truck coming up the street, catching them before they could get to Chris's house. The intersection at Magnolia Drive seemed a mile away.

"It looks like they're over by Dunhill Forest," said Maggie.

She was right. Dunhill Forest was about a mile away to the north, at the edge of the neighborhood. There was a small park there—Dunhill Park—that the kids rode their bikes to once in a while. There wasn't much to do at the park other than swing on the swings, slide down the metal slide, and climb on a small jungle gym. The forest was usually too wet and swampy to bother with. It was also very dense and had no hiking trails, so the kids rarely went there.

"Let's go faster," said Billy. He pulled harder and Chris did the same. The thumping of the wheels sped up slightly, as did the rhythmic squeaking.

"Billy," said Sophie, "do you think the Zobadak men came from Dunhill Forest? Remember how the police told Dad they lost the trail in a forest?"

"I was thinking the same thing," said Billy. "But how would they drive a truck in there?"

"I don't know."

Nothing made sense. Billy felt like his thoughts were a big tangled, jumbled mess inside his head, and he no longer knew what was right or wrong, what made sense and what didn't, what was real and what was imaginary. And he suddenly had a terrible, sinking feeling in the pit of his stomach. What if they were mak-

121

ing a huge mistake? Once again he felt guilty for not telling Mom and Dad about all of this. Who did he think he was, anyway? Why had he let his little sister's feelings prevent him from doing the right thing? He was older; he should know better. And now his sister and his friends were tangled up in this mess too.

"CAAWW! CAAWW! CAAWW!"

All four kids jumped. They stopped pulling the wagon and looked around for the source of the sound. Across the street, next to a huge mound of raked leaves, stood Justin, grinning at them.

"Hey, Crow Boy! What'cha got in the wagon?" he shouted.

"None of your business, Justin," Chris yelled back. "Why don't you just leave us alone?"

"Why don't you come over here and make me," Justin taunted, brushing his long, greasy hair away from his eyes. His high-pitched, irritating laugh floated across the street.

"Forget him, you guys," said Sophie. "We don't have time for this. Just keep going."

"Justin, what's your problem?" shouted Billy. "Why can't you leave us alone?"

"I'll make you a deal, Crow Boy!" Justin shouted. "I'll leave you alone if you show me what's under that sheet."

"We're not showing you anything," said Billy. His voice was beginning to shake with frustration. Sophie was right. They didn't have time for this.

"Why? What is it? A giant box of bird seed? Heeee-heeee-heeee! CAAWW! CAAWW! CAAWW!"

"It's not bird seed!" Billy shouted.

"Billy, forget it," urged Sophie. "Ignore him!"

"I don't want him following us," Billy replied.

"CAAWW! CAAWW! CAAWW!"

In spite of his frustration, Billy had to admit Justin did a pretty good imitation of a crow.

"That's a lot of bird seed, Crow Boy! Are you going to eat all that by yourself?"

"Justin, shut up!" Chris yelled, fists clenched. "You're not funny!"

"Uh-oh!" tittered Justin. "Crow Boy Number Two is getting mad! Heee-heee-heeee! Hey, listen! Why don't I just come over there and take a look myself?"

"Don't you dare!" shouted Billy. He came around and stood in front of the wagon, blocking it. Chris stood next to him.

"Oooohh, I love dares!"

"Hey, Justin!" Maggie suddenly shouted. The others were surprised to hear her voice. She was usually so quiet. "I heard about your cheese problem!"

Justin stopped giggling and glared at her. All the humor left his face and his cheeks began to grow red. Sophie, Billy, and Chris looked back and forth between the two, thoroughly confused.

"Yeah!" said Maggie, brushing the dark red curls away from her eyes. "Your mom told my mom about it. That must have been a ton of cheese you ate! I heard you couldn't poop for a week! And then I heard your mom had to put her finger in—"

"SHUT UP!" Justin screamed, his face as red as a fire hydrant. "Shut up, Sneezy! I'm not going anywhere until I see what you have on the wagon! And there's nothing you can say to make me go away!"

"JUST LEAVE US ALONE!" Billy screamed.

"No way, Crow Boy! Here I come! CAAWW! CAAWW! *CAAWW!*"

"Great, you just made him really mad," Sophie whispered to Maggie.

Justin began flapping his arms up and down like wings. He came across the narrow patch of grass between the sidewalk and the street, his feet plowing through the edge of the leaf pile.

"Caaww! Caaww! I sure am hungry! I could really go for some bird seed! Caaww! Caaww!"

He stepped off the curb, kicking leaves in front of him, and began crossing the street, arms flapping, still screeching, "Caaww! Caaww! Caaww!"

"Kkaaww! Kkaaww! Kkaaww!"

Justin stopped suddenly. The expression on his face was one of pure bewilderment. His head swiveled back and forth as he searched for the source of this new sound, then he began turning around in circles.

"Kkaaww! Kkaaww!"

At first the kids weren't sure what was going on. They heard the sound, but Justin's mouth wasn't moving. Then they saw it: a large crow perched on the mailbox directly behind Justin.

"Kkaaww!"

"Get out of here, you stupid bird!" Justin shouted, waving his arms in the air.

It just stared at him, head cocked.

"Kkaaww!"

Suddenly, another crow glided in from somewhere behind the kids. It swooped across the street and landed on the grass where Justin had been standing only moments before.

There was another "Kkaaww!" from up in a tree across the street, and the kids saw two more crows perched among the red leaves.

"Billy, look," whispered Sophie.

From above came the sound of flapping wings. Three crows flew in from down the street, legs extended as they came in for a landing. And there were more birds up in the sky, most of them circling.

"Billy, we have to go," Sophie urged.

Billy glanced back at Justin who was turning in circles again, eyes rolling with confusion and growing fear.

"What's going on?" Justin shouted. He turned and stared across at Billy. "Is this some kind of trick? Did you do this?"

A huge crow landed in the middle of the street, right in front of Justin, and looked up at him.

"Kkaaww! Kkaaww! Kkaaww!"

Justin screamed—a high pitched, girlish scream—and ran away down the street toward his house, waving his hands over his head as if the crows were trying to land on him.

"Billy! They're coming! We have to go now!"

Billy and Chris sprang into action. They picked up the handle and pulled hard. It took a lot of effort to get the wagon started, but once it was rolling it became easier. Sophie and Maggie pushed gently on the nightstand, careful not to let it slip off the wagon. The corner of Magnolia Drive was approaching quickly but it still seemed too far away. Billy felt if they could just get around that corner, they would be much safer.

They heard it before they saw it.

The rumbling of an engine, like the growl of some large, angry beast. The sound came from somewhere up ahead of them, in the direction they were going. Billy squinted his eyes, straining to see as far as he could up the street. He could see no sign of the truck, but it sounded close.

"Run!" he shouted. "Come on, Chris! Pull!"

The girls ran alongside, trying desperately to hold the nightstand steady on the wagon as it bounced and vibrated along the sidewalk.

Billy saw it then, at the intersection of Fairlane and Turnberry Street, only two blocks away. A puff of black smoke drifted across the street from right to left. The rumble of the engine suddenly grew louder and the truck came slowly around the corner in a swirl of smoke, turning in the direction of Billy and Sophie's house.

Billy realized almost too late that they were at Magnolia Drive. They were going much too fast to turn, and they came down with a jarring bump into the street. The nightstand bounced on the wagon and slid sideways.

"Slow down!" Sophie shouted, clinging to the side of the nightstand.

Billy and Chris slowed down just enough to make their right turn in the street, then began running up the middle of Magnolia, pumping their legs to gain speed.

"Those bushes!" said Sophie, pointing.

They steered the wagon toward the first driveway on the left, where a small, scraggly bush stood at the bottom corner next to the mailbox. The roar of the truck grew steadily louder behind them.

"Slow down!" Sophie shouted again. "It's going to fall!"

Billy and Chris had to force themselves to slow their pace and let the wagon coast the rest of the way. All four of the kids took hold of the nightstand, trying to keep it from tumbling off the wagon onto the street.

The wagon slowed until the front wheels bumped against the curb. In response, the nightstand slid forward and almost tipped off the front end. They pushed it back on as the truck engine backfired with a loud BOOM that echoed up and down the street. All four kids jumped. The engine was so loud now that Billy could feel the sound vibrating in his chest. They pulled the wagon around the edge of the curb and onto the bottom of the driveway until it was mostly hidden behind the bush.

"Get down!" Billy shouted. "Here they come!"

The four kids huddled around the wagon, ducking their heads as far down as they could, Sophie and Maggie holding their hands over their ears. The bush was way too small to completely hide them, but Billy hoped it was enough. It would have to be. He realized that an edge of the sheet was loose and flapping in the wind out beyond the bush and he reached out and pulled it back in, shoving it under the edge of the nightstand. Then he peeked around the edge of the bush.

Within seconds the truck emerged in the intersection, idling slowly up Fairlane Avenue. Its dull, black sides were rusted out at the bottom and the metal was shaking from the throbbing of the engine. Black smoke poured out of the smokestack and from under the hood as well, churning about the truck in a ragged cloud.

The truck was strangely lopsided, as if its frame were crooked, or perhaps one wheel was larger than all the others. It did not seem well built. It had a haphazard, patched-together look, like random pieces from a junkyard bolted together to make a new truck. And its cab had an odd, stretched-out appearance that made it look like it was specially built to hold tall people. A clanking sound came from somewhere on the truck's body, the sound of two pieces of metal rapidly banging together.

Inside the cab sat the same two tall, thin men in their brown business suits. The Zobadak men.

Billy felt a chill run up his spine. He ducked back behind the bush, afraid they would suddenly turn their heads and look in his direction. He heard another loud backfire, like a shotgun blast, and with it came a billowing, rolling plume of smoke that rose straight up into the air, curling in on itself. Crows glided through the smoke as they followed the truck, sailing ahead and then circling back.

Risking another look Billy poked his head out from behind the little bush again. The truck was continuing up Fairlane Avenue and Billy saw the flatbed with its metal stakes disappear behind the corner house.

Breathing a sigh of relief, he was about to stand up when suddenly he heard the roar of another engine. It was like being inside a nightmare. He watched the second truck roll slowly across the intersection. This one was about the same size, and had a similar crooked and stretched-out look. Its flat black paint was peeling and its parts were rattling, but here the similarities ended. This truck was covered with some kind of tall tree branches—leafless, barkless, and bleached white like bones. They sprouted upward from the hood, the roof, and even the flatbed, and they shook and clawed at the air as the truck rumbled by.

Even through the haze of smoke, Billy could see the driver. In a brown suit. He seemed tall and very thin. And maybe even older than the first two men, if that were possible. Billy watched the bizarre truck disappear as it continued up Fairlane.

When it was gone the four of them stayed behind the bush. They waited in a crouch for several minutes, until they were sure no other trucks were coming, then stood up.

"What the heck was that?" Maggie breathed.

"I don't know." Billy grimly reached down to grab the handle of the wagon. "But we have to go. We have to get this to Chris's house as soon as we can."

"Billy, I'm scared!" Sophie cried out. She grabbed his arm, her eyes terrified. "What about Mom and Dad?"

"They'll be okay," he said with a conviction he did not feel. "They can take care of themselves."

"But did you see that? There's *two* trucks now! That means more of those creepy men are coming to our house! They could be going inside right now!"

"Mom and Dad will get out if they have to. They won't let themselves get hurt."

"But they're probably looking for us right now, and they don't know where we are! And they're probably worrying."

Billy sighed. He didn't know what else to do or say. They couldn't go back. Not now.

"Listen, you guys," said Chris, "let's just get this to my house. Hurry up—it's not that far. We can call the police from there. And then you guys can run back home if you want."

Sophie nodded, and they started rolling again, down the middle of the street. It was much smoother than the sidewalk. Chris's house was less than a block away, and he had already cleared a corner at the back of the garage where they could hide the nightstand.

Quickly, without a word spoken, they pushed the wagon up the driveway, past the cars and into the garage. The garage was a separate building behind the house. It was full of old junk: boxes and crates and old furniture and rusty bikes. There was no room inside for even one car.

"Nobody ever comes in here," said Chris.

They backed the wagon down a narrow path between the piles of junk and stopped at the back of the garage. There they heaved the nightstand and carried it across to the corner. Billy draped the sheet back over it while Chris pushed boxes and various other things in front of it until it was completely hidden.

"Leave the wagon here for now," said Chris.

When they emerged from the garage, they realized the noise from the trucks was much quieter. It sounded like they were far away. They also heard sirens approaching in the distance.

"Why don't you guys call your house first?" Maggie asked, but Sophie shook her head.

"No, I want to go home right now," she said. "Come on, Billy, let's hurry up."

"Okay," he said, starting down the driveway. He glanced back at the others. "We're still going in the nightstand tomorrow, right?"

Maggie and Chris both nodded.

"Then we'll call you later to make a plan."

"Billy, come *on!*" Sophie was already on the sidewalk, looking back.

"I'm *coming!*"

They both took off running. Chris and Maggie glanced at each other, then they ran too, sprinting to catch up.

26

"Brope doesn't trust us."

"He doesn't trust you. You and your birds."

"They're not my birds. How many times do I have to say that sentence?" Bob turned around stiffly, kneeling on the passenger seat. He looked out the back window, trying to see through the smoke that plumed out behind them. They were out of the neighborhood now and back on the busy main street. Moving along at ten miles per hour, impatient cars sped past them in the left lane.

"Is Ginkgo coming?" said John, sitting in the driver's seat as usual.

"I can't tell," Bob replied.

"You can't see anything," snapped John. He let go of the steering wheel and turned around to peer out the back. The truck, suddenly driverless, veered to the left across the street, forcing cars to swerve and slam on their brakes to get out of the way.

"Do you see him?" Bob glared at John.

"Maybe. It's hard to tell."

Brakes squealed and horns blared around them. The truck rumbled slowly along at a diagonal across the oncoming lanes, forcing the traffic to part, cars weaving to the right and left, fighting for room to avoid a head-on collision. Other drivers screamed at them, shaking their fists in the air and waving the one-fingered driver's wave.

"I think that's him right there," said John. "I see the branches."

"You better make sure," Bob said, squinting to see where John was pointing. "Ginkgo doesn't know the way back."

The truck bounced up onto the curb in a swirling cloud of smoke, its metal body rattling. It rolled over a mailbox, crushing it under its wheels. Pedestrians screamed and scattered. A bike parked on the sidewalk got hooked by its handlebars to the bumper of the truck and dragged along the sidewalk. Once again, the raucous crows followed in their path, landing on parked cars, trees, buildings, and lampposts, only to take off again as the truck moved further along the sidewalk.

"That's him," motioned John. "He's following us."

It was true. The second truck was cutting across the lanes between the congested traffic following the path left by the first truck. It rode up onto the curb and over the same mailbox, while the first truck slammed at an angle into the front of a store and began scraping along the bricks, sending out a shower of sparks behind it.

"He drives too slow," commented John, looking over his shoulder.

"You drive too fast," said Bob.

John creakily turned back around and grabbed the steering wheel. Using both hands, he pulled on the wheel to guide the truck to the right. It flattened a street sign before clattering over the edge of the sidewalk and back into the street, veering across the oncoming lanes and creating even more chaos as cars swerved to get out of its way.

John waved back at the friendly drivers who were waving at him. The bicycle came unhooked from the bumper and tumbled under the truck, folding and crumpling under the front wheel, then the back wheel, before coming to rest in the middle of the street, a tangled knot of crushed tubes and spokes.

"Ginkgo didn't even go into the house," said Bob, who was still facing backward, watching the other truck that now followed closely behind them, crushing the bicycle even more as it came. Bob's eyes weren't very good, but he could see the branches poking up through the billowing smoke.

"He didn't need to," said John. "He's the surveyor. He can survey from the grass."

"What do you think he found?" Bob asked.

"We'll know after he goes to Brope," said John.

Awkwardly, Bob turned back around to face forward. He rubbed the bump on his forehead, which protruded at least an inch now, cone-shaped with a rounded end.

"You are going to have to take care of that thing," John suggested.

Ignoring him, Bob said, "I want to be John now. You can be Bob."

"We already had that conversation."

"But I'm ready now," pressed Bob. "I'm becoming John Wayne."

John's mouth swung open, hung there for a moment, then closed with a creak.

"John Wayne would not have needed a surveyor," continued Bob. "John Wayne would have just taken the big truck."

"You're not John Wayne. You're just Bob."

"But I'm kind of like John Wayne."

"You're nothing like John Wayne."

"How would you know? You didn't see the John Wayne movie."

"Well—because of your crow problem for one thing. I don't think John Wayne had a crow problem. And I don't think John Wayne had a new limb growing on his head."

"How would you know?" Bob repeated.

There was a long silence between them as the truck took a sudden right turn and jounced up over another curb and across a sidewalk. It careened across a ditch, almost tipping over, and rolled off through the field, kicking up clumps of dirt behind it.

"I don't know why it matters to you," said John. "He's not going to let either of us drive the Ballagahaldo truck anyway."

"Why not?"

"Because," said John, growing irritated. "Haven't you seen it? We're not big enough. Not even close."

27

By the time Billy and Sophie got to their house, out of breath from running, the trucks had already disappeared down the street. Mom and Dad were on the front lawn, watching the cloud of smoke in the distance. When they heard the kids approaching, they both turned, their relief almost immediately giving way to anger.

"Where were you two?" Mom shouted. "We were looking everywhere for you!"

Without answering, Sophie ran straight to Mom and wrapped her arms around her. Mom hugged Sophie back, and the lines on her face softened from anger to worry.

"We were at Chris's," Billy answered, looking down at the ground. "We waited for the trucks to go by."

"Come here," said Mom, opening up one arm to him.

He went to her and buried his face in her chest. She gathered them together and hugged them tightly. Billy started crying, even though he wasn't sure why. Perhaps the stress of the past hour had finally caught up to him.

"It's good that you stayed away from those trucks," said Dad, looking back up the street where the black haze was beginning to thin out. "But you should have told us where you were going. From now on, I don't want you two going anywhere without telling us. Do you understand?"

They both nodded and answered with muffled voices, "Yes."

At that moment, two police cars pulled up in front of the house, lights flashing. The door of one of the cars opened and an officer got out. The other car sped away down the street, siren wailing, in pursuit of the trucks.

Chris and Maggie were standing awkwardly on the sidewalk by the edge of the property, Maggie wrinkling her freckled nose at the smell that still hung in the air. Billy and Sophie joined them as the police officer approached. They listened to Dad explain how the two trucks stopped in front of the house and how the man in the second truck, the truck with the branches, got out, walked onto the front lawn, and just stood there. Mom and Dad were watching from the front window and that was when Dad called the police.

The man stood on the lawn for about five minutes. Dad said he held some sort of Y-shaped stick in his hands—like a divining rod—which he stuck into the ground. Dad pointed to the stick that still stood in the middle of the lawn. Then, Dad explained, the man walked back to his truck and drove away. Dad didn't think he was one of the two men who came to the house the first time. This guy was even taller than the other two. He must have been over seven feet tall, Dad said.

Once again, the policeman assured them the men would be captured and put in jail soon. This time there was an even bigger black stain down the middle of the street. Two stains in fact. With such a trail, it would be impossible for them *not* to find the men from the Zobadak Wood Company.

Billy looked a bit sour at that. He was not convinced. By the end of the weekend, he was even more sour. For the rest of Saturday and all of Sunday, the entire family stayed inside with the doors locked. No one was allowed to leave the house. Dad spent a lot of time on the phone and Mom sat motionless at the computer. Billy and Sophie were never far from their sight. It was like being in prison, and Billy grew increasingly frustrated. They would never get a chance to go back in the nightstand if things kept up like this.

As it turned out, they got their chance after all. Exactly one week later.

28

For once things worked out perfectly. The following Saturday, Mom and Dad had to go to the police station to fill out paperwork and file reports. They said it might take about three hours. They were going to take the kids with them, but Billy asked if he could spend that time at Chris's house, and Sophie asked to stay at Maggie's. Mom and Dad said yes, as long as it was okay with everyone's parents. And it was. All they had to do was promise not to go back home for any reason, just in case the Zobadak men came back.

Both of them had prepared their backpacks the night before. Billy took a flashlight, a pocket knife, a compass, the spyglass from Uncle Gary, and some rope he'd found in the garage. You never knew when you might need some rope. He wore the worst, most torn-up pair of jeans he could find and a plain gray T-shirt that was too small for him. He didn't want to get in any trouble for ruining his clothes. Since it was late October, he also took a jacket, deciding he could leave it in the "Lobby" once they got inside.

Sophie took her own flashlight, which was basically a kiddie toy flashlight shaped like a cow that made a "moo" sound when you turned it on. The light only stayed on for about thirty seconds so you had to keep pressing the button. It was a little embarrassing, but it was the only flashlight she had. She also brought a notebook and pen just in case they needed to draw a map. She grabbed her music box but thought better of it and put it back. Instead, she simply wrote in her notebook the number of the box and the words from the bottom of the music box. On her way out of the room, she slapped the threadbare blue cap on her head, ignoring the pile of brand new hats stacked in the corner, Mom's futile attempts to replace Sophie's favorite. Both of them took a peanut butter and honey sandwich, a bag of potato chips, and a juice box.

As soon as Sophie was dropped off at Maggie's house, the girls went straight to Chris's, where the boys were waiting on the driveway in front of the garage.

Chris was more prepared than anyone else. For one thing, his backpack was so full it looked like the seams might split. Sophie couldn't imagine what he had in there, but that was only the beginning. Covering his chest was a plastic breastplate—the kind a knight would wear—with an image of a rearing, battle-ready horse molded into it. On his head sat a plastic knight's helmet, with a visor that could be raised and lowered. He had a scarf tied around his waist with a plastic sword stuck behind it on one side and a cowboy gun in a holster on the other side. In one hand was a long walking stick. In the other was a plastic shield with the same molded horse on it.

The girls burst into laughter.

"What's so funny?" Chris frowned.

"I tried to tell him," said Billy ruefully.

"You're not really going in like that, are you?" Sophie asked.

Chris looked genuinely surprised, which only made the girls laugh harder. Maggie doubled over, one hand over her eyes, the other on her stomach, trying to catch her breath. Sophie pressed her lips together and stared up at the roof of the house in an attempt to force herself to stop laughing. She almost succeeded, but when she looked back at Chris, laughter welled up again.

Maggie, trying to hold it back as well, turned to Sophie, and Sophie looked back at Maggie, and they both exploded into laughter again.

"You sprayed me!" giggled Maggie.

"Well, you sprayed me!" Sophie said, barely able to get the words out.

"You guys!" Billy finally shouted. "We're wasting time! Will you please stop that?"

"Okay," breathed Sophie, finally getting a hold of herself. She held up her hands. "Okay, I'm sorry. We're not laughing at you."

"Yes, we are! What are you talking about?" cried Maggie, and both girls erupted again, bent over and holding their stomachs.

"I can't breathe," choked Sophie.

"Go ahead and laugh," Chris pouted. "Just because I'm the only one that's prepared here—you're gonna wish . . ."

"Come on Chris," said Billy. "Forget them. Let's go." The boys turned and began walking into the garage and Sophie and Maggie hurried behind them.

"Wait for us, Sir Lancelot!" Maggie called in her best damsel-in-distress voice.

When they got to the back corner of the garage, Billy lifted the sheet that covered the nightstand. He removed the drawers and leaned them against the garage wall. Then he took the key from his pocket. He eyed the others.

"Are you ready?"

They nodded.

"No more goofing around, you guys," he said to the girls. "This is serious."

"Okay, okay," said Sophie, taking a deep breath. "We know it's serious. Let's go."

"What's our plan?" Chris wanted to know.

There was a long silence. Billy folded his arms and looked up toward the ceiling of the garage, deep in thought.

Finally he said, "We're going to find Uncle Gary and tell him what's going on with the Zobadak men. That's the whole plan." Without another word, he crawled under the nightstand, unlocked the inner lid, and pushed it up. There wasn't enough room to climb up with their backpacks on, so Billy went first and Chris handed all four backpacks up to him, one at a time. Chris's backpack was heavy, and Billy almost dropped it on top of him. Chris then handed up his shield and walking stick.

When all four were inside the nightstand, they sat for a moment in the little hallway next to the trapdoor while their eyes adjusted to the dim light. The "Lobby," Billy remembered. His stomach was full of butterflies and he could feel his heart pounding. He closed his eyes and told himself to relax.

It was much warmer inside the Lobby and the girls immediately took off their jackets. Chris wasn't wearing one; he had no room under the armor.

"Did anyone bring a watch?" Billy asked, pulling off his own jacket.

"I have one," Maggie replied. She pointed to a pink digital watch hooked to the strap of her backpack.

"What time is it?"

"Hang on a sec." She squinted at the watch. "12:12."

"Okay," said Billy. "Mom and Dad said they would be back around three o'clock, so that gives us almost three hours. That should be plenty of time, right?"

"Well," said Sophie, "last time we were here, we went to the right, down the main hallway. We didn't go all the way to the end, and there was a little opening there that we didn't go into. Remember?"

The others nodded.

"And don't forget about that secret passage you found," Sophie continued. "And then there's the whole area to the left we didn't explore at all. Oh, and another thing: those footsteps we heard came from above us. So that means there's an upper floor, right?"

Billy exhaled, rubbing his forehead.

"Okay, but still," he said. "Three hours should be enough. Right?"

"Yeah," Sophie replied. "I hope so."

"Well, come on. Let's get started," said Chris, standing up and pulling his backpack over his shoulders. He picked up his shield and walking stick and stood looking down at the others.

"Let's go to the right again," said Billy in a whisper, securing his own backpack. "We'll check out that little hallway on the end, then we'll go back the other way and explore the left hand side."

Moving quietly to the end of the Lobby, Billy peeked around the corner to the right and left. There was no sign of anyone, so he stepped out into the main hall and turned to the right. Out of curiosity he slid open one of the drawers in the wall next to him. It contained a pile of black claw-like objects, each of them as long as one of Billy's fingers, but much wider. The index card inside the drawer read, "Beaks of the Kraken—North Pacific Ocean."

"Whoa," Billy whispered. Unable to resist he opened the next drawer. Inside was an object that looked like a long, straight horn that twisted as it tapered to its point. The card read: "Horn of Unicorn—Hercynian Forest."

"No way," Sophie said over his shoulder.

It can't be, Billy thought as he closed the drawer and began creeping forward. The others followed close behind, floorboards squeaking under their feet. Billy stopped when they reached the passage on the left, which led to the large room with the insect collection. He felt they should start naming places so it would be

Brad Gallagher

easier to talk to each other about where they'd been. Turning back, he whispered, "Let's call this the Bug Museum."

The others nodded. Sophie gave a thumbs-up. Continuing past it, they approached the end of the main hall and stopped before the entrance to the little hallway branching off on the right side. For several minutes, the kids stood there staring at it without speaking.

Unlike everything else they had seen so far, this passage was as black as midnight. The opening was narrow and low at the top. Billy guessed an adult would have to turn sideways and duck his head to get through it. Moving closer, the four of them gathered around the opening and peered into the darkness.

"How far back does it go?" Chris wondered.

"I don't know," said Billy. "I can't see anything." There was a long silence as they strained to make out anything at all inside the little passage. Remembering his flashlight, Billy took off his backpack and dug around inside until he found it.

He took a deep breath, turned it on, and aimed it into the darkness.

142

29

Two steps led down to the floor of the narrow passage. There were no drawers here. The featureless wooden walls stretched away into the distance, and Billy's flashlight wasn't powerful enough to penetrate very far. Dust and cobwebs drifted lazily in the beam of light. Sophie took out her cow-shaped flashlight and aimed it into the passage.

"Moooooo!" said the flashlight when she turned it on. Chris and Maggie jumped at the sound, but the added light didn't do much to illuminate the hallway.

"I don't think I wanna go in there," Billy finally said. "Chris, you go first. You have the armor and shield. I'll follow you."

"I'm not going in there," squeaked Chris. "If you guys go, I'll protect us from the rear."

"I don't know," Billy responded. "Maybe we should go back the other way."

"Oh, get out of the way, you two," Sophie said, with exasperation. "I'm going in."

She pushed past them and the boys were too surprised to stop her. Poking her head through the opening, she squinted into the distance beyond the light beams. Her flashlight turned off automatically after about thirty seconds, so she hit the button again, and once again it moooooed. The sound echoed loudly in the darkness, both familiar and eerie in the mysterious hallway.

"It stinks in here," commented Sophie. "It smells old." She took a step down, holding onto the wall on the right. She listened, then took another step down.

"Do you see anything?" Billy asked. It was still too dark. The air smelled musty, like it hadn't stirred in years.

"No. I think it's a long hallway but it's—" She took three careful steps forward and stopped. "It's hard to tell how far back it goes."

She took four more steps. Her flashlight went out and she quickly pressed the button again.

"Moooooo!"

She turned around and looked back at the others, their silhouettes peering in at her from the opening to the main hallway.

"Aren't you guys coming with me?" she asked.

Suddenly there was a loud, deep creaking that seemed to rise up from all around them. It was the deep groan of wood, of very large boards from the sound of it, rubbing and shifting and straining against each other. The floor beneath their feet vibrated.

"The hallway is moving!" Sophie cried.

"Come back here!" shouted Billy.

The loud groaning noise quickly faded away, but in its place were hundreds of smaller squeaks, creaks, and pops from every direction.

"Sophie!"

Her flashlight was pointing back at them and Billy couldn't see her. The light shook.

"I'm going in," he said, getting up from his crouched position and taking a step down.

"Wait!" came Sophie's voice. "Don't come in here!"

Billy stopped, straining to see what was happening in the hallway, frustrated by his dim flashlight.

"What's going on?" he shouted.

"I don't know," she said. "But it feels like the whole hallway
is getting ready to fall down. The whole thing started shaking and
tilting. Go back up. I'm coming out."

Billy backed up into the main hallway and the three kids
waited, hearts pounding in their chests.

"Moooooo!"

"Sophie, be careful!" shouted Maggie.

Steadying herself with her left hand against the wall, Sophie
began to step gingerly back toward the main hall. Another deep
groaning of wood rose up from somewhere beneath her and the
entire hallway began to shake again, boards rattling and clunking
against each other. Something small, maybe a nail, landed on the
floor just behind her, bouncing once. Above her head was the sound
of cracking wood. Something banged loudly against the ceiling,
sending a reverberating echo racing down the passage behind her.
Curtains of dust cascaded through the beams of her flashlight.

Sophie stopped moving and waited for the hallway to settle
down again. The noises began to subside, but the little hallway
swayed back and forth as though it were balancing precariously
on stilts. It CREAK-CREAK-CREAKED like a gigantic rocking
chair as it swayed.

"Sophie," Billy urged. "Just run. Run across to the steps."

"What if everything falls down?" she said, her voice trembling.

This is my fault, he thought. *I should have gone in there first.
Or I shouldn't have let her go in at all. What kind of big brother lets
his little sister go first into a dark tunnel?*

Somehow it had never occurred to him that they might actually get hurt. What if something really bad happened? Mom and
Dad would never find them. They would call the police and the

145

police would search in all the wrong places and no one would ever know what happened.

And what if the hallway collapses? he thought suddenly and, immediately on the heels of that, *collapses into where?* The thought filled him with terror.

As if in answer to his question, there came a snapping, tearing noise above them and the little hallway suddenly dropped several feet, stopping with a loud THUD! Sophie shrieked. The floor now tilted downward at an incline away from them, still rocking back and forth.

"Don't move," Billy said. "Don't cry. Don't even breathe."

"Billy, I'm scared," she said in a near whisper.

"I'll go get my dad!" shouted Chris, turning and starting back up the main hallway.

"Wait!" Maggie grabbed Chris's arm. "Just hang on a minute," she said. "Sophie, it's okay. Just hold on. Everybody, calm down. We don't have time to run around explaining things to people. Let's just figure this out. We can do it."

"Moooooo!"

She's right, Billy thought, his mind working furiously. *We have to do this ourselves.*

"Okay," he said, taking a deep breath. "Sophie, can you tell how far you are from us? Like, how many steps?"

"Um, I think about four steps," she replied. "Not far, but I don't think I can move."

"All right. Listen: I'm going to stand on the bottom step. Chris, you hold on to me. Grab the back of my shirt, I guess." Billy went to the opening and carefully took two steps down. "Now, Sophie," he whispered to her. "When I count to three, take one big step and then jump. I'll catch you." Turning back to Chris he said, "As soon as I have her, Chris, you pull us back. Maggie, you too."

Chris and Maggie nodded.

"Moooooo!"

"Sophie, are you ready?"

"I don't think this is a good idea. Billy, go get Mom and Dad." Sophie's voice quavered out of the darkness, and even though he couldn't see her, Billy could tell she was crying.

"I can't!" he said. "They're not even home!" He took a deep breath. "Sophie, don't worry, it's going to be okay. I promise. Just take one big step and then jump. Can you see me?"

"Yes."

"Okay, get ready. Chris and Maggie, are you ready?"

"Yeah," they both said together, taking a firm grip on Billy's backpack.

"One—two—*three!*"

Nothing happened.

"Moooooo!"

Billy's voice cracked. "Sophie? What's going on?"

"I wasn't ready," she said quietly.

There was a long, slow drawn-out CREEEEAAAAAK that seemed to emanate from somewhere far back in the hallway.

"Are you ready now?" He fought to keep his voice patient. After all, she was only nine years old.

"Not yet."

"Sophie, come *on!* Don't think about it, just jump. Okay? You have to do it."

"Okay."

"One . . . two . . ."

Sophie suddenly took one big step and then launched herself forward, crashing into Billy. Thrown backward he knocked Chris and Maggie down. All four kids tumbled in a heap into the main hallway.

"Moooooo!"

An ear-piercing squeal of twisting wood came from the dark hallway. There was a crash of a large board falling to the floor and a quick series of cracking and snapping sounds of splintering wood.

Billy sat up. In the gray shadows near the opening, it looked like the entire narrow hallway was teetering to the left and angling downward even more. It made him feel strangely off-balance to look at it.

"It's not even connected to the main hall," he said with disbelief.

He was right. The main hall vibrated a little, but it felt solid beneath them. They untangled themselves and sat looking at each other, breathing hard. Sophie took off her cap, turned her face away from Billy and wiped her cheeks with the back of her wrist.

"Are you okay?" he asked.

"I don't know. Yeah, I'm fine."

The four of them sat quietly on the floor of the hall, listening as the creaking and snapping from the dark hall gradually subsided. When all was quiet they continued to sit for several minutes, just enjoying the sound of their own breathing.

"You have dust in your hair," said Billy, breaking the silence. He reached up and ruffled Sophie's ponytail, brushing the dust out of it.

The gesture immediately reminded them both of Uncle Gary and the way he used to shake the sawdust out of his hair before coming into the house. They looked at each other and smiled.

"Well," said Chris. "I guess we're not going *that* way. So, now what?"

Taking a deep breath as she replaced her cap, Sophie slipped off her backpack and unzipped it. She removed her spiral notebook and pen, opened it to a blank page, and began drawing.

"What are you doing?" Maggie asked.

"Making a map," Sophie answered.

She made a double line down the center of the page and wrote the words "Main Hall" next to it. Then she made the four short hallways on one side and added "Lobby" with the trapdoor at the end of it.

"That's a really good idea," said Billy, looking over her shoulder.

She drew the large room that branched off from the other side with its ten long aisles, writing "Bug Museum" over it. And at the end of the hallway she drew the narrow passage, shading it black with her pen and labeling it the "Dark Hall." She paused for a moment, then wrote "DO NOT ENTER" next to it.

Then she began extending the lines of the main hall in the other direction where they had yet to explore, glancing up from the page to draw what she could see from their current position.

"You guys, we made a lot of noise," said Maggie.

Billy and Chris looked at her. Sophie kept drawing.

"I was just thinking," Maggie continued. "You know those footsteps we heard last time? Well, whoever that was—he probably heard us."

"Yeah, you're right," said Billy. "I didn't think of that."

"What if he's on his way here right now?" said Chris.

Sophie glanced back up, peering into the distance at the far end of the main hall. She stopped drawing. There was movement down there. A small spot of color—yellow and green. Like a butterfly. But not a butterfly. Her mouth fell open and the breath stopped in her chest.

"Is that . . .?" she whispered.

The others looked at her.

Sophie stood up, holding her forgotten notebook in her hand.

"Oh, my gosh," Sophie whispered, so softly the others could barely hear her. "Oh, my gosh—I think that was . . ." She began walking, slowly at first, then faster up the main hallway. Billy, Chris, and Maggie sat on the floor, staring after her.

"What's going on?" said Chris.

"I don't know," said Billy, worried. "Sophie! What are you doing?"

Sophie whirled around, eyes wide, with her finger to her lips. "Ssshhh!" Then she turned back and kept walking.

Maggie suddenly got up and followed her. Billy grabbed Sophie's backpack, shoved the cow flashlight into it, stood up, and trotted after her.

"You're not leaving me here by myself," muttered Chris, fumbling with his shield and walking stick. As he stood his cowboy revolver fell out of the holster and clattered on the floor. He picked it up. The visor of his helmet fell over his eyes and he used the gun to push it back up, then hurried after the others.

30

"Sophie, slow down!" Maggie whisper-shouted. "What are you doing?"

Sophie was already past the Lobby and on her way down the main hall in the other direction. She moved at a fast walk, trying not to make noise, but the floorboards creaked and she grimaced. She passed two branching hallways, one on the left and one on the right, without even glancing into them.

As she approached a third hallway on the left, she began to slow down, painstakingly creeping on her tiptoes. Turning back to Maggie she held up her hand, gesturing for Maggie to stop. Then she looked forward again, craning her neck to see.

Billy and Chris caught up to them and stood behind Maggie, the three of them trying to see as well, even though they had no idea what they were looking for. Sophie began creeping forward again, slowly this time, peering intently all around.

"What is she doing?" Chris whispered to Billy. "Is she nuts?"

Billy shrugged his shoulders. He didn't take his eyes off his sister as Sophie peered into the opening of the third hallway for a moment and then kept moving forward. She stooped over, closely studying the floor. Then she got down on her hands and knees and began crawling, looking all around.

She was near a section of wall that contained a series of panels instead of drawers. Each panel seemed to have been made from a different type of wood and each was outlined with decorative trim. As she approached this section, searching back and forth along the bottom where the wall met the floor, she felt around with her hands, exploring the panels and the trim and the floorboards by the wall.

"Sophie," Maggie whispered, approaching her tentatively. "What did you see?"

Sophie looked up and sighed. Standing she put her hands on her hips and looked one more time up the main hall. When she turned back to Maggie, she had a look of pure joy on her face.

"I saw a fairy!" she said in hushed excitement. "I mean, I think I saw a fairy!"

Maggie's mouth fell open.

"You mean, like, a fairy-fairy? An actual fairy?"

Sophie nodded, eyebrows raised, lips pressed together in a grin that seemed to be trying to hold itself back for fear of exploding.

"You're serious, aren't you?" asked Billy, incredulous.

"Yes, I'm serious! I mean, I'm pretty sure! I mean, I'm definitely positive! Almost!"

"You're talking about a little person with wings, right?" Billy asked, trying to keep the skepticism from his voice. "That kind of fairy?"

"Yes!" Sophie jumped up and down, unable to contain herself. "It was right here! By the floor! I saw its wings fluttering—they were yellow and green! I thought it was a butterfly at first, but then it stood up on the floor and looked at us and it was a fairy! I know you think I'm crazy, but it was right *here!*"

"Where did it go?" stammered Maggie. "I wanna see it!"

"I don't know. When it saw me looking at it, it flew up and went this way and just disappeared. Somewhere right over here by the wall. I couldn't tell where it went. It was just gone."

All four kids began feeling the wall, pushing and knocking on the panels and wiggling the trim work, trying to find anything that might be a secret opening like the one they'd found in the Bug Museum. They found nothing. Backing up to the opposite side of the hallway, Billy scanned the wall for anything that might give a clue to where Sophie's fairy had gone. If that was really what she saw.

"Are you sure this is where it was?" he asked, trying to keep the skepticism from his voice. Who was he to tell his sister that fairies didn't exist? If *this* existed, why not fairies?

"I think so," said Sophie.

Billy looked up the main hall. For the first time, he had a good view of this end of the hallway which they'd previously only seen from the Lobby. Three more side hallways branched off from the main hall before it came to an end, where it appeared to make a right turn. Still carrying Sophie's backpack he began walking toward the end of the main hall. He was suddenly almost desperate to find the end—to establish some sort of perimeter or outer limit to this place. He wanted to find the end and work back toward the Lobby. At least then they would know how big it was.

A fairy. He didn't really believe it. It couldn't be true, of course. But they had seen so many strange things lately, he wasn't sure what to believe anymore. At this very moment, he was walking down an impossible hallway inside an impossible nightstand. How big of a leap would it be to accept that Sophie really had seen a fairy? And if *that* were true—if there were fairies in this place, then this place might be bigger than he'd thought. And more dangerous. He was distracted from his thoughts by Chris, who rattled up beside him, plastic armor and sword clacking together.

"Billy, I'm a little freaked out right now," he said.

Billy didn't answer. He kept moving toward the end of the main hall. He didn't even glance down the branching corridors as he passed them.

"Where are you guys going?" Sophie called after them.

"Just to the end here," said Billy. "I want to check out the end of the hallway."

His voice sounded strange in his ears and he realized he was shaking. It wasn't just the fairy. Some deep part of his mind was beginning to realize something about this place; he wasn't even sure what it was yet, but it scared him. It was like bubbles coming to the surface of deep water: you knew something was down there, but you just didn't know what.

Sophie and Maggie were coming now, hurrying to catch up, and Billy stopped just before arriving at the corner where the main hall made its right hand turn. He took in a deep breath, held it, then stepped around the corner. The passage went on for another ten feet or so, where it abruptly came to an end. Billy felt a brief wave of relief wash over him before he realized there was more to it than that.

On the wall at the end of the hallway stood two doors. But they weren't regular doors. They were small, like cupboard doors, low to the floor. Each door had a small black knob with fancy scrollwork on it. *Probably just more storage, like the drawers,* thought Billy.

Together, the four of them crept to the end of the hallway. Billy stooped, grabbed one of the knobs, and turned. The door creaked as he pulled it open. What they saw on the other side was not at all what they expected.

"That's not a cupboard," Chris said, stating the obvious.

They crouched around the opening, looking through it. On

the other side, the passage continued for several feet, then met with a set of stairs going up.

"Oh, great," Billy whispered. "*Now* what?"

"Where do you think they go?" asked Chris.

"I don't know," said Billy. "Let's just go up and find out. Who knows . . . maybe Uncle Gary is right up there at the top of the stairs."

"Okay, let's do it," Sophie agreed.

Billy crawled through first. Standing up on the other side, he waited for the others to come through. Without even thinking about it, he bounced up and down a few times to make sure this hallway was stable. The floor creaked under him but seemed solid.

Sophie, Maggie, and Chris came through. For at least five minutes, they just stood quietly at the bottom of the stairs, peering up into the shadows at the top.

"Listen," Billy whispered. Around them was a menagerie of wood sounds: little pops and creaks, clicks and ticks, squeaks and thumps, and bumps. Some near, some far, some above, some below, some right or left, some impossible to locate. It was nothing alarming, like the Dark Hall had been. It was more like the entire place was gently settling or shifting as the weight of the children moved around.

A soft scurrying sound made everyone look to the right. Maybe it was a mouse inside the wall. *Or a fairy,* Billy thought.

The stairway was only wide enough for them to go in single file. It seemed twice as long as the stairs at home, and they went straight up without a turn or a landing. Billy thought he could see the top step but he couldn't see anything beyond. Taking a deep breath Billy said, "I'll go up first."

"You want my shield?" Chris offered.

"No, thank . . . um. Yeah." Billy took the shield and, looking upward, put his foot on the first step.

"Wait," Maggie whispered, grabbing his arm. "What's that sound?"

They all listened again. It was very faint, almost inaudible, and Billy had to hold his breath to hear it. It was a knocking or a banging sound. Five or six faint BANGS followed by a moment of silence, then another five or six. It repeated that pattern for a minute, then stopped altogether.

"That sounded like a hammer," Billy said, turning back to the others.

"Do you think it was Uncle Gary?" asked Sophie.

"Yeah, I think so. What else could it be?" With renewed hope Billy started up the stairs. The others followed. The steps were particularly creaky, which made it impossible for them to move quietly. Anything or anyone at the top of the stairs would definitely know they were coming.

The stairs seemed to go on forever, and all four of them were breathing hard as they drew near the top. Billy slowed down and Sophie bumped into his back, almost knocking him off balance.

He peered over the top step. He wasn't surprised to see another hallway. This one ran right and left, perpendicular to the stairs. On the wall across from the staircase were more drawers. Row after row stretched from floor to ceiling.

Adjusting his grip on the plastic shield, Billy realized his hand was sweating. He lifted the shield to his face so that only his eyes showed above it. Wishing he had one of those flimsy plastic helmets Chris was wearing, he led the way up the remaining two steps and entered the hallway. He looked quickly right and left.

In both directions the hallway was curved so that he could only see five yards or so before it disappeared around the bend. There were drawers of every shape and size on both walls, with no apparent organization to them. The entire hallway was painted a light cream color and the drawers were decorated with colorful and intricate designs: painted curls and frills like gold lace and colorful flowers, fruits, twisting vines, trees, animals, and all kinds of landscape scenes. To his left was a closed door in the wall.

"Wow." Chris looked back and forth with admiration.

Sophie began drawing in her notepad, trying to catch up with all they had seen.

"You guys," warned Chris. "This could go on and on forever. If we're not careful we're gonna get lost in here."

"Maybe not," said Billy. "Look at how it curves. This hallway might be one big circle."

"But there's a door," Chris replied. "There could be doors all the way around, leading to other hallways."

"Let's check," Billy whispered. He took a few steps down the left hand passage, stretching his neck to see around the curve.

"Wait," said Sophie, sketching in her notebook. "I need to finish this."

Maggie opened one of the drawers. She took out a bundle of old looking letters tied together with a string. "To Freddie Franco (my True Love)," she read from the handwritten address on the top envelope. She turned the bundle over in her hand, smelled them, then put them back and closed the drawer.

"AaaCHHOOO!" she sneezed.

"Okay, I'm ready," Sophie announced.

They made their way cautiously along the hallway. Billy tried the door as they passed it, but it was locked. Further along were other doors, just as Chris had predicted—one about every five feet. Billy tried each door but each one was locked, until he tried the eighth one. The handle turned with a CLICK. Billy glanced at the others before pulling the door open.

Inside was a small room, no bigger than a closet, with several small drawers in the back wall. On the right wall toward the floor was another cupboard door.

"Oh, don't tell me," said Chris.

Billy opened it and stooped down to peer inside. It was dark, but he could see the first three steps of a very narrow spiral staircase going up.

"More stairs," he muttered.

"Oh, come on!" wailed Chris. "This is crazy! You guys, we'll *never* explore this whole place! It's like a maze in here!"

"Sshhh," hushed Sophie. "Keep your voice down."

"I don't wanna keep my voice down," Chris complained. "Every time we go down one hallway, we find three more. We'll be lucky if we can even find our way out of here!"

"Well, what else are we supposed to do?" Billy said.

"I don't know," Chris shot back. He seemed to be getting angry. "Maybe go back home and play a game of baseball or something. You know, kid stuff. We're just kids, remember? We shouldn't even be in here. This is…" he gestured helplessly around him. "I don't know—this is an adult place."

"We have to find Uncle Gary," said Billy.

"Why? Why do we have to find him?"

"Because he's the only one who knows anything about the Zobadak Wood Company. He's the only one who can help us. And—and we need to know if he's all right."

"Okay, fine. I know. But why us? This is an adult problem. Shouldn't they be handling it?"

"They would never believe us," Billy protested.

"But you didn't even try!" Chris was shouting now, his gray-blue eyes blazing, and Billy, Sophie, and Maggie were surprised at how angry he was.

"Chris," Sophie broke in, trying to calm him down. "What's going on with you? We're not lost. I know exactly where we are."

"I think he's scared," Maggie offered, not unkindly.

"Of course I'm scared," Chris shouted. "Why aren't you guys

scared? I mean, what's wrong with you? Look at this place we're in! It's not even possible for this place to exist! And there's foot-steps and weird noises and somebody with a hammer." He pointed at Sophie. "And now she's seeing fairies! Come on, you guys! This is too much. I don't think I can do it—it's just too much . . ." Tears began rolling down his cheeks. He pushed the visor of his helmet further back on his head and wiped at his cheek, leaving a gray smear of dust.

"Chris, listen to me," Billy said, stepping forward and grab-bing Chris by the shoulders. "I still don't think it's as big as it seems in here. I mean, think about it. My uncle can only build so much." Even as the words came out of his own mouth, Billy didn't believe them. They sounded flat and empty.

"No, you think about it," Chris shot back. "How do you know it's just your uncle in here? How do you know there's not a hundred people building this place? And how do you know they haven't been building it for a thousand years? I mean, look around. This place is old, you have to admit. This place is way older than your uncle. And not only that, where the heck are we? We're not in the nightstand. We're not in my garage, I know that. Are we even on planet earth anymore? I mean . . ."

Chris's voice trailed off, the size of his thoughts becoming too big for words. He lifted his arms in frustration and let them drop back to his sides.

Billy opened his mouth to reply, but nothing came out. Chris was right, of course. If it was possible for this place to exist at all, it was also possible for it to be gigantic. And Billy realized that there was a part of him that already knew all this. He'd only been pretending not to know, perhaps so he wouldn't lose his nerve.

He looked at Sophie, and the expression on her face told him she was thinking more or less the same thing. In fact, she looked scared, too, which only made him feel worse. What was he getting them into? He had been so focused on what he was doing that he'd forgotten to be careful.

"Guys, guys, guys," Maggie said. "You all need to relax, okay? We're not lost, right? Chris, if we went back right now, it would take us about five minutes to get to your garage. And we're not going to get lost either. Sophie's drawing a map. And if we need to drop breadcrumbs like Hansel and Gretel, then that's what we'll do, okay?"

"That won't work," said Chris, sniffling.

"Why won't it?" asked Maggie.

"Mice'll eat 'em."

They looked at each other.

"Or fairies," said Billy, a bit reluctantly.

Sophie turned her head toward the wall and her shoulders began to shake. At first Billy thought she had begun to cry. Then he realized she was laughing.

Maggie smiled, covering her mouth with her hand, her almond-shaped eyes narrowing.

"Stop it, you guys. It's not funny," Chris said, but he couldn't keep a smile from creeping into the corners of his own mouth.

"It is *kind* of funny," said Billy, grinning. "You have to admit."

Chris shook his head.

"I'm not admitting anything," he said, but it was too late. He barely got the sentence out when he suddenly burst into laughter, unable to hold it back anymore. He bent over, putting both hands against the wall, and soon there were fresh tears on his face. The four of them stood laughing, and for those few minutes, all their problems were forgotten. Finally their laughter subsided and they simply stood there smiling at each other. *These are my best friends,* thought Billy.

"I'm still mad at you guys," said Chris, but he didn't sound very mad.

"Speaking of bread crumbs," said Maggie. "Is anyone else getting hungry?"

"Yeah," Sophie agreed. "Let's eat lunch and we'll figure out what to do next."

Pulling off their backpacks they sat down on the floor. Billy and Sophie took out their peanut butter and honey sandwiches and juice boxes. Maggie had a baloney sandwich and a bottle of water.

Chris opened his backpack and took out a plastic container filled with beef stew. Then he removed a small Spider-Man Thermos with chicken soup. A plastic bag with little cheese cubes. Another plastic bag with baby carrots. Another plastic bag holding some cookies. A bottle of root beer and a napkin, fork, knife, and spoon. He arranged everything around him as though he were setting a table for royalty while the others watched him in wonder, munching on their sandwiches.

31

They decided that they would continue around the curved hall-way. If they ended up back at the stairs, they would go back down and return to Chris's garage. Then they would come back on another day and explore a little more, one section at a time.

After eating Chris seemed a little calmer, and all four of them felt better in general, so they shoved their garbage into their back-packs and gathered up the rest of their belongings.

"Oh, I almost forgot," said Chris, reaching into his backpack. "Here, Billy. I brought an extra gun for you." He held up an Old West six-shooter cap gun just like the one hanging in the holster on his hip.

"What am I supposed to do with that?" Billy was mystified as to why Chris would bring a cap gun in the first place.

"I don't know," Chris replied. "For extra protection."

"But it's just a cap gun," Billy protested weakly. He wanted neither the gun nor to hurt his friend's feelings.

"Do you want it or not?" Chris held the gun out to him.

"No, I don't think so. I mean, thanks for bringing it," he stammered, "but I don't want to carry that thing around."

"Okay, your loss," Chris said. He seemed a little hurt as he shoved the revolver back into his pack and zipped it up.

Maggie rolled her eyes at Sophie.

"Boys are *so* lame," she whispered. Sophie nodded her head and snickered.

"I heard that," Billy said.

They started walking again. The doors continued on the left wall, which was the outer side of the curve, about every five feet. Billy tried the knobs on every door, but most of them were locked. The few that were unlocked opened onto the same closet-like rooms with drawers and cupboard doors of various sizes. Two more of the cupboard doors opened up to staircases, one ascending and one descending. But some of the cupboard doors opened up to just plain storage shelves, and those contained a variety of things. One had an old globe whose continents didn't look quite like the ones on the globe in Billy's classroom. Another cupboard held shelves lined with jars full of formaldehyde in which floated various dead reptiles and amphibians: snakes, lizards, toads, geckos, etc. On a shelf in another cupboard was a large jar filled with flat, brown, crusty-looking things. The label on the lid read "SCABS." Billy closed the door with a shudder and didn't open any more cupboards after that.

The right-hand wall inside the curve continued with ranks of colorfully painted drawers. Opening them at random, they found mostly old letters and diaries and notebooks. It was tempting to read some of them, but they wanted to keep going. They had to be out of the nightstand by 2:45 at the latest to beat their parents home. They must have been about halfway around the circle when Billy discovered a door on the right hand side.

"Hey, look at this. Should I try it?" Billy scanned the three faces next to him.

"Yeah, try it," Maggie said, nodding her head. "There's probably a round room in the middle or something."

"Who knows, maybe Uncle Gary's in there," said Sophie.

Billy grasped the knob and twisted, but it didn't budge.

"Oh, well," he shrugged. "So much for that."

They continued forward, but a sudden THUMP above them froze everyone in their tracks.

"What was that?" Chris whispered.

"Ssshh, listen," Sophie hushed.

There was another THUMP, then something clattered and bumped and began rolling and tumbling. It sounded very much like somebody falling down a set of stairs.

"Aaagghh!" came a rough voice, followed by the startled yowl of a cat.

The noises came from the direction of the door they had just tried, and the kids instinctively backed away from it as the tumbling and bumping and banging grew louder. Suddenly something crashed against the inside of the door and the noise stopped.

"Confoundit!" a muffled voice shouted from behind the door.

The kids backed away further, staring at the door.

"Let's get out of here," said Chris.

"Wait!" said Billy. "Just hang on a minute."

The door swung open and a scruffy looking brown cat immediately ran out, scrabbling toward the kids. When it saw them, it stopped, hissed, and took off in the other direction, claws skittering on the wooden floor.

"Get back here, you mangy little fur bucket!" said the voice from the open doorway. An arm reached out to grab the cat as it went by, but it was too late. "When I catch you, I'm gonna make me a new pillow!"

"Is that your uncle?" Maggie whispered to Sophie.

She shook her head. "I don't think so."

"Then let's get out of here!" whispered Chris. "Come on!"

"Maybe he can help us," said Billy.

Tucking the sword under his arm, Chris fumbled the cowboy six-shooter out of its holster and held it up with a shaking hand.

At the bottom of the doorway, close to the floor, a grizzled head popped out, its thin and uneven hair in disarray. They couldn't tell if the man was very old or just filthy and unkempt. His beard and sideburns grew in patches and he had a scar on one cheek. He was struggling to turn over and get up, after having apparently fallen down a set of stairs. His other arm swung out into the hallway, holding a crutch that banged against the doorframe and the opposite wall.

He apparently didn't see the kids standing in the hallway, so they waited quietly for him to untangle himself. As Chris adjusted his heavy backpack on his shoulders, the plastic sword slipped out from under his arm and clattered to the floor. The man stopped thrashing about and squinted in their direction.

"What in the name of Johansson's ghost are *you* doing here?" he blurted out in a voice that rattled like a can of marbles.

"Billy—talk to him," Sophie prodded.

Billy took a step forward.

"Uh, hi," he mumbled. "Are you, um—are you okay?"

The man finally managed to turn himself over and crawl out into the hallway. For the next several minutes he struggled to stand, swinging the crutch about with one hand and using the doorframe to pull himself up with the other. His clothes were dirty and ragged. He wore an old suit jacket with a huge hole in one elbow and mismatched buttons, which had been carelessly buttoned in the wrong holes. Everything about him looked crooked. One leg was longer than the other, and he wore a tall, red platform shoe on the short side. He leaned to the left on his crutch. His head was cocked at an odd angle, and his gray hair was longer on one side than the other and sticking straight out.

Billy couldn't help thinking of the old nursery rhyme: "There was a crooked man who built a crooked house . . ."

"Do I look okay?" the man snapped. "Go ahead, be honest!"

"Umm . . ."

"You're kids, aren't you?" he asked, squinting at them.

"Yes."

"Well. I didn't see that coming. What is this, some kind of field trip?"

"Uhh, no . . ."

"Don't they go to the zoo anymore?"

"No—I mean, yeah, they still go to the zoo."

The man took a step forward, leaning to the left as he tried to see around the curve of the hallway, and for a moment Billy thought he was going to topple over.

"How many of you are there? Twenty? Thirty?"

"Oh, no—there's just four of us. Um, my name is Billy, and this is my sister Sophie. And these are our friends, Chris and Maggie."

"Why is that one pointing a gun at me?"

Billy turned around.

"Chris, put that away! It's not polite."

Chris dropped his shield, trying to shove the gun back into its holster.

"You're darn right it's not polite!" the old man squawked. "Anyway, guns ain't allowed in here. I hope that's not a real gun."

"No, sir," said Chris, his voice a frightened squeak. "It's just a cap gun."

"A *cap* gun? That uses real gunpowder, don't it? Them ain't allowed in here either! Do you have any idea what would happen if a spark hit the floor and caught fire?"

All four kids shook their heads, staring wide-eyed at the man.

"Woooooshhh!" he flung both arms in the air, his crutch smacking against the ceiling and causing a little shower of dust to trickle down into his hair. "Up in smoke! Like a barn full o' monkey fur!"

"I'm sorry," stammered Chris. "I didn't mean to—"

"Give it to me." The man held out his hand and lurched forward, his two different shoes making a CLUNK-THUMP, CLUNK-THUMP sound that the kids instantly recognized.

Chris pulled the gun back out of its holster and extended it forward, tapping Billy on the arm with the barrel.

"Here, give it to him," said Chris.

Billy took the gun, turned it around, and handed it to the man butt-first, deciding not to mention the other gun in Chris's pack. Without a word, the man took the gun. Keeping his eyes fixed warily on the kids, he reached into his jacket pocket and pulled out a set of keys on a chain. Then, turning away from them, he limped back to one of the doors on the outer wall and used a key to open it.

The kids watched as he got down on his hands and knees and began opening and slamming drawers and cupboards. Finally, he took a large glass jar out of one of the cupboards and set it down on the floor of the hallway. It appeared to be full of water. He unscrewed the lid and dropped the gun into the jar with a plop. Twisting the lid back on, he returned the jar to the cupboard, stood up, shut the closet door, and locked it.

"Now then," he said, turning back to the kids and shoving the keys back into his jacket pocket. "Are you kids lost?"

"No, sir," said Billy.

"Are you sure? It's real easy to get lost in here."

"Yeah, I'm sure."

"How'd you get in here?"

Billy hesitated. He wasn't sure if he should tell the man how they got in. He looked back at the others. Sophie shook her head.

"Well," said Billy. "Do you mind if I ask your name?"

"Of course not. Why would I mind?"

The man stared back at Billy, eyebrows cocked. Billy waited for him to give his name but the man said nothing, continuing to stare back at Billy as though waiting for something.

"Uh," said Billy, confused.

"Why would I mind?" the man repeated.

"Oh, um—no reason. So—what's your name?"

"My name is Krandall. Krandall Blemish."

"Nice to meet you, Mr. Blemish," said Billy, remembering his manners. "So, do you live in here?"

"Of course I live in here," Krandall replied. "I'm the janitor. Or the custodian. Or the caretaker. Or the undertaker. Or whatever it's called. I don't remember the exact name. There's too many words; I can't keep track of them all. Anyways, don't I have enough responsibility as it is? Well, don't I?"

"Oh, uh, yes, sir. You do." Billy fumbled to give the right answer.

"Darn right. Anyways, what makes you think I could get out of here even if I tried?"

Billy didn't understand the question. Again, he looked back at the others for help, but they only shrugged their shoulders.

"What do you mean?" he asked.

"What do you mean, what do I mean?" Krandall snapped, his voice rattling. "Use your noggin, kid! I'm an adult. Adult: big. Kid: small. I can't get through the joints anymore!"

Billy was becoming more confused with each sentence the man spoke.

"I was six years old when I wriggled into my dresser," said Krandall, staring off into space as if lost in memory. "Six years old. But I remember it like it was yesterday. I don't remember what I ate for breakfast today, but I remember the day I climbed into my Buglu Drawer."

The kids were suddenly dead silent. Chris stopped fussing restlessly with his backpack and gear, Maggie stopped sniffling and Sophie and Billy were holding their breath without even realizing it.

"Stupid kid, that's what I was," Krandall went on. "I was so mad at my folks that day, I just wanted to leave and never come back. So I ran away. Most kids run away from home by walking down a street, or hiding in a field for a few hours until they get hungry and bored and lonely. Not me. I found the Buglu Drawer when I was four years old, so, clever me, I had a better plan. I ran away into the furniture. Into my bedroom dresser. That was the year 1955. Right after my sixth birthday. Didn't take me long to get lost, I'll tell you that. Days went by, and the more I wandered, the lost-er I got. Months and years went by, and then one day I finally found the way back to my dresser. But I was too big to crawl back out. I sure tried, though. Yes, sir. I sure did try."

For several moments, the hallway was in complete silence. There were a few creaks of wood here and there but Krandall only stared into space and the kids just stared at Krandall. They didn't know what to say. His story was horrifying, and they didn't know whether to be scared or sad or confused or happy to have found someone who might be helpful.

"Oh, pickle-biscuits!" Krandall suddenly blurted, breaking the silence. "You kids don't wanna hear about my sad story. Are you running away from home or something?" he demanded.

"Oh, no. We're not running away," said Billy. "We're looking for someone. Maybe you can help us, Mr. Blemish."

"Call me Krandall. You're looking for something you say?"

"Actually we're looking for a person. It's very important that we find him. Are there any other people in here?"

"Oh, sure. A few."

"Do you know a man named Gary Fyfe?"

"Gary Fyfe," Krandall repeated and studied the floor, deep in thought. His body began leaning to one side, and the kids thought that he might have fallen asleep.

"Mr. Blemish? I mean, Krandall?"

Krandall's head snapped up, and he looked around in apparent surprise at surroundings. He cleared his throat, hawked, and swallowed.

Brad Gallagher

"Gary Fyfe, you say? No. I don't know any Gary Fyfe."

Billy's disappointment at hearing this was so heavy, it was like someone had just dropped a boulder into his backpack. If Krandall Blemish was telling the truth, and he really had been inside this place since 1955, then surely he would know if Uncle Gary was in there somewhere. Billy didn't realize until now how much he had gotten his hopes up. It almost felt like losing his uncle all over again.

He turned to the others and knew immediately they were feeling the same way. Sophie was biting her upper lip and looking down at her hands. Chris and Maggie were looking at the floor.

"What do you want him for, anyway?" Krandall asked.

"Oh, he's my uncle and he's been missing for half a year. We're trying to find him. He's hiding because of this stupid company that's looking for him and causing all kinds of trouble."

"Heh!" said Krandall. "Owes money, does he?"

"Yeah, I guess. Well, not really money. I think they're trying to get something back that was shipped to him. Some kind of wood."

Krandall stiffened, squinting at the kids.

"It's a *wood* company you're talking about?" he asked.

"Yeah."

"What's the name of this wood company?"

"Zobadak. It's called the Zobadak Wood Company."

Krandall flinched when he heard the words. He spun around to look behind him, then turned back to the kids.

"Zobadak?" he said, his voice hitching as the word became lodged in his throat.

"Yes."

"They didn't follow you here did they?"

"No."

"Are you sure? Do they know how you came in?"

"No."

"Are you sure?"

170

"Yes!" said Billy. "What is it? What do you know about them?"

"By the devil's blue toe, I hope they didn't follow you here!"

"Why?" Billy asked, alarmed by Krandall's sudden outburst of panic. "What is Zobadak? I wish you would tell us who they are."

Krandall pulled the keys out of his pocket again and limped towards the kids, grabbing door handles and shaking them to make sure they were locked. The third door he tried was unlocked and he shoved a key into the keyhole, cranking it over.

"Don't you know what the Zobadak Wood Company is?" Krandall shouted at them, his voice quavering.

"No," said Billy, glancing back at Sophie, Chris, and Maggie. Chris had his shield up and was pulling the visor of his helmet down. He picked up his sword, leaving the walking stick on the floor of the hallway.

"Let's go, you guys," he said, moving backward down the hall. "I don't like the sound of this and I don't wanna be here anymore."

Krandall continued along the curved hallway, past the kids, grabbing and shaking door handles.

"Wait!" Billy cried. "Krandall! What is the Zobadak Wood Company?"

Krandall stopped and looked up at him, eyes wild and darting with panic.

"Don't you know?"

Billy shook his head.

"That's Brope's company!"

"Uhhh, what?" said Billy, more perplexed than ever.

"Hey, you guys?" Maggie said softly.

Krandall disappeared around the corner, and they could hear him rattling knobs and slamming doors as he clomped away.

"Who's Brope?" Billy muttered, more to himself than to any-one else.

"You guys?" Maggie repeated.

Sophie grabbed Billy's arm.

"Should we go after him? He knows about Zobadak. We have to find out what he knows!"

"Who's Brope?" Billy shouted down the hall. "Mr. Blemish! Krandall! What does that mean?"

"You guys, I hate to bring this up right now, but . . ." said Maggie.

"What is it Maggie?" Sophie turned to her.

"It's almost 3:30."

"What?" Sophie exclaimed. "How could it be that late?"

"I don't know; we lost track of time."

"Billy, we have to go! Mom and Dad got home half an hour ago! They're going to be looking for us!"

"Yeah, okay," said Billy, reluctantly.

"Good idea!" said Chris. "Let's get out of here and never come back!"

The others looked at him reproachfully, but Chris was already on his way.

32

They went back the way they had come, even though it was probably the long way around the circular hallway, back to the stairs. There was no sign of Krandall Blemish, who had probably disappeared up some side passage. As they descended the stairs, Sophie flung a steady stream of questions at Billy.

"Who's Brope?"

"I have no idea."

"Do you really think Krandall has been in here since 1955?"

"How should I know?"

"What did he mean when he said he was too big to get back out?"

"I don't know."

"The nightstand is big enough for an adult to climb out of."

"He didn't say nightstand. He said dresser."

"Oh, yeah. That's right. So does that mean there's another Bigy Bigy Buglu Drawer in a dresser somewhere?"

"I don't know. Yeah, I guess."

"It would have to be connected to this place too, wouldn't it?"

"I guess."

"Do you think there's other ones besides that?"

"I don't know."

"How many other people are in here?"

"I have no idea!" he said, annoyed.

"So if Uncle Gary's not in here, where would he be?"

"Sophie, I don't know!" Billy stopped at the bottom of the stairs and whirled around to face her. "I have no idea! Why do you keep asking me questions? I don't know, okay? I don't know anything!"

Sophie was taken aback by his sudden outburst.

"I was just asking," she faltered.

"Well, stop it! All I know is, we didn't find Uncle Gary, we still don't know where he is, and now we're in big trouble with Mom and Dad because we're a half-hour late getting home. Chris and Maggie's parents are going to be mad too because they were supposed to be watching us."

With that, he crawled through the cupboard door and back into the main hallway. The others followed, and without another word they continued back toward the Lobby.

When they passed the wall with the various different wood panels where Sophie had seen the fairy, she stopped for a moment to take one more look around. Seeing nothing, she sighed and kept walking.

They heard the rumbling as they entered the Lobby and approached the trapdoor.

"What is that?" Maggie asked.

Chris held his backpack over the opening, ready to drop it down to the garage floor.

"Chris, wait!" Billy grabbed the backpack and the four of them listened.

The rumbling was impossibly deep. They heard objects rattling inside Chris's garage. It seemed the entire garage was shaking. Something metal clanged as it fell to the floor and rolled.

"Is that an earthquake or something?" Chris asked.

Sophie and Billy stared at each other, seeing the dawning realization in each other's eyes.

"Truck," they both said simultaneously.

"No," said Chris. "There's no way. It would have to be in my driveway to be that loud."

They looked at him, aghast.

"Oh, God," choked Chris. "Oh no. You guys, I don't like this. You should have never brought this stupid nightstand to my house."

The rumbling deepened and something much larger toppled over in the garage below. Glass broke somewhere, tinkling on cement.

"They found us," Sophie cried, her voice choked with horror.

"Don't go down there," Maggie whispered. "Whatever you do. . . ."

Billy peered down through the opening. He saw the gray of the garage floor, but nothing else. At that moment, another thought leaped into his mind like an animal fleeing a forest fire, clawing through the jungle of terror that seemed to expand throughout his entire body. Tearing off his backpack, he tossed it aside.

"What are you doing?" Sophie stammered.

He looked at her, his face pale with desperation and fright. He didn't think he would be able to get the words to come out of his mouth without either crying or screaming, but somehow he did.

"Mom and Dad!" he shouted, and without another thought, he swung his legs over the edge and began climbing down.

"Billy!" Sophie screamed.

He let go of the rungs, letting himself drop straight down to the floor of the garage. Ducking under the bottom of the nightstand, he stood up, legs shaking so much he could barely hold himself upright.

The noise was so loud and so deep that the floor of the garage was shuddering, and he began to think maybe it was an earthquake after all. It vibrated in his chest and in his teeth; even the hair on his arms seemed to vibrate. He couldn't see past the mountain of junk in the garage, so he took three steps to the right where he could look up the narrow pathway in the middle. To his enormous relief the driveway was empty but his relief didn't last long. Whatever was making the sound, it was probably coming from his street—from Fairlane Avenue—from his house. Hurrying back to the nightstand, he stuck his head underneath.

"It's clear!" he called up. "There's no truck here!"

Sophie was already on her way down, but Billy didn't wait for her. He ran out of the garage, blinded by the glare of the afternoon sun. With his hands out in front of him and his eyes half closed, he took off down the driveway and onto the sidewalk, sprinting toward Fairlane Avenue.

Before he had cleared three driveways, he stopped in his tracks. Through watering, sun-blind eyes, he saw something that made absolutely no sense. The entire neighborhood seemed to be shrouded in a black fog that hung like a ceiling over the houses. The smell of burnt oil and wood seared his nostrils, and he knew, with a horrible sinking feeling, that the Zobadak Wood Company men were back.

But it wasn't trucks he saw this time. All around him, people stood on their front lawns, transfixed like statues, all staring at the same thing. He sensed it even before he saw it: over the rooftops, a forest was moving through the smoke down Fairlane Avenue. Or maybe it was a machine. Billy saw massive wheels that looked more like oil-stained metal gears, as tall as people, rolling past the intersection of Fairlane and Magnolia. Above the wheels was a monstrous dark machine, taller than the houses, made of rusted iron and steel-banded logs, chains dangling from its sides.

The engine sounded like a freight train with broken gears grinding—or a tornado full of sheet metal, echoing up and down the street. And beneath the noise of the engine was a cacophony of metal clanging and steam hissing, cranks rattling and pulleys squealing.

On top of the machine, crooked chimneys stuck out at odd angles, belching black smoke. At the front end was some kind of tall tower, like a lighthouse, with a spotlight at the top turning in circles, slicing into the smog.

And from everywhere on the top and sides, there sprouted dark, gnarled, leafless trees that seemed to claw at the sky. The machine—or the forest—was as long as ten houses, and the back end of it passed by the intersection, dragging chains and cables in the street behind it.

Sophie, Chris, and Maggie stood next to Billy, staring with open mouths.

"Wh-what—what—what—?" Chris stuttered.

Billy watched the thing's humped, tree-covered back moving slowly away through the smoke that drifted over the rooftops. It was leaving. Which meant it had already been to their house. It had already done what it came to do.

Snapping out of his trance, Billy took off.

33

Sirens approached the Fyfe house for the third time in three weeks, only this time, they seemed to be coming from every direction.

Billy stumbled, almost falling, when his foot landed in one of the deep ruts left behind in the grass. There were two long wheel ruts gouged across every front lawn on Fairlane Avenue, one on each side of the street. The street itself was black with oil and ash.

Catching himself he kept running, darting back and forth between the clusters of people outside. Turning to glance behind him, he saw the churning cloud of smoke that almost completely obscured the machine as it rumbled away, straddling the street. He could still see the spotlight turning and flashing in the tower high above the treetops.

His pulse roared in his ears as he approached the house, terrified but unable to stop. Their neighbor, Philip, was standing on his lawn with a cell phone to his ear. He saw Billy approaching and quickly pocketed the phone and moved to intercept him.

"Billy! Thank God you're okay!"

Ignoring him Billy swerved past him, but Philip grabbed him gently but firmly around the shoulders.

"Don't go over there! It's not safe!"

Struggling to get away, Billy screamed, "Where are they? Where's my Mom and Dad?"

"Billy, stop! Listen to me!" Philip shouted. "You can't go over there!"

Straining to free himself from the neighbor's hold, Billy caught a glimpse of the house, and suddenly all his strength drained away. His legs became rubber and folded beneath him.

The house—their home—wasn't even a house anymore. It looked as if it had somehow opened up like a flower. Wooden beams, joists, and studs stuck up in every direction out of the pile of crumbled brick and bent siding surrounding the wreckage. All the wood of the house was warped into twisting corkscrews and curls. Forests of splintered two-by-fours jabbed up out of the rubble, baring claws of bent nails.

Their belongings were scattered everywhere among the rubble and across the lawn, everything white with drywall dust. Their toys and blankets, the big television, the couch cushions, the clothes and dishes and Mom's books and Dad's DVD collection. Everything broken and torn. And in the driveway sat both cars covered in dust. They were home when it happened. Mom and Dad were home.

"Where are they? Where are they? Let me go. I have to find them!" Billy fought to pull himself away, but Philip held on tight.

"Billy, listen to me!" Philip shouted. "Where's your sister? Where's Sophie?"

At that moment there was a piercing scream from behind them. Sophie stood with both hands up against the sides of her face, staring at the tangled mass of twisted wood and shattered brick that was once their house. Where they used to sleep and eat and play and argue and cuddle on the couch.

"Sophie!" Philip exclaimed, kneeling and grabbing her and

hugging her tightly to his chest. "Oh, you poor kids!"

Sophie burst into tears, her body shaking with terror, confusion, and grief.

"What happened to them?" cried Billy.

"Kids, listen to me," said Philip. He tried to sound calm, but his voice quavered and his face was ashen. "They're not dead, okay? I know that for a fact. Okay?"

"How do you know that?" Billy demanded.

"Because I saw them leave."

Both kids pulled back to look at him.

"Leave where?" Billy asked with awakening hope.

"Well . . ." Philip hesitated and looked down at the ground. "They went with the men on that—truck."

"Oh, no." Sophie shook her head, fresh tears spilling down her cheeks.

"What do you mean, they went with them?" Billy whimpered. "You mean the men took them?"

Philip looked back up at the kids and nodded his head.

"Yes," he said. "But the important thing is that they're alive, okay? The police will find them and get them back. They can't get away this time."

"No," Sophie sobbed. "Oh, no. Oh, my God, Billy. What are we going to do?"

"Listen, kids," said Philip. "The police are coming right now. You hear those sirens? You just stay with me until they get here, okay? The police will know what to do."

Sophie wailed, covering her face with her hands.

Billy, too shocked to cry or even speak, turned away from the house to look up the street where the horrible truck had disappeared, leaving a black trail of ash, oil, torn-up lawns, and astonished gawkers in its path. As before, Chris and Maggie were standing on the sidewalk, their cheeks wet and smeared with soot.

Philip stood up and waved his arm in the air as three police cars pulled up to the curb from the other direction. Not far behind them, a fire truck approached, its siren howling.

"Stay right here, kids," said Philip, holding the palms of his hands towards them in a gesture at once calming and gently commanding. "I'll be right back. Just stay here."

He hurried to the nearest police car where two officers were climbing out.

Billy looked at Sophie, then at Chris and Maggie. Turning again to what was left of the house, he saw the handle of Mom's vacuum cleaner sticking up out of a big pile of dust and rubble. At that moment, he knew what he had to do.

"We have to go," he said, looking back at Sophie. "We have to go back."

"Billy, don't," Sophie sobbed.

He started walking toward Chris and Maggie, then stopped and came back. His head was reeling.

"We have to, Sophie," he said urgently. "We have to go back there. We have to find Krandall. He can help us. He knows about the Zobadak Wood Company."

"Just stop!" cried Sophie. "We can't do anything! We should have never gone in there in the first place! We should have told them! We should have told Mom and Dad!"

"I know!" Billy was shouting now. Face wet with tears, eyes red, he paced back and forth like a caged animal. "Don't you think I know that? This is all my fault! I'm the one who should have told them! It's my fault they're gone! It's my fault, and now I have to try to fix it!"

"We can't fix it! Billy, don't you get it? We're kids! We're just kids! We can't do anything! Didn't you see that truck?" Sophie sobbed.

Billy stopped pacing and grabbed his sister by the shoulders. Behind her, he saw Philip talking to the police and gesturing toward the kids. The police looked over at them.

Everything seemed so clear to him at that moment.

"Sophie, listen to me." He tried to keep his voice as calm as possible. "You stay here, okay? You'll be safe. I'm going back inside the Buglu Drawer."

Sophie began shaking her head.

"Just listen," he continued. "If we both go with the police, they're going to put us in a special police place or something to protect us. And then maybe they'll put us with another family. We'll never get back here again. And they will never believe us if we tell them what we know. They'll never believe us, okay? They'll say we're just talking crazy because we're upset. Right now, Krandall is the only person we know who has any idea what's going on. That means this is my only chance to try and help Mom and Dad. Don't you see? I have to go back in there. If I don't, they could be lost forever."

The police began walking toward them.

"I have to go right now! You stay with them. I'll come back and find you as soon as I can, okay?"

"Billy . . ."

He pushed up the bill of her cap, kissed her on the forehead, then turned and ran.

34

He heard the wind rushing in his ears, he heard his heart pounding against his ribcage, he heard the policemen shouting, "Hey!" behind him and their keys jangling as they ran after him. He heard more sirens and barking dogs and people talking frantically, but none of these sounds meant anything to him as he hopped the fence marking Philip's back yard and sprinted between the houses towards the next street.

He knew all the shortcuts, all the little paths behind garages and sheds, all the crawlways beneath hedges and bushes. He had taken this route a thousand times before, and he knew it as well as he knew his own bedroom. He moved through it so quickly and efficiently that within minutes the police were blocks away and he could no longer hear them calling his name.

An old duct-taped plastic kiddie swimming pool leaned up against a wooden fence behind the garage of a colonial on Pickadilly Lane. Behind this swimming pool, two slats of the fence were broken away. Billy slipped through the opening, crawling through damp leaves, and pulled the swimming pool back over the hole. He was now behind Chris's garage.

Peeking around the corner at the driveway, he saw nobody out front. He quickly rounded the corner and disappeared into the garage. In less than three minutes, he was pulling himself up into the Lobby. They would never find him in this place. Not unless Sophie, Chris, or Maggie told.

In the little hallway he sat down on the floor with his forehead on his knees and waited for the stitch in his side to go away. Exhausted and afraid and suddenly very thirsty, he began to cry and sob uncontrollably. It was like a flood had broken down a wall and now everything came pouring out. It was beyond his power to stop it or hold it back.

Billy had no idea how long he sat like that, wanting to go onward to find Krandall but unable to move, feeling desperate and desperately alone, waiting for the tears to stop, exhausted. It could have been two minutes or two hours, but at some point he fell into a restless sleep, his mind sinking helplessly into dark dreams where he found himself crawling through endless trapdoors and tunnels, trying to find something he had lost.

In the confusing moments after he awoke, Billy couldn't quite grasp where he was. The light filtering in from the opening in the floor next to him was much dimmer than before and he could just make out the shape of Sophie curled up on the floor across from him. They must be in the basement, where they sometimes "camped out" in their sleeping bags on weekends. Only they didn't have their sleeping bags for some reason.

He sat up yawning, rubbing his eyes and adjusting the position of his back because of the little drawer handle that poked into it—and that was when reality began to settle back in. They weren't in the basement. They were in the Buglu Drawer. And their parents were gone.

Immediately on the heels of this memory came a stream of questions. Had he fallen asleep? How could he have? What was

Sophie doing here? Why wasn't she with the police? Had she led them here? Reaching across, he gently shook her shoulder.

"Sophie," he whispered. "Sophie—wake up."

She lifted her head groggily and murmured, "Hmmm?"

"Wake up," Billy repeated.

Sophie sat up and looked around, blinking. Her eyes were puffy and red.

"What's going on?" she mumbled.

"You tell me," said Billy. "What are you doing here?"

"Oh, yeah," Sophie yawned, slowly coming out of her cloud of sleep. "I got away."

"You got away?" he asked incredulously.

"Yeah. When you ran, everybody was so busy trying to find you, they forgot about me. I just ran in the other direction. You were asleep when I got here. I didn't want to wake you up."

Billy was dumbfounded. He didn't know whether to be relieved or shocked or frustrated or angry. All he knew was that he had never been happier to see her in his life.

"Don't look so surprised," she said. "There's no way I was going to let you explore this place without me. Anyway," she teased, "you'll just get lost."

He grinned.

"There's no way I'm getting lost," he vowed. "But still, I'm really glad you came."

"Yeah, I know. So what's our plan?"

He looked around. "Well, we left our backpacks up here, so we still have all our stuff. That's good. And maybe we should look through Chris and Maggie's packs and take whatever we need. And then—"

"We don't have to do that," Sophie interrupted. "They're going to be here in a little while. They can carry their own stuff."

"What?"

185

"It took me a while to sneak through the neighborhood without being seen. And they knew where we were going, so by the time I got to Chris's garage they were waiting for me."

"Oh." His mind was racing furiously.

"So they're both back at home right now. They're going to get some extra food and, when their parents think they're asleep, they're going to sneak out and meet us here."

"Even Chris?"

She nodded, pulling her cap on. "It was Chris's idea."

Billy was so overwhelmed with relief and gratitude that he almost couldn't speak. The thought of creeping through the dim hallways of the nightstand all alone had been almost too much to bear. But now he would have not only Sophie but his friends with him as well. Somehow, while he was fast asleep, one of his biggest problems had been taken care of.

"You guys . . ." he began. The words caught in his throat and he couldn't finish.

"I know, I know," she said. "Forget it. Let's just stick together and do this."

"I don't even know if we're doing the right thing," said Billy. "What if this is another big mistake and I just make everything worse?"

"We are doing the right thing. You're the one who made me realize that. You have to stop blaming yourself. It was your idea to move the nightstand out of our house. If we hadn't moved it, they would've taken it or destroyed it or something."

"Yeah, but if I had told Mom and Dad about it, things might have worked out differently."

"Maybe, but maybe not," Sophie shrugged. "It doesn't matter now, and we don't have time to worry about it. We just have to figure out what to do next."

They sat for a long time without saying a word. It felt late. Eventually there was a sound from below in Chris's garage. It was the sound of footsteps moving across the floor, kicking a glass bottle as they came. Then there was a voice, whispering up to them.

"Hey, are you guys up there?"

It was Chris.

"Yeah, come on up," Sophie called back.

They heard him bumping, banging, and flopping around inside the shaft as if he were fighting with something. A muffled "Ouch!" came up through the trapdoor.

Billy and Sophie looked at each other.

"What's he doing?" Billy asked.

Sophie shrugged.

"Help me out with this," came Chris's strained voice.

A box emerged, almost too large to fit through the opening. Billy and Sophie quickly grabbed it and pulled it up, struggling under its weight. Chris came up behind it, breathing hard, and collapsed to the floor.

"What the heck is in there?" said Billy.

"Supplies. And food."

Upon hearing the word "food," Billy suddenly realized how absolutely famished he was. Opening the box, he began digging through the contents. Inside was a confusing variety of items: canned vegetables, five apples, a box of cookies, a loaf of bread, several cans of soda, a bottle of ketchup, four spoons, a corkscrew, a hammer, a screwdriver, a dictionary, an extension cord, a disposable camera, a toothbrush, a bottle of glue, five woolen hats, five pairs of gloves, and one sock.

"Did you bring a can opener?" asked Sophie.

"No," Chris said. "I couldn't find one. I thought we could use the hammer and screwdriver if we have to."

Billy didn't care. He opened the bread and took out two slices, poured ketchup on one of them, slapped the other one on top, and devoured it. The sandwich was equal parts terrible and delicious.

He finished it in less than a minute, then tore into the cookies.

"What's the dictionary for?" Sophie wondered aloud, rummaging through the supplies.

"I don't know. It just seemed like it might come in handy."

A few minutes later they heard another set of feet carefully making their way across the dark garage. When they reached the back corner, Maggie's voice called up to them.

"I have two bags. I'm going to hand them up one at a time."

Chris reached down and pulled up two paper shopping bags with handles. Maggie climbed up behind them.

"It's cold out there," she said, swinging the lid of the trapdoor closed as Sophie began inspecting the contents of the bags.

"You should have waited," Sophie said reproachfully to Billy, who was finishing his second ketchup sandwich.

She'd brought a bounty of food: cold pizza slices in plastic wrap, canned tuna (and a can opener), lunch meat, bottles of water, peanut butter, cheese slices, a bag of chips, granola bars, cupcakes, a roll of paper towel, forks, and butter knives. With obvious pride in her voice, she announced her final prize.

"I also brought a Magic Marker."

"What's that for?" Chris asked.

"We can use it to keep from getting lost. When we come to hallways that go in more than one direction, we can draw little arrows on the floor pointing the way back to the Lobby here. So we can remember where we came from."

"That's a great idea!" Sophie exclaimed as she began assembling a turkey sandwich for herself. "You're awesome, girl!"

They exchanged a high-five, their eyes alight with camaraderie.

"Yeah, I know."

"Oh, brother," Chris groaned and rolled his eyes.

"Actually, it *is* a good idea," Billy mumbled around a mouthful of pizza.

"Chris brought a dictionary," Sophie whispered to Maggie and they both giggled.

"Oh, don't start," Chris snapped. "Just you wait, you're gonna be glad we have it."

For the next hour they sat eating, drinking, and talking about nothing in particular. For a little while Billy and Sophie almost forgot about the horrible situation they were in. Almost, but not quite. Even so, the food somehow made Billy feel better.

It was after ten o'clock when they finished. They packed what they could fit into their backpacks and stood up, looking at each other.

"Are we ready?" Billy asked.

The others nodded.

"Okay. Let's do it."

35

As they made their way to the end of the main hall and up the stairs to the circular hallway, Maggie talked almost non-stop.

"Fairlane Avenue is still full of police and fire trucks and work trucks. The power is out in half the neighborhood. That giant machine broke some power lines at the end of the street when it came through. Your house is surrounded with yellow tape and they have these big lights shining on it. All the news reporters are there. I saw Dan Haggis from Channel Four News talking to a camera. He's my mom's favorite news person. She thinks he's handsome, but I think he's kind of goofy looking. His nose is crooked and he has a unibrow. But there's crowds of people everywhere. You guys are like celebrities."

"Did the police catch that truck?" Billy asked. "It was so big and slow, they must have been able to find it."

"Well . . . not yet. It went across a field where the police cars couldn't drive. And then it went into Dunhill Forest. They've been searching the whole forest on foot, but they haven't found anything yet. They were talking about it on TV. They called it 'the most mysterious event of our time' or something like that. They aren't even sure what they're looking for. Somebody took a video of the truck, but it's really shaky, and all you can see are a bunch of trees moving through the smoke. They kept showing it over and over."

"The police aren't going to be able to help us, Billy," said Sophie.

"I know." He understood now that he had done the right thing by coming back to the nightstand, but it didn't make him feel much better.

They reached the circular hallway at the top of the stairs and immediately began walking around it, trying doors as they went. All of the doors were still locked, but when they came to the stairway Krandall had tumbled down, they found the door hanging open just as Krandall had left it.

"Krandall!" Billy called up the stairs. "Mr. Blemish!"

There was no answer.

"You're practically whispering," Sophie said. "No one's going to hear you like that." She took a deep breath, cupped her hands around her mouth, and bellowed, "KRAAAANDAAAALLLLL!," causing the other three kids to jump. Her voice echoed in the hallway and up the stairs.

Still no response.

"Let's go up," said Billy.

Maggie stooped with the permanent marker in her hand and drew a small black arrow on the floor near the wall, pointing back the way they had come. And with that, they started up the stairs.

It was hard to imagine anyone, let alone an old man like Krandall, surviving a fall down a set of wooden stairs as long as the one they were on. They climbed at least twice as many steps as the stairway coming up from the main hall. These seemed older too, and they creaked so loudly Billy decided they didn't need to holler to announce their presence.

When they finally reached the landing, they had to stop to catch their breath. Chris was fumbling with his shield and walking stick gasping for air under the weight of his overstuffed backpack.

On the right side of the landing was an opening to another passage that took an immediate right turn. Expecting another hallway or another set of stairs, Billy went through the opening and was met with something entirely different.

"Hey, you guys, look at this." He stepped hesitantly forward and the others followed him into a small round—or to be precise, a decagonal—room. There was a cot against the opposite wall, piled with blankets and a cowboy sleeping bag. Under the cot was a row of shoes. Billy wasn't sure, but it didn't look like there were any actual pairs, as no two shoes looked the same.

Next to the cot was a small end table bearing stacks of yellow-spined magazines. They were copies of *National Geographic,* which his Dad subscribed to. He kept boxes full of them in the basement. He couldn't seem to throw them away, but he never looked at them again after he'd read them.

Against another wall stood a large cedar chest. Its lid was open, and piles of clothes were spilled out and scattered on the floor around it. More clothes hung from hooks on the wall above it.

Other walls displayed what appeared to be blueprints or plans for furniture. Some were in frames, others were merely pinned to the wood with thumbtacks, their yellowed edges curled and ripped. And one entire wall was filled with rows upon rows of little hooks from which dangled keys of every shape and size. Instinctively, Billy's hand went to his pocket where he felt the skeleton key still safely tucked away. It was one of the few things left from their house.

A dining table was scattered with miscellaneous plates, cups, and silverware, and in the midst of the dishes was a chess set. Behind the table was a set of shelves containing boxes of cereal, canned meat, and other "imperishables."

That was one of Mom's favorite words—imperishables. Those were foods that didn't need to be kept in the refrigerator. She used to take frequent mini-shopping trips to buy perishables, like milk and eggs. But when she shopped big, she'd call out something like, "Henry, I'm going for the imperishables! I'll be back in a couple of hours!"

Mom would have never approved of this little room. In general it was a filthy, disorganized mess. The garbage can was overflowing. A plunger stood next to the dining table. Various tools and other odds and ends were scattered everywhere.

"This must be Krandall's room," guessed Sophie.

"It smells like old cheese," Maggie observed. "Or dirty gym socks. Or socks full of old cheese."

"That's gross," said Chris, who was then forced to admit, "but you're right. It kind of does smell like that."

Billy approached one of the large sheets of paper hanging on the wall. At first, he thought it was a plan for some kind of strange, complicated desk. He saw legs and drawers and little numbers with arrows all over the place. But there seemed to be too many extra lines running back and forth, up and down across the paper. Moving closer, he saw a circular shape that looked very familiar.

"Hey," he said, mostly to himself, "this isn't a furniture plan. I think this is a map."

"A what?" said Sophie, coming over to stand next to him.

"A map. Look at this. I think we're right here in this room. See? And the steps go down here to this bigger circle. The round hallway."

"Hey—I think you're right," said Sophie, tilting her head.

Chris and Maggie joined them.

"And look," Billy continued, tracing a set of lines down the map with his index finger, "here's the other stairway going down to the Main Hall."

"Boy, that Main Hall doesn't look like much of a main hall," said Chris.

"Yeah, you're right." Billy scanned the map with dismay. He saw the area they had explored so far and it was only one small corner of the map.

"This place must be huge," said Sophie. "How are we going to find anything in here?"

"And this is only one map," added Maggie. She sniffled and wiped her nose with the back of her hand. "Look—there must be ten more maps in here."

The others were similar. At a glance, they could have been mistaken for furniture blueprints. One looked almost like a dresser. Another looked like a tall china cabinet or something. Billy wondered if they were purposely disguised to look that way so that no one would suspect they were maps. There were even little notes handwritten on them, indicating what type of joinery to use, or the direction of grain.

"AaaCHHOOO!" sneezed Maggie. "Ugh. Allergies."

"Billy, this is too much." Sophie said. "What are we going to do? We don't even know how these maps connect to each other or anything. It could take a year to search this whole place."

"I don't know. Let me think."

"It's not in here!"

"What? What's not in here?" Billy turned to Sophie, confused.

"I didn't say that," Sophie replied, wide-eyed.

"No, it's not!"

They both turned to Maggie, who looked back at them and shrugged.

"I didn't say anything."

"Shut up! I'm not talking to you!"

It was definitely a young girl's voice—sounding muffled but close by. The voice had an English accent. The four of them looked around the room for any clue as to where the voice was coming from.

"I thought you said you put it back in here!"

On the wall near the foot of the cot was a cupboard door. It was close to the floor and Billy hadn't noticed it until now. The voice seemed to be coming from behind that door.

Billy held a finger to his lips and mouthed, "Be quiet."

He approached the cupboard door and cautiously opened it a scant inch. Peeking through, he saw a hallway beyond. But there was no sign of another person.

"Well, it's not!" shouted the girl's voice.

Billy opened the cupboard door all the way and poked his head through, looking right and left. The hallway went in both directions, but the voice came from the right. Looking back, he said, "Come on, you guys. Let's check it out."

He crawled through. Sophie and Maggie followed him. Chris brought up the rear, struggling with his sword, shield, and walking stick to get through the opening.

"Come here and see for yourself!" the girl demanded.

"I put it in there this morning," came an answering voice, this one sounding like a slightly older girl, also English. "Just relax."

Billy followed the hallway until it ended in another "T." He turned left, walking as softly as he could while listening to the voices.

"Okay then, show me, smarty-pants."

He turned down a narrow corridor that branched off on the right. Unlike the previous hallway this passage was lined with drawers. It went straight for about ten paces, then turned right, then left, then down two steps and right again. Billy lost track of how many other small passages they hurried past on the right and left. Sophie and Chris hurried to keep up, and Maggie lagged behind as she marked the way with arrows.

"Wait up, you guys," she called after them.

"Billy, slow down," Sophie called. "We're going to get lost."

"See? I told you."

"Well, you must have taken it out then."

"No, I didn't. I haven't even seen it since you had it yesterday in the garden."

"But I put it back right here!"

Billy stopped suddenly and Sophie crashed into his back, almost knocking him over. Chris was huffing and puffing.

"Ssshhh!" Billy hushed. "Listen."

"I'm telling! Mom! Lisa took my Boo-Boo Bear and she won't give it back!"

"I did not!"

The voices seemed to be coming from one of the drawers in the wall. Carefully, Billy pulled the drawer open. Inside was a small stuffed bear, no bigger than a mouse. It had little black beads for its eyes and nose. Billy lifted it out and turned it over in his hand, examining it. Then he handed it to Sophie, who looked it over, perplexed.

"It's cute, Ahchoo!" said Maggie.

"Sssshhh!" said Billy, Sophie and Chris together.

"I put it back in the drawer this morning! I'm not lying! Ginny probably took it out and lost it and now she's trying to blame me!"

"Billy," whispered Chris. "Pull the drawer all the way out."

Billy nodded. He grasped the drawer in both hands and slid it all the way out of the wall. Gently setting it down on the floor, he looked into the rectangular opening where the drawer had been. It was dark inside, except for a narrow strip of bright light running horizontally across the back panel. He could hear noises—footsteps and voices—and they were definitely coming from the opening.

As his eyes gradually became accustomed to the bright light, he began to see shapes on the other side. A picture on a wall. And a chair below the picture. And the edge of a window, where sunlight streamed in. Billy realized he was looking through a gap between two pieces of wood, and on the other side was a room. A room in somebody's house. The footsteps came closer, two sets of them.

"Did you look behind those batteries and things? And the spare lightbulbs?"

Suddenly, a person's body came into view. A hand reached in and began pushing things around, although Billy couldn't see what they were. Then a face appeared, looking straight toward Billy. He jerked backward, slapping a hand over his mouth to keep from screaming.

"See, I told you! It's not here! You lost it!"

"No, I didn't!"

"Yes, you did! You lost Boo-Boo!"

"What—?" Sophie began, but Billy waved his hand to stop her from speaking.

"Aaa—aaah—AAAhh . . ." another of Maggie's sneezes built up.

Billy waved both hands, shaking his head frantically, and Maggie clamped her hands over her mouth and under her nose. When the sneeze came, it made a squeaky flapping sound against her cheeks.

"Mom, she lost Boo-Boo!" The despairing, weeping voice of the girl receded into the distance as her footsteps took her away to another room, and the other set of footsteps followed quickly behind.

As he picked up the drawer and replaced it, Billy told them in a whisper what he'd seen.

"It's another Bigy Bigy Buglu Drawer," said Sophie, her hazel eyes round. "It must be. That little bear fell through a crack somehow. And ended up in here."

"Do you know what that means?" said Billy. "That means there could be a bunch of them. Like, hundreds."

"Or thousands," said Chris.

197

"And they're all connected—" Maggie sniffled.

"To this place," Sophie finished.

"That's why Krandall said he came in through a dresser," said Billy. "That's where his Buglu Drawer was. And the opening in that piece of furniture was smaller, so when he grew up, he couldn't fit anymore. But those two girls, I don't think they know anything about it. And—and—" He stopped, confused and overwhelmed.

"Billy, we have to find Krandall," Sophie fretted. "This place is too big."

"Wait, listen," Maggie interrupted. "There it is again."

They listened and they all heard it: from very faint and very far away came a pounding sound, like someone hammering nails. The same sound they had heard earlier back on the first staircase.

"What is that?" Chris whispered.

In answer to his question, another voice suddenly echoed up through the hallways—this one making no attempt to hush it-self—and this one definitely not the voice of a young girl.

"Varmint! Get back here!" the voice rattled. This was followed by another sound that drowned out the fainter, more distant hammer-and-nails pounding: the unmistakable CLUNK-THUMP, CLUNK-THUMP, CLUNK-THUMP of a crooked footstep and crutch.

The kids looked at each other and shouted simultaneously.

"Krandall!"

36

They hurtled through unfamiliar hallways, turning right, left, left, and right. All they knew was that if they failed to find Krandall, they would be hopelessly lost. Maggie ran behind Chris with the unused marker in her hand. She had given up trying to mark their path. If she stopped to draw her little arrows, she would be left behind. At each intersection, Billy paused for no more than two seconds to listen and locate Krandall's shouting and footsteps.

"You flea-bitten, fish stealin', blanket-clawin', night howler! Where are you?"

The voice sounded somehow close and distant at the same time. It was difficult to tell which direction it was coming from.

"Left!" Sophie shouted. "Billy, go left!"

"No, he's right here," Billy responded, opening a door that led into another hallway. The CLUNK-THUMP, CLUNK-THUMP seemed a bit closer, and Billy leaped through the doorway and ran to the right.

"When I catch you, it's lights out! By the jelly-stained jacket of my great Aunt Josephine I'm going to turn you into a furry brown hat with a tail!"

Krandall's voice rattled on and on in a stream of colorful language that at one moment seemed just around the corner and at the next echoed back from some faraway passage. The kids would turn in another direction and he would abruptly sound closer again. They were in a long straight hallway now, with numerous narrow hallways and closed doors on both sides.

"Billy, stop!" cried Sophie, panting.

"No, keep moving! I think we're right behind him!"

"No, we're not! Billy, please! Just stop for a second!"

Billy stopped, the breath tearing in and out of his lungs. He leaned against the wall, closed his eyes, and listened. The clunking and thumping of Krandall's footsteps faded into the distance.

"Krandall!" Billy screamed as loud his exhausted lungs would allow. "Kraaandaaaaaaalll! Mister Blemish!"

Chris collapsed to the floor in a pile of armor and plastic weapons, his face red. When he brushed off his helmet, his mop of brown hair was drenched with sweat. Maggie sat down across from him, the marker still held pointlessly in her hand.

"He's gone," said Sophie breathlessly.

"Krandaaaaallll!"

"Billy, he's gone," she repeated. "And now we're completely lost."

"No. We can still find him. You guys, get up! Come on! We can still find him!"

"No, we can't! He's gone. I can't hear him at all anymore." Sophie sank to the floor next to Maggie.

"You guys are giving up! I can't believe it!" Billy was outraged. "You're just going to sit down and give up?"

"We're not giving up," Sophie cried. "But the more we run around, the deeper into this place we get! And I don't even know what direction we came from anymore."

"It doesn't matter!" Billy shouted. "We don't have to go *back;* we have to find him! Come on, we can still find him if you guys just get up!"

"Stop it, Billy! We're lost! Don't you get it?"

"I don't care! I don't care if we're lost!"

"What are you talking about?" Sophie smacked the floor with both hands. "You know how big this place is. How can you not care if we get lost?"

"Because Krandall is our only chance to find Mom and Dad!" Billy argued furiously with his sister. "He knows about the Zobadak Wood Company, in case you forgot. And now he's gone. We let him get away by sitting around!"

"We did not let him get away! He got away because you kept running around and you had no idea where you were going!"

"I was following his voice!"

"How do you know? This place is a giant maze. There's no way you could tell which hallway he was in. But you just kept running!"

"Well, you were running too," he defended himself. "You must have thought it was a good idea!"

"We were running just to keep up with you. If we get separated in here, then we're really in trouble."

"Oh, so now it's all my fault!"

"I didn't say that!"

"Yes, you did! You probably think everything is my fault! It's my fault we didn't tell Mom and Dad about the nightstand. It's my fault they got taken away by those men. It's my fault we lost Krandall. And now it's my fault we got lost in here!"

"You guys, stop fighting!" Maggie interrupted. "It's not helping anything."

"Billy, I never said everything was your fault."

Billy slid down the wall, crumpling into a heap on the floor, and covered his face with his hands, trying to block out the world.

"I never said that," Sophie repeated. "I don't think it's your fault."

"Well, maybe you should," he sobbed. "Because it *is* my fault. Everything is my fault. Mom and Dad are gone because of me."

"No, they're not. You didn't know—"

"You're right, I didn't know anything. But I went ahead and made all the decisions anyway. And every decision I made was wrong."

Sophie closed her eyes, leaning her head against the wall.

"Billy, you can't think like that," she said, breathing a deep, trembling sigh. "If we did things differently, maybe it would be a hundred times worse right now. You don't know."

"I'm not sure how it could be any worse," he moaned, his voice so low and choked they could barely hear him.

"I think we should go back," said Chris. "We should try to find our way back the way we came and get out of here. My parents will help us. We should get out of here and go tell my parents."

"We don't even know which hallway we came out of last," said Maggie.

"You guys should just leave me here," Billy squeaked.

"Don't be ridiculous," said Sophie, wearily.

The four of them sat for a long time, without speaking, in the dim hallway. Billy wasn't sure how long they sat there but it seemed like hours. He slid sideways, lying on the floor with his head resting on his arm. Staring at the oak floorboards in front of him, he didn't care if they ever got up again.

Sophie was right. As usual. They were lost for real now. Seriously lost. And now the fear growing inside him—the fear of what it meant to be lost in this place—threatened to overwhelm everything else he felt. It took Krandall years to find his way back to his dresser. How long would it take them? And now poor Chris and Maggie were lost too, even though this wasn't their problem.

Billy felt like he was slipping into a giant black hole in the ground. He had never been so tired. And "sadness" didn't even come close to what he was feeling. He guessed there must be another word for it that he just hadn't learned yet—a word adults kept for themselves. An adult word because kids weren't supposed to know about this kind of thing. It was too much. Too big and wide and deep, and only an adult would know how to handle something like this. Billy didn't want to know what that word was. He hoped he never found out.

He became aware of Chris's heavy breathing next to him. He must have fallen asleep. Billy knew he would fall asleep too if he closed his eyes for even a minute, and he didn't dare. Someone had to stay awake in case they heard Krandall again.

Glancing across at Maggie, he saw her check the watch hanging from the strap of her backpack. She looked up and saw him looking at her.

"Almost 3:00 in the morning," she said softly.

Billy nodded. It was the latest he had ever stayed up in his life. They were going to have to do something sooner or later, but not right now. Later was good.

Suddenly, Maggie sat bolt upright, startling him.

"Hey, you guys," she whispered, pointing down the hallway. "Look at that."

Billy looked. The passage seemed endless, disappearing into the far shadows. But something was on the floor of the hallway, only a few yards away. At first he thought it was one of their backpacks. It was about that size. But as he stared at it, the object shifted and moved toward them. Heart suddenly pounding, Billy lifted his head up, straining to make out what it was through gummy, blurry eyes.

"What is it?" he asked, hoarsely.

"I can't tell," Sophie said.

"Too big to be a fairy," Maggie whispered. "Unless it's a really fat fairy. Figures, I would get to see the fat fairy."

Then the object moved closer and they realized what it was.

"It's the cat," Sophie said.

It stood in the middle of the hallway, staring at them. It held a fish in its mouth. The fish seemed almost too large for a cat to carry, and it twitched once as if it still had a bit of life left in it.

Warily, the cat approached them, crouching low, its padded feet utterly silent on the wooden floor. When it came within five feet or so, it suddenly sprang forward and leaped over their out-stretched legs, landing with a soft thump on the other side. It bounded away down the corridor and was gone, the prized fish still clamped in its jaws.

Billy looked back in the direction from which the cat had come, vainly hoping to see Krandall approaching in pursuit of the apparently thieving animal. The hallway was empty and quiet as a tomb except for the deep breathing of Chris, who continued to sleep.

"Where do you think the fish came from?" Maggie whispered.

Billy shrugged and laid his head back down on his arm. It didn't matter. Nothing mattered anymore.

"Who knows," said Sophie, taking a deep breath and stretch-ing. She was staring down the hallway in the direction the cat had gone, resting her cheek on her bent knees.

Billy watched her, feeling the exhaustion creep back in. Maybe he could close his eyes, just for one minute. Just to rest them a little.

"Signs," mumbled Sophie.

"Hmm?" he asked without opening his eyes.

"There are signs over those doors."

"Oh." He didn't care about signs or cats or fish or anything else. All he cared about was finding Mom and Dad. And getting them back. He thought about something that had happened only a few weeks ago. Mom had been watching an old movie, and she'd asked Billy if he wanted to sit and watch it with her. He didn't really like those old black-and-white movies. He thought they were boring. So he'd said, "No," and gone off to play a video game. She hadn't seemed to mind at the time, but right now, in his imagination, she was very disappointed that he hadn't wanted to sit with her.

He would give anything to have that chance again.

37

"Billy!"

He was curled up on the couch with Mom, watching a movie on the television. The movie was actually pretty good, much to his surprise: it was an adventure about a group of explorers searching the jungles of South America for a temple of gold. The explorers were crossing a rickety old suspension bridge over a deep canyon. Billy's head was in Mom's lap, and she was gently stroking his forehead. He was wrapped in a blanket, warm and safe and peaceful, but then Sophie came into the room, screaming and yelling.

"French fries for a quarter!" she shouted. "French fries for sale! Only a quarter!"

She held a shoebox in her hands nearly overflowing with a pile of French fries and she marched back and forth in front of the TV, like a peanut salesman at a ball game.

Why does she have to be so obnoxious? he thought, lifting his head off Mom's lap.

"French fries! One quarter each! French fries! Quarter!" She started jumping up and down, the fries spilling out of the box all over the carpet. Mom laughed.

Why is Mom laughing? She hates it when we bring food into the living room.

Suddenly he was back in the hallway, in the Buglu drawer. He opened his eyes, blinking.

"What's going on?" he asked.

"Billy! You guys! Get up!" Sophie shouted. She shook Billy's shoulder, then turned to Chris and began shaking him. "Get up! Chris! Wake up!"

"What is it?" Maggie yawned.

"Billy, look at that! The sign over that door! Maggie, wake up Chris!" Billy sat up and stared at Sophie, irritated.

"Sophie, what is it?" Maggie repeated, shaking Chris's shoulder obediently.

"I already fed the dog," mumbled Chris.

"Chris, wake up! Come on, you guys! Billy, did you see it?"

"See what?" Billy rubbed his eyes, trying to get the crust out of their corners.

"The sign over that door! Right there! It says 'French Quarter'!"

"It says what?" Billy asked, completely confused. Nothing made sense.

"French Quarter!"

The memory of the words came back into his head like the crack of a whip and he sat upright, suddenly wide-awake.

"Where?"

"Over that door!" Sophie squealed, running down the hallway and pointing at one of the doors, jumping up and down. "Right here!"

Billy stood up and ran over to her, almost knocking over Chris, who was still trying to pull himself up out of sleep.

"What does that mean?" Maggie pleaded.

"I think it's part of a message that Uncle Gary sent us," Sophie answered gleefully. "It was on the bottom of my music box."

"What?"

"Never mind, just get your stuff. I think this is where Uncle Gary is!"

Billy tried the doorknob, but it was locked. His heart sank. He pounded on the door with his fist and shouted, "Uncle Gary! Are you in there?"

Silence was the only answer.

"Uncle Gary!" Sophie shouted.

Billy, Sophie, and Maggie shouted together, as loud as they could. They listened, but there was no answer.

"Billy! Do you have the key?" Sophie asked.

"Yeah, but it's not for this door. It's for the lid of the nightstand."

"Try it anyway."

Billy dug into his pocket and pulled out the key. Bending down to examine the keyhole, he saw that it was made for a skeleton key. He shoved the key into the lock and turned it. To his amazement, he was able to turn it all the way around. There was a metallic clunk from inside the lock, and he turned the doorknob.

Chris was still getting up, gathering his things. "Where are we going, guys?" he asked groggily.

Billy glanced back at Sophie, who nodded her head. Then he pulled open the door. On the other side was a very short hallway with an arched ceiling, ending with two downward steps.

"Uncle Gary?" Billy carefully crept down the two steps. He was in a square, mid-sized room, about the size of one of the classrooms at his school. The ceiling was high and vaulted, with four triangular arches curving up to the center, where the support beams made a big "X" shape. The wood trim between the walls and arches was elaborately carved with curling vines, flowers, griffins, cherubs, and all kinds of little faces. "Grotesques," Uncle Gary had once called them.

All four walls were lined with drawers, each drawer surrounded by a narrow molding of darker-colored wood, carved in a variety of patterns. In the center of the room was a large table or cabinet with drawers underneath the tabletop on all four sides. On the opposite wall was another door. There was no Uncle Gary.

Billy crossed the room and flung open the other door. Beyond it was another hallway. The style here was similar but even more ornate, with scrolls and grape leaves and fruits and animals and people seemingly carved into every available surface. The ceiling was arched to a point and even the support beams were decorated. This hallway stretched into the distance, where it appeared to either turn or dead end. On both sides were more arched entranceways.

"Hellooo?" Billy shouted, the sound of his voice bouncing around erratically through the high ceilings.

"Oh, great," said Sophie. "Another maze of hallways."

Billy stepped forward and began walking along the arched passage. The carved wooden faces in the walls seemed to watch him as he passed.

"Uncle Gary!" he shouted again, louder this time. Surely, if anyone were close by they would hear him. He stopped moving, tired of walking pointlessly through empty hallways. "Helloo!" The echo of his own voice was the only answer.

Maybe it was just a coincidence, he thought. French Quarter. Maybe it meant nothing at all. Maybe it was just there to give them one more false hope so their hopes could be squashed one more time.

But surely Uncle Gary wanted them to notice something about the music box. Why else would he put that particular number in Sophie's birthday card—the number that matched the box that contained her music box?

He stood in the murky shadows of the hallway, trying to think of anything that might help them, when Sophie's voice came drifting through the air from the room behind him. She was singing.

"You are my sunshine, my only sunshine . . ."

Billy turned to look at her. Her backpack was off and she carried it to the table in the middle of the room. She put the backpack on the table and looked up at Billy, smiling.

"You make me happy when skies are gray . . ."

It was the song from the music box. Her voice was strangely sweet in the oppressive gloom of their surroundings. Unzipping the backpack, she took out the spiral notebook she had brought with her. The one she had long ago stopped drawing her maps in.

"You'll never know, dear, how much I love you . . ."

She turned to the first page of the notebook and silently read what was written there. Then she looked up at one of the walls, moving closer with the notebook in her hand as her eyes scanned back and forth across the rows of drawers.

"Sophie? What are you doing?" Maggie asked.

"The number from my music box," Sophie answered, moving slowly along the wall until she reached the corner of the room, reading the drawer numbers. "Remember Billy? We thought it was a date."

"It's an address," Billy said, growing excited as he tried to recall the number. "French Quarter. Um—umm—French Quarter . . ."

"1885," Sophie finished for him, holding up the notepad. "French Quarter—1885."

"That's it!" Billy exclaimed. "You guys, look for a drawer with the number 1885 on it."

"Okay, if you say so," said Maggie, perplexed. She began scanning the wall that Sophie hadn't looked at yet. "Are these numbers even in order?"

"Yeah, they are," Sophie replied. "But I don't think 1885 is in this room. These are all under a thousand."

"I have no idea what's going on," said Chris, still trying to adjust his plastic breastplate to a more comfortable position. Finally giving up he dropped everything he was holding, unbuckled the armor, and threw it down on the floor in frustration.

"It was written on the bottom of Sophie's music box. We'll explain later," said Billy. "Just help us find drawer number 1885. If it's not in this room, it must be close."

He went back into the vaulted hallway. The walls here did not have any drawers, but when he came to the first intersection, he saw two other rooms on the right and left, similar to the first one. He went into the right-hand room and his eyes moved across the walls.

"Here's 1,150 . . . 1,270 . . . 1,335 . . ." he read aloud. Instead of metal plates, the numbers were inlaid into the drawers with a lighter colored wood.

Sophie and Maggie hurried together into the room across the hall and began searching. Chris, unencumbered by his armor, picked up the shield and sword and walked further up the hallway to the next set of rooms. After searching for several minutes, they heard Chris shout.

"What was that number again?"

"It's 1885!" Maggie shouted back.

"Okay. Yeah. I think I found it."

The other three hurried back out to the arched hallway. They found Chris in the next room to the right. The drawers in this room were particularly large. He pointed to one of the bottom drawers.

"Right here," he said.

"Open it," said Sophie.

They rushed across the room as Chris bent over and grabbed the handle. It was shaped like the head of a lion, with a large metal ring in its mouth. With both hands Chris pulled, leaning back and straining. The drawer was large and heavy. Billy grabbed the front edge as it began to open, adding his strength to Chris's, and the drawer slid out ponderously, making a deep, hollow scraping sound.

"It's empty," Maggie said in dismay.

"No, wait," said Sophie. "There's something here."

She reached in and pulled out a small envelope. On the front was written the word "Kids."

They looked up at each other in disbelief. Billy was almost overwhelmed with the wave of relief and growing hope that washed over him. It had to be from Uncle Gary. It just had to be.

"Is that us?" Chris asked. "Are we the kids?"

"Of course, dingleberry," Maggie said. "Come on, Sophie! Don't just stand there. Open it."

"I'm afraid." Sophie stared at the envelope. "What if it's not for us? What if it's just another old thing in one of the drawers?"

"What's wrong with you guys?" said Maggie, snatching the envelope from Sophie. "You're being ridiculous."

"Go ahead, Maggie. Read what's inside," said Billy.

Maggie opened the envelope and took out a folded sheet of paper. She unfolded it, peeking with one eye at the words on the top of the page, then looked up at Sophie and smiled.

"What does it say?" Sophie implored.

"'Dear Billy and Sophie.'"

Sophie squeaked with excitement, hands clamped over her mouth.

"Read it, read it," urged Billy.

Maggie read:

Dear Billy and Sophie:

I don't know if you will ever get this letter, but I'm putting it here just in case. If you found it, that means you got the clues I sent you and figured it all out. I am very impressed. You kids are so smart, and I'm proud of you.

I'm also worried because if you're reading this, there's a chance you might be in trouble. There are some dangerous things happening and I truly hope you did not get involved. If you did, I am very, very sorry.

You probably have a thousand questions.

Climb into the drawer. Watch your heads. Pull the drawer closed from the inside. Crawl to the back.

Love,

Uncle Gary

PS Please keep this letter with you. Do not leave it lying around.

38

"It's him!" Sophie cried out. "It really is! Billy, we found him!"

She ran across to Billy and hugged him. Under normal circumstances he would have recoiled with an "Ewww, gross!" but now he hugged her back as tightly as he could, so tight his arms grew sore, but she didn't complain.

"Come on, Sophie," he said. "Let's go! Let's do what the letter says."

"I don't think I want to go in there," said Chris. "It's like a coffin or something."

"Okay," said Maggie. "You stay here and wait for us. The rest of us are going in."

"Uh, no way," Chris backtracked fast. "You're not leaving me here by myself."

Releasing Sophie Billy took the letter from Maggie and read it again. Then he carefully folded it up and put it in the back pocket of his jeans. Without another moment of hesitation, he climbed into the drawer, got down on his hands and knees, and crawled forward. His backpack scraped against the upper edge of the opening, but he could still fit inside without taking it off.

"Come on, you guys," he said, feeling his way forward into the darkness. "It's really long. There's enough room for all of us in here."

Sophie climbed in behind him, then Maggie and Chris. Once they were all in, they groped for something to grab onto. Billy found little wedges of wood in the upper corners that supported the rails for the drawer above them.

"Okay, everybody. Pull," he said. "Pull it closed."

They all pulled together. It took all of their strength, but slowly the drawer began to slide shut. They could feel it grinding against the wood below, making a low, hollow roar that surrounded them on all sides. When it closed, there was a heavy THUD, and they were immersed in absolute darkness.

"Ow! Watch your foot, Maggie. You kicked me in the head!"

"Sorry."

"Be careful."

"I'm going toward the back now. Stay with me."

"I can't see anything."

"You don't need to. Just crawl."

"Hey, that's my finger! Why are you backing up?"

"My backpack got hooked on something. Okay. I'm going now."

"This is really creepy. How long is this thing?"

"AaaaCHHOOO!"

"Bless you."

"It's so hot in here."

"Did somebody fart?"

"You're gross!"

"It was you, wasn't it?"

"Shut up. I don't know what you're talking about."

"Come on, you guys. Stop goofing around."

"Wait a minute. Be quiet. Do you hear that?"

They stopped crawling and listened. It was the pounding again. The hammer sound.

"Does it seem closer?"

"Yeah. It does."

"Keep going, Billy."

"I see something! It's lighter up ahead."

"Why aren't we using our flashlights?"

"Good question."

"We don't need them anymore. Look at this."

The others saw it too. The drawer was dimly illuminated ahead of them. Sophie watched Billy's silhouette move toward it.

"It's coming from above," Billy whispered. Suddenly he stopped crawling.

"What is it?" Sophie said. "Why are we stopping?"

"We're at the end of the drawer." Craning his neck he looked up. Above him was a square opening: a shaft with a ladder, similar to the one inside the nightstand. The light was coming from the top of the shaft. It wasn't bright, but after the complete darkness of the drawer they had just crawled through, Billy had to squint up into it.

Somehow this light seemed different. It seemed white, like sunlight, as opposed to the dim, yellowish glow of the incandescent bulbs hanging in all the hallways. He stood.

"I'm going up," he said. "Stay with me, you guys. I don't know what's up here."

"Going up where?" asked Chris, bringing up the rear. He could see almost nothing.

With shaking hands, his heart pounding in his chest, Billy reached up and grabbed one of the metal rungs over his head. Stepping up with one foot, he began to climb. The square of light over his head grew rapidly even as the pounding of the hammer grew louder. Whatever was making that sound was right up there beyond the borders of that bright square.

On the seventh rung, his head emerged from the top of the shaft. Momentarily blinded by the light and the sting of sweat in his eyes, he wanted to wipe them but was afraid to let go of the rung. His hands were too slippery. Climbing the rest of the way up, he crawled out onto the floor. Feeling a wall behind him, he leaned against it. He pulled the bottom of his shirt up and dabbed at his eyes.

"What's up there?" Sophie called from below.

"Um," he said, blinking and squinting around him. "Oh." It was all he could think of to say.

"Billy?"

"Come up here, you guys," he said. "Hurry."

39

"Is that what I think it is?" Chris asked, standing on the rungs of the ladder, with his head poking up out of the hole. "Oh, man. Hey. Can we go back? I left my armor back there. I want to go get it."

"Then go get it. I'm not going back," Sophie said, breathlessly.

"What if there's, like, wolves or something out there?" Chris said, his voice quivering.

"Look at it again, Chris," said Billy. "It's not what you think."

Before them was a forest. Hundreds of large trees, some of them enormous, stood in dense ranks that marched away into the distance. But they weren't outside. They were inside a gigantic room with a ceiling that spread like a wooden sky high over the treetops. The light they were seeing was actual sunlight, streaming in from windows in the ceiling.

It took a long time for Billy to understand what he was seeing, because the trees were so strange. The first thing he noticed was that none of them had leaves. And they seemed to have no bark on their trunks. As he began to notice more particular details, the truth of what they were seeing began to dawn on him. A broom leaning against one of the tree trunks. A stepladder leaning against another. A bed of sawdust covering the forest floor. Two sawhorses with a familiar-looking flannel shirt draped over one of them. Tools. A stack of boards off to the left.

Billy stood up and took a few tentative steps forward.

"Those aren't real trees," he whispered. Approaching closer he began to see the details of the trees themselves: the individual boards that formed the trunks, and the varying grain patterns that made each board distinct. In the trunk of the nearest tree, he saw a little handle, apparently the handle for a small drawer built into the tree.

"They're not real trees," he repeated, more loudly this time, turning back to the others who were now following him. "Somebody made these."

"No way," said Chris, looking around with his mouth open. "That's not possible. There's too many."

"He's right," said Maggie, who began sniffling from her allergies, her nose wrinkling anew. She brushed away the dark red curls plastered to her forehead.

"This is incredible," Sophie said. "It doesn't even seem real. Billy? Am I dreaming right now? Are you sure we're not still sleeping in the hallway back there?"

"If we are, then I'm having the same dream," he answered.

The trees were beautiful; the pattern of the grain was deep and rippling, with a strange bluish tint. And no two trees were the same. Just like a real forest, each tree was a different size and shape, some tall and thin, some wide and squat, some straight, some crooked, some with oddly shaped bulges in their trunks. Each tree seemed to have its own personality, and strangely each seemed to be trying to say something—to convey a message or evoke some feeling.

One tree looked like an ancient oak, with a wide, twisted trunk and gnarled branches that made it seem like an old man, weary, arthritic, and brooding, but very wise. Another, tall and thin with upward slanting branches, seemed to be full of youth and energy, reaching for the sky. Another was surely some kind of warning, with frightened splayed branches that seemed to Billy to be warding off evil. One odd little tree was simply curious and slightly amused, maybe even a little mischievous. One was pulled in tight, trying to withdraw itself from the world while the tree next to it seemed wide open, ready to take in whatever came its way.

Billy realized he could look at any one of the trees and immediately know something about its personality. He wondered if the others felt this way.

The smaller branches higher up formed an intricate and tangled canopy that the sunlight filtered through, and the entire forest seemed to be shrouded in a hazy blue glow.

"Who would do something like this?" Maggie said. "AaaCH-HOOO!"

"It would have to be a crazy person," said Chris. "A complete nutcase."

Billy was at the very edge of the forest. He reached out and touched the wood of the nearest tree, running his hand down the smooth, polished trunk. Looking down, he saw at the base of the tree a handwritten number: "128." That was when he knew for sure. They had found him, and he laughed out loud.

"Uncle Gary," Billy said. "It was Uncle Gary who built this."

"Oh," stammered Chris, embarrassed. "Well, I didn't mean, like, your uncle is a nutcase or anything, I just meant . . ."

"It's okay," said Billy, and it really was. He felt like he was about to burst with a mixture of admiration, pride, and awe. The forest might have been the most amazing thing—the most amazing example of craftsmanship—he had ever seen. Of course, a person would have to be crazy to build a forest out of wood, but Billy was beginning to understand something. He didn't know if it even made sense, but at the moment, it felt like the truth. He realized that maybe a person had to be at least a little bit crazy to accomplish anything truly remarkable. Because if you weren't a little bit crazy, you were too aware of how impossible some things were. If you weren't a little crazy, you would know all the reasons why something like this couldn't—or shouldn't—be done.

"Uncle Gary built this," Billy said, mostly to himself. "You're right. I guess he is crazy. He's a complete nutcase. But look at what he did. He made this."

"Should we go in there and look for him?" Maggie sniffled.

Sophie was looking at another tree, a huge, wide-trunked, gnarled thing. She found a knob of wood sticking out that looked like a branch starting to grow. Pulling on it, a drawer opened in the side of the tree. The drawer had been almost invisible when it was closed.

Looking inside, she said, "Nails."

At that moment the pounding started again, echoing eerily through the trees. It seemed to come from somewhere deep inside the forest. Peering in the direction of the sound, Billy could see nothing. It was impossible to tell how far back the forest went.

"I'm going to call him," said Billy, looking at the others. They nodded, and he took a deep breath and began shouting, "Uncle Gary! Uncle Gaaarrrryy!"

The pounding continued.

"All of us together," said Sophie. "On three. One—two—three!"

"UNCLE GAAARRRRRRYYYYYY!" Their voices reverberated through the hollows and depths of the forest. A moment later, the pounding stopped.

"Again," Sophie urged.

"UNCLE GAAARRRRRRYYYYYY!"

Then they heard footsteps approaching, slowly at first, but picking up speed. Soon the footsteps began to run.

"I'm scared," said Chris, backing away from the trees. "You guys . . ."

A voice from the forest said, "Kids?"

"Uncle Gary!" Billy called again. "Is that you?"

And suddenly, as if from out of nowhere, he came into view, running between the trees toward them.

"It's him," Sophie breathed, moving closer to Billy and grabbing his arm. "Oh, Billy, it's him. It really is."

"Kids!" he shouted when he saw them. Leaping over a fallen log, ducking under a branch, Uncle Gary came to them, slowing to a walk with a look of pure, joyous surprise on his face. With his long skinny arms open wide, he scooped them up, Billy and Sophie together, and hugged them, sprinkling them with sawdust.

"Kids!" he repeated. "You found me! I can't believe it!"

For a long time he just held them tight, rocking gently back and forth with his eyes closed. And they simply allowed themselves to be held, their faces buried in his dusty shirt, relief coming off of them in waves. For the first time in what seemed like days, Billy felt like they weren't alone, with only themselves to depend on. He felt like he had been carrying a terrible weight of responsibility on his shoulders for so long, and he allowed that responsibility to fall away and become absorbed by Uncle Gary.

"I missed you so much," said Uncle Gary.

Maggie sneezed.

Uncle Gary noticed Maggie and Chris standing there and he opened his arms wider, gathering them in as well.

"This is Chris and Maggie," Billy introduced, his voice muffled against Uncle Gary's shirt. "They're our friends."

"It's a pleasure to meet you both," Gary said. "You kids are amazing. Just amazing. I don't know how you did it. Those crazy clues I left weren't very good. I was trying to be so careful. But somehow you figured it out."

Finally releasing the kids, he sat down on the floor with his back against a tree, smiling. Reaching into his shirt pocket, he pulled out a toothpick and put it in the corner of his mouth and patted the ground beside him.

"Sit down," he said. "I want you to tell me all about it. Did you run into Krandall?"

"Yes," said Billy. He and Sophie remained standing.

"Oh, good. He's a strange old fellow, but he's harmless. Krandall knows more about this place than I ever will. I told him to watch for you. Did he help you out?"

"No, not really," Sophie answered. "He didn't even know who you were."

Uncle Gary chuckled. "I guess I'm not surprised. He asks my name almost every time I see him. Oh, well. I'm not sure how you found the French Quarter without his help."

"We just ended up there," Sophie said. She glanced at Billy.

"Amazing. You know, I have to tell you something. I was hoping you kids would never find that secret door in the nightstand. It's so easy to get lost in here. You have no idea how big this place is. I left those clues for you in case of emergency only. You see, I had some trouble back at home that I had to get away from. I'm sorry I didn't get a chance to say goodbye but I was planning on coming back home when everything settles down. Hopefully, things are getting back to normal now and—"

"They're not," Billy interrupted, looking at the floor.

"What do you mean?"

"Uncle Gary, they took Mom and Dad!" Sophie blurted, her eyes brimming with tears.

"Took them?" Uncle Gary leaned forward. "Who took them? What are you talking about?"

"The Zobadak men," said Billy. "The men from the Zobadak Wood Company. They came to our house."

Uncle Gary's face fell.

"When?" he asked.

"Yesterday," Billy answered, his eyes tearing up as well.

"Oh, no," Uncle Gary stood up, pressing the heels of both hands against his forehead. He began pacing back and forth. "Oh, no, Billy, do the Zobadak men know about the nightstand?"

"No."

"You're sure about that?"

"Yes."

"Tell me what happened. Tell me everything."

Billy told him, beginning with the first visit from the Zobadak Wood Company men. He told Uncle Gary about the crows and the trucks. He told him how he had found the door in the nightstand and how they had explored it and later moved it to Chris's garage.

When he mentioned the gigantic, tree-covered machine that had rolled down Fairlane Avenue and what it did to their house, Uncle Gary's eyes grew dark.

"The Truck of Ballagahaldo," he whispered under his breath. "It must be."

Finally, barely able to speak, Billy told him what had happened to Mom and Dad and how he had run from the police and ended up back in the nightstand, and how Sophie, and then Chris and Maggie, had followed him.

"You poor kids." Uncle Gary looked utterly stricken. "Oh, you poor kids. I'm so sorry you got involved in this. I didn't want that to happen. I never thought they would come to your house. Never in a million years." He had a faraway look in his eyes as he murmured to himself, "What have I done? This is all my fault."

"I should have told them," Billy cried. "If they knew about the nightstand they would have been able to hide in here. They would have known what was going on and maybe they wouldn't have gotten caught."

Uncle Gary held Billy at arm's length, looking into his face with an expression of such sudden, grave seriousness that Billy was alarmed.

"Listen to me, Billy. Both of you listen closely. You guys did *not* do anything wrong. In fact, every decision you made was the right one. Believe that, because it's the truth. If you had told your parents about it, the wood men would *still* have taken them away and probably you too. And not only that, they would now have the cabinet. And I know you don't understand everything that's going on—you don't understand what this place is and what it means—but if the wood men had found this cabinet and gotten inside, it would have been a disaster. A disaster so terrible I don't even want to think about it." He shuddered involuntarily. "Billy, your idea to move the nightstand out of the house was brilliant. It saved many lives. And more than that."

The kids stared at him, confused and awed.

"*I'm* the one to blame here," Uncle Gary emphasized. "Only me. No child should have to face a situation like this. No child should be forced to make such decisions. I had no idea the Zobadak Company would pursue me so aggressively. And—and—I never imagined they would take that truck out. I didn't even know it was possible. They risk the whole world finding out about them." He stopped pacing and rubbed his temples.

"Okay. First things first. We have to see what we can do about Hank and Molly."

40

"That machine is in Dunhill Forest somewhere," said Sophie. "The police are searching but they haven't been able to find it yet."

"They'll never find it," said Uncle Gary flatly. "The Truck isn't in that forest."

"But people saw it go in there," Maggie insisted. "And anyway, how could something that big get away?"

"Oh, I'm sure it went into Dunhill Forest. But that's not where it is now."

"I don't get it," Billy fretted. "I don't get any of this. I don't even know where *we* are."

Uncle Gary sighed deeply and said, "Okay, I'm going to try to explain this to you." He sat down on a pile of sawdust, leaning back against one of the trees. Particles of dust drifted lazily in the still air around him as he stared into the trees, chewing his toothpick and choosing his words. The kids watched him, listening to the many wooden squeaks, clicks, and pops from every direction.

Finally he spoke:

"You must never talk about this to anyone. This is a secret that has been kept for two hundred and fifty years, maybe even longer. In fact, this might be the world's last secret place. It has to stay secret. Do you understand?"

They nodded solemnly.

"It's all about joinery," he began. "I know you two have heard me talk about it before." He nodded towards Billy and Sophie, then turned to their friends. "Joinery is a word furniture makers use. It's the way pieces of wood are connected together. If you open a drawer and look at the side of it, you will often see wedge-shaped pieces that fit together like a puzzle. That's called a dovetail joint. There are many different kinds of joinery for many different purposes. Some types are very strange and complicated. Before the industrial revolution, before the mid-1800s, furniture was made by hand. But now the old ways are mostly forgotten. These days most furniture is made by machines. But there's magic in joinery when it's done by hand."

"Okay, but—" Billy started.

"Hang on, let me finish," Uncle Gary said. "Now, the old cab-inetmakers were always obsessed with secret drawers. Many an-tiques have them. Some old desks have as many as twenty or more secret compartments. Back then, some incredibly complex pieces of furniture were made. There are secret drawers inside of secret drawers, there are mechanical tables that transform into vanities or desks, chairs that transform into library steps, desks with clocks and little dancing people that emerge from their tops. There are dressers that hide bookcases and writing desks and cosmetic stor-age cases. All of this came from a single desire: to make the piece of furniture more than met the eye; to fill it with surprises. To make it larger on the inside than on the outside, so to speak. This was the philosopher's stone of furniture makers." He brandished his toothpick meaningfully.

"Kids, right now you are inside the world's largest piece of furniture. It's a cabinet. But this place is inside the angles and the gaps and the seams of furniture. It's not a fourth dimension exactly. It's more like dimension three-and-a-half. I know it sounds like magic, but it's really all about math and angles and geometry. Back in the 1750s a secret guild of cabinetmakers, the Augsburg Joiners Lodge, discovered a kind of joinery they called a 'fathom joint.' It was very special because it opened up spaces that didn't exist before. The fathom joint allowed them to build this place and then connect regular pieces of furniture to it. If you wanted to, you could go out through a desk in China. Or a dresser in Scotland. Or a bookcase in Alaska. It doesn't matter how far apart individual pieces of furniture are; they are still connected. We are inside the spaces between furniture. That's the best way I can think of to explain it."

"Does this place have a name?" Chris asked, dazed.

"Oh, yes." Uncle Gary tossed his chewed toothpick away and pulled another one out of his shirt. "It's called the Curiosity Cabinet. A cabinet of curiosity, or *Wunderkammer,* is a room or a chest of drawers that contains many unusual and interesting objects. Many wealthy people used to own *Wunderkammers.* It was a status symbol. They would collect curious things, then store and display their collections in these cabinets. But only a few people ever knew about this one. Many things were put in here that had to be kept secret or safe. Many objects that people believe to be lost are actually in here somewhere. This is the Curiosity Cabinet. And this is just my opinion," he added, "but I think it's the most amazing, wonderful creation ever built by man. The most incredible piece of craftsmanship and artistry. Many people have worked on it over the years. I feel privileged to be a part of it."

Uncle Gary's voice took on a note of awe. "Some of the world's greatest woodworkers and cabinetmakers have contributed their talents. Oeben and Riesener and Roentgen and Weisweiler and Socci. And John Channon worked on it. The Murray Cabinet is connected, believe it or not. And Thomas Sheraton never made any furniture because he spent most of his time working in here."

The kids stared at him, lost. Uncle Gary held up his finger and began to cough. He turned his head to the side, coughing and hacking into his sleeve, his shoulders shaking and particles of sawdust raining from his hair and clothes.

"I'm sorry," he said finally, clearing his throat. "I'm not used to talking so much. And I get carried away when it comes to this cabinet."

"So," said Maggie, "we're, like, in a giant, secret museum?"

"Well, yes. But it's more than that. There are things in here that were too important or too valuable or even too dangerous to be left on public display. Leonardo daVinci's missing Medusa shield is in here. And Shakespeare's first folio. And all eight of the missing Fabergé eggs. And the sword Excalibur, though I've never seen it. Oh, and the thunderbird photograph. You'd like that one, Billy. I could go on and on. Rumor has it that the Holy Grail is hidden somewhere in here. Of course," he scoffed, "I don't really believe that."

"Where does all this stuff come from?" Billy asked.

"Well, some collectors put their entire collections in here instead of giving them to museums. Some people hid their most valuable possessions in here. Many things were just pushed through and forgotten. You see, very few connections are large enough for people—at least adults—to actually climb inside. Most are very small: only large enough for small objects to fit through. So, when people needed to hide something, they would open a small panel and put their rings or their money or important papers inside. But today most people don't know anything about it, and things get lost accidentally. Many people have antiques in their homes and have no idea they're connected to this place. And sometimes things just fall through the cracks and end up in here."

"Like Boo-Boo Bear," said Maggie.

"Like what?" Uncle Gary wrinkled his brow.

"It doesn't matter," said Sophie. "I don't care about Boo-Boo Bear. All this doesn't explain where that machine went."

Uncle Gary looked at her grimly and said, "I know. I'm getting to that."

There was a flickering of light above them. When they looked up, they saw dark clouds moving across the sky through the windows in the ceiling. The light inside the forest room grew dimmer and rain began to patter against the glass. They heard a low rumble of thunder.

"There is another type of joinery," Uncle Gary continued. "Very rare and complex and very mysterious. It's called a grafter joint. I used to think it was a myth until I actually saw one myself. It's used to connect living trees. Grafting is really nothing new. Many farmers use it. Grafting is when two different live trees are split and the two halves are tied together. The wood actually grows and weaves together, and the two trees become one tree. A grafter joint is a bit like the fathom joint, only it can connect one tree to another one in a completely different forest. Now the Zobadak Wood Company is doing something like that. They are using a grafter joint, but somehow, they can graft many trees together so they get an opening large enough for a truck to drive through. They can drive into one forest and come out through another. It's how they deliver wood, as I recently found out." He pressed his hands against his face as if to block out the thought.

"Who are they?" Billy urged. "The Zobadak Wood Company. Who are those men? And who's Brope?"

Uncle Gary's head came up and he stared at Billy with a confused expression.

"Where did you hear that name?" he said.

"Um. Krandall said it. He said Zobadak is Brope's company."

"Oh. Krandall told you? Well, that explains it," said Uncle Gary. "Forget about Brope. It's just an old fairy tale. Krandall gets confused. He hears stories and gets them mixed up with reality. I'll tell you about it some day, but it has nothing to do with Zobadak."

"Okay," said Billy, glancing at the others. He was beginning to feel a little like Krandall himself. Confused didn't begin to describe it.

"As for the Zobadak Wood Company, they know nothing at all about the Curiosity Cabinet or the nightstand. And we have to do everything we can to keep them from finding out. Okay? That's why I didn't tell anyone where I was. And I certainly didn't expect you to figure things out so fast. But I'm sure glad you did."

"But what do they want?" Billy asked helplessly. "What are they after?"

"They're after this wood." Uncle Gary gestured at the trees and the stack of wood near the edge of the forest. "The Zobadak Wood Company has been a supplier of rare wood for many years. But not many people know about them. They don't advertise or anything. They sell exotic types of wood that can't be found anywhere else. This wood you see here is very special. It was never meant to be sold. It's called Blue Oak. It's a tree that used to grow on one particular island near Britain. Sadly, the Blue Oak is now extinct. That makes this the rarest wood on earth."

"So you stole it?"

"No, I didn't steal it." Uncle Gary smiled. "I ordered it and paid for it. The problem is, the Zobadak Wood Company has some employees who are not very smart. They didn't realize how valuable it was until after my order was shipped. When they did realize it, they started sending me bills asking for more money. A lot more money. Of course, they knew I wouldn't be able to pay. They just wanted the wood back. I refused, so they came looking for me. They were going to take it back by force."

"That's why they took our parents?" Sophie exclaimed. "Because of this stupid wood?"

"I'm afraid so, yes."

"Well, give it back to them! If they'll let Mom and Dad go, then just give it back! Let them have it!"

"Unfortunately, I can't do that."

"Why not?" Sophie demanded.

"I'm sorry. I wish it were that simple. But there's too much at stake here. And these people are criminals. I know that now. Even if I did give the wood back to them, they still might not return Hank and Molly. There's so much I need to tell you, but we don't have much time. If we're going to get your parents back, we have to act fast while they're still on the Truck."

"How?" cried Sophie. "It's impossible. We don't even know where it went. And we don't even know if they're still on the Truck."

Uncle Gary sighed, looking at Sophie with a mixture of sadness and encouragement.

"Come here," he said, approaching her with his arms open. He hugged her tightly and spoke in a soft voice. "Listen to me, Sophie. I know you're scared. And I can't imagine how crazy and confusing all of this must seem. But I need you to trust me now, okay? You've known me all your life. I'm still the same Uncle Gary. And I feel terrible that you got thrown into all of this. I wish we could just sit around here and talk and laugh and tell stories like we always did. I have so many stories to tell you. And we'll do that again, I promise. But right now we have to take care of business. Listen to me now, Sophie. Are you listening?"

"Yes," she sniffled.

"There's another way to get them. Possibly. All I need from you is to trust me and don't lose hope. Okay?"

She nodded.

"Okay, Billy?"

"Okay."

"Maggie and Chris—are you two okay?"

They both nodded.

"All right. I want you guys to sit down and try to relax. Even take a quick nap if you can. You must be exhausted. This is a safe place. You don't have to worry about anything here. I have to go and talk to somebody. There's some information I need to get. I'm going to leave you here, but I'll be back in less than an hour. Everybody okay?"

"Okay," said all four kids simultaneously.

And with that, Uncle Gary turned and walked straight toward the wall. When he reached it, he slid back a panel the kids didn't even know was there. Beyond it was a hallway.

Another hallway. And Uncle Gary disappeared into it.

41

"Where are you going?"

"I'm going to stand at the front of the Truck."

"You can't do that. We stand in back with the trees."

"You go stand back there with trees. John Wayne would not do that."

"But you don't belong at the front of the Truck."

"John Wayne belongs where John Wayne goes."

John's joints squeaked as he looked back toward the trees. Then he turned to Bob again. Bob, who was now calling himself John Wayne. The Truck rumbled and groaned beneath them.

"You are not John Wayne," said John. "You are Walnut Bob."

"Walnut is a kind of tree. Do I look like a tree?" The growth on his forehead was now over four inches long and tapered to a thin, upward-curving point. Tiny green buds were sprouting at its tip.

"You are not making sense," John said. "None of us look like trees. We are not supposed to. But that doesn't mean we are people."

"That is true. But I'm different now. I am changing. I can feel the change growing inside. I'm not Bob anymore. John Wayne showed me the way."

"I don't understand."

"I don't expect you to understand, Elder John." John Wayne hitched up his pants and checked the gun hanging on his belt.

He turned his head to the side and spat, but nothing came out. He began walking.

"Come and stand in back with the trees," said John.

"I can't do that," said John Wayne as he swaggered away.

"Brope will grow angry."

John Wayne stopped, swaying as the Truck heaved on the uneven ground.

"He's going to turn you over," creaked Elder John.

"He wouldn't do that," said John Wayne. "I'm one of his oldest."

"Maybe that's the problem. You are getting slow and strange. Brope blames you and your crows for letting the Gary Fyfe get away."

"They are not my crows. I know that now. I found out. They follow all of us because they like the smell. They are hungry. It was your banister's fault the Gary Fyfe got away."

"Brope still blames you," Elder John argued, adding, "Brope didn't want to send the Truck. You said you knew for sure the wood was in the house. He opened up the house completely. No wood. Only those two people. And why did you take those two people?"

"They are called hostages. They know where the Gary Fyfe is. They are going to tell Brope. The Laurel smoke will make them tell."

"What if they don't tell? Brope will grow angry toward you."

"Brope doesn't scare me anymore."

John Wayne coolly scratched the branch on his head and began walking again.

"He should," Elder John said, his jaw squeaking. "Come stand with the trees."

John Wayne kept walking, teetering and creaking on his stiff legs.

"I'm going to fix everything," said John Wayne. "You will see."

"What are you going to do?"

"I'm going to stand in front and keep lookout."

"Look out for what?"

"Bandits. Outlaws."

42

"Why are you staring at me?" Maggie asked through her stuffy nose. She shifted to make herself more comfortable against her tree.

"I'm not . . . I was just . . ." Billy stammered, his face turning bright red.

Sophie leaned over and whispered something in Maggie's ear and Maggie smiled crookedly.

"Yeah, right," she said. "A red-haired freak like me? I don't believe it."

"What are you guys talking about?" Billy demanded.

"Oh, nothing," Sophie answered innocently.

The four kids leaned up against trees at the edge of the forest, listening to the rain patter against the windows in the ceiling. It was hot in the forest room, and Sophie used her cap to fan herself. Chris kept hearing noises in the forest and was convinced it was haunted, but they didn't see anything supernatural.

Between looking for ghosts Chris flipped through the pages of his dictionary, grimly determined to make it useful.

"Listen to this," he said. "According to the dictionary, crows are sometimes carrion eaters. So I looked up 'carrion' and do you know what it is?"

The others shook their heads.

"It's the decaying flesh of a dead body!" he uttered in a deep, ominous voice. He suddenly twitched, sat up straight, and looked into the trees. "Did you hear something?"

"That's interesting," commented Sophie. "Billy, you remember how those Zobadak men smelled?"

"Yeah. They smelled like garbage. Or like rotten meat."

"You think that's why the crows came?"

"It makes sense." Billy shrugged.

"You know what that means?" Chris blurted. "That means they're zombies!"

"Oh, stop it, Chris. You're being ridiculous," Maggie said.

Billy and Sophie looked at each other, sharing the same thought: *after seeing how the Zobadak men acted, maybe it wasn't so ridiculous.*

"Look," said Maggie, pointing at Billy and Sophie. "All you're doing with that dictionary is creeping everybody out. Will you please put it away?"

"Sure, I'll put it away," Chris answered smugly, returning the book to his backpack. "I think I've made my point. You're glad we have it, now, aren't you?"

"Oh, yeah, we're real glad. We all feel much better now."

When the sarcasm faded they sat quietly for several minutes, each of them deep in their own thoughts. The rain outside seemed to be picking up, and they heard water dripping in some far away part of the room.

"It's been forty-five minutes," Maggie said, looking at her watch and yawning.

"He should be back soon," Sophie said.

"What do you think he's going to do?" Chris asked.

Billy only shrugged. He didn't know what Uncle Gary could possibly do to help them.

"Um, Sophie," said Maggie. "If . . . um . . . I mean, like . . . if we don't find your parents? You can—you know—come and live with me and my mom. I know she wouldn't mind."

Sophie's eyes suddenly welled up, but she nodded and smiled. "Thanks, Maggie."

"Yeah," said Chris. "And you should live with us, Billy. My brother is a huge jerk, but you just have to ignore him."

"Thanks, but we would have to be in the same place. Sophie and me."

"Yeah," said Sophie. "And anyway, stop talking about it. I don't like this conversation. We'll find them. I know we will."

"Dog feathers!"

All four of them jumped and then scrambled to their feet at the sound of the voice that seemingly came out of nowhere. But it was a familiar voice. A door opened in the wall across from them, the same door Uncle Gary had disappeared into earlier. Uncle Gary came out with a roll of papers in his hand. He was followed closely by Krandall, hobbling along on his crutch and his one red platform shoe. Krandall was pushing a yellow janitor's bucket on wheels with a mop.

"But she said she told you two weeks ago," argued Uncle Gary.

"She didn't tell me nothin'!"

"Okay, fine. But do you know where it is or not?"

"'Course I do!"

"And did you seal it up?"

"I reckon I did. Dang hazard is what that closet is. And a disturbance of the peace." When Krandall saw the kids standing at the edge of Uncle Gary's forest, he stopped and stared.

"Johansson's ghost!" he exclaimed. "Those are kids!"

"Yes, that's my niece and nephew and their two friends. You met them yesterday."

"I did?"

"Krandall," Uncle Gary put a hand on Krandall's shoulder, startling him and causing him to twitch slightly. "Listen. We don't have a lot of time. I'll explain later. You just need to take us to that closet now."

"So I'm a tour guide now for kids on field trips? Like I don't have enough to do cleaning up behind everybody? Hairy canary! Look at this place! It's a mess!"

"I know," said Uncle Gary. "I promise I'll take care of it but—"

"It's dirtier than Blackbeard's beard-brush in here! Look at that! You got trees growin' in here! What am I, a farmer now? Do I need to go get my tractor? Where's Gary? Gary! Gaaarrrryyy!"

The kids stood up, watching Krandall holler into the trees for Uncle Gary, as Uncle Gary took him by the shoulders and tried to calm him down.

"I'm right here! Krandall, stop shouting."

"Oh, there you are! Did you see what those kids did to this place?"

"No, Krandall. They didn't do it. We're going to the closet, remember? The one we talked about? You need to take us there right now."

Krandall squinted at him suspiciously. He clawed nervously at the hair that stuck straight out on the left side of his head, but it popped right back up behind his hand.

"You don't mean the, uh," Krandall lowered his voice and leaned in closer to Uncle Gary, "you don't mean the *Loud* Closet, do you?"

"Yes, Krandall. The Loud Closet."

Krandall heaved a sigh. "All right. Follow me," he said, shaking his head. And with that he turned and began limping away.

"Leave the bucket here," said Uncle Gary. "We won't need it where we're going."

Krandall released his grip on the mop handle and continued walking.

Turning to the kids Uncle Gary said, "Grab your stuff, kids. Let's go."

They picked up their backpacks, shoving snack wrappers into them. Chris shouldered his pack and bent to pick up his shield and sword.

"Oh," said Uncle Gary. "Maggie. Chris. It's almost 6:00 a.m. You probably have to get back home so your folks don't worry, right?"

"Well, yeah but . . ." said Maggie.

"Now's your chance," he said, pointing to the doorway. "There's a shortcut. If you go through there, turn left, then left again, down the stairs, then go through the third door on your right and then just keep going until you come to a crossing—"

"We're not going home yet," Chris interrupted. "Not until they get their parents back. No way."

Maggie glanced at him, surprised.

"You sure?" Uncle Gary asked.

"Yep," said Maggie and Chris together.

"You have some loyal friends there," Uncle Gary said to Billy and Sophie. "You're very lucky."

Billy smiled.

"Thanks, you guys," said Sophie. "But you don't have to do that."

"Yes we do," said Maggie. "We're not leaving you."

They hurried to catch up with Krandall, who walked surprisingly fast despite his crutch and his one short leg. This time they didn't go out through the same door. Instead they followed the wall all the way across to the end of the room, where Krandall slid back another panel. Going through they entered a narrow hallway.

Billy's head spun as they followed Uncle Gary and Krandall through twisting hallways, through doorways, down stairs, up stairs, between sliding panels built into the walls. It seemed the more he learned, the less he knew. He had been sure that if they ever found Uncle Gary, all his questions would be answered. But after speaking with him, he realized he now had twice as many questions.

"So, do you know where this machine is going?" he asked.

"No, I don't," Uncle Gary answered.

"Have you seen it before?"

"No."

"But you've heard of it? I mean, you know something about it?"

"Yeah, I've heard of it. I probably shouldn't be telling you too much about it. But I was a kid about your age the first time I heard about the Truck. My grandfather told me about it. Gave me nightmares. He used to say, 'When kids misbehave, they get grounded. But when they really, *really* misbehave, the Truck of Ballagahaldo comes for them.'"

"The Truck of Ballaga . . . what?"

"Ballagahaldo. My grandpa said that you can hear it coming from ten miles away. Sounds like a tornado with an engine. So that gives you a little time to hurry up and fix your mistakes and apologize. But if you don't, it will park in front of your house and wait for you—and it won't leave until you're on it. When I got a little bit older, I figured it was just another kid's story, like the boogeyman. But many years later, I found an old history book with a chapter about the Truck of Ballagahaldo."

"I'm surprised I've never heard of it in school or anything," said Billy.

"Don't be surprised. It was removed from history books. Very few people have ever heard of it. And most of the people who have heard of it think it's a myth." Uncle Gary shrugged. "Many pieces of history get lost for one reason or another. The Truck was just a very big and expensive experiment that failed. Ballagahaldo is the place where it was built. It's a remote island in the South Pacific Ocean. It was made during the Industrial Revolution, in the mid-1800s, when people were learning more about machines and how to make machines do the work of people. They built the first steam engines then for trains. The engines ran on steam from burning coal, but the Truck of Ballagahaldo runs on steam from burning wood. The wood comes from trees that the Truck continually grows on its back, so in theory, it should never run out of fuel. But it was very large and very slow and it never worked well. It's a horrible machine. The company that made it went out of business, and the Truck was abandoned to rust away on the island. It's really a miracle it still works at all. It must have been fixed or rebuilt by the Zobadak Wood Company. They sell a lot of wood from the island of Ballagahaldo, so it makes sense. And I've been hearing a lot of rumors lately about it. When you told me what happened, I knew the rumors were true."

Billy didn't know what to say. The story was bizarre, to say the least. Uncle Gary always had a knack for telling stories. But surely he wouldn't make something like this up—not when it was such a serious situation. If Billy hadn't seen it with his own eyes, he never would have believed it.

"I still don't get how it came to our neighborhood," said Sophie. "And then how it got away."

"I don't entirely understand it either," said Uncle Gary. "But it doesn't matter right now. First things first."

"Where are we going?" asked Billy.

"We should be almost there. Krandall, how much farther is it?"

"We'll get there when we get there!" Krandall shouted over his shoulder.

They had just reached the bottom of a set of stairs and were walking down another very long, straight hallway when Krandall suddenly stopped.

"I reckon we're there."

The floor vibrated under their feet, and they heard a deep but distant rumbling.

Krandall turned around to look back at the others. He banged the end of his crutch against the door to his right.

"That's it right there," he announced, his voice rattling. "The Loud Closet. Stand in line, kids. Single file, now. No pushing."

Uncle Gary placed his hand on the door and leaned his ear against the wood.

"I can feel it."

"Don't blame me," Krandall rasped. "Skookis did it. The darn fool."

"I know," Uncle Gary soothed him. "No one's blaming you."

"And now I'm the one who's gotta fix it." Suddenly, Krandall began speaking in a high-pitched voice, in an apparent imitation of a woman. "Kraaaanndallll! Skookis made a hole to the Oval Office of the White House! Can you go patch it up? Kraaaannndalllll! Skookis let a herd of cattle get into the Rose-wood Cathedral! Can you go shoo 'em out and seal up the joint? Kraannnndallll! Don't forget to shovel up the manuuuuurrrrre!"

"I know, Krandall. It's very frustrating."

"And now this! It's the worst one yet!"

"Listen, when we're done here I'll go talk to her about Skookis. I promise."

"Lotta good that's gonna do," Krandall snapped.

Billy glanced at Sophie.

"Who's 'her'?" he asked in a whisper.

Sophie shrugged, whispering back, "Who's Skookis?"

Billy shrugged.

"I'm opening the door," Uncle Gary said. "Stand back a bit, kids."

"Now hold on a minute," Krandall mumbled. "Don't get jumpy." He grabbed a large ring of keys from his belt and fingered his way through them until he found the one he was looking for. He unlocked the closet door, then nodded at Uncle Gary.

The kids backed up. Billy's heart pounded. He had no idea what was behind the door or what it had to do with them. Chris backed up more than a bit, holding his shield before him.

"Go on, then," said Krandall. "This is what we came for."

Uncle Gary turned the handle and the noise spilled out like a flood into the hallway. It was like the sound of a tornado spinning through a metal scrap yard, or a hundred train engines rolling through an earthquake, or a hurricane full of giant gears whipping through a forest of splintering wood.

The kids backed up further. Krandall's mouth was moving as he mumbled something, but they couldn't understand him. Uncle Gary stared through the doorway, then looked back at Billy. For a brief instant, he looked very much like Billy's dad. A chill ran down Billy's spine, all the way to his heels and back up. It was at that moment he realized what the sound was and why it seemed so familiar.

"That's the Truck," he said. "That's the sound of the Truck."

Uncle Gary nodded solemnly, then stepped through the doorway.

43

Billy approached the doorway to the Loud Closet, followed closely by Sophie. She grabbed his backpack and they both peeked in.

It was a walk-in closet, not much bigger than the one in their parents' bedroom. The walls on both sides had a rod for hanging clothes, and above that a long shelf, but there were no clothes on the rods and the shelves were bare. On the floor, right in the middle of the closet, stood a yellow janitor's floor sign that read, "CAUTION." It still wasn't clear where the sound was coming from.

Uncle Gary was at the far end of the closet, on his hands and knees, poking around at the wood on the floor and walls. Standing up, he came back to the doorway and shouted, "Krandall! Where is it?"

"You gotta pull up the—ahhh, get out the way! I'll do it!" Krandall pushed through the doorway, limped to the back of the closet, and crouched in the corner, facing the wall on the left side. He pulled a section of molding off the bottom of the wall and tossed it onto the floor next to him. Then, placing his fingers in the narrow spot that had been covered by the molding, he slid a thin strip of wood sideways.

He looked back at them and said something the kids couldn't quite make out over the rumbling. Turning back to the corner, he placed both hands on the wall and pushed down. A square section of the wall not much larger than an 81/2 x 11 sheet of paper dropped down into the gap left by the sliding strip. Then he pushed on it and the panel swung open. Immediately the volume of the noise doubled and a short gust of wind blew in, carrying with it the smell of burning wood. Krandall stood up, scowling.

"I thought you sealed it up!" Uncle Gary shouted to Krandall over the noise.

"Well, I guess I didn't!" he shouted back. "I'll get right on that as soon as I'm done moppin' the floor over there in your forest!" He stepped out into the hallway.

"Go have your look, kids!" he encouraged. "The bus leaves in ten minutes!"

Billy didn't move. The noise rumbled in his chest, making it hard for him to think. Uncle Gary was lying on the floor in the corner, with his head inside the opening in the wall. Sunlight poured through the opening, illuminating his shoulders, and wind ruffled his clothes.

When he pulled his head out and sat back on his heels, his face was a mask of grim dismay. Noticing Billy in the doorway, he shouted, "Stay back! Don't come in here!" He got up and came to the doorway. He pushed Billy back into the hallway and firmly closed the door.

"What is it?" Billy said, alarmed.

"I didn't expect this," Uncle Gary said. He seemed to be talking to himself. He jabbed a fresh toothpick in his mouth and chewed on it as he paced the floor. "William and Mary. This is worse than I thought. I expected the Truck, but I didn't expect this. Oh, boy. Okay. We'll just have to deal with it, that's all."

"What?" Billy cried. "Deal with what? What's going on?"

Uncle Gary stopped pacing and looked at the roll of papers in his hand, suddenly remembering them. Sitting down on the floor, he unrolled them and began studying them closely. He clenched the toothpick in his teeth as he traced his finger along various lines on the page. Billy knelt on the floor across from him. Sophie came forward, looking over his shoulder at the paper on the floor. Chris and Maggie stood just behind her.

"What is that?" Billy asked. The paper was so brown with age he could barely make out the lines on it.

"Copies of the original blueprints for the Truck." Uncle Gary tilted his head, squinting. "But—it's different. That tower—I don't see it on here."

"You mean the lighthouse?" said Billy, remembering the terrifying sight of the giant machine rolling away down Fairlane Avenue with its spotlight turning.

Uncle Gary looked up at him.

"I almost forgot," he said. "You saw the Truck. Did you say a 'lighthouse'?"

"Yeah," said Billy. The others behind him nodded as well. "It looked like a big lighthouse. It was on top of the Truck. There was a spotlight shining out of the top of it."

"Can you tell me where it was on the truck?" Uncle Gary asked. "On the front or the back or—"

"The front," Billy answered, cutting him off.

"You're sure?"

"Yes. It was definitely at the front end."

"Okay," said Uncle Gary looking back down at the paper on the floor. "Man, oh, man. It's bigger than I thought."

"How are we going to find them?" Billy asked.

"Well," said Uncle Gary. "If I'm reading this right, the Truck is almost pure machine. The entire body of it is nothing but gears and pistons and boilers and furnaces. There are narrow walkways for the workers to get around inside, and that's about it. But up on top, near the front, there's an old control booth—right here." He pointed to a small square on the blueprint, near the front of the Truck.

"It's where the driver of the Truck used to sit. I think that booth is still there. I think it's right at the base of the lighthouse— maybe just behind it. If Hank and Molly are still on the Truck, they're probably either inside that booth or in the lighthouse."

"But, what if they're not on the Truck anymore?" Billy's voice sounded small.

Uncle Gary stood, rolling the prints back up.

"I think they are," he said. "The Truck is still moving. That means it hasn't got to where it's going yet. As long as it's still rolling, they're probably still on it." He opened a drawer in the wall, shoved the prints in and slammed it shut.

"Listen, everybody. I'm not worried about finding them yet. We have a bigger problem right now."

"What is it?" Billy asked, standing up.

"That opening in there," he pointed toward the closet. "It's too small. I need to be able to climb through it before I can get to the Truck. And we need to be able to get Hank and Molly back in here."

"It's too small?" Sophie repeated. "What are we going to do? Can you make it bigger?"

"I think so, but I need to get some tools. And a few other things. Listen. I want you guys to stay right here, okay? Don't move from this spot. And don't go into that closet. It's too dangerous. Do you hear me?"

They nodded.

"I should be able to get my things and be back here in fifteen minutes or less."

"How long will it take you to fix the hole?" Sophie asked.

"I don't know. Maybe half an hour. Maybe less, I hope. Krandall."

"Uhh!" Krandall had been dozing off, leaning against the wall. When he heard his name, he twitched and dropped his crutch.

"Krandall, I'm going to get my tools. I'll be right back."

"Yeah, that's great! That's a really good thing you're doing there, Jerry. You get those tools. Get 'em good!"

"It's Gary!"

"Yeah, him too."

"Krandall, I want you to stay here. I'm going to need you. Don't leave this spot. Stay right here with the kids. Okay?"

"Oh, sugar scars on Sunday!" he huffed. "Would you just leave already?"

Krandall bent and pulled a wide drawer out of the wall. Then he turned and sat down in it, leaning his head back against the wall and closing his eyes.

"All right, then," said Uncle Gary, turning back to the kids. "I guess he's not going anywhere."

"Please hurry," said Billy.

Uncle Gary gave Billy and Sophie each a quick hug and a kiss on the forehead.

"Hang in there, kids," he said. "We'll get through this. I promise." Then he was running back up the hallway, up the stairs, back the way they had come.

For a few minutes more, they could hear the floorboards creaking under his feet, and then he was gone.

44

Krandall's inelegant snore competed with the muffled rumbling from the closet. The old man whistled through his nose between snores, his mouth hanging open.

"I know what you're thinking," said Sophie.

Billy sat in the hallway across from her. He had been staring at the closed door of the closet, listening to the incessant thrumming and grinding of the Truck that somehow sounded both very close and very far away. His big eyes shifted to Sophie.

"You must be thinking the same thing," he countered. "Or else you wouldn't know what I was thinking."

"Maybe," she said.

"Are you guys thinking about eating?" Chris asked brightly. "'Cause that's what I'm thinking too. I'm starving."

"No, they're not thinking about eating, doofus," said Maggie. "They're thinking about looking in the closet."

"Oh."

"Maybe just a quick look," said Billy. "Just to see. And then we'll come back out here and wait."

"I'm not sure that's a good idea," Chris said, his hand unconsciously moving to his shield. "I mean, your uncle said we shouldn't go in there."

"I know, but we just want to look, that's all," Billy responded. "It doesn't hurt anything just to look."

"What if Krandall wakes up?" Maggie asked.

All four of them looked at Krandall. His head was lolling to one side in a way that looked painful. As they watched, a string of drool ran from the corner of his mouth to his shoulder.

"I don't think he's going to wake up," Billy observed.

Sophie averted her eyes, pushing up the bill of her cap. "Let's just do it," she said. "Real quick."

Billy, Sophie, and Maggie stood up.

"Oh, man," Chris complained, climbing wearily to his feet. "Don't you guys ever just relax?"

When Billy grabbed the metal doorknob, he felt the vibrations on the palm of his hand. He looked at Sophie.

"You ready?"

"Yeah, come on."

He turned the knob and pulled open the door, and once more the noise filled the hallway. With it came the smell of burning wood. As he stepped into the Loud Closet, Billy's eyes were locked on the square opening in the corner where sunlight streamed in, projecting a bright square on the opposite wall.

The loud noise vibrated in his chest. As he approached the back end of the closet, he had a strange feeling of vertigo—almost dizziness, but not quite. In an odd, disconnected way, it almost felt like the closet was moving. He put a hand out to steady himself on the wall.

"I don't like this!" someone shouted behind him. Probably Chris.

Ignoring him, Billy knelt down in front of the opening. He closed his eyes and held his breath for a minute, trying to get his courage up. *Just look,* he thought. *Just one quick look.*

Opening his eyes, he crawled forward and stuck his head into the opening. At first he didn't understand what he was seeing. Treetops moving slowly by. Below them. He seemed to be looking down at a forest from above. The wind blew in his face. As he lay on the floor looking down at the trees, he felt the sensation of swaying or pitching. *Are we flying?* he wondered illogically.

Then his mouth went dry. The Truck was directly beneath him. Leafless, twisted trees covered its top side, and scattered among the trees were numerous crooked brick chimneys, belching out black smoke. Immense logs along the sides were bound together with great bands of steel. Giant gears turned and cables twisted. He was looking down at all this. That meant . . .

That meant they were high up in the lighthouse at the front of the Truck. They weren't flying. The hole was on the outside back wall of the lighthouse. No wonder Uncle Gary had looked so scared. No wonder Uncle Gary didn't want them in here. They could fall. In fact, Billy realized, the hole was just big enough for a kid to slip right through. The thought made his stomach roll over.

Craning his neck he looked up and saw the top of the lighthouse only about ten feet above them. He could see the railing surrounding the top, chains clinking against the supports. The spotlight swept by, illuminating the haze of smoke around them.

He looked back down. The wind blew in his hair as he scooched forward a bit more, hanging onto the edges of the opening. He looked straight down to see the round wall of the lighthouse stretching away below him. Black smoke flowed around it. There came a piercing shriek of steel and a deep clanking from somewhere inside the machine as it trundled slowly forward. Billy felt the lighthouse shuddering and swaying back and forth. The Truck was moving along a rutted dirt road through a forest. The trees of the forest looked strange to him, almost tropical. He saw the long, broad leaves of palm trees flailing in the wind on both sides of the Truck.

Billy pulled himself out of the opening and was suddenly back in the closet. He lowered himself to the floor, feeling sick and utterly hopeless.

"What is it?" Sophie shouted over the clamor.

All he could do was point and crawl out of the way so she could look for herself.

Tossing her cap out to the hallway, she squirmed forward and stuck her head through the opening, her hands gripping the sides so tightly her knuckles turned white. A minute later she backed out. Her face was pale, and tear tracks left streaks across her cheeks. She shook her head as if to disagree with their predicament.

"What are we going to do?" Billy shouted.

"Nothing!" Sophie cried. "There's nothing we can do! It's over!"

She got up and went back into the hallway, crying. Chris approached the opening cautiously, stooping over.

"What's wrong, Billy?" he asked.

But before Billy could answer, Chris caught a glimpse of the view through the open panel and suddenly stood bolt upright. He backed away.

"Oh, no!" he yelled. "No way! I'm terrified of heights. I'm not going anywhere near that. No way!"

Finally Maggie came forward. She glanced at Billy, who was now sitting on the floor of the closet with his hands over his face. Without a word she got down on the floor and looked out. A moment later she slid forward, sticking her head through the opening.

Billy sat there and watched her—watched the wind whipping her red curls and her T-shirt about. She lay there without moving for so long, he was beginning to think something was wrong. He was about to reach over and pull her back in when she suddenly backed out and sat up, looking at him. Her dark eyes were wide.

"I see them!" she exclaimed.

"What?" The noise from the Truck was so loud that Billy almost had to read her lips.

"I see them! I think I see them!"

"See who?"

Maggie leaned forward and grabbed Billy's shoulders impatiently, shaking him.

"Your parents! I think it's them!"

Billy got up on his knees.

"Where?" he shouted.

"Straight down!" Maggie stood up and ran into the hallway. "Sophie! I see them! Did anyone bring a pair of binoculars?"

"What do you need?" Chris asked.

"Binoculars!"

Billy was confused for a moment, but then suddenly he remembered. Running out to the hallway, he grabbed his backpack and yanked the zipper open. The first thing he saw was the coiled rope he had packed. The rope.

"Don't even think about it," he said aloud to himself. But he was thinking. He was thinking all kinds of things. Digging to the bottom of his backpack, he pulled out the spyglass Uncle Gary had given him so long ago. It seemed like years. He pulled the ends apart until the three shining brass tubes were fully extended. Hurrying back into the closet, he got down on his stomach and put his head through the opening.

"Look straight down," he heard Maggie say. "There's a building."

At first everything was a blur. Billy twisted the end of the telescope until he saw black tree branches swing suddenly into focus. In the magnified circle of the lens, he saw a close-up of the trees that grew on the back of the Truck. Moving the telescope down further, the base of the lighthouse came into view straight below.

And there, at the base, was a low brick building. It was in shambles. There was no roof, only four walls, and they were partially crumbled. But it looked like the original control booth Uncle Gary had found on the plans. It was the same shape. He moved the circle around the walls until he came to a panel covered with gauges and levers and cranks that he assumed must be the old control panel.

Then, moving his spyglass across the middle of the floor, he saw them. It *was* them. It was definitely them. He couldn't see their faces, but it was Dad's flannel shirt, the faded blue and green one he always wore. And next to him was Mom in her orange hooded sweatshirt. Not orange exactly—it was burnt umber. That's what she called it. Most people didn't look good in that color, but she did. That's what she always said.

She'd worn that sweatshirt when they went to the police station the last time he'd seen them. When they'd dropped him off at Chris's house and driven away. They had waved at him from the car and he had waved back, but he had half-waved over his shoulder without looking as he was walking up Chris's driveway because he was so busy and had important things to do and didn't have time to look at them as they drove away. And that was the last time he'd seen them until now. It was Mom and Dad. There was no question about it.

"Is it them?"

Sophie's voice, far away.

But something was wrong. They weren't moving. Why would they just be lying on the floor like that? It didn't make sense.

"Billy! What do you see?"

He pulled out of the opening, banging the back of his head on the top edge and almost dropping the telescope.

"Something's wrong!" he shouted.

"What is it? Do you see them?"

"I see them, but they're not moving! They're just lying on the floor of the control booth!"

"Are they sleeping?" Chris asked.

"Are they dead?" Sophie cried.

Billy walked out of the closet and into the hallway.

"Billy! Are they dead?" Sophie followed him out.

"No! I don't think so. I don't know!"

He stooped and pulled the rope out of his backpack. His body was on autopilot—moving and doing things without his brain telling it to. In his mind he heard nothing but a constant buzzing, like an old radio tuned to the empty space between two stations.

"What are you doing?" Sophie screamed, her voice on the edge of hysteria.

"Oh, no you don't," Maggie grabbed his arm. "You'd better not be thinking about going down there."

"How long ago did Uncle Gary leave?" he asked her.

Maggie looked at her watch.

"Almost fifteen minutes ago," she answered.

"He'll be back any minute. When he gets back, he has to fix the hole to make it bigger. That's going to take him another half hour or whatever. When he fixes the hole, he has to stay up here because he and Krandall have to pull them up. We're not strong enough. I'm going down there."

The others looked at him, rendered speechless by the cold logic of his explanation.

"But . . ." began Sophie.

"You could fall and get killed," said Chris. He looked terrified. He looked more afraid than Billy felt.

"No, I won't," Billy answered as he carried the rope back into the closet, looking for something to tie the end to. The hanging rod. He began tying one end of the rope around it. "You remember that tree house we found in Dunhill Forest? Way up in that big tree?"

"Yeah. So what?" Chris responded.

"You remember those little boards nailed to the trunk of the tree for climbing up into the branches?"

"Yeah. You climbed up it, but I stayed down because I was afraid. So what? What does that have to do with anything?"

"This isn't that much higher."

"Are you kidding? This is twice as high! Maybe three times!" Chris's voice squeaked.

"Well, maybe, but I can do it. The heights don't bother me."

"You're crazy!"

After the fifth knot around the bar, Billy guessed it would hold. He tugged on it, and it seemed solid enough. Then he began tying the other end around his waist. He felt strangely calm.

"Billy, I don't think you should do this," Sophie urged. "It's insane! I think you should at least wait for Uncle Gary to come back. Maybe he'll know what to do."

"I know what Uncle Gary will say," Billy returned. "He'll say, 'No way.' He won't let me go, and then he'll waste all kinds of time trying to figure out another way, and then finally he'll have to agree. We don't have any other choice. And we can't waste any more time."

"But what if you fall? Billy, I couldn't stand to lose you too! I couldn't stand it! I'd be all by myself!" Tears spilled down Sophie's cheeks in a seemingly endless stream. "I don't want you to go down there!"

"Sophie." Billy felt a wild bubble of panic rising up inside and took a deep breath to calm himself again before continuing. Beneath the calm was a churning whirlpool of every emotion he had ever felt. Happiness over finding Mom and Dad, dread of what might be wrong with them, terror over what he was about to do, anger with Sophie for trying to talk him out of it, sadness because of what Sophie—what they all—were feeling, love for Sophie and Mom and Dad and Uncle Gary and Chris and Maggie and . . .

Turn the autopilot back on, he told himself. *Turn the autopilot back on.* He took her by the arm and walked her back out into the hallway, dragging the rope behind him.

"Sophie, listen to me," he said. "I'll be okay. You're not going to lose me. It's just like climbing the rope at school. It's no big deal. But I have to do this. I *have* to. We already lost Mom and Dad once, and it's practically a miracle we found them again. We can't lose them this time. We just can't."

He hugged her and she squeezed him so hard it hurt. It only lasted a minute, and Billy was beginning to wonder if she would ever let him go. But then she did. It was time.

As he turned to go, Maggie was looking at him strangely from the other side of the doorway.

"What?" Billy asked her.

"Nothing," she said. "Just . . . be careful."

"I will. Thanks," he answered, and for a fleeting moment he thought he recognized the expression on her face. Was it admiration? Or affection? *No, don't be ridiculous,* he told himself. Still, an unexpected thrill fluttered in his stomach and somehow he suddenly felt much braver. He smiled at her, then stepped through the doorway.

In the closet Chris stood at a safe distance from the opening.

"Take these with you!" he shouted over the noise, holding out his shield and the extra cap gun he had been carrying in his backpack.

Billy looked at them skeptically. He was about to say, "No, thanks." He couldn't imagine why he would need them.

"Just take them!" Chris shouted again, more emphatically. "Please!"

Rather than argue and hurt Chris's feelings, Billy took the gun and shoved it into the waistband of his pants. Then he grabbed the shield and slung it over his left shoulder.

"I'm not even going to say anything to you," Chris yelled. "Just get back here!"

Billy nodded. Then, without another thought, he got down on his hands and knees and backed towards the opening. He slid backwards until his legs were hanging over the edge. He took a deep, shaking breath and closed his eyes. *Okay,* he thought. *Here we go. Just like climbing a tree. I'm gonna do it. Here we go. . . .*

Gripping the rope as tightly as he could, he wiggled backward. It was a tight squeeze, especially getting past with the shield on his back, and for a moment he wondered if he would make it through at all. Suddenly there was a lurch and he was dangling in the open air.

Even above the wind and the incredibly loud rumbling and roaring of the machine below him, he could still hear his breath tearing in and out of his lungs. He allowed himself to just hang there for a minute, swinging back and forth, bumping against the wall of the lighthouse, feeling the wind blowing around his body. He hugged the rope with his eyes closed.

Do I open them? he thought. *I don't need to open them. I can go all the way down without looking. Anyway, they say you shouldn't look down, right? You shouldn't look down. So, don't look . . . don't look . . . don't look . . .*

Billy opened his eyes and looked.

45

The view below took his breath away.

The Truck was moving through a lush tropical jungle, on a dirt road between two green mountains. The banks on both sides rose gently into hills, the hills turned into steep slopes, and the slopes became vertical cliffs hanging with vines. The Truck was too wide for the road. It scraped and crashed through palm trees and coconut trees on both sides. Billy watched bright red and orange birds take off, startled, and fly squawking in every direction.

Below him the Truck rumbled, groaned, clanked, and hissed. From his position high above, he saw mostly leafless black trees. He had the disorienting illusion of being on a small forested hill moving through another, entirely different, type of forest, as if his hill had come loose from some faraway mountain and was sliding down through the jungle.

Between the trees, running the length of the Truck right down the middle, was a straight trench. It was some kind of opening into the mechanical insides of the Truck. Just inside the trench, Billy saw a moving chain. It looked like a gigantic bicycle chain, bouncing and rattling as it advanced.

For a horrifying moment Billy imagined himself falling into the trench and getting pulled by the chain down into the engine of the Truck. But then he saw that the trench didn't run all the way up to the control booth. If he dropped straight down, he would be near the control booth.

And that was where he needed to go.

As he spun slowly on the rope, the control booth came into view and he saw Mom and Dad still lying in the same position. Still sleeping of course. It worried him to see them so still, but maybe they were just exhausted from their ordeal. *Everybody needed to sleep,* he told himself, *even if there was a lot of noise around.*

It took every ounce of willpower to release one of his hands from the rope—his fingers stiff from gripping it so tightly—and slide it down the rough fibers to a lower position. He allowed his legs to relax just enough so they slid down a little, too. Then he unclenched his other hand and brought it down.

It became easier each time he did it, and soon he was moving steadily downward, his hands and legs remembering the rhythm on their own without him having to think about it.

The plastic shield slipped off his shoulder and he fought to keep it out of his way, but every time he lowered himself the edge of the shield bumped him in the cheek. Finally he couldn't stand it anymore and straightened his arm, allowing the shield to slip off. It tumbled down, flipping and fluttering like a giant leaf. He hoped it would land in a place where he could retrieve it, but a gust of wind snatched it and carried it off, far over the jungle on the right side of the Truck. Chris was going to be mad. Billy watched until it disappeared into the trees, then continued his descent.

Turning to face the lighthouse now—only inches from his face—he studied its wide, coarse-grained pattern, and he realized the lighthouse was actually made of wood. Of course, that made sense. If he understood things correctly—and he wasn't sure if he did—the Curiosity Cabinet would not be able to connect with anything unless made of wood. It was all about the joinery, the way pieces of wood were joined together.

Then he realized the lighthouse was not simply made of wood: it seemed to have been made out of one big piece of wood. Which of course was impossible. But no matter how closely he examined it, he could not see anything that looked like a seam or a line where separate boards came together. It looked like it had been carved from one giant tree trunk.

No, that wasn't quite right either. It wasn't "carved." What did Uncle Gary call that machine he used? A lathe. The lighthouse looked like it had been turned on a giant lathe. It looked like a fancy table leg with grooves and ridges going around it at the top and bottom.

Crazy. Don't think about it, he told himself. *None of this makes sense. Not one bit of it. Hopefully I'll wake up pretty soon.*

Mechanically, hand over hand over hand, he lowered himself further. He tried to ignore the wind that pushed him, making him swing back and forth, sometimes slamming him into the side of the lighthouse. He tried to ignore the black smoke that occasionally swirled around him, making him cough, blinding him. He tried to ignore the pain in his hands, which was getting harder and harder to do. His hands were sweating, and he had to grip the rope tighter and tighter to avoid slipping. Several times he slipped momentarily and burned his hands, his feet and legs desperately twining around the rope to stop his descent.

It wasn't a very good rope for climbing, he decided. It was too thin. He wondered if it would even be strong enough to lift his parents. *Don't think about it,* he told himself again. A chill ran down his spine. *Don't think about it.*

He twisted slowly on the rope and now he was facing the body of the Truck again. He was surprised at how much progress he had made. The base of the lighthouse was growing very near, maybe only two or three stories below. But then he looked out at the forested back of the Truck and saw something that caused his breath to stop in his throat. He clung to the rope, suddenly not wanting to continue, and at the same time knowing he'd never be able to climb back up.

He hung there swinging on the rope, staring into the trees, wondering why he hadn't seen before what he was seeing so clearly now.

46

Sophie, Maggie, and Chris stood crowded around the opening, taking turns looking through, when Uncle Gary came sprinting up the hallway with a wooden toolbox in one hand and a coiled rope in the other. He skidded to a stop and quickly assessed the situation. "Billy went down there, didn't he." It wasn't a question.

"Yeah," Sophie shouted over the noise.

"I had a feeling," sighed Uncle Gary, tossing the rope on the floor. He squeezed his eyes shut, rubbing them with his thumb and forefinger. "You guys had a rope?"

"Yeah. Uncle Gary, we found Mom and Dad!" Sophie exulted. "They're in that control booth you were talking about!"

"I know."

"You know? Why didn't you tell us?"

"Because at first I wasn't sure if it was them. I didn't want you kids to worry unnecessarily. And I definitely didn't want you to go down there. You're sure it's them?"

"Yeah." Sophie held up the telescope.

"Oh," said Uncle Gary. "Well—I sure wish Billy had waited. That boy is just like his father—when he gets something in his mind, there's no changing it. I should have taken you guys with me. But we can't do anything about that now. I need to get started right away widening that hole. Come on out."

He motioned for the kids, and Sophie took one last look down at Billy. He was still on the rope, but it looked like he was close to the bottom. Finally. She squeezed her eyes closed for a brief, fervent moment and then got up and went out into the hallway.

"Should we wake Krandall?" Maggie asked.

Uncle Gary regarded Krandall, still fast asleep and leaning precariously to one side.

"Nah. Let him sleep. We'll wake him when we need him."

Uncle Gary entered the closet, placed his toolbox on the floor, and knelt in front of the hole. Sticking his head through he took a quick look down at Billy to make sure he was all right. Then he inspected the frame of the opening. He looked at both sides, tracing his finger up and down along the edges, feeling the joinery.

The kids watched him from the doorway. He didn't seem to be doing anything. He was just kneeling there, looking at the right side, then the left side, then the right side again. After several minutes of this, Uncle Gary sat back on his heels and just stared. He reached into his shirt pocket and pulled out a toothpick, poking it into his mouth. Then he leaned forward and inspected the left side again. Then he sat back and stared some more, eyebrows creased.

"Uncle Gary!" Sophie shouted at him, impatiently. What was he doing? They didn't have time for this.

He either didn't hear her or he was ignoring her. Sophie waited, almost out of her mind with frustration. She stooped and picked up her old cap, put it on, then took it off, then put it back on. She was about to shout at him again when he suddenly nodded his head, as though answering a question no one else could hear. Reaching into his toolbox he pulled out two clamps, braced them against the top and bottom of the left side of the opening and tightened them. Then he dug around inside his toolbox and pulled out a small hacksaw. Inspecting the joint again, he found a place that seemed to satisfy him and began sawing.

"How long is it going to take?" Chris said to Sophie.

"I have no idea," she answered. She wanted to ask Uncle Gary, but she didn't want to slow him down. If he had to stop and answer questions, it would only take longer.

She watched him saw at the wood for what seemed like an hour. He stopped to blow the sawdust away and then began sawing again, turning the saw back and forth at different angles.

Sophie couldn't tell what he was doing from where she stood, but what she saw didn't seem to make any sense. He didn't seem to be accomplishing anything. The hole didn't look any bigger. He wasn't taking out any pieces of wood. He just kept making cuts and moving the saw at different angles. Finally he put the saw down and grabbed a chisel and a small hammer. Placing the chisel against the frame of the opening, he began tapping gently.

Sophie's frustration grew. Why didn't he just take a big saw or an ax and just hack out a big chunk of wood and be done with it? What was all this gentle tap-tap-tapping? Unable to stand it anymore, she shouted, "Uncle Gary!"

He looked up, squinting, seeming almost surprised that the kids were still there.

"Are you almost done?"

He nodded, wiping sawdust away from his eyes, and went back to his tapping with the chisel and hammer.

"Will you check on Billy?" she asked.

He stopped working and looked up again, clearly irritated.

"What?" he said.

"Will you check to make sure Billy's okay?"

Placing his tools on the floor, Uncle Gary leaned forward and put his head through the opening. After two hours—which were really only twenty seconds—he pulled back out and looked up at Sophie with a confused expression.

"What's taking him so long?" Uncle Gary said.

"What do you mean?"

"He's still on the rope. He's just not going anywhere."

47

Arms shaking, muscles screaming with pain, Billy hugged the rope and stared up at the top of the lighthouse. The rope stretched away from him into the heights. He gazed at the tiny dark square it disappeared into on the wall of the lighthouse near the top. That tiny opening led back into the closet and safety. He thought he saw a head poking out of the opening, looking down at him. Was it Uncle Gary? He couldn't tell.

He'd thought that if he hung quietly long enough, his arms would somehow find the strength to haul him back up, but he knew now that was impossible. That left him only one choice: to finish his descent.

A sudden gust of wind and smoke blew him in a circle and Billy swung back and forth, spinning. He opened his eyes and looked again at the small, leafless forest growing on the back of the Truck as it circled by again and again. He knew the dizziness would soon overwhelm his fear and he would have to either finish climbing down or simply let go and fall.

He could see them in a blur each time the forest spun by. Just standing there among the trees. Standing and staring forward, facing the front of the Truck. Facing *him*. The Zobadak men. Representatives of the Zobadak Wood Company, in their brown suits. There were at least ten of them spaced randomly across the back of the Truck. "The woodmen." Wasn't that what Uncle Gary had called them? That name seemed really, really appropriate right now, in a way he didn't even want to think about. In a way that terrified him.

His spinning gradually slowed to a stop. Before he had time to feel relieved, he began spinning in the opposite direction, this time gradually picking up speed. *This is ridiculous,* he thought. *I have to go down. I have no choice.*

The woodmen hadn't moved at all since he'd first seen them. At first he'd figured they were simply waiting for him to get down to the Truck, but he wasn't so sure anymore. They just stood there, stiffly upright, arms at their sides. They hadn't moved a muscle, and now he was wondering if maybe they hadn't seen him after all. He didn't know how that was possible, but why else would they just be standing there in the trees?

Suddenly a sprinkling of sawdust fell over him. He blinked and shook his head, trying to clear it away from his face. Then realizing what it was, he looked up. It was Uncle Gary. Billy couldn't see anything in the opening above, but it had to be him. He was working on the hole, widening it.

Billy shook his head again, this time to clear his mind of all the fear and panic and crazy thoughts. Clear it all out. *It's time to go,* he thought. *They need me. Mom and Dad are just below and they need my help.*

Billy took a deep breath and released his frozen grip on the rope, lowering himself hand over trembling hand. Relaxing his leg muscles, he allowed himself to slide down, ignoring the burn on his legs through his blue jeans and the worse burn on his hands. He counted his hand movements, if only to keep his mind from thinking about anything else: one, two, three, four, five . . .

Each time his spinning brought the back of the Truck into view, he expected to see the woodmen walking toward him, and each time he saw the same thing: they stood like statues. Or mannequins. Maybe that's what they were. Mannequins set up to display their particular outdated style of brown suit. All the same, like car salesmen from the seventies, Mom had said.

Suddenly his feet touched the solid surface of the Truck and he was down. He let go of the rope, feeling the tension in his arms and shoulders release with a burning sensation. He gingerly rubbed his aching, bleeding hands together, trying to get the circulation back into them. He could barely move his fingers.

Billy had never been in an earthquake before, but he imagined it must be something like this. The shaking and rumbling coursed through his entire body, and it seemed the very air around him was vibrating. He stood up, trying to get his bearings.

I'm on the Truck, he told himself. *I'm on the Truck of Ballagahaldo.*

The world spun and tilted. Billy lost his balance and fell down. He decided to wait a minute before attempting to stand again. The surface beneath him was uneven and rippled, and he realized he was on a layer of dirt and tree roots, as if the entire top of the Truck was woven out of roots. Beneath it he could feel the clanging and thrumming and grinding and pounding of the steel machinery.

As he was preparing to stand again, the rumbling was shattered by an even louder sound—a deep, bellowing wail, like a long, drawn-out blast from an immense tuba, that came from far above at the top of the lighthouse.

"What is that?" Sophie yelled, pressing her hands to her ears. The noise went on for about twenty seconds.

"I don't know," Uncle Gary replied. "Sounded like a foghorn. A big one." When the noise stopped he went back to work, tap-

tap-tapping with a small chisel the size of a pencil.

Krandall had snapped awake when the noise sounded, and now he was standing in the hallway, startled, looking back and forth.

"Show's over!" he announced. "Everybody back on the bus!"

When the sound stopped Billy took his hands away from his ears and looked around. The dizziness seemed to have mostly faded and he thought he could stand. The control booth was no more than ten feet away. From where he sat Billy could not see any entrance into it, but the brick wall was crumbled at one corner and he thought he could climb over it. He stood up and began walking toward the control booth, stepping carefully to avoid twisting an ankle on the tree roots.

He had been avoiding looking toward the trees on the back of the Truck, but now he glanced over. The first thing that caught his eye was a flock of crows circling in the air just above the treetops. Those darn crows again. He hated those crows. The trees were also full of crows and he was suddenly confused. Had they always been there or had they just arrived? Up above the flock circled in and out of the smoke that belched from the various chimneys. At times it was hard to tell what was smoke and what was a swooping knot of crows.

Don't stop, Billy told himself. *Just keep going, keep going, you're almost there. . . .*

Turning his attention to the bottoms of the trees, he saw the woodmen, only they were no longer standing still.

"Oh, no . . ." he whispered, ducking around the wall of the control booth. He hurried along it to the corner that was nearest the forest, getting a clear view of the men as they came forward. They were looking directly at him and walking in their strange, stiff manner, like their joints had been put together too tight. He didn't know if any of them were the same men who had come to their house because they all looked the same. Well, not exactly the same, but close enough. They were all very tall and thin and they seemed very old, with wrinkled, expressionless faces. They came forward slowly but surely.

He suddenly remembered what Chris had said about them being zombies. And yet, in spite of their smell and their movements, there was a part of him that knew without a doubt they were *not* zombies. They were something strange all right, but it wasn't that.

At the broken corner of the control booth, Billy reached and took hold of the crumbled brick, simultaneously jumping and pulling himself up. The bricks were loose and began to pull out of the wall, but he somehow managed to claw his way onto the top. He dropped down to the floor inside the booth.

The control booth looked a bit like a small office, with tables and chairs around the perimeter. Most of them were tipped over and obviously hadn't been used in a long time. Along the front wall, up against the base of the lighthouse, was a massive control panel with big metal levers sticking out. Billy saw cranks and gauges and a huge steering wheel that looked like it belonged on a ship. Scattered about the floor was a mess of crumbled brick, rusted gears, and metal scraps, along with broken glass, tangles of wire, and steel cable. Everything was covered with a thick layer of black soot. In the middle of the floor, amidst the junk, lay the motionless bodies of Mom and Dad.

Billy ran to them.

"Mom!" he cried, kneeling next to her and shaking her shoulder, calling out again, "Mom!"

She didn't move.

"Dad!" He reached across her and shook Dad's shoulder. Still no response.

"Can you hear me? Mom! Dad! It's Billy! Can you hear me?" He kept repeating the words over and over, not sure what else to do or what else to say, his mind working frantically for some idea of what to do next. He crawled around to get a closer look at Mom's face, tears streaming down his cheeks, and he held her face in his hands.

"Mom! It's Billy! Are you okay? Mom, can you hear me? Please wake up!"

Turning again to Dad, he shook him.

"Dad! Please!" Leaning back on his heels, he looked up at the sky. "What am I supposed to do?" he howled out loud.

Think—*think*. On all those TV shows and movies when someone was unconscious, what did they do? How did they figure out if anyone was alive? Check for pulse. Check for breathing. Check for body temperature.

He felt Mom's forehead. It definitely wasn't cold. It was hot, actually. But that didn't mean anything because everything was hot. The air temperature was sweltering. Not only were they in some kind of tropical jungle, but the heat rising from the Truck made it even hotter. They were riding on top of a giant, wood-burning furnace, and Billy realized he was sweating so hard it was dripping into his eyes.

Check for breathing.

He put his ear next to Mom's mouth and closed his eyes, listening. It was useless; everything was too loud. He looked at their backs to see if they were rising and falling with their breath, but he couldn't tell that either. Thanks to the Truck, everything was shaking.

How did they do that pulse thing? He'd learned it in school. In health education. Mrs. Roboski had taught them. She'd even had a dummy she demonstrated on. Justin kept laughing and disrupting the class and saying the dummy was Mrs. Roboski's boyfriend until she finally sent him to the principal's office. Once Justin was out of the way, the rest of the class learned something.

What they'd learned was that you can check for a pulse at the neck or the wrist. Billy put his fingertips against the side of Mom's neck. Trying to relax so he could concentrate, he felt for a moment, then moved his fingers to another spot and felt there. He moved them again and…was that it? Yes! A faint thrumming beneath the skin. THUMP-THUMP . . . THUMP-THUMP . . . THUMP-THUMP . . .

She was alive! He breathed a sigh of relief that turned into a sob, and he had to quickly get a hold of himself. Turning to his father, he repeated the same process, trying to find the same spot on the side of Dad's neck. And there it was.

"Oh, thank you! Thank you! You're alive!" he cried out loud. He lowered his voice to a whisper. "Hang on, Mom and Dad. We're going to get out of here now. Hang on."

At that moment the door of the control booth swung open, banging against a piece of scrap metal on the floor. In the doorway stood one of the woodmen.

48

"Stand back, everybody!" Uncle Gary shouted, as he tightened two more clamps onto the left edge of the opening. "Get away from the closet door! There's a lot of pressure on this wood and when it lets go, it's really gonna pop!"

Sophie had no idea what he was talking about, but she backed away from the opening, pulling Chris and Maggie with her.

"Well, I'm about done waiting around for you people," Krandall complained. He had awakened from his nap on the wrong side of the bed, or rather drawer. "I got work to do," he continued. "You let me know when you're all done with your little playtime happy-go-round here!" He turned to leave, but Chris leaped at him, grabbing the back of his shirt, which gave way with an unmistakable ripping sound.

"You tore m'shirt!" Krandall yelled. "That was my good one too!"

"You're not going anywhere," Chris said firmly.

Inside the Loud Closet, Uncle Gary picked up a U-shaped chisel and placed it very carefully against a precise spot on the frame where he had been cutting and chiseling. Placing the hammer against the chisel, he turned his head to protect his face, squeezed his eyes shut and whispered, "Here goes . . ."

He struck the end of the chisel, and there came a sudden, very loud wooden SNAP like two large boards clapping together with great force. Little triangles of wood flew in every direction, skittering around the closet like popcorn and bouncing out into the hallway. The sound reverberated through the walls.

"What in the name of Rachel Jackson's corncob pipe was that?" Krandall exclaimed.

Uncle Gary turned back to the opening, inspecting the edge. It was a bit rough, but it seemed to have worked. He had never widened an existing connection before. He hadn't even been sure it would work, but it seemed to be holding.

With trembling fingers he loosened the clamps one at a time. There were four in all. He winced as he took the last one off. The wood creaked, but held. It was actually working! As he blew the sawdust away and brushed the larger wooden flecks with his hand, he just hoped it was wide enough.

Far below the woodman reached into his jacket and pulled out a business card, extending it forward through the doorway on a stiff arm. Billy lunged at the metal door, throwing his shoulder against it. The door slammed on the woodman's wrist and bounced back, as if it had struck a solid branch. The arm didn't flinch or pull back but stuck through the opening like it didn't feel a thing, the business card still pinched between thumb and forefinger.

Without thinking Billy snatched the card out of the woodman's hand and tossed it aside. Then he shoved the arm out and closed the door. As he did so, he thought he saw splinters sticking up out of the wrist.

I didn't see that, he told himself. *I didn't see that. I did not see that.* He might have been shouting out loud or only thinking in his head. It didn't even matter anymore.

There was an overturned chair nearby, just out of reach. He let go of the door and ran for it. As he picked it up and turned around, the door began opening again.

"Excuse me," came a voice from the other side. Somehow, in spite of all the noise, he heard the voice clearly, with its strange, high-pitched squeak. "My name is Don," the woodman said.

Billy jammed the back of the chair under the doorknob, throwing his whole weight against it to close it again. Then he wedged the chair legs against the floor. He had seen the trick many times in movies, but he had never tried it before and had no idea if it actually worked.

There was a table against the side wall, cluttered with rusty wires and strange equipment. He leaped onto it. Standing on tiptoe he could just barely see over the crumbling top of the wall.

There were even more woodmen than he'd originally thought. Twenty or more moved slowly and stiffly through the trees in the direction of the control booth. Some were very close, and when they saw his head over the wall, they reached into their jackets and pulled out business cards, extending their arms out toward him.

"Leave them alone!" he screamed hoarsely. "Leave my parents alooonnnne!"

His voice was completely drowned out by a sudden heavy clanking sound from deep inside the Truck, as of some gigantic ratchet or gear grinding. There was a burst of smoke from the trench where the giant bike chain rattled along. And then one of the large trees from the forest tipped over and collapsed into the trench. When it landed it was yanked rapidly forward, snapping and crumpling and torn to splinters by the chain before being swallowed entirely into the depths of the trench. The crows that were still in trees took off squawking to join the flock as it circled madly overhead.

Billy jumped down, his head whirling. It seemed to him like the whole world had gone insane. He ran back to Mom and Dad, kneeling between them and gently shaking their backs.

"Come on, wake up," he whispered. "Please wake up."

That was when a rope landed, as if from out of the sky, onto the control panel at the front of the booth. It landed with a heavy FLUMP! that was actually loud enough to startle him. Looking up, he saw that it led all the way back up to the opening in the wall of the lighthouse, just below the top. He saw somebody waving an arm to him.

Billy jumped up and ran. It was a much thicker rope than the one he'd come down on. There was a loop tied on the end, and a piece of paper was sticking out of the knot. He snatched the paper out. A message was sloppily scribbled on it, unmistakably in Sophie's hand. He felt a warm surge of relief just looking at her writing.

The note said simply, "Put the loop under Mom's arms and slide it tight. Please be careful."

49

"Pull!"

Uncle Gary stood in front of the opening, feet apart, rope held tightly in his hands. Krandall, standing behind Uncle Gary, tossed his crutch onto the floor of the closet and stooped to pick up the rope.

"Nonsense!" he bellowed. "Box o' nonsense is what this is!"

"Just pull!"

They pulled. Hand over hand, they pulled the rope up into the closet. Soon it began to pile up on the floor. Sophie wasn't sure if Krandall even knew what was going on, or if he knew what they were pulling up. But he was amazingly strong, and he pulled the rope with an energy and speed that apparently surprised even Uncle Gary, who glanced back at him and quickened his pace.

"Sophie!" he called a moment later, shifting the toothpick in his mouth with his tongue. "Pull the extra rope out into the hallway as we bring it up! Don't let it get tangled!"

Sophie, Maggie, and Chris dragged the pile of rope out into the hallway and stretched it out straight. No one spoke a word. There didn't seem to be anything to say. Sophie was glad they had a job to do. At least they were busy. But as they carefully laid the rope in neat loops, back and forth, they were all thinking the same thing. Was Billy okay?

Krandall was yelling as he pulled the rope. He was going on and on about something that, as usual, made very little sense.

"Five pairs were in here! Five!" he shouted over the wind and the rumbling machine outside. "And Marie Antoinette's coat hung in here for years! Can you believe that? Smelled like peppermint. And Napoleon's corduroys. This was all before it got loud, of course. All that stuff had to get moved. Now I can't remember where I put it!"

With a feeling of disbelief, Billy watched his mother rising higher and higher toward the top of the lighthouse. She looked horrible, just hanging there like a limp doll swinging back and forth but he was actually beginning to feel hopeful. It almost didn't seem possible, but they might make it out of here after all.

She was going up much faster than he had come down, but it still seemed to take forever. When she was about halfway up, the flock of crows, moving like a single organism, swooped toward the lighthouse. For a moment, Billy's heart leaped in his chest. He thought they were about to attack her. Instead they flew behind the lighthouse, circled, and came around the other side, moving toward the back end of the Truck. Billy turned in a circle, watching them as they disappeared into the cloud of smoke. They came out of the cloud off to the left, flying over the jungle.

Billy realized the jungle had fallen away on that side. Where there had once been steep slopes rising up on both sides, now only one side went up and the other dropped into a deep canyon. He couldn't even see the edge. He had no idea how wide the road was, but the Truck had to be close to it. *Whoever's driving this thing,* Billy thought, *had better be careful or it could go off the edge. Speaking of which—who exactly is driving this thing?*

279

Somehow the thought had not occurred to him until this moment. He craned his neck to look up at the top of the tower. That was probably where the driver sat. Was it one of the woodmen up there?

And speaking of driving, where exactly were they going? The Truck moved forward slowly and steadily, but he couldn't see their destination because the lighthouse was in the way. Uncle Gary had said something about how they had to get Mom and Dad off the Truck before it reached its destination. What was its destination? What if they were close? What if they were almost there? He had no way of knowing.

The crows swung around the front side of the lighthouse again and Billy looked up. Mom was gone. For a brief, terrifying moment, he thought she had fallen or been plucked off the rope by the crows. But then he saw a tiny head appear in the opening—Uncle Gary's maybe—and an arm came out and waved to him. They had her. She was up. She was alive and safe now.

Oh, thank God, he thought. *She's going to be okay.*

And then the rope came down again—a coil that fell and fell and fell, unwinding as it came, slamming onto the wall on the left side. Billy ran across, climbed up onto the control panel, and pulled the rope in. Glancing over the wall he saw that the woodmen had completely surrounded the little room he was in. There were twenty, maybe thirty of them. They were feeling the wall with their hands as if searching for a way in.

One of the woodmen stood just below Billy. He turned his face up toward Billy and said in a voice that creaked like an old door, "Gary Fyfe, please. My name is Rob. We represent the Zobadak Wood Company. May we come in?"

Billy backed away, stumbling on one of the levers that stuck up out of the control panel, and fell backward, banging the back of his head against a large valve wheel. Pain shot through his head, down his neck, all the way into his back. He rolled off the control panel, rubbing his head and blinking to clear his blurred vision.

He grabbed the rope and crawled across to his father. He was still asleep. Either that or unconscious. Wiping the sweat and tears from his eyes, Billy looped the rope under Dad's right armpit, then the left. He pushed the sliding knot as tight as he could against Dad's back. Looking up to the distant face that watched him from the opening, he waved both arms in the air to signal that Dad was ready.

At that moment the door of the control booth burst open and the Zobadak woodmen swarmed through.

50

"The Grand Duchess of Wellington had the world's first miniskirt! Made from the wool of a four-horned ram! Blue plaid, as I recall. She had a big mole over her right knee. Very unsightly! Lots of hair stickin' out of it, if you believe the stories! It was on account of that mole the miniskirt went out of style right away and didn't come back for another hundred and fifty years. Not too many people know about that miniskirt. Ugly as a bag o' beetles, it was. Hung in this closet right on the end there!"

Krandall talked non-stop the entire time, without once pausing to catch his breath. His listing of the closet's former inventory went on and on with one bizarre story after another, to the point where Sophie wondered if they could possibly be true—or if the closet could possibly hold that many items. And he never seemed to grow tired as he hauled up the rope like a fisherman hauling up a net.

Uncle Gary gritted his teeth, his face running with sweat. He was clearly having a much harder time pulling Dad up than Mom. Out in the hallway, Chris and Maggie worked to keep the rope organized. They were going to need it one more time, for Billy.

Nearby, Sophie knelt over Mom. She gently stroked her forehead, looking for any sign of consciousness, any twitch or quiver that would indicate she was coming to. At least she was alive. But what was wrong with her? Why wasn't she waking up?

"Mom? Mom, can you hear me?" Sophie repeated over and over. She snatched the cap off of her head and tossed it aside. "Momma? It's Sophie. Can you hear me?"

Nothing. She barely seemed to be breathing. Without knowing why—perhaps because she was tired of just saying "Mom, can you hear me," perhaps because she wanted Mom to keep hearing her voice so she'd know she was safe, perhaps because Mom used to say how much she liked to hear Sophie sing, Sophie began to sing:

"You are my sunshine, my only sunshine—You make me happy when skies are gray—You'll never know, dear, how much I love you—Please don't take my sunshine away…"

A tear fell from her eye and landed on Mom's cheek, rolling back toward her ear. Sophie wiped it away and kept singing. Even though the song itself made her cry and even though she was tired of crying, it seemed like the right thing to do.

"You are my sunshine, my only sunshine…"

Now another voice joined hers. It was Maggie, who was busily pulling the rope down the hallway to keep it straight. She didn't seem to realize she was singing as she worked. When Chris began singing too, Maggie looked over at him, surprised. Chris never sang. He certainly wasn't very good at it, and he'd be the first to tell you so, but he sang anyway, and somehow his off-key voice added something to the song. Made it more beautiful for some reason.

"You'll never know, dear, how much I love you…"

The three of them sang like it was the most natural thing in the world—as if it were just exactly what you were supposed to do in this particular situation—and to Sophie it seemed the most beautiful song she had ever heard. It said everything that needed

283

to be said. It magically put into four simple lines the entire sea of emotions and thoughts and fears and hopes that whirled and stormed inside of her. Those words seemed to contain all the meaning she wanted Mom to hear, and her emotions poured out with the notes. She sang not just to Mom, but to Dad who was being hauled up, and to Billy who was still down there, and to Uncle Gary who seemed so distraught and tired, and to Maggie and Chris who seemed so afraid yet never gave up and never stopped wanting to help.

"Please don't take my sunshine away . . ."

And Mom's eyelids fluttered.

"Mom?"

They opened for a moment, then closed, then opened again.

"Mom! Can you hear me? It's Sophie!"

"Sophie," Mom whispered. She licked her lips and her mouth seemed so dry, but she smiled anyway. "Don't stop singing."

Weeping, Sophie hugged her.

"You're okay! Oh—you're okay! Maggie! Chris! She's okay!"

Inside the Loud Closet, Krandall was shouting, "Black, if you read the history books! But I can tell you firsthand they were blue! Not even navy blue, either. More of a powdery sky blue. And they weren't lederhosen, either. They were more like chaps. Like the cowboys wore. Only satin. And King Louie IV used to wear them when he rode out to visit the peasants and play a game of bous-kashia. How they admired his chaps!"

"Krandall!" Uncle Gary called. "Help me get him in here!"

"What in the name of Barnum's broken backscratcher is that?" For the second time Krandall was completely taken by surprise to see a human being appear in the opening at the end of the closet. But Henry's shoulders were stuck, and for a terrifying moment Uncle Gary was convinced the hole wasn't big enough. He didn't want to lift Henry's arms up over his head because he might slip right out of the rope and fall back down. But in one quick, decisive action, Krandall reached down and grabbed Henry under the arms, then turned him at an angle and dragged him up through the hole. Henry's favorite shirt was torn, his arms red and scraped, but he was inside the closet, safe at last.

"Get him out to the hallway!" Uncle Gary yelled as he began coiling the rope for one last time. "Hurry up! We have to get Billy!"

Krandall dragged Dad out to the hallway and dropped him unceremoniously on the floor. Then he began feeding the rope into the closet, where Uncle Gary worked furiously to coil it up again so it wouldn't get tangled in a knot when it was dropped back down.

Sophie kissed her still unconscious father and ran into the closet to help. Falling to her hands and knees, she crawled to the hole and looked over the edge, ready to drop the rope. Instead she backed out, her eyes wide with fear.

"Uncle Gary! He's in trouble! Billy's in trouble!"

51

"My name is Ron. And these are Don, Rob, Tom, Lon, and John. We represent the Zobadak Wood Company. May we come in?"

The woodmen clustered and elbowed through the doorway and came forward, pulling business cards out of their brown jackets. Billy leaped up onto the control panel and carefully made his way past the many levers, gauges, and wheels to the farthest corner. He was afraid he was trapped, and he looked wildly about.

"We are looking for the Gary Fyfe. We need to speak with him about a shipment of wood that was made by mistake. We need to get the wood back."

Desperate Billy looked for some way out of the control booth. There was only one door. The woodmen walked toward him slowly and awkwardly, and he thought maybe he could run past them. But there were too many—and they were still coming through the doorway. The front of the booth, where a window used to be, was no help; it stood tight up against the tower.

The crumbled corner where he had climbed in wouldn't work either. He could see the head of one of the woodmen looking at him over the ruined top of the wall. The man's arm was reaching over the wall, holding a business card out to him.

The only other way out was to climb over the wall and drop down. The control panel was wide: it went across the front of the booth from the right side to the left. Standing on the panel Billy was able to look over the wall. It looked like a long drop, but if he climbed over and hung by his arms, it might not be too far. It seemed about as high as a one-story house. Maybe a little higher.

"Excuse me," came a creaking voice from behind him.

One of the Zobadak woodmen was almost at the panel and reaching toward him.

Jumping up onto the top of the wall, Billy crouched for a moment, looking down. There were no woodmen on this side; apparently they had gone around to the door. Behind him, Ron or John or Tom was trying to climb up onto the control panel.

Billy swung his legs over the edge of the wall and turned around so he was lying on his stomach. Then he lowered himself off the edge of the wall and hung by his fingers. He looked down, realizing it was a bit higher than he thought.

"Excuse me." The head of the woodman appeared over the wall, looking down at him.

Billy let go. For a moment he was in freefall, his stomach rising, and then he crashed down onto the surface of the Truck, crumpling into a heap. He rolled onto his back and lay there for a moment, trying to decide if he was injured. His butt was sore, and there was a throbbing pain in his shoulder, but other than that he seemed to be unhurt. He sat up, then stood, feeling the Truck shift and rock beneath him.

Now what? He looked toward the back end of the Truck. The dark forest trembled and swayed, churning with black smoke. There were more of the woodmen coming through the trees. As he watched them another tree suddenly toppled over, pulled snapping and crunching into the chain trench where it was devoured by the engine.

He couldn't go that way. He couldn't go back around the booth. The only other way was forward. Maybe he could go that way to get around to the front of the Truck.

Turning he started walking around the base of the lighthouse, stumbling and tripping over the tangled bed of tree roots underfoot. Steadying himself with his hand against the wall of the lighthouse, he came around the bend. Before he had gone twenty steps, another woodman suddenly appeared before him. Billy stopped, took a step back, stumbled and fell.

"Well, all right then," drawled the woodman. Creaking, he stepped toward Billy. He had what looked like a small branch sticking out of his forehead.

Tall and thin, slow and stiff, he seemed to Billy like some kind of insect. Or like a tree. Staring at the twig-like object on the woodman's head, the thought came tumbling into his mind. *That's exactly what they remind me of,* he thought. *Trees.*

"You got some nerve, setting your foot onto my ranch," said the woodman.

Billy looked at him with a mixture of curiosity and horror, realizing he recognized this one. This was one of the two guys who had come to their house. Bob. The one who had stood in back was named Bob.

But he didn't talk like the others. The others always said the same things, almost like they only knew ten sentences and said them over and over. But this one was different. In a weird way he almost sounded like a cowboy. Or like he was pretending to be a cowboy and doing a lousy job of it. Even his posture was different: his legs bowed out slightly as though he were trying to look like a cowboy.

"I know how to handle troublemakers like you," the woodman said, his voice creaking like an old rocking chair.

Billy stood up to run back the way he had come, but stopped. There were at least twenty woodmen advancing from that direction. The smell of rotten meat wafted through the air, mixing with the smoke. He was cornered, with the lighthouse behind him and the wall of the booth on his right. There was nowhere for him to go.

A shadow suddenly blocked out the sun, and when Billy looked up to see what it was, all hope left him. The crows were swarming down, like a blanket of darkness.

"Throw the rope! Why aren't you throwing the rope?"

"I can't see him! The crows are everywhere! And I think he's too far away. He's on the other side of the control booth. The rope won't reach across to that side."

"Then let me go down there!" Sophie grabbed the coiled rope and tried to pull it out of Uncle Gary's hands. Exhausted as he looked, his grip was like steel.

"No way. You're not going anywhere. *I'm* going down."

"*You* can't go!" Sophie cried. "You're the one they're looking for!"

"I have to do something!" Uncle Gary shouted back. "I'm the one that got him into this!"

"Let me go!" Chris shouted from the closet doorway.

"Oh, stop it, all of you!" Krandall hollered. "You sound like a piñata party!"

The foghorn blast came again from the Truck, cutting off any hope of conversation. Uncle Gary dropped the rope through the opening and it spun wildly as it unrolled on its way down. He got down on his hands and knees and began backing out through the opening.

Sophie suddenly felt a hand grasp her by the arm, and she was pulled out into the hallway, knocking Chris over and falling on top of him.

Krandall lunged past her into the closet. He bent over and grabbed Uncle Gary by the shoulders of his shirt and hauled him up, lifting him several inches off the floor. He carried Uncle Gary out into the hallway and flung him to the floor. Krandall's mouth was moving the whole time but no one could hear what he was saying. As he was turning back to the closet, the foghorn stopped. They heard him muttering ". . . like I'm some kind of babysitter! Following everybody around, wiping up messes, picking up toys, washing the dirty laundry! Who am I, Marjorie the laundry lady? Marjorie the babysitting, housecleaning laundry lady! Kraaaandaaaaallll! Gary left a big mess down on the Truck of Balagahaaaldooooo!"

The closet door slammed shut, blocking out his tirade, blocking out the rumbling and rattling of the Truck and the cawing of the crows and the creaking of stressed wood. Uncle Gary stood up and leaped at the door, but it was locked from the inside. He cranked the handle, pounded on the door, shouted for Krandall, but to no avail.

"What's he going to do?" cried Sophie, alarmed.

Uncle Gary pounded on the door again and cursed under his breath.

"I don't know," he said, hanging his head. "I don't know. I'm not sure if he even knows what's going on."

"But . . ." said Sophie, her mouth opening and closing silently. She didn't know what to say.

Uncle Gary slumped on the floor and put his head in his hands.

"What are you doing?" Sophie asked. "We have to get in there! Can't we—I don't know—break down the door or something?"

"It's solid oak," Uncle Gary mumbled, not looking at her. "We'll never get in there."

"But. . . ." the tears were coming back. "If we don't get him back—I don't know what I'm going to do."

"Me too, Sophie," he sighed. "Me too."

52

Curled up on the root bed, his hands covering his head, Billy waited for the attack of the crows. He clenched his teeth and squeezed his eyes shut, steeling himself for the pecking beaks and digging claws that were surely moments away.

Nothing happened.

He heard them cawing and flapping. They seemed very close, but he felt no talons digging into his back and no beaks stabbing at his head. Holding his breath he opened a narrow slit between two fingers and peeked out. Billy could hardly believe his eyes.

The crows were attacking, all right, but they were attacking the Zobadak woodmen. There were so many crows, it looked like a moving mound of shiny black feathers and flapping wings, writhing and churning. An arm with a brown sleeve came out of the pile, pinching a business card between two fingers. A crow leaped across the mound to it, snatched the card away, and flew up into the air. Every once in a while, Billy saw an expressionless head protrude, only to be attacked and buried beneath a cluster of squawking birds.

The woodmen tried to walk and move, but the crows moved with them and the flapping mound slowly drifted this way and that, breaking apart and coming back together.

They're helping me, Billy thought. *They're actually helping me. All this time I was afraid of them, but they've been helping us all along. Maybe they're only after the carrion smell, like Chris said, but it still comes to the same thing: they chased away the Zobadak men when they broke into our house, they warned us when the two small trucks were coming, and now . . . Now I have to get out of here. Now is my chance.*

He stood up and turned to his left—the only direction he could go—and ran. He ran right into one of the Zobadak woodmen. The woodman grabbed his wrist in a grip as solid as ironwood and held it tight. Billy screamed, trying desperately to pull away, but the woodman only looked down at him with a blank face that seemed to show no effort or emotion whatsoever.

It was the weird one, if such a thing could be said about these men. It was the one with the branch on his forehead, who talked like a bad cowboy. Billy had forgotten he was standing there to the left, away from the others.

The woodman regarded him calmly. There were five crows perched on his head, flapping, cawing, and pecking furiously, but he didn't even seem to notice they were there.

"My name is John Wayne," the man said. "Not Bob. It's John Wayne. That's why I'm taking care of business."

"Let me go!" Billy screamed, pulling and yanking at his arm. The hand that held onto his wrist didn't even seem to budge.

"You ain't goin' anywhere, pilgrim, 'til I get some information," the woodman said. The crows fell over his face, digging in their claws to hang on. The woodman casually brushed them away.

"I don't know anything! Let me go!"

"You are the Gary Fyfe's family member. I saw you in the

house. There are two saplings of the Gary Fyfe family. One and two. You are one. You know where the Gary Fyfe is and the Gary Fyfe knows where the Blue Oak wood is. The shipment was a mistake. Now yer comin' with me and talk to Brope."

"No—NOOO!" Billy kicked and punched and screamed and pulled, but the woodman only stood still, looking down at him with his flapping hat of crows.

The tremendous foghorn sounded again from above, like the bellow of some great prehistoric beast. Startled by the sound the crows took to the air in one massive, spooked flock, swooping away and down into the wide valley that opened on the right side of the Truck. They circled around to the front of the Truck but didn't land again. The woodmen who had been buried under the attacking crows began walking toward Billy and his captor. Their clothes hung in tatters, but they showed no sign of injury. No blood. No claw marks.

The foghorn stopped.

"They are all going to know my name now," said the woodman who held him. And then, the woodman did something utterly bizarre. Instead of reaching into his jacket and pulling out a business card like the others, he reached into the waistband of his pants and pulled out a bent stick, pointing it at Billy.

"Put your hands inside of the air before I pull the trigger," the woodman drawled creakily.

Billy stopped struggling. It was useless anyway. He looked up at the cowboy-talking woodman with a mixture of terror, confusion, and—what was it he felt exactly?—dawning realization. Somehow, this one knew something about cowboys, and he was trying to imitate one. Billy didn't know why, or what it all meant, but—what if…?

Please let it be there—please let it still be there . . . Billy's free hand went to his waist, to the handle of the cap gun that still stuck

293

out of the waistband of his pants. Somehow—miraculously—it hadn't fallen out through all of this. He grabbed the gun and pulled it out. Then, with a crazily shaking hand, he lifted it up and pointed it at the woodman.

"Say your prayers!" he shouted, hoping his voice didn't sound too terrified.

The woodman looked at the gun. His face remained expressionless, but something changed. Then he heard a sound—it might have been his imagination, or it might have been some noise from within the engine of the Truck, but—there was something different about it. And it seemed to come from the head of the woodman, just above him. It sounded like a series of small drawers opening and closing, one after the other. It reminded Billy of someone searching through a dresser for something.

"Get ready for the dust!" Billy shouted. He couldn't remember ever hearing a cowboy say that—didn't even know if it made sense—but he couldn't think of anything better at the moment. And it was a little bit cool, maybe. He cocked the hammer, noticing the fresh ring of red caps inside.

"Let go of me right now or I'll shoot!" he threatened.

The woodman's mouth opened, then creaked shut.

Billy pointed the gun in the air and pulled the trigger. There was a sharp but really pathetic popping sound, along with a tiny puff of smoke. Billy hoped it was enough to make an impression. Teeth clenched in his best menacing showdown snarl, he pointed the gun at the woodman again.

The woodman looked at the cap gun, then at the bent stick in his own hand, then back at the gun. His grip on Billy's wrist opened up.

The other woodmen were almost upon him. Without another thought, Billy ran in the only direction he could— around the cowboy woodman and toward the front of the Truck.

As he came panting around the base of the lighthouse, the Truck lurched and tilted to the right, throwing Billy off his feet. Looking back he saw the woodmen following him, undisturbed by the motion.

Billy scrambled back up. From where he stood next to the lighthouse, he could see the deeply rutted dirt road ahead of them. On the right side the land fell away down a steep slope, and he could see the thick jungle far down below, with the intermittent sparkling of a river running through the trees. The wheels of the Truck had to be very close to the edge.

Billy was running out of places to go. If he tried to climb down off the Truck, there was a good chance he'd be crushed under the enormous wheels. And even if he wasn't, he had no idea where he was or how to get back home. He had to get back up to the top of the lighthouse somehow, back to the opening he'd come through.

He looked back at the lighthouse. On the front side, he saw something that gave him hope. An arched entranceway into the lighthouse stood wide open without any kind of door. If he could get in there, he could climb to the top from the inside. He'd still have to find a way out to the opening somehow, but at least he'd be a lot closer to his destination.

The lighthouse was built very close to the front of the Truck, leaving only a narrow ledge running across to the other side. Steel posts stuck up every ten feet or so, where a railing used to be. There was nothing between the posts to hold on to, but as long as he stayed close to the lighthouse, Billy figured he would be safe.

It wasn't far. But as he got closer to the entrance, the ledge became narrower. He moved sideways, his back against the outside wall of the lighthouse. He could see the road moving beneath him, almost straight down from where he stood, and he kept imagining himself falling off the edge and plummeting down to the road. If the fall didn't kill him, the advancing Truck surely would.

Don't look down, he reminded himself.

He looked up and out, in the direction the Truck was traveling. The road sloped downward, descending into the bottom of the valley. It seemed far too narrow for the Truck in places, and he wondered how it could possibly stay on the road without falling off the edge on the right. To the left, that side of the Truck dragged through the trees and undergrowth of the rising hills.

Straight ahead the road wound back and forth as it descended into the valley, sometimes disappearing around a bend and re-appearing further on. But there was something else up there. About a mile ahead maybe, though Billy wasn't very good at estimating distances. The jungle at the bottom of the valley was shrouded in a blanket of black smoke. Was the forest on fire? There seemed to be something among the trees. Buildings maybe. They were square anyway. But there was too much smoke to see clearly. Was that where they were headed? Was that the destination? Was Brope down there?

The wall against his back ended abruptly, and Billy fell backward into the entrance to the lighthouse, toppling onto the floor. Heart pounding, he sat up and looked around, half expecting a crowd of woodmen to surround and capture him. But there were no woodmen.

There was only a ramp that led up inside the lighthouse. Billy stood and slowly walked up the incline. The inside of the lighthouse was hollow. Of course. But the ramp wound upward in a spiral, around the inner walls. There were no stairs.

Walking forward, he could see up the middle of the lighthouse. Cables and thick wires hung down from somewhere high above. Black liquid—probably oil—dripped down, spattering onto the wide black stain covering most of the floor. The spiraling ramp continued up, around and around, all the way to the top. Pausing for a moment to look behind him, giving his brain one last chance to talk him out of it, Billy started up.

53

Krandall, sitting at the end of the closet next to the hole, with the rope held loosely in one hand, drifted off into a deep and comfortable sleep. He dreamed that he was riding on a horse, good old Bayard no less, in the wide-open fields of the Great Plains, under a warm and brilliant sun that hung in the wide blue ocean of the sky. The free wind blew over him, carrying with it the smell of mothballs and cedar. Articles of clothing floated by on the wind: there was the Grand Duchess's miniskirt, short as ever, and Bram Stoker's garlic-scented turtleneck, the little yellow sweater belonging to Queen Mary Stuart's Skye terrier dog, that rascal, and Prince Vseslav's wolfskin tunic. There was the flowery, purple blouse worn once and only once by Rasputin on the day he almost lost the respect of the royal family. The blouse seemed to wave at Krandall as the wind carried it across the rolling fields.

"There you are, you devil!" Krandall said. That blouse had been lost for years; he had almost forgotten all about it. His legs twitched in his sleep as he spurred his horse on. Slumping on his side, head pressed against the wall of the closet, a string of drool ran from the corner of his mouth.

Out in the hallway Uncle Gary pounded on the door again and listened.

"Nothing," he said. "I wonder if he climbed down to get Billy. If that's what he did, we could really be in trouble. I don't know how they'd ever get back up."

"We have to do something," said Sophie, lines of worry etched across her youthful face. "We can't just sit here."

"I just don't know," Uncle Gary said. "Even my tools are in there. I'd try to take the whole door off its hinges if I had my tool box."

"Can we find something in one of these drawers?" Chris asked. "Maybe a big rock or something. And smash the door down?"

Uncle Gary shook his head.

"This whole section is mostly clothing. And I'm not going anywhere and leaving you guys alone again. I want to be here in case something happens." With his fist, Uncle Gary pounded on the door so hard it rattled in its frame.

"Krandall! Can you hear me! Kraaannndallll!"

Rasputin's blouse was calling him onward—waving and calling his name. Taunting him. Grinning, he nudged his horse again and went after it. Swinging his lasso over his head he flung it out, hoping to loop it over the shirt so he could pull it in. But the shirt was too quick and darted away over the next hill. Krandall went after it.

"You get back here, you silly shirt!"

54

The long walk up the incline seemed to go on forever. Billy studied the inside of the lighthouse as he went: how the walls and the ramp all seemed to be carved out of a single massive piece of wood. He wondered if that were actually possible. Did trees grow that big? Even if they did he had no idea how someone could hollow it out like this, leaving only the spiral ramp inside.

At first Billy looked in wonder at the amazing patterns of the wood grain that moved past him, the endless variety of waves and swirls and patterns and shapes. He saw faces in the wood along with animals and boats and all kinds of intricate objects and scenes. The wood grain almost seemed to be telling a story, as one object or scene led into another in ways that actually began to make a strange kind of sense to him.

By the time he neared the top, Billy no longer cared about any of it. Exhaustion had taken over. Even his fear over what was in store for him was completely overwhelmed. His breathing sounded like a saw cutting wood as it wheezed in and out of his chest, and all he could do was stare down at the ramp before him and keep trudging forward.

Suddenly the foghorn sounded again, vibrating the entire lighthouse. Billy was startled out of his trance. Looking up he realized he was almost there. The ramp ended in another doorless, arched opening. The sound of the foghorn echoed down the inside of the lighthouse, ricocheted off the bottom and came back up, reverberating and crashing into itself, sending sound waves bouncing in every direction.

Billy was overcome by a sudden dizziness. The lighthouse seemed to be swaying back and forth, tipping and pitching like a ship on rolling waves. He was almost thrown off balance. Catching a glimpse over the edge of the ramp, he saw the hollow middle of the lighthouse stretching down below him like a deep, waterless well.

Collapsing onto his hands and knees, he crawled away from the edge and pressed himself against the wall. He broke into a sweat, feeling waves of nausea and vertigo wash over him. Closing his eyes, he took deep, slow breaths, trying to calm himself.

After several moments the foghorn stopped. Billy sat with his eyes closed for another minute, listening to the hanging cables clanking against each other. Finally he ventured a look up the ramp again.

The doorway to the top of the lighthouse was only a few feet above him. He studied it, wondering where the driver was. After all, he reminded himself, someone must be driving this thing. Another one of the woodmen probably, but fortunately they were slow. Maybe he could even sneak by without being seen. Climb out of a window and try to get the attention of Uncle Gary in the opening. Maybe Uncle Gary could throw a rope up to him.

First things first. Billy stopped himself with an effort. First he needed to see what was up there. *Who* was up there. He crawled the rest of the way to the top until he reached the doorway to the lantern room. That's what they called the top of a lighthouse. Billy remembered that from the time his family had vacationed on Lake Michigan and taken a tour of a lighthouse. He decided now, if they ever went there again, he'd skip the lighthouse tour. He was all done with lighthouses, thank you very much.

He waited quietly, watching for any sign of activity in the lantern room. Woodmen or regular men or somebody. The lantern room was round, with windows all the way around. From where he crouched by the door, he could see the sky outside the windows, thin shreds of smoke drifting by.

In the center of the room was the enormous lantern, sitting atop a metal frame that housed a mass of gears and cables and pulleys, all dripping with black grease. The mechanism was for moving the beacon light in a circle, but it was stationary now, the light shining straight ahead.

Billy stood up and carefully stepped into the room. It wasn't large, but it was definitely bigger than the one he'd seen at the lighthouse on Lake Michigan. There was a space all the way around the lamp where someone could walk. At the front was a control panel, apparently for driving, but it was a very strange control panel. For one thing it was vertical instead of horizontal. Made of wood it was covered with doorknobs and hinges and what looked like oddly-shaped round drawers. More wooden doorknobs hung from the ceiling by cables. Billy could see nothing that looked even remotely like a steering wheel.

And he could see no sign of life. He looked carefully around the room, his heart pounding in his chest. Strangely, even though he saw no one, he felt a presence. There was someone or something else in there with him. He could feel it.

Billy realized he was almost hyperventilating. Suddenly fearful that somebody would hear him breathing, he tried to hold his breath. It was no good. He needed the air. His breath trembled as it tore in and out of his mouth, and there was nothing he could do to stop it. Billy realized that he was terrified. More terrified than he had ever been in his life.

Something was there. Something was inside the lantern room with him. But he couldn't see it. His eyes fell on the only other thing in the room besides the spotlight and the control panel. It was a piece of furniture. A bureau of some kind. Uncle Gary used to talk about bureaus. He'd said "bureau" was a fancy name for a chest of drawers or a dresser. This bureau was different from any other dresser he'd ever seen. It was large, with long legs ending in wheels, and it had many small drawers. *Too small to be useful for storing very much of anything,* Billy thought. The drawers were in the front, on the sides, even on the top. It made no sense.

His eyes darted about, searching for anything else that could be in the lantern room, but there was nothing else to be seen. He looked out the window. The view was frightening. From high above he looked down at the road they traveled on. He saw the entire panorama around him, from the valley dropping away on the right all the way across to the steep incline on the left and the gnarled trees on the back of the Truck behind them, where chimneys poured smoke into the air. He saw the flock of crows, sweeping through the air below him. Still, he had that feeling. Someone or something . . .

The Truck suddenly tilted again on the uneven road. Every motion was exaggerated at the top of the lighthouse and Billy hung on to avoid falling over. The bureau rolled across the floor, stopping just short of hitting the far wall. Billy watched it, seeing its front for the first time, its bizarre arrangement of irregular knobs and what looked like telescoping drawers within drawers. The lighthouse rocked back in the other direction, and Billy prepared himself to leap out of the way in case the heavy piece of furniture rolled back toward him. Oddly it didn't.

Instead it rolled to the left a few inches. Then suddenly it rolled backward, against gravity up the incline of the floor, where it slammed into the wall.

Billy watched it, wide-eyed, mouth hanging open. *This is not right,* he thought. *Something's not right here.*

One of the drawers—the only large one, in fact—slid open as if pulled by invisible hands. Then it slid shut. As it did so the wood of the drawer scraped against the sides, making a low squealing sound.

The sound was familiar. He would never have noticed it in other circumstances. In fact he wouldn't have recognized it if the word hadn't been on his mind already. Because it wasn't just a sound of wood squealing. It was a *word.* When the drawer slammed shut, it sounded like *"Brope."*

Billy took a step backward.

The drawer came open again—and slammed shut again.

"Brope!"

Stepping around behind the lantern, he kept his eyes locked on the bureau. And the bureau turned with him.

It's watching me. It's watching me.

Panic rose like a snake up his spine until he thought he might scream.

Looking frantically for a way out, he saw that the windows all had latches. That meant they could open. He moved toward the side facing the rear of the Truck, above where he guessed the opening to the Curiosity Cabinet to be. The bureau turned with him, keeping its front facing him. It rolled sideways to keep its distance.

It's afraid of me, Billy thought crazily, only the crazy thought was true and he knew it with every fiber of his being. *This thing is somehow alive and it's afraid of me. I startled it.*

He reached up to the window latch behind him, keeping his eyes on the bureau. Once more, its drawer opened and slammed shut.

"Brope!"

"It's calling Brope!" Billy breathed out loud. "It's afraid and it's calling for Brope!" The window squeaked on its hinges as he pushed it open.

Suddenly the Truck lurched violently and the lighthouse swung to the right. Billy grabbed onto the window frame and hung on. Looking back toward the front of the Truck, he saw the jungle swing into view, shaking and tilting, and he realized that the Truck had gone off the edge of the road with no one steering it.

He caught a glimpse of the road veering off to the left before the Truck pitched forward and began rattling and bouncing down the slope into the valley. Picking up speed it crushed trees and tore up great clumps of dirt, sending birds and animals fleeing in every direction. The Truck twisted, and there was a sudden, piercing scream of tearing metal. Something deep inside the Truck snapped, and a glowing, billow of smoke and flames shot up out of the chain trench.

The floor tipped further and further as the Truck listed forward, until Billy was hanging from the window frame with his feet dangling in the air. Looking down he saw nothing but green jungle approaching the front window. The bureau swiveled around to face the control panel, its drawers sliding madly open and closed in every direction.

Desperate, Billy pulled himself up and climbed out the window. He dropped down onto the narrow walkway around the top of the lighthouse. Gripping the railing he stared for a moment at the jungle speeding past on both sides, as some distant, rational part of his mind told him this was the most dangerous place he could possibly be.

Without thinking about what he was doing, he scrambled over the railing and down onto the back wall of the lighthouse, hanging from the edge of the walkway.

The Truck continued to lurch and heave, plowing through the jungle. A low BOOM vibrated through the entire Truck, and a heavy twanging sound and a broken gear spun up through the air, smacking into the lighthouse just below Billy's legs.

Looking down he saw chimneys collapsing along the back of the Truck. The trees hung on for dear life, but many were torn away by the surrounding jungle, while others caught fire from the flames belching out of the chain trench.

Billy's grip on the edge of the walkway began to slip. He turned to face the lighthouse and tried to get a better hold. Another explosion came from behind him, and a steel cable with a pulley on its end whistled up through the air and slammed through the windows of the lighthouse over his head, sending a shower of broken glass down over him.

Billy screamed and the walkway slipped out of his fingers. He began sliding down the slanted wall of the lighthouse—down toward the old control booth below—down toward the Zobadak men, who were still standing around the booth, looking up at him as if nothing much were happening. He scrabbled and clawed with his arms and legs to find something to hold onto, but the wall was smooth and there was nothing to grab, so he slipped downward, faster and faster and—

"There you are, you silly shirt! Get back in here!"

And suddenly he wasn't sliding anymore. A strong hand gripped his upper arm and pulled him back upward.

It was Krandall, his body half out of the opening, reaching out now with his other hand to grab the back of Billy's shirt. Teeth clenched he pulled Billy in through the opening with one smooth motion.

Billy collapsed backward on top of Krandall, his head spinning. The closet rattled and screeched around them as the wood twisted and strained.

"Get off me!" Krandall shouted. "Stop your playin' around! This is no time for games! You're gonna miss the bus!"

Billy looked up at him, confused and disoriented.

"And take that shirt off! What are you doing with that? That's Rasputin's shirt!"

"Huh?"

Another explosion came from outside the opening, and a billow of smoke rolled into the closet.

"Aaachhh!" shouted Krandall. Coughing and waving his hand back and forth, he stooped over Uncle Gary's toolbox and began rummaging around. He pulled out a hammer and a large chisel.

"Hang on! I gotta seal this thing up! One more mess for Krandall to take care of!"

Billy pressed his back against the wall as he stared out of the opening across from him. The jungle whipped by outside as the Truck gathered speed in its furious descent. He saw the wall of the valley behind the Truck and the narrow ledge where the road was receding into the distance. As the Truck plunged faster, rocking and bouncing, its enormous wheels flattened everything in its path. Stripped gear teeth and glowing chunks of metal flew upward, arcing into the forest, leaving trails of black smoke behind them. The floor of the closet seemed to tip at a steeper angle, and Krandall approached the opening with difficulty, holding the hammer and chisel in one hand, steadying himself on the wall with the other.

When the Truck collided with the bottom of the valley, the impact was so deep and so immense that Billy felt rather than heard it. The shockwave seemed to roll up through the Truck, through the closet, through Billy's entire body, followed by a heavy WHUUMMP!

Krandall slammed against the forward wall of the closet, dropping the tools. The closet seemed to roll backward, tip upside down, and jerk sideways—but somehow, at the same time, it felt stationary, so Billy wasn't sure if it actually moved or not. Both he and Krandall slid across the floor in a tangle and crashed against the door.

A second jolt came when the body of the Truck cracked in half, metal shrieking and howling. The closet went dark as the daylight from the opening suddenly vanished. Clumps of dirt and shreds of jungle foliage spewed into the closet.

Something outside popped with a loud, metallic PING! There was another explosion that sounded distant, followed by a long, drawn-out groan as the Truck rolled slowly onto its side and finally came to rest. The closet floor tilted—or seemed to tilt—back in the other direction.

And then all was silent, except for a continuous hiss of steam jetting out of a cracked boiler somewhere.

55

Billy brushed dirt off his clothes and crawled across to the opening. Looking out he saw the forest floor about ten feet below him. The lighthouse had broken off the Truck and was lying on its side, its top end partially held up by trees. The opening faced downward and Billy saw part of the wreckage to his left. The rest of the jungle floor was littered with broken gears, huge splinters of wood, cables, and shredded pieces of metal, some of them coated with oil and still burning.

As his vision cleared he also saw the bodies of the woodmen. They lay tangled and broken among the wreckage. One of them was directly below the closet opening. As he studied it a strange feeling of unreality began to wash over him.

The woodman's body was in pieces, but there was no blood, no exposed flesh or bone. It appeared to be hollow inside—the arms, the legs, the body—all hollow. It was made of wood, its broken parts split, cracked, and splintered. It did not resemble a doll or a mannequin. On the contrary, Billy had the distinct impression he was looking at a piece of broken furniture. The various parts seemed to be connected together with some kind of strange joinery—ball and socket joints made of wood and connected with dowels and various other little wedges and grooves. The woodman's skin, which was peeled back in places, was either bark or some kind of veneer.

Billy remembered the spyglass. It was still in the closet, lying on the floor only a few feet away. Fortunately it hadn't fallen out when the Truck crashed. He snatched it up and put it to his eye, twisting the lens until the woodman's body came into focus in close, sharp detail.

The woodman's head was cracked open, but it wasn't empty like the rest of the body. Something was inside. Adjusting the focus and squinting through the drifting smoke, Billy tried to make out what it was. A box of some kind. Only it wasn't square. It was some sort of odd irregular polygon shape. And it was covered with little geometric patterns of different colored wood.

The object immediately reminded Billy of a gift he'd once received from Uncle Gary—a Japanese puzzle box with similar designs. The designs were actually small hidden panels, and when you pushed on certain ones, they slid sideways. You had to slide the panels in a particular order if you wanted to open the box.

Billy was gripped by a sudden urge to jump down and grab the box out of the woodman's head. What might he find inside it? Krandall suddenly appeared next to him, staring down at the remains. Billy began to say something to him, but Krandall clamped his hand over Billy's mouth. When Billy looked up Krandall's face was terrified. The old man put a finger to his lips.

"Sssshhhhhh," he hushed softly.

Billy nodded his head, not entirely sure what was going on. Krandall removed his hand and then pointed at his ear.

At first all Billy heard was the hissing of steam. But then another sound came, far in the distance. A strange, deep, booming, tumbling sound. It almost sounded like large wooden boxes falling or bumping against each other. And beneath that sound, a steady BOOM, BOOM, BOOM. . . .

Suddenly a flock of birds flew by over the treetops, squawking. They were followed closely by a group of monkeys, howling and jabbering as they swung through the trees, going in the same direction as the birds. Something had scared them. Something was coming.

Billy carefully put down the spyglass. The floor of the closet was now vibrating with each BOOM. As the sound grew steadily closer, he heard the rustling and snapping of trees. Something very large was forcing its way through the jungle, pushing trees aside as it came.

"What is that?" Billy whispered.

Krandall slapped his hand over Billy's mouth again, pointing with his other hand to the left, toward the wreck of the Truck. Some of the woodmen were standing up. Others were struggling sluggishly with broken limbs to untangle themselves and crawl out of the wreckage. One of them opened its mouth and spoke.

"The Masterpiece," it creaked. "The Masterpiece."

The approaching noise was so loud, Billy thought it was going to shake the lighthouse right out of the trees that propped it up. A loud buzzing, groaning sound came then, rising in pitch until it became painful and Billy had to cover both ears with his hands. He squeezed his eyes shut, half expecting whatever it was to crash into the lighthouse.

But then the noise abruptly and completely stopped. Both the squealing and the booming.

Billy uncovered his ears and listened. He heard the hissing of the steam and beneath that, a mumbling of creaky voices. It was the woodmen, many of them speaking all at once. They repeated the same word over and over, as if chanting to their god.

"Masterpiece . . . Masterpiece . . . Masterpiece . . ."

There was movement over by the forest. At first Billy didn't see anything. Whatever it was, it was mostly obscured behind the trees. But something was out there. In the forest.

It was gray. It looked like wood, old and weathered and faded from exposure to the elements. And it was gigantic. From his vantage point Billy couldn't see where it began and where it ended. At first he thought it must be a piece of the Truck lying in the forest, but then it moved again.

That was when Billy realized it couldn't possibly be wood. The thing twitched, the way a large animal's skin will sometimes twitch to shake off the flies. From it came a low huffing, snorting sound, and a blast of stale air wafted into the closet. Sour air, with a strong smell of decay.

The woodmen continued to chant.

Moving very slowly and carefully, Krandall turned. His eyes darted about as he searched the closet for the hammer and chisel he had dropped. He found them in the corner and reached over, picking them up one at a time so that they wouldn't clink together. Billy, frozen in place like a statue, watched him. Some distant part of his mind realized that he was literally frozen with fear—he couldn't have moved if he'd wanted to.

Krandall placed the sharp end of the chisel against the frame of the opening where the fathom joint connected the closet to the lighthouse.

Outside there was another sound, like an old, creaky door opening very slowly. The sound came from high above.

With the hand holding the hammer, Krandall gently pushed Billy back, away from the opening. Holding his breath Billy slid back until he was pressed against the opposite wall.

Krandall raised the hammer. Paused for a moment. And then brought it down hard against the chisel. The loud CLANG of steel against steel shattered the silence and Billy watched as the opening began to warp. It took on an odd, tilted shape.

There was more movement outside—the trees shook—and another heavy THUMP! The lighthouse bounced and swayed.

Krandall's arm swung up and down rapidly, and the wood around the opening began to tear loose and splinter. He moved the chisel around the opening as he went, prying the wood from the top and bottom and on both sides.

A sudden frenzied multitude of sounds burst from the jungle outside: howling and groaning, screeching and jabbering, twittering and moaning. And what sounded like hundreds of doors and drawers slamming repeatedly, over and over.

Krandall kept hammering away, ripping large shards of wood away from the joint where the closet was connected to the lighthouse. And suddenly there came a cracking sound from somewhere both close and far away, a deep cracking behind the walls and under the floor and over the ceiling and—

SLAMMM!

The opening slammed shut with a force that shook the entire closet. Somehow, right before Billy's eyes, the hole was gone, leaving nothing but a wooden wall just like all the others. The Truck was gone, the forest was gone, and whatever was in that forest, it was gone too. Krandall stood up and tossed the tools into the toolbox.

"That should do it," he announced, brushing his hands together.

Inside the closet the ringing in Billy's ears was the only sound he heard.

56

"What was that sound?" Sophie cried.

"Oh, no!" said Uncle Gary, standing up.

Sophie stared at him. The look on his face terrified her. Tears began spilling down his cheeks, and she watched as the last remaining shred of strength and resolve left him.

"What was that?" she repeated, grabbing his arm.

He glanced quickly down at her, his eyes red and hopeless, then looked away.

"It was the joinery to the Truck. It's been closed up. The connection is lost."

Sophie's mouth fell open, and her own tears came rising up to her eyes in a wave of grief that seemed destined to drown her. Maggie and Chris stood back by her parents in shock and exhausted disbelief. Maggie's hands covered her mouth as Chris sat down heavily on the floor.

Then the closet door opened.

"Hi, guys," said Billy, looking dazed, exhausted, and a little pale, but unhurt.

The tears cascading down Sophie's cheeks changed magically in mid-fall from those of despair to sheer joy. She leaped at her brother and threw her arms around him, laughing and sobbing at the same time.

57

"We don't know whether to reward you or punish you," Mom said, smiling wanly from her hospital bed. "So I guess the two cancel each other out." She smiled at Henry, resting comfortably in the bed next to hers, in the joint room they'd been admitted to.

"You can punish us if you want," said Billy. He adjusted his chair so that it sat exactly between the two beds his parents, miraculously it seemed, lay in. "We don't care. We just want you to come home."

"Don't be silly. We're not going to punish you." Mom looked at them and sighed. "Uncle Gary told us everything, but we're still trying to sort it all out. You have to admit, it's pretty far-fetched."

"We'll show you," said Billy. "As soon as you get out of the hospital we can show you the Bigy Bigy Buglu Drawer."

"I said it was far-fetched," Mom corrected him gently, "but I didn't say we doubt you. At this point we don't know what to believe."

"Yeah," said Billy with a glance at his sister. "I know what you mean."

"Listen, kids," Dad said. "We don't want you going back in there. Do you understand?"

They both nodded.

"Even if your Uncle Gary does need you," he emphasized, "you stay out of that drawer. When we get out of the hospital, we'll figure out what to do about all of this."

"When are you coming home?" Sophie asked.

"The doctor is still running a few tests," Dad said, looking pale and exhausted. "It was smoke inhalation that made us pass out. But it's mostly cleared up and he said we should be out of the hospital very soon. Maybe even tomorrow."

"That's great!" Billy bounced in his chair.

A long silence followed as the four of them just looked at each other, glad to be alive and glad to be together.

"You know," Mom broke the silence. "What you guys did was so incredibly brave—I can't even tell you how proud we are."

"I didn't feel brave," Billy said. "Not at all. I was scared the whole time. And crying and confused. I didn't even know what I was doing," he confessed.

"Being brave means doing what you have to do even though you *are* scared. And it's doing what you believe is the right thing even though you're never totally sure."

Both kids looked down at the floor.

"Come here," Mom said, holding her arms out to them.

Billy and Sophie climbed into the bed with her, one on each side, and she hugged them both tightly.

"My two favorite things," she said, eyes closed, smiling.

58

The headline from the previous day's *Greenhaven Daily News* read: "**Freak Tornado Destroys One House. Occupants Missing and Feared Dead!**"

"Tornado?" said Sophie. "Why does it say tornado?"

She had just joined Maggie and Chris, who sat across from her in the hospital waiting room. Maggie glanced back at her mom, who sat talking to Chris's parents across the room.

"Because that's what everyone's saying," Maggie whispered. "Everyone thinks it was a tornado."

"But all the people on our street saw the Truck. It drove right up the street."

"Sshh. Lower your voice. It doesn't matter what they saw. Remember what your uncle said? What people see and what people remember are two different things."

"But didn't somebody get a videotape of it?"

"Yeah," said Chris. "I saw it on the news earlier today. You can't really see anything. Just a bunch of smoke and some trees moving through the smoke."

"I can't believe this."

"They were talking about a giant machine when it first happened," said Maggie. "But nobody believed the witnesses. They kept saying people were scared and they didn't really see what they thought they saw. They said the tornado must have picked up some kind of construction machinery and dragged it through the neighborhood and *that's* what people saw. And also that's what made the tracks on everyone's lawn."

"Even my mom said that's what it was," Chris whispered. "She was looking out her front window when the Truck went by. She had a clear view right down the street, and now she's calling it a tornado."

"They started changing their story the day after it happened," Maggie shrugged.

"This is unbelievable!" said Sophie, incensed.

"It's better this way," Maggie disagreed. "If people start investigating too much, sooner or later they're gonna find the Buglu Drawer."

"I guess." Maggie had a point, but still.

The waiting room doors opened. Billy, a fresh bandage pasted across his cheek, walked in with Uncle Gary. He was embarrassed to be seen with the bandage, especially in front of Maggie. And yet, as they approached, there was that strange look on her face again. She smiled at him and he looked down, feeling the prickling sensation of his cheeks turning red.

The others stood up and greeted them.

"How are they?" asked Chris's mom.

"They're going to be fine, Marla," said Uncle Gary. "I just spoke to their doctor, and the hospital might release them tomorrow, depending on how the tests go."

"We're going to stay in a hotel for a while," said Billy. "But Mom and Dad like it here, in spite of what happened. They want to look for a new house in the same neighborhood."

"That's great!" Chris shouted.

"Honey, keep your voice down!" scolded Marla. "We're in a hospital!"

Chris looked sheepish.

"And how are you doing, Billy?" asked Lucy, Maggie's mom. "You look a little banged up."

"I'm good. Just some scrapes and bruises. A big bump on my head. And the doctor made me put this patch on my cheek, but I don't think I really need it. It looks kind of silly."

"It looks cool!" said Chris.

"Can you excuse us for a minute?" said Uncle Gary to the other adults. "I'd like to have a few words with Billy and Sophie."

"Of course," said Marla. "We should get going anyway. And Chris, you need to finish your grounding."

"Aw, man."

"We need to go too," said Lucy. "Come on, Maggie."

"Call me!" Maggie threw at Sophie as she was led away.

"I will."

"Bye, you guys!"

"Bye!"

Uncle Gary waited for everyone to leave, then ushered the kids to the corner of the room.

"Listen," he said in a low voice. "I had a long talk with your parents. Henry is pretty mad at me. He says I should have told him sooner. He thinks I put his family in danger by not being more open with him. And you know what? He's right."

"But, you didn't know—" Billy began.

"Wait," Uncle Gary interrupted. "Please let me finish. I need to say this. What I did was wrong. I put my brother and his wife in serious danger. I put you guys in danger. If any of you had gotten hurt, I don't know what I would have done. I could have never forgiven myself. You guys are the only family I have, and you kids . . ." His voice hitched, and he had to stop for a moment to gather himself.

"I love you kids like you're my own children. And I'm sorry." He put his long arms around them, and no one said a word for at least three minutes.

Billy still had a thousand questions. The woodmen. The Blue Oak. The thing in the lighthouse. The thing in the forest. Brope. What did it all mean? Uncle Gary and the other adults had done a very good job of explaining it all. The woodmen of course were just men in disguise. As for the other things Billy had seen, well, the bump on his head, the stress, the smoke inhalation, and the exhaustion, had caused his mind to exaggerate or distort what was really going on. Uncle Gary also thought Billy had probably passed out when the truck crashed and that he had dreamed part of his experience. The mind plays funny tricks that way.

Uncle Gary had a reasonable and logical explanation for everything, and Billy was actually beginning to believe the explanations were true. He even wanted them to be true. And eventually he realized it was pointless to push the issue any further.

"From now on, *we're* handling things." Uncle Gary's voice broke into Billy's thoughts. "I don't want you guys to worry about any of this. Henry and I are going to take care of it. Understand?"

The hug was over. Uncle Gary held them at arm's length and looked into their faces with an expression of firm determination, so Billy and Sophie nodded.

"The Zobadak Wood Company is a band of criminals, and we're going to deal with them like criminals." Uncle Gary stood up. "Now let's get out of here. I'm tired of being in this hospital."

They began walking together down the hallway leading to the main entrance. Billy made the decision to put away his big pile of questions and just leave it alone for now. That was when Sophie abruptly snatched the number one question off the top and flung it right out into the open.

"So, who's Brope?" she asked, pushing up the bill of her cap.

"You're not still worried about Brope are you?" said Uncle Gary. He continued walking forward, calm and unconcerned. "I told you, it's just a crazy old story. A fairy tale. It's not worth worrying about."

"Oh, we're not worried or anything," Billy jumped in. Perhaps he just could clear up this one thing. "Can't you just tell us the story? Please?"

Uncle Gary sighed.

"Okay. If you really want to know, I'll tell you. But I'm afraid you're going to be disappointed. It's really rather silly."

59

"Let's sit down over there." Uncle Gary pointed to a small court-yard outside the hospital, to a circle of cement benches ringed by maple trees whose late autumn leaves had turned a brilliant yellow. They went to the farthest bench beneath a large tree with low branches that cast a steady stream of leaves out on the air currents. Sitting down Uncle Gary poked a toothpick into the corner of his mouth and thought for a moment.

"About two hundred years ago, in the 1700s, there lived a Dutch cabinet-maker named Zulus Bosch. A very strange old fellow. There are no known pieces of furniture made by him that still exist. But there are stories and other records relating to him. For a while he was actually a member of the original Augsburg Joiners Lodge, which invented the fathom joint and built the first sections of the Curiosity Cabinet. But they kicked him out because—well—nobody really knows why. They probably thought he was crazy. And he probably was, I guess." Uncle Gary shrugged.

Sophie held up her hand. "Wait. Is this true?" she demanded.

"It's true that Zulus Bosch was a real person. But he was a very reclusive and mysterious man," Uncle Gary explained. "Even today most historians have never heard of him. After he got kicked out of the Augsburg Joiners Lodge, he moved to a remote little cottage in the countryside of Switzerland and became a hermit. But long before that, when he was still a child, he lost one of his legs at the knee in an accident with some farming equipment."

The children listened attentively.

"His father was a wood carver and he made a new leg for Zulus out of mahogany. But there was no knee, so Zulus couldn't bend it, and he had to walk around with one stiff leg. Later on, when he became an accomplished woodworker, he began making legs for himself that could bend. He made one after another, trying to perfect the mechanism of the joint. He became obsessed with the idea of creating a new type of wood joinery that could actually move smoothly without the use of hinges or other metal parts.

"He worked for years developing his new invention, which he called the living-hinge joint. Somehow he was able to connect the individual fibers of wood grain from one board to another. These joints could flex and move and twist in a way that had never been done before. He supposedly built furniture that could actually transform into other types of furniture by moving their various parts around. His notebooks are lost now, so no one knows exactly how he did it." Uncle Gary's voice held warm admiration and dropped a note or two when he went on.

"This is where the story begins to get strange: Zulus never stopped working—up on the hill in his workshop, day and night, night and day, for over ten years. And he wasn't very popular among the villagers that lived nearby. They called him a witch and said he was doing some kind of dark magic. You have to understand," Uncle Gary explained. "In Europe at that time, people were very superstitious. They created stories to explain the unknown. And usually things got exaggerated and embellished.

"According to one story Zulus showed up in the village

marketplace one day with a very unusual chair to sell. The chair walked on its own from one spot to another. It was probably some mechanical trick, but the people thought it was magic. They were so scared they ran away screaming. Zulus never went into town again for fear of being arrested and burned at the stake or something."

Billy and Sophie sat mesmerized. Uncle Gary smiled at their rapt faces. "But his real business wasn't making chairs. His masterpiece was a cabinet he'd worked on for many years. It was a new kind of cabinet, large enough for a person to walk into, full of drawers and cupboards and shelves. He called it the Brope Cabinet, although no one knows where he got that name or what it means. They say it was as big as a house. Or maybe it *was* a house. He never stopped working on it, continually adding more and more to it. It was built entirely using his special living-hinge joinery. One source said he used freshly cut wood—still living wood, still moist, splicing the pieces so that they actually grew together.

"Then in 1793—" Uncle Gary took a deep breath and let it out slowly. He looked down at the paver bricks under his feet and seemed to be deciding whether or not to continue. "In 1793," he said slowly, "Zulus Bosch disappeared, and no one ever saw him again. The legend says that one night during a violent storm, his Brope Cabinet got up and walked off into the hills. Some said it was witchcraft that made it come to life. Others thought the cabinet was haunted by an angry tree spirit still lurking in its timbers. It prowled the Black Forest and surrounding hills for years afterward.

"The people of the area were terrified. Every time a strange noise was heard in the forest, they said it was the Brope Cabinet. Every time a person disappeared, they said the Brope Cabinet came and took them. The legend says it trapped Zulus Bosch inside itself before it left, and there his body remained until nothing was left but his bones rolling around in the drawers. And sometimes people traveling on lonely roads through the forest late at night could hear an eerie rattling sound in the trees. It was the rattling of bones. And that's how they knew the Brope Cabinet was nearby."

Billy shivered. He closed his eyes and listened to the restless tree above him. Its leaves seemed to be whispering secrets that drifted away on the breeze before he could quite catch the words. He didn't want to say it, but he wanted the Brope story to be over.

"Every country in Europe had its monsters, of course," Uncle Gary continued. "Werewolves and vampires and ghosts and goblins of every sort. But the Brope story is unique. There's nothing quite like it in the folklore of any other country. According to one tale it roamed the countryside looking for lost children, which it would collect inside rows of coffin-shaped drawers on its back, and it wouldn't stop until they were all full.

"Eventually the tales got wilder and more ridiculous. By the twentieth century, people stopped being afraid because, of course, no one had actually seen the thing. The Brope Cabinet became almost a folk hero. I heard there's one small village in Switzerland that actually has an annual Brope festival. They have a parade, and the main attraction is a big float made to look like a giant cabinet draped in garlands, with goofy eyes and buck teeth. And they have little girls dressed as fairies riding on the float, waving to the crowds."

"That sounds like fun!" Sophie exclaimed. "I want to do that!"

Uncle Gary laughed, but Billy felt ill.

"So," Sophie said brightly, "Brope is a piece of walking furniture?"

"Yep. It's even sillier than your average fairy tale, isn't it? You guys really shouldn't worry it. Anyway, it has nothing to do with our situation."

"Okay, so what does 'Bigy Bigy Buglu Drawer' mean?" Sophie asked, pressing for more information.

"Oh, that," Uncle Gary chuckled. "Your dad wrote that when he was a kid. About your age, Billy. He probably doesn't even remember. The nightstand used to be in our grandfather's house, in the room we slept in when we spent the night there. I have no idea what it means."

"So you didn't make the nightstand?"

"I wish I did, but no. That nightstand is older than I am."

Yawning, Uncle Gary stood up and stretched.

"Come on, guys. We should get going. I'm starving. How about if we head over to the Meat Tree and get some hamburgers?"

Billy stood up absently. His thoughts were a million miles away.

"Billy? You okay?"

"Huh?" Billy looked up. Uncle Gary's face wore a concerned expression.

"You look like you've seen a ghost."

"No," said Billy. "I'm fine."

Uncle Gary patted him on the shoulder and they began walking toward the parking lot.

When Sophie spoke to him, even though it was a whisper, Billy jumped.

"You believe it, don't you?" she said, leaning in close. "About Brope."

"Huh? No, of course not," he whispered back.

"It's okay. I believe it too."

"You do?"

Tugging at his sleeve Sophie slowed down a little bit to put some distance between them and Uncle Gary.

"You saw something, didn't you?" she whispered.

Billy nodded. He had seen a few somethings, although he hadn't said much about it to anyone.

"I saw something too, remember?" she said. "The adults can't explain everything."

Billy knew immediately what she was talking about. The fairy. There had never been a single doubt in her mind that she had seen one. And in that moment he understood there was more to this than met the eye. More than even Uncle Gary knew.

Sophie was right. Adults couldn't explain everything. Sometimes they didn't even see what was right before their eyes. *It's not over for us,* he thought. *It's not over.* The words kept repeating, vibrating with truth, and echoing through the hallways and staircases and corridors of his mind. He reached out and grabbed Sophie's hand without even realizing he was doing it, and together they followed Uncle Gary to his old green station wagon.

60

Sometime in the middle of the night, Billy awoke with a start. He opened his eyes and looked up at the unfamiliar ceiling of the hotel room. Uncle Gary snored away on the couch across the room. Sophie slept in the other bed.

It was a noise that had awakened him. Unless it was just part of a dream. He thought he'd heard something from the nightstand next to him, which was completely ridiculous. This was just the hotel nightstand, not the Bigy Bigy Buglu Drawer.

But there it was again. Billy sat up, heart suddenly pounding, and listening intently.

The small quick tapping sound came again. Almost like a little hammer, but too fast to be an actual hammer. Then the sound changed, becoming something like a saw, yet still it was much too fast. No one worked that fast. Then he heard a soft but definite THUMP from right there in the drawer next to him.

"Am I dreaming?" Billy said aloud. The sound of his voice in the quiet room told him he was wide awake. Uncle Gary continued to snore, and Sophie was quiet and still. Billy couldn't tell if she was asleep or not.

He reached out and opened the drawer and his mouth fell open. Inside, surrounded by little piles of sawdust, was his pirate cannon. The one from Uncle Gary, carved out of a whale tooth by a real pirate. The one Justin had stolen.

How could this be? He lifted it out of the drawer and turned it over in his hands. Sure enough, it was the same one. He even recognized the dark yellow stain near the end of the barrel. Glancing back in the drawer, he realized there was something else. A small folded piece of paper.

As he reached for it, he heard a faint giggling from inside the nightstand, immediately followed by a ringing bell, like a bicycle bell. The sound quickly faded and disappeared.

Billy pulled the paper out of the drawer and carefully unfolded it. There was a sloppily written note inside, in what looked like a child's hand:

Dear BillyFyfe,

Here. Have back your wale tooth cannon. Yay! Don't worry. That kid Justin never saw me. He snores like a motorcycle. I'm getting me one of them some day. A motorcycle. Krandall gonna be so mad. Ha-HaHa! I love when Krandall get mad.

You better watch out Billy! I heard a speshal rumor! Brope is coming! He has a speshal dror just for you!

You crashed his big truck. That was COOL! But now he mad. So sad.

Olly olly oxen free! Just kidding.

Love,

Skookis

PS Hide this note. Don't tell no bodies.

PPS I saw you picking your nose.

PPPS Do you want to be frends?

PPPPS I'm going to get the puzzle box brain.

When Billy looked up from the note, Sophie was sitting up in bed, watching him. Wordlessly he handed the note across to her. As she read chills raced in spirals around his body from the top of his head to the bottoms of his feet and back up again.

This was definitely not over.

Epilogue

"Juice Tin?"

"No! It's *Justin!* Like, as in—you know—Justin."

"Like 'just in case'?"

"Uh, yeah. I guess."

"Hello, Just In. My name is John Wayne."

"Ha! You mean, like the cowboy? Hee-hee-heee!"

"Yes. Exactly like that cowboy. Thank you for noticing. Did you know the boy and girl that lived inside that house over there?"

"You mean Billy and Sophie?"

"Yes, those."

"My mom said I shouldn't talk to strangers. What are you, some kind of police detective?"

"Yes. I'm that. A detector."

"You mean a detective?"

"Yes."

"What's wrong with your voice, old man?"

"I'm old. Do you know where the Billy and Sophie are?"

"I don't know. But the last time I saw them, they were acting pretty weird. It was before that tornado landed on their house."

"How did they act weird?"

"They were moving something on a wagon. Some kind of big thing."

"A thing?"

"Yeah. Some kind of thing. It was hidden under a sheet."

"Do you know where they were taking it?"

"I'm not sure. But they were probably going to Chris's house. I offered to help them move it but then they got mad at me. And they started making fun of me. And then they made these crows come after me. I don't know how they did it."

"Take me to the Chris's house."

"Uh. Yeah, sure. Come on."

"Walk slower, please Just In."

"Okay. Hey, old man, what's that thing on your head? And why is your arm all crooked?"

"It broke."

"Whoa. How did that happen?"

"In a crash."

"Shouldn't you go to a doctor or something? You should have a cast on that."

"No, thank you. I will prune it."

"Uhhhhhhhhh, okay. You know what, dude? You're pretty freaky."

"Creaky. Yes."

"Yeah, that too. Creaky freaky. Hee-hee-heeeeee! Creaky freaky! I'm going to call you that!"

"You're going to call me John Wayne."

"Whatever. Hey, there's Chris's house."

"Which one?"

"That one. The one with the big tree on the front lawn."

"The weeping willow?"

"Yeah. The weeping willow."

"Thank you, Just In, for your help."

"Sure. Any time. I always try to be helpful. That's just how I am, you know?" The boy shrugged and flipped the greasy strand of hair away from his eyes. "Hey, let me know if you need anything else, okay?"

"Here is my card. Take it. Call that number if you see the Billy and Sophie again. The boss wants them."

The End

Acknowledgments

I want to offer my sincerest thanks to the following individuals without whom this book would not have been possible: my longtime friend Ron Dingman for his detailed editorial help and his imaginative feedback and ideas on the early drafts; my other longtime friend Mark Beardslee for his editorial help, his many excellent suggestions regarding plot and story details, and his usual high enthusiasm that I have come to depend on; Mr. Bob Howe and the amazing people at the Michigan Elementary and Middle School Principals Association (MEMSPA) for putting on the author's contest and providing such a great avenue for writers to have their work read and published; Brian and Anne Margaret Lewis at Mackinac Island Press for all their support, enthusiasm, and guidance throughout the process and for providing such an incredible opportunity; Charlesbridge Publishing; the editor Rebecca Chown for her exceptional work and countless improvements to the story; Tom Mills for the great, atmospheric cover art; Mary Hewelt for the recommendation; Rachel Smolarz for reading the first draft and offering suggestions; Sue Gallagher for the original spark; Jim and Barb McCormack; my parents for giving me a love of books and a deep curiosity about almost everything; and my kids, Paris, Nathan, and Kaia for inspiration, for keeping me young and for reminding me what it's like to be a kid.